Prince Etcheon

AND

THE SECRET OF THE ANCIENT

Prince Etcheon

AND
THE SECRET OF THE ANCIENT

JoAnn Arnold

Horizon
Springville, Utah

ISBN 978-0-88290-956-1

Published by Horizon Books, an imprint of Cedar Fort, Inc., 2373 W. 700 S.
Springville, UT 84663

Distributed by Cedar Fort, Inc., www.cedarfort.com

Library of Congress Cataloging-in-Publication Data

Arnold, JoAnn.
  Prince Etcheon and the secrets of the ancient / JoAnn Arnold.
    p. cm.
  ISBN 978-0-88290-956-1 (acid-free paper)
  1. Religious fiction. I. Title.

  PS3601.R585P75 2008
  813'.6--dc22
                                2008034325

Cover design by Angela Olsen
Cover design © 2008 by Lyle Mortimer
Edited and typeset by Melissa J. Caldwell

Printed in the United States of America

10 9 8 7 6 5 4 3 2 1

Printed on acid-free paper

Other books by JoAnn Arnold

Miracles for Michael
Journey of the Promise
Pages from the Past
The Silent Patriots

Contents

CONTENTS

Acknowledgments

Before Horizon Publishers merged with Cedar Fort, Inc., Duane Crowther was the person I answered to. He became my mentor and my friend and remains so. His wife, Jean, however, was the reason Duane became my mentor and friend. She read my first manuscript, "Miracles for Michael," and then insisted he read it. My eternal thanks to Jean.

Also, Mr. Crowther advised me on how to prepare a manuscript and explained the importance of having at least five people read a manuscript before submitting it. I took his advice seriously and would like to thank my husband, Brent, Donald Boyle, Winnie Stevenson, Leora Potter (who doesn't really care for fantasies but agreed to read it anyway), Loretta Nielson, and Lyman Dayton (a professional screen writer), for taking time to read the manuscript, *Prince Etcheon and the Secret of the Ancient*.

As Mr. Crowther knows my battle with commas, I think he appreciates their help as well.

I thank Duane Crowther, Lyle Mortimer, and all those at Cedar Fort who continue to support my work.

1

The Village

I HAVE WONDERED IF I SHOULD tell you this story, though it is true. For there is the mystery of its time—whether it is in the future of the past that was or the beginning of yet another future still to come. Nonetheless, it would be unfair to keep the story from you, for it is your story as well.

Whether I am good at storytelling is yet to be seen. I am fully aware that knowing a story and telling it so it is understood in its truthfulness are two different things. Nonetheless, I shall try to tell it as it was, and as it is.

It is Tarainisafari who must carry the responsibility for what I know and for what I have done. It is she who told me the things that made my soul accountable in the beginning (or what I thought, at the time, to be the beginning).

Tarainisafari came into my life the day they placed Granna Fela into her grave. Granna was the only relative I had in this world, as far as I knew. Those who lived in the Village of the Meadows did not know Granna before the day she arrived with a child of two years in her arms, nor did any visitors from beyond the village ever come to visit. In our cottage there were no records or stories that would tell of those who came before her. No stories of aunts, uncles, or cousins. But most disturbing of all—there were no stories of a father or a mother who had loved me. Yet I knew that Granna loved me and that sustained me.

I loved the pleasant little village, filled with gentle folk, who kept to themselves unless there was a need for them to step outside their doors and walk a ways with a troubled soul. The day I buried Granna, the whole village walked with me to the burial and waited with me while the wooden casket was lowered into the cold and darkness of what would be the home for her bones, while her spirit went home to heaven.

I will always remember that day and the kindheartedness of the people. But all their attempts to fill my emptiness were in vain, and I regret that, for it was not in lack of their undertaking. A little cottage, lonely and quiet, was calling me home.

As I turned to the twilight of the evening and set my feet on the road to my future without Granna Fela, darkness cast its shadow upon the forest, and the melodic echo of a voice coming from its depths touched my ears. I could not help but be drawn to it. A soft light sprinkled through the trees, dancing to the rhythm of the music as a voice whispered softly in the rustling of the leaves, "Do not be afraid."

It drew me into the glow of light, and I found myself in a most remarkable place, where appeared the most enchanting female I had ever seen. She was slender in her appearance; her beauty glistened in the glow of light that surrounded her. Her eyes, reflecting ageless wisdom, sparkled in their transparency. Her hair, the color of the sun, fell to her waist. The gown she wore did not match the season of the time, only the timelessness that seemed to surround her; its material flowed with iridescent colors, giving no color an advantage over another, but separating them and then bringing them together again.

A gigantic, gnarly tree stood in the background in its own majesty. Its limbs circled about her as if to protect her—from what, I did not know.

When the woman stood, her height was close to mine. She looked deep into my eyes. "Etcheon, grandson of Feladelphia," she said as if she already knew me, "this has been a most extraordinary day for you."

I looked at her somewhat surprised. "How do you know of me and my day?"

She smiled, but did not have time to answer my question because an eagle fluttered its wings against my head and settled itself on the outstretched arm of its mistress. The white feathers that adorned its head and decorated its tail told me it was of the species of the bald eagle. It seemed to be communicating something through the *ka-ka* of an eagle's noise.

"Barok has reminded me that I have not introduced myself to you. My name is Tarainisafari."

2

Then the scene in front of me disappeared, and I found myself alone in front of the cottage. I looked around and wondered if I had been walking in a dream. Quickly, I reached for the door and opened it to all that was familiar to me, and the dream was forgotten.

That night I slept and another dream came to me. I sat with Granna as she told me of the things that would prepare me to continue my life without her. It was a time of learning, not so much in the ways of the life in me, but a more beautiful life in her.

The next day, I was surrounded in memories as I walked about the cottage, doing those things Granna would have me do. As night fell, a knock came to my door. Thinking it was the kindness of one of the many women from the village bringing me a sweet pie or loaf of bread, I opened it without a thought to anything else. Instead, a man stood before me dressed in a strange apparel unlike any I had ever seen before. A long black cloak was wrapped around his shoulders, his silver hair tucked beneath its collar. His hat, also black, was worn low over his eyes as if to shadow his face. From what, I could not imagine, for there was no moonlight that evening.

Though I was considered to be tall in stature, he was taller by half a cubit and was large in size. Behind him a horse of even greater circumference, stood in waiting. He asked if he might come in when I made no move to be polite.

"My name is O. P. Otherton," he said quietly. "I am here to read the will of Feladelphia, she who was your guardian." He opened a peculiar looking bag and pulled from it a paper on which I could see the signature I recognized as Granna's. At that point I took him at his word and invited him into the cottage.

He ventured a smile of one who was not a stranger to reluctance and extended his hand in the simple gesture of shaking mine. I, in turn, extended mine, after which he sat down at my invitation. I asked him if I could take his cloak and bring him some refreshment. He thanked me, removed his cloak, but did not give it to me. Instead, he laid it next to him and asked for a cup of water.

He graciously accepted the water, lifted the cup to his lips, and took a generous sip. Then, without comment, he set the cup beside him and removed several pages from his bag. I sat quietly, watching with anticipation, while he looked through them.

"You are Etcheon, the grandson of Feladelphia, are you not?"

"I am."

"I only ask," he replied, his eyes peering at me over the top of the page he was reading, "because it is necessary that you verify that fact to me. I know who you are, or I would not be here."

When he spoke again, it was with a tone of sadness. "First, I must say that I am sorry for your loss. Feladelphia was a very kind and generous woman. Second, I will tell you that your life is now in danger."

I was stunned at his last words and asked for an explanation.

"You will understand when I am finished." His brows furrowed over his eyes as if there were secrets hidden there for no one to see. Then he began to speak of things I never would have imagined I would hear.

"Feladelphia called herself your grandmother, though in reality she was not," he said in a quiet tone. "She brought you here, away from all that she had and all she knew, to protect you from those who would see that you no longer existed."

He took from his pocket a monocle and fogged it with the moisture of his breath. He carefully wiped the monocle with his handkerchief and placed it over his eye, at the same time giving me a look of compassion.

My heart was pounding, and I sat in silence . . . listening . . . waiting for him to say more, but he did not. Instead, he stood, picked up the cup of water, and walked to the window. Lifting the lace curtain, his eyes became narrow, darting here and there, concentrating on what might be lurking beyond the garden, the fence, or the road. His actions concerned me, and I wondered what he was looking for. I asked him as much.

"You will understand when I am finished," he repeated. He turned from the window, and though a worried expression fixed itself upon his face, he attempted a smile in my behalf.

"I bring to you these documents," he continued with a deep sigh, returning to his seat. "More importantly, I am the only one Feladelphia trusted with this knowledge because I am also her brother." He raised the cup of water to his lips and took yet another sip. "Those who desire your life have been watching and waiting for this day. It was very difficult for me to come without being followed, if I was not followed."

"Please," I said, "tell me what it is that I am to understand. The mystery of it all is becoming a burden."

"If that was the only burden you would carry from this day, it would be a great relief to both of us. But the true burden comes with the knowledge of what you will find written on the pages before me." He handed me an envelope; the seal upon it was of curious markings.

"What you see is your family crest upon the seal. Inside the envelope you will find its replica in gold, which you should keep well hidden on your person from this day forward. You will also find within the envelope the document of your birth as well as a letter of explanation from your parents. Do not open it until after I have gone."

Next he cleared his throat, adjusted his monocle, and studied yet another paper he held in his hand. After a moment, he handed it to me. "Please read this silently. Then, if you have any questions, I will try to answer them."

I took the paper from him and began to read:

To Etcheon, my grandson by choice, I leave the following instructions: Three days after I venture from this earth you are to collect my personal belongings together. Those things you have no need of, you are to give to Mrs. Ratherberry. She will distribute them among those who have need. When the room is bare of my belongings, brush every brick. Remove and repair those that wobble.

This day is the beginning of a new life for you. In this new life, you must listen to the voice that speaks from within you. There is nothing more I can tell you, only this: In every moment, trust yourself.

As I read the words Granna had written, tears began to cloud my vision. I reached up to wipe them, uncomfortable in their presence.

"Do not feel sorry for tears," Mr. Otherton said, handing me his white handkerchief. "Tears repair the heart."

I used the handkerchief for the purpose it had been handed to me and then waited for him to continue.

"These documents you must keep in a safe place, but always nearby," he explained. Then he handed me a finely tooled, soft leather pouch. "Keep everything I have given you inside this pouch and keep the pouch close to you at all times. Do you understand?"

I nodded, and he nodded to accept my answer. Picking up the cup of water, Mr. Otherton finished drinking. He picked up his bag and looked at me one more time. In his eyes I could see there was compassion on my behalf.

"Take care, young Etcheon," he warned. "And thank you for the water." With those simple words he handed me the cup, wrapped his cloak around him, placed his hat upon his head, and cautiously opened the door. His eyes were alert, and his forehead bore the perspiration of a worried soul. "I can only pray that I have not been followed at this time, for if I have, we are both in danger. I will not know until I return to my home. I can only say one thing more. If I have failed, you will know. If I have succeeded, you will know."

"But how will I know?"

"If nothing has happened by midnight on the morrow, you will know I was not followed. If, on the other hand, I have failed in my responsibility, you will also know, for they will come for you. Guard yourself from any stranger that may knock upon your door. Do not let them see you."

He paused as if another thought came to his attention. "You will learn soon enough all that your future brings, so I will not burden you more. But I will tell you this. You must leave this village as soon as it is possible."

Mr. Otherton placed his hand on my shoulder and bid me farewell in a quiet voice. I watched as he quickly climbed onto his horse and rode into the darkness, leaving me alone once again. I closed the door and—for the first time in all the seasons of my life—I secured the latch. I darkened the room before stepping to the window, just as he had done, and let my eyes search beyond the garden, the fence, and the road—for what, or whom, I did not know.

In my hand I found I was still in possession of Mr. Otherton's handkerchief. Though it did not belong to me, I was content that I still held it—it was all I had left of him.

The cottage was strangely quiet now. The pouch, documents, and letter Mr. Otherton left for me were setting where his bag had been. Only now there was something else with them. When I looked closer I discovered a small sachet.

I placed the white handkerchief upon the pouch, next to the sachet and documents. Then I sat, still and silent, simply staring at what was in front of me. I cannot say how long I waited before I found the courage to open the letter. I only know that when I reached for it, my hands were trembling.

I broke the seal. The weight of the gold crest caused the envelope to open, and the crest fell to the floor. I knelt beside it and traced with my finger the outline of a tiger standing on its hind legs holding a staff in its left paw, a crown in its right. On the tiger's back, a pair of wings gave it the appearance of being in flight. I picked it up and held it in my hand as I reached for the pages waiting inside the envelope. The first page, I discovered, was a certificate of birth.

This document is written for the sole purpose of proof and witness to the birth of a baby boy on the 12th day, of the 3rd month, of the 61st year of the New Kingdom.

The name given him by his father, King Etcheon, and his mother, Queen Arcadia, is Prince Etcheon the Younger.

The bloodline of this child is pure, and his name is forever. No one can take it from him.

I, Mythias, have written this document with my own hand in order to protect the birthright of the child, Prince Etcheon the Younger.

As I touched the raised lettering, my throat felt dry, and my heart throbbed within my chest. I was the child of royalty. I whispered the names of my mother and father so I could hear them with my ears and let them to linger in my heart.

Placing the certificate carefully on the table, I unfolded the letter. My breathing seemed to be stilled as I read why I was placed in the care of Granna Fela and, when the time came, what was expected of me. What I read disturbed and frightened me, and I began to wonder if my seventeen years had given me the maturity to be the person I now needed to be. It was then that I began to understand what Mr. Otherton meant when he said, "The true burden comes with the knowledge of what you will find written on the pages . . ."

The sachet came to my attention once again as my fingers touched the strings that held its contents secret. Inside, I discovered a gold neck chain. Wrapped within the chain was a mantle, round and large enough, it seemed, to hold the crest. I placed the crest inside the mantle and slipped the chain around my neck.

With the gold crest hidden and hanging from my neck, I tucked the documents and letters into the pouch and placed it beneath my bed. I closed my eyes, knowing that at the end of the second day after Granna's death, what I had been given was beyond my imagination.

Early, on the third morning after Granna's death, I turned to the unfortunate task she had given me concerning her personal belongings. I carefully placed them inside a large cotton bag, taking time to walk to the window to search beyond the garden, the fence, and the road, every now and then. What I thought I would see, I did not know, only that I continued my vigil throughout the rest of the day, remembering the words of Mr. Otherton about the midnight hour.

As the sky darkened, so did the cottage. There I sat in the darkness, listening, waiting, but all was quiet, and I soon fell asleep.

2

Carainisafari

I WAS AS RELIEVED FOR MR. Otherton as I was for myself when I awoke and found all was well. Even though I only knew him for a short time, he was Granna's brother, and he had given me a gift more valuable than a kingdom.

I would not venture out today, but instead stay inside the cottage and do the things Granna had asked to be done in her note. But I would continue to watch for any stranger that might hide behind the gate or walk up to my door.

As I worked, I was reminded of all Granna had done for me. She taught me the bow and the sling. She taught me the computation of numbers, the science of the earth, and the seasons of time. She made me a gentleman and an intellectual, and then she left me. I missed her deeply and painfully at that moment and found myself drawn to a small shelf just to the left of the mantle.

Two unicorns, sculptured in white and gold with horns on their heads and wings spread in flight, stood as if they were protecting five small, leather-bound books that nestled between them. Each book contained a story, written in language not spoken in the village, but one that Granna taught me when I was a child.

I pulled the first storybook from the shelf and sat on her bed. I was just about to open the cover when I heard a sound coming from the road beyond the gate. Without hesitation, my sling in hand, I stepped quietly through the back door. Using the cottage and the foliage as a cover, I moved silently into a position where I could see the road clearly.

Near the road I caught sight of a deer racing through the trees. I waited, but nothing more happened. The road was silent as were the trees beyond it. I slipped silently back into the cottage, secured the latch, and continued my dusting.

Three bricks seemed to wobble at my touch. Remembering Granna's instruction, I carefully tugged at one. It gave way, falling into my hands. I removed the second and the third. Then I peered into the shadows of light that filtered through the darkness of the hole beyond the bricks. There I saw the outline of what appeared to be two bundles.

I reached into the darkness and pulled them toward me. One was larger than the other, but both were tightly woven about with cords to protect their contents. They were neither heavy nor awkward. I laid them carefully on the floor and set the bricks back in their places. At that moment, I knew that Granna had not wanted me to clean the bricks as much as she wanted me to find what was behind them.

I sat down and was just about to untie the cord of the first carrier when I heard the sound of dry limbs breaking from somewhere behind the cottage.

I quickly hid the carriers beneath Granna's bed and once again picked up my sling, moving cautiously to the edge of the window. With a finger, I moved the curtain slightly and peered out. In the thicket I saw moving shadows. Someone was watching the cottage.

It was then that I heard the voice of Mayor Ratherberry calling out my name. Relief surged through me. I set my weapons down and opened the door to greet him.

"Hail there, young Etcheon." Mayor Ratherberry waved and dismounted his horse. He came toward me, his eyes soft with concern. "I have come to see how you are faring this day."

I admitted that it had been a rather difficult morning, explaining Granna's request concerning her belongings. "I am to deliver them to Mrs. Ratherberry who will give them to those in need."

"Ah, yes," he replied with pride at the mention of his wife's activities. "She is like a mother hen gathering her chicks about her and tending to them. It is one of her many fine qualities."

I nodded in agreement and asked him if he would mind delivering Granna's things to his wife.

His smile was generous. "I would be more than happy to do that for you."

"May I ask one more favor?"

"But of course."

"I must go away, for a time. How long, I do not know. Would you mind stopping by the cottage, now and again, when you are passing by, and see to its upkeep?"

"It would honor me to do so, my young friend," he said with sincerity, and though I could see he wanted to ask my business, he graciously refrained from doing so.

When the bag was tied to his horse, he turned to me one more time, tears glistening in the corners of his eyes. "You have never been away from Meadows since the day you came as a child. You are young, but more importantly, you are innocent. Do not let your innocence show. Keep it hidden beneath a quiet expression." He embraced me, I think as a father would embrace his son. Then he climbed into his saddle and returned the way he had come.

I watched him as he disappeared beyond the hillside, and a feeling of loneliness swept through me. I did not know where I would go. I had never been beyond the perimeter of the village before, and I did not want to leave it now.

I turned back to the cottage and opened the door, when a strange odor touched my nostrils, and I heard the sound of footsteps against the floor.

"Not to run," a voice called out to me. A scraggly, yellowish man, wearing a long stained jacket over dirty, patched trousers, appeared in the doorway of Granna's bedroom. Stringy dark hair fell about his shoulders. A wrinkled hat hung low over his eyes, leaving them in the shadows, yet the pupils cast a glow about his face, revealing odd features covered by thick whiskers. In one arm he held the books—in the other, the unicorn bookends.

"Got what we com fer," he hissed, his voice raspy, as if he was not used to speaking. "No harm'll com if'n ya mind." He glanced behind me. Then the glow of his eyes returned to me. "Not fer ya to be thinkin' of scapin'."

I turned to see a man, similar to the first, but bigger—his appearance even more petrifying. In his hand he held a dagger. Beyond him, I could see two more men, waiting beside the gate. Their fearsome ugliness was no different than the second.

The sensation of terror chilled my spine and the taste of fear coated my mouth. "What do you want of me?" I asked, knowing I could not run, for they were behind and in front of me. "I am nothing but a village peasant. Those books you hold against you are nothing but silly storybooks."

"Nay." The man grinned, his dirty fingers wrapping themselves tighter around the books. His wide grin revealed unsightly teeth. "They's gold to him who wants 'em, and boy what reads 'em." His laugh was raspy and ugly. "Talks gone." He nodded to the man with the knife, and I felt a twinge of pain against my throat.

"Much pain can be, without takin' life," the second man spoke quietly in my ear, his breath thick with the smell of dead rats. "No trouble; no more blood 'cept the drop on yer shirt." His filthy hands grabbed me, none to gently, and dragged me from the cottage.

It was then that all things became a blur. I heard a roar, and I saw, out of the corner of my eye, a streak of black. Then the knife fell to the ground. The body of the one who had held it fell with it, his neck broken. I turned to see the books and the bookends drop from the hands of the second man as deep gashes from large claws caused large slits and holes in his face and neck, yet no blood flowed. He fell to the ground next to the hat that had veiled his face, and I could see his ugly, twisted features.

The two men near the gate turned from ugly humans to sneering, hideous wolf-like creatures—fangs dripping with their own dribble. Their enormous eyes, searing with fire, turned to me, and I could not move. They howled as they lifted their paws. But before they had taken even one step toward me, two Great Danes attacked from behind, forcing them to the ground and tearing at them until they lay dead.

Still a third creature stepped from the trees—larger than any of the others. His voice, when he called out my name, was gentle, but his eyes told me he was not. His giant hands reached out and grabbed the Great Danes, dangling them as if they were puppies. He took one step, then another, toward me, his narrow eyes reaching deep into mine, holding me captive.

"Not so simple to flee frum me," he snorted, coming closer as the ground trembled under the weight of his huge body. Then a cry of an eagle took his attention, and he looked up to see massive, sharp talons, just before they dug into the sockets of his eyes, tearing deeper and deeper. He cried out in pain and dropped the Great Danes to fight against the bird, whose size was larger than any eagle I had ever seen.

The hands of the creature waved about his head, tormented by the pain, trying to grab the eagle. But soon his hands were holding his ears against the shrillness of the eagle's battle cry. Finally, one last breath escaped his lungs, and he fell dead.

Even as his body fell, it began to decay. So did the bodies of the others who died before him. Soon there was nothing but ashes scattered about. A cool breeze appeared and swept them into its force, carrying them up into the air and away.

I could not explain what I had just seen. I could only stand frozen—watching the dogs clean their bodies until there was nothing left of the creatures on them. The eagle had disappeared, only to return with his talons free of what had oozed from the creature. He settled himself on the fence beside me, his kind eyes touching mine while his beak opened and the sounds that escaped formed themselves into words.

"You will be all right now," he said. "Retrieve the carriers, and we will lead you to safety inside the forest."

I looked at him and simply nodded my head that I understood, though I did not. I reached down to pick up the books so I could take them with me, but they were gone as well as the bookends. "Where . . . ?" I could make no sense out of what I had just seen, or what I could not see. Neither did I know how to talk to an eagle.

"There will be time to talk later." The bird fluttered his wings impatiently.

I frowned at him, and my mind became alive again. "Am I in a dream? Or are you real, and I am understanding the sounds that come from your beak, as if they were words?" I flung my arms in exasperation. "How did you know about the . . . the . . . whatever kind of creatures they were?"

"I am Barok," the eagle replied. "I am your friend and protector. The rest of the story is much too long in the telling, and there is no time to dawdle. It will all be explained to you, soon enough." He flapped his wing gently against my ear. "Go quickly. There may be more of these creatures behind us."

I took a deep breath and did as he asked. I had no desire to see another creature as ugly and frightening as those who had come to my door.

Before the sun had reached its highest point, I stepped from the little cottage that had been my home. Two carriers, still unopened, were strapped to my back and against the pouch, along with another suit of clothing. My sling was in my pocket, my bow in my hand.

I turned, one last time, and looked at the cottage. Sadness felt heavy in my heart. Where I was going or how long I would be gone, I did not know. But I had come to the conclusion that what had happened and what was happening now was not a dream, and I was to trust my life to the animals that had come to my rescue.

The two Danes now stood on either side of me. The wounds encountered in their battle against the creatures were no longer visible. The eagle, his size shrinking in front of my eyes until he was small enough to fit upon my shoulder, seemed content and called to the Danes to lead the way.

We traveled swiftly and in silence for a great distance, not keeping to any pattern or path, but varying our direction from the east to the west and back again—never straying from a northerly course. How deep we ventured I cannot say, but the forest became quiet as darkness began to fall, and I found myself growing weary.

She watched him as he approached the edge of her clandestine realm. The animals had reached him in time, though the timing could have been better. Etcheon would not have had to encounter the changelings, nor know of their existence, had the mayor of his village not stopped by. He would ask her about them, and she would have to tell him the truth, whether it be this night or another. He would have to know.

She watched him approach. He was the fair-haired son of a fair-haired son of the clan of Purcatious—meaning pure of blood. He was as his father — intelligent, tall, strong, and agile. He was as his mother in the clarity of his deep blue eyes and his gift. She could sense the integrity and strength of his ancestors within him. Feladelphia had prepared him well for that which he had yet to learn.

She calculated the time. Another year would pass before he would step beyond the tree. "Help me, Ancient one," she whispered, her hands touching the warmth of gnarled bark as she rested her head against its strength. "Let me make no mistakes in preparing him for that which he must do."

Barok fluttered his wings. I too saw the light coming from a distance. I could hear the softness of the music that echoed through the trees.

"Open your pouch and release the unicorns," Barok commanded, lifting his talons from my shoulder and flying to a branch.

"But I do not have them," I protested. "They disappeared before I could pick them up from the ground."

"That is true, and now they are in your pouch."

"And what am I to do with them once I release them from my pouch?" I questioned. I opened my pouch and was surprised to actually see them inside. I gave the eagle a dubious glance before I removed them, holding them up for him to see.

There was no need for my concern as to what would happen. As quickly as they were in my hands, they became alive, their bodies stretching and growing until they were the size of a horse. They shook their golden manes, their horns catching the light of the sun. They lifted their hooves high in the air and let their feathered wings lift them into the sky. As soon as they had disappeared, Barok settled himself on my shoulder, seemingly unimpressed.

"What just happened?" I managed to sputter through my gaping mouth.

"They were the protectors of the books for the length of time the books were away from their realm. Now close your mouth before a flying insect finds a new home."

I shook my head and rubbed my eyes. "Is this something that I will have to get used to?" I asked. "Creatures who can change forms . . . bookends who come alive . . . an eagle who can grow and shrink as easily as he can talk?"

The eagle shrugged. The Danes granted me a sympathetic glance, but no answer was given me. Instead the music that seemed distant, just a few minutes before, now filled me with its tender melody, and my questions no longer concerned me.

"Hello, Etcheon," I heard a voice whisper within the music.

"Hello, Tarainisafari," I answered back as if saying her name was not new to me. To say it tickles the tongue, so I will simply call her Taraini from this point on.

"Welcome to my home," she said, and smiled as I stepped from the coolness of the darkened forest into the warmth of her light.

I looked at the beautiful woman before me. A unicorn stood at her right side, its wings now all but invisible. The Danes stood at her left, while an owl peered at me from a limb of the ancient tree.

My eyes turned back to Taraini. "May I ask where we are? It has been a very strange day, and I feel like I'm caught in a whirlwind—twisting inside out."

She looked around her just as I had done. "We are here," she said simply.

"Then can you tell me where 'here' is?" I asked again.

"It is a place without distinction, without the riches of great lands. It is a place of peace, a realm of safety—one that no one can violate. Can you accept that answer?"

I hesitated. "For now I will, but I hope for a clearer explanation at some time in the future."

Removing the carriers from my back, she called for the Danes to take them. "Come," she said, beckoning to the entrance of her home. "I have prepared a welcome feast for you." She stopped and turned to me. "I'm sorry, I have not thanked you for bringing Sadusaius back to me. I have missed him, but he was very proud to have been given the responsibility as caretaker of the books." She turned her back to me once again and motioned for me to follow. The second unicorn was nowhere in sight.

When I stepped inside the cavity of the ancient tree, I found a room of vines and limbs that had wound themselves around each other until they had designed and created finely crafted cupboards and tables, chairs and bookcases, and all the necessary furnishings to provide comfortable, if not elegant, surroundings. The room was truly remarkable.

A staircase circled around the wall of the tree until it disappeared in the darkness far above me. There seemed to be no end to its size.

Taraini smiled at my wonder and bid me to sit at a table filled with foods I had never seen before. Their flavor, though different, was as sweet and tasty as those I knew. As we ate, we talked of the village and the people who lived there.

"You will be happy to know that all are safe in the village." She smiled, setting her fork beside her plate. "The creatures were sent by another as insects imbedded in the coat of Mr. Otherton's horse. They are Changelings—a name given them because they can change from one form to another. It was to our advantage that it took them three days, in the atmosphere of your village, to change from insects to the ugly creatures who came to your door."

I shuddered at the thought of them. "I have seen enough this day to know that nightmares can become realities."

"It was not something you were meant to see." Her hand reached out across the table and touched mine. "We are sorry that you had to, though it may be good, as time goes on, that you did. Nonetheless, you were in no danger because Barok was there to protect you."

"I am truly grateful to those who rescued me," I replied, thinking of all she had said. "You spoke of the one who sent the creatures as if you knew who it was."

"It is the one who desires power above that which he has," she replied, and I thought I caught a glimpse of anger in her eyes. "You will begin to understand in time."

"Tell me how you know me." It was a question I craved an answer for.

"I know you because you are a part of me as I am a part of you."

I frowned at her, and her face puckered in sympathetic response. "It is not a simple answer I know, but it is the answer nonetheless."

"I do not understand," I told her truthfully.

She stood and took my hand, leading me back into the night. "My home is the age of creation," she said as if to change the subject. Then, giving her full attention to the massive tree in front of us, she continued, "The Ancient knows everything that was, everything that is, and everything that is yet to be. Its wisdom is far beyond that of the greatest philosopher. Its knowledge would fill the universe." She touched the bark with reverent hands. "It has created my world—my kingdom—and is my protector. But there is something you must know. The Ancient knows of one future for you and your people. It is for you to decide if there is another."

I touched the bark of the Ancient as she had done, and something stirred inside of me. It felt as if a memory, lost long ago, wished to return but could not find the way.

"The day will come," she whispered, "when you must step beyond the bark of the Ancient and into another time of this world. There you will find that which hides inside of you."

She reached out and soothed my brow with the touch of her fingers, then summoned the eagle. "It is late, and you are tired. Barok will show you to your room where you will find everything you need. Sleep well and tomorrow we will open the carriers." She smiled. "Good night, Prince Etcheon the Younger."

The eagle waited for me at the foot of stairs woven of limbs. "Follow me, lad," he called to me. Spreading his wings, he disappeared into the darkness of the staircase.

I followed, finding him in the front of a door. With a touch from Barok's wing, the door opened, and I found myself in a room of twigs and branches, twined and intertwined until they were shaped as a bed, a washstand, a chair, and a wardrobe. The room, I could see by its shape, was one of the enormous branches that extended from the body of the Ancient.

I heard the door close behind me. I stood there thinking that this had been the most remarkable day of my life. Everything around me was strange. . . and beautiful . . . and peaceful . . . yet mysteriously puzzling. My mind and body were suddenly exhausted, and I dropped to the bed—asleep within seconds. I awoke to the sun on my face and an eagle sitting at the foot of my bed.

"Ah, there you are. I wondered when the sun would awaken you." He eyed me with his piercing pupils. "You slept well, I see, which is good, for we have much to do today. Breakfast awaits the prince. Let him dress quickly." Barok paused. "Perhaps it would be better to say let him change his clothing, for I see he forgot to undress before he slept." He perched himself on the wardrobe and, with his beak, opened the door. "Inside you will find your clothes for the day. Hurry now. I shall see you at the bottom of the stairs." Barok flew from the room.

Taraini welcomed me with a gentle smile when I walked down the stairs and invited me to sit at a table filled with fruits and breads. "Eat, then we will see what lies hidden inside the pelted folds that hang from your shoulder."

I ate what she had placed on my plate while we talked of trivial things. When my plate was empty, she handed me a folded parchment. "Open it and read it aloud, please."

I did as she asked.

tcheon,

I am writing this letter on the 6th day of the 8th month of the 63rd year of the new kingdom. As I sit here, I am watching a young mother embrace her child as she reads him a story. That child is you, my son, and it is difficult

to pen this letter knowing that we may never see you again.

Tears are forming on your mother's cheeks while my heart is aching. It is only because of the love we feel for you and the knowledge that we are protecting your life, that we do this.

Today we will deliver you to Feladelphia, who has made arrangements to take you to a place, and a time, that is unknown to us and to all who know us. There, she will see to your education and your protection. Yet in all that she will teach you, she cannot teach what she does not know.

There is another who will attend and teach you after Feladelphia is gone. Listen and learn well, my son. A great responsibility lies ahead of you. It is a responsibility that will require much from you, for in the end it will be you who saves us if we are to be saved.

We can only pray that you are well and those who search for you have failed in their quest.

Our lives depend upon your life; our kingdom upon your victory or defeat.

Your loving father,

King Etcheon

I folded the letter carefully and placed it back into the pouch. "It is you my father refers to when he speaks of another, is it not?" I asked.

"It is," she replied. "Now undo the cord of the smaller of the two carriers."

I laid the letter down, carefully freed the knot, and lifted the pelted covering. Inside laid a golden dagger confined in a leather sheath—its handle engraved with my family crest. Beneath the dagger, I found a beautiful scarf made of silk. There was also a curious looking compass.

She smiled. "The dagger belongs to your father—the scarf to your mother."

I touched the silk with my fingers, then cradled it in my hands, and lifted it to my cheek.

"The scarf will be a part of you again," Taraini said softly. "I will wrap it so it can be carried within your pouch without becoming soiled." Her eyes told me she understood my reluctance in letting it go as she reached for the scarf and guided my attention back to the carrier.

I picked up the dagger and removed it from its sheath. It was an amazing piece of workmanship. "This belonged to my father."

Taraini nodded. "This also will now be a part of you. You are to wear it as you do the crest."

Before I could touch or ask about the odd-looking circular gold compass, Taraini folded the pelt, covering it, and instructed me to open the second carrier.

Inside I found a vest made of the same material as that of the sachet. It was unlike anything I had ever seen. I took it from the carrier and studied it closely. "Tell me," I said, "what is this made of?"

"Its material is from the bark of the Ancient," she replied, with no further explanation.

Beneath the vest I found a white tunic, a pair of dark brown trousers, a belt, a pair of soft leather boots and, what I assumed to be a covering for my head. The covering was made of the same material as the vest. Its crown molded to be raised slightly above the crown of the head. Its brim was tapered upward in the back, yet down in the front to protect the eyes.

"It is a clataè," she explained, taking it from my hand.

"It is remarkable," I replied, "as is the vest."

"The Ancient of Trees thanks you for your approval of its gifts," she nodded. "The vest is indeed soft to the touch, yet it is strong as metal. Nothing can penetrate it. It is the same with the clataè. There will be times when their protection will become your power." She returned the clothing to the carrier, wrapped the cords, and tied them. Then she handed it to me. "Place the carriers in your wardrobe while I prepare a lunch for us. When you return, Barok will show you the horse you will ride through the meadows and woodlands of this tiny kingdom."

"Tell me about the vest," I said to Barok later, as we neared the most magnificent horse I had ever seen.

"I can tell you nothing that you do not already know," he replied, fluttering his wing against my cheek. "So I will tell you something you do not know. The horse you will ride is named Walkelin."

He perched himself on the beautiful stallion's back. "He is a gentle horse, strong and fast, with a quick mind."

The horse's coat was the color of cinnamon; his mane—black and silky. He was large and powerfully built. He was also pleasant, as he nuzzled me with a velvety nose in friendly greeting.

"Where is his saddle?" I asked, looking about and seeing none.

Barok cocked his head and peered at me. "He does not wear a saddle. Neither does he wear a bridle."

"Then how do I ride him?"

"You simply sit upon his back. If you need to hold anything, wrap your fingers through his mane." He flew about me, seemingly enjoying my dilemma.

"Can I communicate with him as I do you?" I asked.

"In time, if that is your wish."

"If it is my wish?"

Before he could reply, the unicorn appeared. He did not stand as tall as Walkelin, nor was he as muscular. Instead, he was slim and graceful in his movements. His white coat and golden mane gave the impression of a magical appearance. The horn on his head glinted in the sun. The large pupils of his eyes seemed almost transparent in their color, yet they reflected light as if they were crystals. He was just as he appeared as the bookend Granna insisted that I dust every morning. Now I wondered if I had, at times, offended him with my complaining. I reached up, stroked his mane, and whispered in his ear, "I apologize for any dust I might have overlooked."

Sadusaius neighed softly. I had been forgiven.

Taraini was waiting when I returned to the garden with the horse and the unicorn. "It is a beautiful day for a picnic," she said, as the unicorn knelt for her to mount.

Walkelin knelt for me and once I was astride, the Danes took their place on the path in front of us while Barok soared just above the shadows of the trees.

As we rode to the south, the quiet that surrounded us brought with it a calm breeze, and I began to acquaint myself with Taraini's kingdom. There were no riches that would speak for man, nor great lands that they would desire for their own—only trees, small meadows, and gentle streams.

We traveled for perhaps two hours when the animals stopped. "You have seen all that exists within the perimeters of my realm," Taraini explained as she slipped from the unicorn's back. "Here we will eat lunch and talk."

I laid a coverlet on the grass under the shelter of a tree and accepted a plate of sweet breads and fruit that she offered me.

"What do you think of my kingdom?" she asked, looking about her while relaxing by the hollow of the tree.

"I am enchanted with its beauty, yet curious of its existence."

"And what does your curiosity require for satisfaction?"

"To know if we are deep within the forest near my village."

"We are within no other forest but our own."

"I do not understand."

She smiled softly, and her voice became tender. "I will explain. We are where the Ancient of Trees has placed us, for now. As you can see the Ancient has provided me with a peaceful home, at the request of my father. Here I have studied much of the wisdom and knowledge it holds within its bark, as my father did before me. Here, time is irrelevant and where my life becomes your life, so that you can learn, as I have, who you are meant to be."

"Yesterday, when you spoke the words that the day will come when I must walk beyond the tree and step into another world of this world—what did you mean?"

She dropped her eyes, shadowing them beneath her lids. "Perhaps I should not have revealed those words so quickly." Then she raised her eyes to meet mine. "But, again, perhaps you are ready. It is not for me to judge. Only you will know."

She said no more about the subject, but instead took the final bite of the sweetbread she held in her hand and began putting all that was not eaten back into the basket. Though we lingered yet a little while, she refrained from speaking of it again.

It wasn't until later that evening, when we sat under the limbs of the Ancient, that she answered my question.

"The time will come," she began, "as I first explained, when you will leave this forest and enter another time and another place within this world. There lies the kingdom of your people, though it is now ruled by another."

"In this time and place you speak of, do hideous creatures, like those who attacked me, exist?" I asked, remembering I was ill-prepared to have defended myself. If Barok and the Danes had not been there to protect me, I surely would have died.

"Do not think of them for now. The day you step beyond the tree, you will be able to defend yourself against all who try to harm you."

She gazed into the sky as if she were looking for something. "See that constellation in the distance?" she pointed directly above her.

I followed the direction of her finger. "I see it," I said.

"I think of it as belonging to you. Let it always be your guide." She turned back to me. "There is something else I must tell you. It is not with mortal weaponry that you will face your most fearsome foe. Instead, it will be that which lies within you. Because you are who you are, and with all you will yet learn, no wizard will have power over you. He will not be able to control your mind. He will not be able to shake your spirit. Your power will be greater than his power. Your light greater than his darkness." She stood. "Now you must rest. Tomorrow we begin your training."

She watched him as he climbed the stairs to his room. It had been wise of the king and queen to follow the council of the Ancient—though their sacrifice seemed almost unbearable, for they would never know their son as a child.

It had been difficult to refrain from telling him more, but she must also follow the council of the Ancient in allowing the animals to tutor him—to prepare him as only they could, so the gift that slept inside him would begin to feel life in his desire to use it for good.

3

The Danes

IT WAS EARLY WHEN BAROK ENTERED my room through the window and began making his eagle noises. "Save your sleep for another time, Etcheon, my lad. There is much to do this day."

I opened my eyes and immediately peered into those of the eagle, who had perched himself upon my chest.

"Ka-ka!" he cried. "There are your eyes. Now use them to find your clothing and guide you down the stairs."

"Funny bird," I scoffed at him, amused.

He did not reply but flew to the wardrobe. "The clothing inside, you will wear. They are the clothing of your kin."

I removed one of the five tunics, a pair of dark leather trousers, and finely stitched boots from the wardrobe. I felt the richness of their fabric, hesitating to put them on until Barok's wing flapped against the back of my head.

"These clothes are not simply to admire," he said. "They are to be put upon this all but naked body that stands before me."

"Tell me," I replied, unconcerned with his flurry, "what are they made of?"

If an eagle could give a sigh of impatience that is how I would describe the noise that came from his chest. "The day is not long enough for a discourse on that subject," he chided. "Just be pleased with the comfort of their soft material and the protection of their covering." At that moment, he seemed more a mother hen than a commanding eagle, and I could not resist a smile, concealing it as I dressed.

"Do not forget the vest," he reminded me, dropping it on my head. When it was where it belonged, he fluttered about me. "Methinks you are a gentleman, after all. Now come, you have wasted enough time."

As soon as we had finished the morning meal, Taraini led me outside and motioned for me to sit on the large stump, beneath the shade of the Ancient. "We would like you to tell us a story from the first of your books," she said, pointing to my pouch.

"They are simple stories," I replied, wondering how she knew about them.

"Perhaps not," she said. "We are waiting."

I reached my hand inside and removed the first one Granna had read to me. The leather of its cover was weathered but strong, and the memory of it being held in her gentle hands brought a sudden tear to my eye. I quickly wiped it away and opened the book.

"You must tell us the story in the language it is written," Taraini insisted.

The animals moved close, in anticipation, and I began to read, the language rolling from my tongue as if I had never spoken another.

> *El Agle flat vor el daklek ov el myst estva klope eslof lunga el vetaes rym . . .* [The eagle flew above the shadow of the mist that spread itself along the water's edge].
>
> It was a mystery to him until his eyes cut through its haze and beheld a child, a small boy cloaked in the murkiness, hidden from his mother. The eagle heard her call to her child, unable to see him. Nor could she hear his cries: "Help me, Mommy. I cannot see where to go."
>
> Then the mother looked up at the eagle. "Protect him," she called out to him. "For it is the wizard's work that conceals my child from me."
>
> Beyond the mist, the eagle saw four soldiers on swift horses making their way to where the child stood, and he knew the woman spoke the truth. The mist was a wizard's magic, a conspiracy to kidnap the son of a king.
>
> With a cry, telling the woman he understood, the eagle swooped down, grasped the child in his talons, and returned to the sky. But

even as he did so, an arrow pierced his feathers, scarcely missing the muscle of his body. He had to command all the power of his wings to soar above the swiftness of the arrows that could pierce the child dangling from his talons, now too afraid to cry out.

On the ground the young mother stood, watching her son being lifted into yet another mist well beyond her reach. She shuddered at the fear that her child must have in his heart. But there was no other way. She, who was to take him away, had not yet arrived.

Her eyes caught sight of an arrow as it barely grazed the eagle's wing just as he disappeared into the cloud, carrying her child with him.

She laughed at the soldiers, hearing the beating of the horses' hooves against the ground. They had come too late. Her child was safe. She hid herself among the rocks until all was silent once again.

When, at last, she was inside the castle, where the king awaited her return, she fell into his arms, her tears uniting with his as they held each other. "It has been done," she whispered in his ear.

The eagle flew near the sea, until he came to the safety of his nest. There he laid the child upon the soft straw. "No danger will come to you now," he said. "When it is safe, I will take you to yet another place." Spreading his wings, he cuddled the small boy, and they slept.

I stopped reading. I simply held the book in my hand, touching the pages made of fine parchment that never became soiled, even though I ran my fingers over them each time I read and studied them. I never knew why this book, along with four others, sat on Granna's shelf, guarded by two stately unicorn bookends. I never knew why it was so important that I learn the language in which they were written, or why Granna watched over them as carefully as she watched over me.

It was then that a deep awareness shook me. This story was not a story of fantasy but, instead, a story of truth. I turned to Taraini. "The mother knew the child would be in danger when she took him to the sea, did she not?"

"Why do you suppose she took him then?" she asked, lifting her eyes to meet mine.

"Because the greater danger was in not taking him, I would assume."

"You are correct," she replied.

I let my hand caress the pages that lay open. "This is my story, is it not?"

"It is," she said simply.

I turned to Barok. "And you are the eagle who saved me that day."

Barok nodded

"Why did you leave me?"

He cocked his white, feathered head and gazed at me. "I did not leave you. It was you who did not recognize me." He cocked his head and eyed me, carefully. "As it is, methinks it was a simple thing to do for such a fine prince. Now, please continue the story."

The next hour, when the boy awakened, the eagle returned him to the place where he had rescued him. There, another woman waited. In one hand, she held two bundles. In the other, she held a small, round golden astrolabe.

She took the child in her arms and cuddled him. "Do not be afraid," she soothed him. "All things will be well for you." Then she opened the astrolabe, touched the dial with her finger, and with the eagle on her shoulder and the child in her arms, she disappeared.

I studied Taraini's face. "You know Granna Fela."

"I know her as well as you do, and I love her as you do."

"Will I see her again?" I asked, burying the tears that stirred my heart.

"Someday, we will both see her again," she assured me, taking the book from my hand and slipping it into her sheath.

I wanted to remember the other stories. I reached for my pouch, but Taraini touched my hand and shook her head.

"All in its time," she said quietly. "Now, we must begin your training." She reached out and brought the Danes to her. "You will go into the forest and learn from Ranulf." She stroked the black one. "And Gudrod." She touched the neck of the brown one.

I repeated their names, kneeling between them and stroking their necks as she had done. As my hand felt the warmth of their coats, my mind felt a strange connection to their consciousness. The sensation of the encounter startled me, and I withdrew my hands.

"Allow them to communicate with you," she instructed.

I frowned.

She returned my frown with one of her own. "Did you think my Danes were without the skill to converse? Sit with them and let them teach you." With those words, she walked away.

I looked at the Danes, wondering if I should talk or simply listen. I let my mind become quiet. They moved closer and settled themselves on their haunches. The sensation that disturbed me when I touched them earlier began to vibrate once again. I listened without distraction, completely captured. Gudrod would bark, and I understood the meaning of his bark, just as I understood the chatter of Barok. Ranulf's eyes locked mine, flooding my mind with silent conversation.

I moved to the ground and positioned myself between them, placing a hand on the back of each dog. As I stroked them I began to understand that our communication could be as natural as if I were speaking to Taraini.

"It will become simple to you," Gudrod barked. "We will teach you to distinguish between human and animal; between human and human; between animal and animal—through their scent. You will know the odor of fear, the odor of the hunter and of the prey, and the odor of the morning and of the night. These you will know as well as the scent of sunshine and rain."

Ranulf barked. "You will learn to use your instinct as an animal does. Yet it is one thing we cannot teach you, for it is already within you. We can only teach you to recognize its presence. Come now. We will begin." He paused. "First you must place a blindfold over your eyes. You will follow our scent, using your nostrils, and our movements with your ears."

"I think I can already smell the scent of two Danes having a sporting time as they cause one boy grief," I complained while stifling a grin. I pulled Mr. Otherton's handkerchief from my pouch. "But I will do as you ask."

"Is the scent strong enough?" Ranulf asked when the handkerchief covered my eyes.

"You both smell like dogs." I rubbed my nose and made a face.

"Then you are ready."

I heard the rustling of dry leaves. I listened to identify the direction in which they were going. When I knew enough, I crouched to my knees and using my hands to guide me, much as an animal would, I began my first lesson.

For a very long time, I sniffed and listened and pawed my way through the leaves and rocks in my search. Then, without warning, I lost the scent of the Danes. Neither could I hear them. I resisted the desire to remove the blindfold and sat still, listening, forcing myself to concentrate. I could hear the scampering sounds of a small animal. I could hear the breeze as it gently caressed the trees, but I could not hear the Danes.

Something brushed passed me, and I caught the scent that had filled my nostrils earlier. "You have come back to rescue me, after all," I said, hoping it was, indeed, one of the Danes.

"Wake up your senses," Gudrod barked. "Do more than listen to the simple sounds. Sniff more than what is directly beneath your nose."

On the fourth day, it was as if my brain had awakened, and I could smell the scent of the trees as well as that of the squirrels that lived inside them. The Danes were pleased.

On the sixth day, thunderclouds, lightening, and insistent rain became a lesson all in itself, and I found myself listening for the sounds of the forest beneath the splatter of the rain that drenched my clothes. Water dripped from my hair and down my face, but I did not bother to wipe it away. I simply stood there, listening, until the scent of wet wood, dead leaves, live animals, and, if I was not mistaken—two Great Danes—came alive.

I separated their scent from that of the others, letting it lead me. Finally, I could hear Runolf in my head. He was telling Gudrod that he could see me. I glanced around, sniffing the air. The Danes were to the left. Their scent was strong. I had found them.

I called out to them. "I cannot see you, but I smell you, all the same. I can hear you in my thoughts. Do I need to stand before you, before I have passed the test?"

"It was a clever way to find your strength, don't you think?" Gudrod asked, appearing through the trees and gazing at me with steady eyes.

Clever, indeed, I thought to myself as I wrung the water from my tunic and my hair. "Tell me," I said, "did I pass the test?"

Ranulf looked up at me, placing his paw against my leg. "The test was not to find us, but that you could find us in spite of the test itself. Such is life. To find us without opposition would have been simple for you. But when the storm was placed in your path, you reached deeper inside until you found the ability."

In the beginning it had taken great effort to communicate through thought—to read the eyes of the Danes while no words were spoken. But as the days passed, it all became effortless. But if I were asked how I do this, there is no explanation that would satisfy man.

"The Danes have done well," Tarainisafari said to the Ancient as she watched Etcheon come toward her, a Dane on either side of him.

"Does that surprise you?" she heard the Ancient's voice echo in her thoughts.

"No," she replied. "For in him I see the strength of his ancestors. Yet, there remains so much innocence."

The Ancient's thoughts melted with her own. "His innocence will be his greatest resource. Tomorrow we will begin his training in mortal weaponry."

4

The Cestrosphendone

"YOUR SLING IS TUCKED AWAY somewhere, I presume," Taraini said. She put her arm through mine and guided me into the hollow of the tree.

I nodded that it was. "But who will teach me more than I know?" I asked, knowing there was no man in this kingdom.

"I will teach you." She turned away and walked a short distance from me. When she turned back to face me, I could see a sling in her hand. It was of a different design—longer and of much finer quality than my own.

"Never take anything for what it seems," she warned me. Then, placing a small arrow into the shaft of the sling, she demonstrated her ability. "I shall aim for the small limb on the right side of the tree two stadia from where I stand."

I watched as she became one with the sling, her movement quick. Her eyes seemed to guide the direction of motion and suddenly, with only a single rotation and the slightest of hesitation in her arm, the arrow was released and, with great speed, sailed silently to its target with astonishing precision. My mouth dropped open, and my eyes felt as if they were about to fall from their sockets.

"You are surprised that I have the strength?" Her amusement was plain.

"I will admit that I doubted, but tell me of the weapon," I begged. "I have never seen one like it before."

"It is called a cestrosphendone. Though similar to the sling, it is greater in its accuracy and delivery. Does it impress you?"

I nodded, taking my sling from the pouch. It seemed dull and unimposing in comparison, its flexible leather old and weathered.

"Aim for the same target." She handed me a stone and directed my attention to the tree where the arrow was imbedded in the limb and barely visible to my view. With my eyes steady, my balance smooth, and my rotation underhand as Granna taught me, I let the stone fly. I missed my mark by almost a cubit.

"You will soon learn, Etcheon." She had not spoken the words, for her mouth was still. I had taken them from her thoughts. In that instant I began to marvel at the transformation that was taking place inside of me. "How far can it reach?" I asked.

"The pebbles?" she asked innocently, though I knew she was aware that I had read her thoughts.

"The mind."

She gave me a steady gaze. "As far as you will take it. As far as you desire it to go." Taking the sling from me, she replaced it with an impressive braided leather sling, its length over three cubits. "Desire to know and understand this weapon," she instructed. "Tomorrow, you will begin to understand the cestrosphendone that, from this point on, we will simply call the cestro."

Barok did not have to wake me the following morning, for I was awake early, and as soon as the morning meal was over, I insisted that we begin. I became annoyed with myself several times throughout the day but refused to stop until I could master the weapon.

"Perhaps you should rest for the evening," Taraini suggested when the sun had set and my muscles were enflamed with pain. "You have learned far more than you think."

With reluctance I handed her the cestro and found a comfortable spot against the Ancient of Trees.

For twenty days I studied the cestro and perfected the sling. I must say the mastering of it was not an easy task, but the perfecting of it was pure exhilaration.

On the morning of the twenty-first day, Barok awakened me. "Put on your old clothing. Remove the chain from around your neck. Leave it as well as the crest inside your room. Place the sling and the cestro inside your pouch, and follow me."

Taraini was waiting, astride the unicorn. Walkelin stood ready. I could see the mischievous glint in his eye as he challenged me to mount him without his help of lowering himself.

"I am not as innocent as you think me to be when it comes to straddling overgrown stallions," I retorted, in jest. With three quick, striding steps, I threw myself onto his back, grabbing his mane to hold me.

Taraini's laugh was not as loud as Walkelin's snort, and I wondered if he was impressed or surprised. For myself, I was surprised, but I would never tell him so.

"There was a time," Taraini said, as we traveled, "when a man would give his word, and his word was as precious to him as his own life. Then one day, men were introduced to greed, many falling victim to its evil. From that day, a man might give his word and then take advantage of the trusting soul who accepted it, stealing everything, even his life."

She studied me as a teacher would her pupil. "You are the victim of greed, Etcheon, and still as innocent as a babe in your knowledge of its devastation."

I laughed. "Mayor Ratherberry, from my village, advised me to keep my innocence hidden beneath a quiet expression."

"And you have done so," she commented, touching the unicorn's neck with her fingers as a signal for it to stop. "Your Mayor Ratherberry seems to be a man of insight. Now let us dismount and walk. There is something I must show you."

Leaving the horses, Taraini led me to a rather large rock. Though its size was quite remarkable, it was craggy in its appearance—grayish-blue in color and not at all impressive. She said nothing, only nodded for me to follow as she touched a small crack along its surface, then disappeared. "Do not be afraid," she whispered in my thoughts.

"I am not afraid," I replied, annoyed that she did not warn me of what was to happen. I closed my eyes and pressed my fingers against the crack.

"You can open them now," she chided me in her amusement.

I opened my eyes to find myself in a cave somewhat larger than the rock I pressed my fingers against. The glow of a large crystal that Taraini held in her hand gave light to the room, revealing several books carefully placed on raised, flat surfaces. They were set apart, as not to touch each other, yet there was order in their placement. In the center was a small, finely crafted table with a stool beside it.

When I looked back at Taraini, her expression was gentle and her eyes apologetic, though she did not apologize. "There are many things you will learn," she said, instead. "Do not let appearances form their own opinions in your mind."

She let her hand direct my eyes around the room. "In here you will learn of the strategy of men. You will read of wars caused by greed, of hate, and the division of kingdoms. But you will also read of wonderful things that will stir your mind and your heart." She reached down and touched a large, rather thick book, held together with cords and leather. "You will begin with this one. It is well over a thousand years old."

She took two steps, leaned down, and touched another book. It was not as large as the first and was bound with a cover made from something I did not recognize. "When you have finished the first, you will read this one." She walked from book to book, touching each one, and explained that I was to read all twenty-one books.

"Do not read them out of context for they are in chronological order and will bring you forward in time," she instructed, her voice soft but imposing. "Neither are you to take them beyond the walls of this rock. The books are delicate because of their age and must remain within its protective atmosphere. If removed, they will deteriorate until they are nothing but ashes." She paused and looked deeply into my eyes. "Do you understand?"

I acknowledged that I did. I walked about the room, as Taraini had done, touching the books one by one and sensing their ages. She watched me, quiet and observant. When I reached the last book, she spoke, her eyes revealing her sorrow and her voice strained. "You will not be the same when you return to my home. You will have aged with knowledge. You will have grown in wisdom, and you will have discovered the emotions of anger, hate, and greed."

She sighed deeply, letting a moment of stillness pass before continuing. "Be very careful when these emotions surface within you for they are strong. You must be stronger, or they will take hold of you as they did those who have disrupted your world and mine."

How strong were the emotions of hate, anger, or greed? I had no idea for I had yet to experience them, and the thought was somewhat troubling. I accepted the crystal from Taraini's hand, watched her disappear from the room (if one would call it a room), only to return with a basket filled with vegetables, fruit, bread, a plate, utensils, and a cup.

"Barok will bring clean clothing each morning and place it outside the rock." She set the basket on the table. "There is a stream a short distance from here where you can find fresh water for drinking and bathing." She touched her fingers to my cheek. "I will miss you, Etcheon."

With those words she turned away from me. I watched her as she walked into the sunlight. I wanted to cry out to her, beg her to stay. Beg her to protect me from that which might corrupt me. But I did not. Instead I stood there, silent, my mind touching another time.

I looked around and gazed at the books, praying they would bring me answers as I read them. How many days would I be here alone, I wondered. If I read one book a day, I would be here for twenty-one days. I shuddered as I began to feel the same loneliness I felt the day after Granna's burial. Then I heard Taraini command Walkelin to stay with me, and I was grateful.

The weight of her responsibility felt heavy as she walked back into the sunlight. She had no desire to leave him alone for even a short time with the books. He would return to her home either a man of greater determination and courage, or a man filled with bitterness and anger. She could not help him this time, nor could the Ancient. Only the gift of his mother could help him discover his inward strength. Would that, along with his innocence, be his resource, just as the Ancient had foretold? She prayed they would.

She climbed upon her unicorn and before leaving, commanded Walkelin to stay close by. That was all she could do for him.

5

Walkelin and the Books

I OPENED THE COVER OF THE book Taraini gave me and began to read in the quiet and loneliness of the room. Soon I became fascinated with the words I read in the language of my birth. Forgetting my loneliness, I read continually, reaching for food only when I was reminded of my hunger by the gnawing in my stomach.

With the setting of the sun, I finished the last page of a book that talked of a beautiful and peaceful people who studied the things of the earth, the planets, and the galaxies. I closed it carefully—laying it back on the rock from which I had taken it.

I walked out into the night, my cup in my hand, my mind filled with the mysteries of what I had read, and went in search of water. I could feel Walkelin's breath against my neck as he fell in step.

"Do not walk at the back of me," I scolded playfully. "Instead lead me to water."

He whinnied and moved to my side, guiding me to a small lake filled with clear water shimmering in the moonlight. I knelt at its shore and filled my cup.

It was late when we returned to the rock and the books. I did not go back inside, but instead, made the grass my bed, thinking of the one who wrote the book, which told of a kingdom that expanded without borders, until the ground became the sea. There, people lived in peace. There was no fear to trouble them. Their lives were happy. Their deaths came after their hundredth year and were sweet. There was no disease, no pain, and no sorrow. In the purity of their lives, they governed themselves. They studied music, art, the sciences, the earth, and the sky. They gave names to the clusters, galaxies, and the constellations.

I turned my eyes to the stars where one cluster seemed to draw me nearer to the heavens, and I felt a humble tightening in my chest. It was the cluster Taraini had pointed out to me.

It was early morning before I fell asleep, and when I awoke, clean clothes and food waited for me. I felt a disappointment that Barok had not awakened me with his sounds. I longed to tell someone of my discovery.

Taking the food, but leaving the clothes undisturbed, I hurried back inside the rock. I opened the second book and ate fruits and sweet bread while I read children's stories and verses of poetry. There were fanciful tales of unicorns and dragons, of underwater ships sailing the seas. There were fables filled with secret forests, fairies, and little people. The poetry spoke of romantic love and the philosophy of life.

When I placed the second book back on its rock, I knew it by heart.

Each day became as the day before. Barok delivered food and clothing without waking me. I did what I had to do in performing the daily rituals of living. Then I read feverishly, filling my mind with the happenings and the happiness of the pure in heart. I had all but forgotten I was alone, except for Walkelin, who followed me to the lake each time I went.

In twelve days I traveled in time through seven hundred years. But it wasn't until the thirteenth day and in the thirteenth book that I began to notice a change in the framework of the writing. This book told of welcoming a new people who had traveled a far distance. It told of medical discoveries to ease the burden of illness and pain.

On the fourteenth day, in the fourteenth book, the script was written in a more deliberate hand describing battles with no weapons, against a people who had many. "I cannot begin to write of the devastation I have seen," the author began.

> We are a people who have never experienced war nor did we even know the meaning of the word itself, until we were forced to fight without knowing the strategy of fighting. We have no weapons. We are at the mercy of those who have invaded our kingdom and brought with them disease and destruction. They have come to rid

themselves of us and take what is ours. We cannot stop them. We can only hide our children where they cannot find them, make ourselves their target as we run, and lead them away from the hiding place.

The writer continued to describe the ugliness of the invasion, and I forced myself to read on until I could no longer bear it. I suddenly felt as if I was suffocating, and I stumbled outside for air, barely remembering to leave the book behind. My stomach was retching, and I could not stop the sickness. I staggered to the lake and fell into the water, letting its coolness wash over me until the sickness passed.

Walkelin stood silently at the water's edge, watching and waiting as if he understood; and if he understood, why did I not? I had never felt such pain before.

"Taraini!" I screamed. "Why did you leave me here alone to read of such terrible things?" There was no answer. Yet, if nothing else, my display brought me to my senses, and I pulled myself from the water.

Walkelin nudged me gently, and I climbed onto his back. He took me to a meadow where birds were chirping and butterflies dancing. There he stood quietly while I rested against a tree, my strength depleted, and listened to the sounds of the meadow until my spirits were lifted and my mind settled. Yet I could not put the things I had read from my thoughts.

I did not sleep that night until the early hours of morning and then only fretfully. I took my time to bathe and eat. I lingered in the fresh air for longer than I should, for I was not anxious to return to the inside of the rock, and to the book I had run away from the night before. When I opened it again and began to study the pages, the anger that had planted its seed inside of me demanded that I know everything that was written.

For three days, as I read about the horror of war and of the pain and grief suffered by the descendents of the pure in heart, I began to recognize the terrible emotion of hate. The words, difficult to read now because of the corruption of the language by those who ruled, did nothing to restrain the hate, only encourage it.

It wasn't until the nineteenth day when I opened the nineteenth book, the feeling of hate and anger strong within me, that I was introduced to greed.

This book was, once again, written in the pure language of my birth. It told of a clan of Purcatians, as they now called themselves, who escaped from the kingdom during that first war and found sanctuary deep within the forest. Because they were an intelligent people they soon learned the art of survival and remained undiscovered for many years, until one of their own became discontented and desired to have more.

> In his greed, he exposed our secret place to the enemy, a place that, for over a hundred years, had been our sanctuary. Only a few escaped this time, being forced to flee far from our forest and into the mountain pass.

> Did Peilon, the one who deceived us, receive his reward of gold and status as he yearned for in his deceit? I do not know. I can only hope that he has found his happiness here, for he has condemned himself in the hereafter.

I saw greed as a disease of the soul. I had no use for it nor did I desire to be faced with its infection. I continued to read.

> We searched until we found another place to build a kingdom, far away from civilization, deep within the mountains. Years passed and there we dwelled, no longer free of fear, but free to be happy once again. Our children have been taught the art of defense for there is no choice. They have taught their children, who will teach their children, and so on. We must now always be prepared for battle in order to secure our peace.

> It is with sadness that we do this, for it takes from our children their innocence and gives them knowledge we hoped to keep from them. Yet even as I write these words, I question if it was wrong to have deprived them of this knowledge in the first place. The lack of skills of war is the very thing that brought us close to extinction.

> Our lives will never be as they were in the beginning, but our hearts will remain pure, for we have built our kingdom in the same order of the first kingdom.

I closed the book, placed it back on the rock, and walked outside to a quiet evening. I lay down on my bed of grass and fell asleep, strangely undisturbed by thoughts.

On the twentieth day, I opened the twentieth book and continued to read of the goodness of this kingdom. They had returned to their old ways in their study of the earth and the sky, of music and art, and of the sciences. But because of the changing world around them, they continued to study the strategy of war, though they lived for the next hundred years in peace.

I studied their strategy until I understood it. It was clever, evasive, deliberate, and wise.

The morning of the twenty-first day, I awoke early, anxious to read the last book. I had neither taken the time to bathe or change my clothes for the past four days, and I had no desire to do so today.

The first page of the twenty-first book returned me to that same kingdom in a more recent time, and its discovery, once again, by men whose cause was greed. The author of these writings explains,

> We have trained our sons for four generations for this cause. Our success is in our ability to outthink the enemy and to use only that, which is superior in weaponry to eliminate them. They think the bow and mortar with fire are the sure offense, but our slings and our cestrosphendones have proven more effective, not only from a distance, but from hiding places outside our walls unknown to the enemy. We have the advantage for we fight on familiar ground. Everything is well placed. We hit from behind, above, the side, and the front. They are not prepared for our tactics. In our minds we have become a warlike people for the safety of our children. But those who know the strategy of the weapon and the battle do not boast of their skill. They keep it hidden, until the day they may need it.

The writer told of a wise king who brought the sling and the cestro to his people. The name was King Etchon. There the writing ended.

I turned to the next page and found the writing to be in a different hand. It dated the time to be sixty-five years later and listed the descendents of King Etchon.

King Etchon – Queen Oran ⁓⁓ Anointed on the 1st day of the 1st month of the 1st year of the New Kingdom.

King Etchon II – Queen Nayal ⁓⁓ Anointed on the 6th day of the 4th month of 20th year of the New Kingdom.

King Etchon III – Queen Beca ⁓⁓ Anointed on the 4th day of the 9th month of the 42nd year of the New Kingdom.

King Etcheon – Queen Arcadia ~~~ Anointed on the 8th day of the 1st month of the 60th year of the New Kingdom.

I could feel the tears burning my eyes as I read the names. These were my ancestors. Their names were written on parchment, sealed away and protected in the cavity of a rock.

I returned to the story that told of other kingdoms that were built near the sea, away from the mountain. These kingdoms did not know of my people's existence, for their city was hidden from the eyes of all who passed by. Nor did any army seek to find them for the word of their strength had reached other lands. Fifty-seven years passed and the army of the Purcatians became complacent. The practice of the weaponry lost its flavor.

The story of so many years ago, repeated itself. One who wished for more adventure, riches, and status outside his realm, led the army of an evil king through the walls of the Hidden Kingdom where they murdered and imprisoned an empire that asked only to be left in peace.

Tears of anger scorched my eyes, and the taste of hate coated my tongue. I screamed of them to the heavens. Anger and hate grasped my mind and my soul, pulling me into their ugly and consuming darkness. I fought the emotions that burned within me, reaching out to grasp the whispered words of Taraini's warnings, but the emotions were too strong, and I fell to the ground, weak and helpless.

How many hours I lay there, I do not know, only that a voice inside my head begged me to make myself read to the last page. The voice continued until I pulled myself against the table and reached for the book, forcing myself to continue.

There has been deception among our own people, causing me to desire the death of those who have been tempted by selfishness and greed. Yet it is the good among us who have paid the price of this evil. All but a few youth have been taken captive. The enemy rumors that our king and queen have been placed under a spell and lay in a tomb of glass. Their torture is that their minds are conscious, their eyes can see, and their ears can hear. Yet they are as if they were dead.

I cannot understand the workings of a sorcerer of magic, if there is such a thing, yet I have not seen the tombs; therefore, I cannot make judgment.

I am now in hiding with the children, who have been spared. We remain within the walls of our kingdom, for it is the safest place, now that the army that invaded think they have taken all. But soon they will return for the riches that lie within our mountains. I pray that the son of King Etcheon returns in time, for we must remain here until he does.

Suddenly, it seemed as if my heart had stopped beating. My eyes locked onto the words, and I repeated them. *How long ago had the words been written?* I thought to myself. I would not find the answers until I read further.

Yiltor (oh, how I hate to even write his name) has already begun his search for the child. But he will not find him. Another has taken Young Etcheon and fled with him through the portal. There he will be prepared for the day he will return in his vengeance. Those who have conquered us because of our own foolishness are afraid of him already, for he carries the purity of his ancestors and the gift of his mother.

I will end my writings and place this book on the rock on top of the hill for the eagle to find and take away. I sign my name as witness of all that has happened.

~~~ I am *Klogan.*

I closed the book once again and held it to me, not knowing what to feel. Feeling nothing, I heard nothing but the words of all the books I had read. They were in my conscience and my heart, flowing together until they were one.

In time all the emotions I had experienced began to return to me. I pushed them away. I did not want to have them inside me, but I could not stop them from entering. To fight them, I grabbed the sling and the cestro, made my way to the outside of the rock, and searched for stones until my pouch was full. One by one, I placed the stones in the pocket of my sling and flung them through the air at a target far in the distance with only my emotions to guide them. When my right arm tired, I switched to the left. Listening to my instincts and allowing the sling to become part of me, I made the left aim as accurate as the right.

When, at last, my left arm became weary of the task, I fell to the ground and cried like a child, until the tears were dry. Then I closed my eyes in sleep.

When I awoke, Walkelin was nuzzling my arm, which was sore and stiff to his touch. The warmth of his breath, nonetheless, felt good, and I wrapped my tired arms around his head. He lifted me up and pushed me to the clean clothes that hung on a limb of a tree all the days I refused to bath. I gathered them into my arms, noticing a small bar of soap sticking out of a pocket, and allowed my horse to lead me to the lake. Then, with a deliberate nudge, he pushed me into the water. I could not help but laugh, knowing how I must look and smell.

"Today is the twenty-second day of our confinement, Walkelin," I said, looking at him from the middle of the stream, removing the filthy clothes from me. "Yet I have no desire to leave until I know how to control the thoughts inside my head and my heart."

He neighed and threw his head in response. I recalled the words of Barok when he said I would be able to communicate with my horse when I was ready.

My eyes narrowed as I studied Walkelin. "It was you who reached into my head and demanded that I finish reading the book when I felt I could no longer stand the pain of it."

He threw his head once again and stamped his hoof against the ground.

"All right, I'm hurrying," I said, and scowled, in spite of the smile that crossed my face.

"I think you smell better already," he snorted, and I felt as if I were alive again.

"The books have taught me something I want to share with you," I said to him when I was presentable. "Where light abides, where one controls his thoughts and his emotions—there, the strength of his being survives."

I threw myself on Walkelin's back, my clothes wet against my clean body, my hair still dripping. "Run!" I shouted.

He reared his head and snorted. "I will take you where you have never been before at a speed you have never traveled before."

"Can I stay on your back if you move at a greater speed?"

"Let your body relax against mine, as if you are a part of me," he advised. "Then we will be one."

I could feel the tension in his muscles as they rippled. I grabbed his mane and suddenly the breeze became a wind against my face. His hooves barely touched the ground in his speed. We flew through the trees, across the meadow, and beyond the perimeter of Taraini's kingdom.

When at last we stopped, I climbed down and fell to the ground, laughing. "It was more than I could have imagined."

He raised his head, and I thought I could see a smile in his expression. I stood. "It was your intention to let me feel your power."

He said nothing, only nuzzled me with his velvety nose. I stroked his neck and put my face next to his. This horse had stayed with me through the most painful part of my instruction. He belonged to me and I to him.

"When you put your faith in me and we become as one," he said, "no one can harm you, for your life will be as my life."

"I will never doubt you," I said to him. "My life is your life."

He raised his head high and neighed loudly. Then he looked at me. "I will take you back to the rock now. You must prepare to return to Taraini and her family."

As we turned to follow the path that would take us back to the Ancient of Trees, I found that it was, indeed, invisible to the outside world. It was as if we slipped through a wrinkle in time. I leaned close to Walkelin's ear. "Will you answer my question if I ask it?"

"I know the question without you asking," the horse answered. "Because I took you beyond this realm, it is only fair that I answer. This kingdom stands not in time, as you know it, but in timelessness itself. That is its protection. To think of it as a wrinkle is an excellent prospective."

"Thank you."

"You are welcome," he replied.

She watched them as they came toward her. The horse's gait was steady and the rider's back straight. As they drew closer she could sense the change in Etcheon. He carried the expression of a man. She could feel the strength of goodness, and she was pleased. It did not surprise her, however, when a tear fell upon her cheek. Already she missed the boy that would now only exist in her heart.

6

Kevelioc

WHEN WE RETURNED TO TARAINI'S home, she called to us and waved. When we stood beside her, I dismounted while she smoothed Walkelin's mane and rubbed his neck. Then she turned her attention to me, placing the palms of her hands on either side of my face.

"We are gladdened at your return. It seems as if you have been away from us for a year though it has been only half that," she said. "Come now and enjoy our celebration of your return."

Before I could ask her what she meant concerning the time of our absence, Barok landed on my shoulder. His wings fluttered against my face while his feathers tossed my hair and tickled my ear.

"Well, lad," he said, "the change is all we expected it to be. You have not disappointed us. You left here a naïve boy. You were unaware of the darkness in a world of which you knew nothing. What you learned while inside the rock aged you with its pain and matured you with its reality. It gave you new courage. It strengthened your resolve. It turned you into a man."

He ruffled me with his feathers once again and flew from my shoulder to the ground where he grew to his full size. Cocking his head he looked deep into my eyes, and I found myself in the clearness of his pupils. What I saw startled me, and I stepped forward for a better look.

"You see it?" he asked, extending his head so that his eyes were right before me.

"In your eyes, I see a stranger."

"What you see is the boy, who stepped away and let the man take his place."

I turned to Taraini. "Have I changed? What did you mean when you said it seemed as if I had been away for a year though it was only half that?"

She laughed softly. "To you it was twenty-one days. To us it was six months and one day, and, yes, you have changed."

I shook my head. "The wrinkle extends even inside this realm."

She gave me a look of surprise. "That is an odd similarity, but accurate—perhaps." She sat beneath the shade of the Ancient. "Sit beside me and read to us the story from the second book. Then you will understand."

I took the second book from my pouch, opened it to the first page, and began to read.

El syld deplay bolk ta el dert . . . [The child threw the book to the ground.]

"I am tired of reading the same story again and again," he cried to his mother. "Tell me a story filled with adventure."

"You tell me a story, instead," his mother replied.

"But I do not know a story without a book." He frowned and stamped his foot.

"Look into the sky and tell me what you see." She took his hand and he sat beside her.

Laying his head upon her lap, he gazed upward. "I see the clouds," he muttered impatiently.

"Look deeper, study them, then tell me what you see." She touched his forehead with her lips and waited.

He sighed and let his eyes linger on the clouds as they floated by. "I see a horse," he whispered finally.

"If you can see it, then it is yours," she said gently. "Reach up and bring it to you."

"I don't know how."

Her words were soft and quiet as she whispered in his ear. "Close your eyes. See the horse in your mind and beckon it to come."

The boy closed his eyes and began to imagine the horse. He watched it as it raised its head and shook its silver mane. He beckoned it to him, and the horse came, its coat shimmering against the shadows of the clouds. It was the most beautiful horse he had ever seen.

He climbed upon its back and together they traveled through forests, over mountains, and across meadows. There was nowhere they could not go. Even through the sky they flew as if the horse had wings. They became strong and invincible. They fought dragons and giants, bringing peace to the people of the villages.

Then one day the horse began to fade from him. "The time has come that you must return to your home," it said, its voice echoing among the billows. "And I must return to the clouds."

"But why must you go from me?" the boy cried, reaching out to his horse.

"Your mother has been watching over you this past hour," the horse explained, "and needs you to awaken."

"But it cannot be simply an hour," the boy said. "For we have been gone many years, and you have become my friend."

"You have placed yourself within a dream," the horse replied, "wherein time becomes neither here nor there. Only the dream itself matters. Do you understand?"

"Perhaps," was the boy's sad response. "But why should it end if I do not desire it?"

"Because your mother desires it." The boy's mother's voice reached his ears, calling him from his dream as the horse began to disappear back into the clouds. "Wake up, my child. We must return home."

He opened his eyes to his mother's sweet smile. "How long have I been away?" he asked.

"Only a short time." She seemed amused. "Tell me, did your horse come to you?"

The boy nodded. "Yes, he came, and now he is my story."

"Tell me your story," she said, and he did, leaving nothing untold.

It was a wonderful adventure, and it pleased his mother. When he finished, he looked into her eyes. "Why, in my story, I was gone for many years to me, yet just an hour to you."

She took the hand of her son. "Now, I will tell you a story," his mother replied and, as they walked she told her child the story of time.

"Os me daus epsle en unthr spet?" I asked as I folded the script and looked into the many eyes staring at me.

"Has the language of your father become natural to you, now?" Barok squawked in humor.

I gave him a questioning look. Then I understood. In the telling of the story, the words flowed in the language with which I was becoming more and more contented. "I'm sorry," I said, "but it is, after all, the language I have been studying for the past . . ." I could not finish for I did not know how long I had been away in time so I asked. "Were my days lived in another realm?"

"Not as you would think," Taraini explained. "You decided in your mind that it would take twenty-one days to study the books. Within the rock, time is irrelevant; therefore, it took you that amount of time to learn all there was to learn."

"But here, we had to go on as usual," Barok said with a yawn.

"And it took six months and one day to do so," echoed the Danes, lounging on their paws.

I was amused at their response in spite of the idea of fitting time in space, according to will. "The boy's adventure in his dream was as my adventure inside the rock, but I was awake," I argued.

"So was the boy's mother," Taraini said.

"That does not help me understand," I sputtered, my frustration growing inside me. "Answer me this; can I control time?"

"If you are strong enough within your mind."

"But only my time?"

Taraini fixed her eyes upon me. "If that is the strength of your power."

Her answers only brought more questions. "If there is greater power, is it possible for me to restrain time for more than myself?"

"It is." Taraini watched me closely, offering no further explanation.

"Enough questions," a large black panther growled from behind me. "There are more important things ahead of us at the moment." He smacked his lips. "Like food."

"It is time to introduce you to Kevelioc." The sound of Barok's *yee-ka-ka* sounded like laughter. "I believe he is more hungry than curious."

I watched the panther out of the corner of my eye, wondering where he had been hiding all this time. But it was something I would not concern myself with for now. I would simply enjoy the most delicious food I had tasted since . . . twenty-one days, or six months and a day . . . it was all the same to me.

As we ate, (and forgetting time, for the moment), I told of all that I had studied, leaving nothing of my thoughts and my feelings out of the story. "Yet if the story in the book is true, and I do not doubt that it is," I said, biting my lip in the thought, "I still have much to learn, to prepare myself for something I cannot yet comprehend."

"All in due time," the panther purred. "All in due time."

"The time draws near when we must send him on his journey," Taraini whispered to the Ancient while the others slept. "Tomorrow Kevelioc will take him beyond the perimeter." She laid her head upon her pillow. "He is anxious to learn the evolution of time."

"Then it is time to teach him."

I woke up with Barok on my chest, his eyes awaiting mine.

"Ah, it is good for you to see me, this morning," he said. "You have a busy day ahead of you. Prepare yourself. You are to travel beyond the perimeters of this kingdom and into the mountainous woodlands with the panther."

I frowned at the eagle and brushed him from my chest. "Why have I not met this panther before?"

"It was not time until now," Barok enlightened me.

"Well, I do not think he cares for me," I complained, rubbing the sleep from my eyes. "Why would he wish to be bothered with me now?"

Barok cocked his head and made a noise I could only interpret to be a chuckle. "Because he has much to teach you, lad. That is why he wishes to be bothered with you." He flew to the wardrobe and waited.

I sighed heavily and pulled myself from the bed, trying hard to imagine what I could possibly learn from the grumpy, unfriendly panther. Nonetheless, I dressed. When the laces of the vest were tied, and the chain that held the crest was once again around my neck, I felt whole again. "Tell me," I said to Barok as I belted the dagger to me and placed the pouch over my shoulder, "why could I not wear the crest while I studied the books?"

"It is simple to explain," the eagle cocked his head, "now that you understand the relevance of time. But I will leave its explanation to Taraini. Come now. Your morning meal awaits you."

Taraini was waiting for me when I descended the stairs. "I understand Barok greeted you as if he were the sun and helped you dress."

"I only suggested he put on these clothes—I did nothing to help him get into them," Barok scoffed. "That he did for himself. As you can tell, I mentioned nothing about the clataè, and he thought nothing about bringing it down with him."

"Should I go back for it?" I asked apologetically.

"I shall go for you," Barok said. "You must eat." With that, he flapped his wings and was gone.

"Please sit." Taraini pointed to one chair while lowering herself into another. "I suppose Barok has already told you what is to happen."

"I believe he gave me a short explanation," I replied before biting into a delicious apple pastry. "But may I ask—what are the ways of the panther?"

Taraini covered her mouth with her napkin to hide her amusement. "I could answer that, I suppose, but I think Kevelioc could give you a better explanation."

Barok flew into the room and dropped the clataè on my head. "Wear it a little lower in front, to shade your eyes," he suggested.

I made the adjustment and found that I could see through the brim as if it were not there.

Reaching up, Taraini touched it and brought down a mask that covered my face. "There will be times when the mask must be worn to protect you as well. It is a shield. Nothing can penetrate its strength." She raised the mask and put it back in place, tilting the brim slightly lower, giving more shadow to my face.

"Tell me what it is made of," I said, removing the clataè and studying its leather material.

"The material is the making of the Ancient and only the Ancient knows the components of its molecules."

Emotion stirred within me. "Why am I so favored?"

She answered. "Born within you lies a powerful gift—handed down to you by those of your kind, through your mother. With that gift comes great responsibility." Her answer only added to the questions that filled my head, yet when her hand touched mine, it quieted my soul.

"I am ready to go with Kevelioc now," I said simply.

"You will go without provisions," she explained. "You will learn the ways of the panther, just as Barok said." She gave me a sly grin. "You will know what they are before you return." Then she nodded to the panther, who, somehow without my awareness, stood beside me.

His movements had been quick and silent. I had not even heard the sound of his breath. There seemed to be no signs of communication between us. I only assumed I was to follow when he turned away from me and left the room. I found it difficult to stay up with him when we entered the forest.

When he reached the perimeter of the kingdom, he stopped and turned to me—his eyes large and luminous—his stare intimidating. I could hear a deep sound resonating from his throat.

"We will now be exposed to the dangers that dwell beyond the border of this kingdom," he growled. "Use your instincts as you follow me. I will teach you to run with speed, to jump with force, and to climb with agility. I will teach you the persistence of the hunt, the quickness of the kill, and the element of surprise."

With those words, he crossed through the perimeter. I followed, staying close behind him as we moved deeper and deeper into the wild. I heard sounds I could not recognize—calls and chatter that were unidentifiable to my ears. I found myself completely dependent upon the shiny, black, unfriendly creature in front of me.

Less and less sunlight penetrated the foliage as we traveled, and the path became darker. On each side of me I sensed creatures lurking; I could see tiny glossy eyes staring from behind the trees and undergrowth. I had never seen so little and sensed so much. I struggled to get my mind fixed as to direction and visibility for I seemed to have very little of either.

Suddenly, from behind me, something knocked me to the ground and pressed its teeth against my throat. My heart seemed faint within my chest, and I could not move.

"You have much to learn," Kevelioc hissed in my ear, and then backed away from me while still pinning me to the ground with his front paw. "I could have killed you in an instant."

"I believe your responsibility is to teach me, not scare me to death." I reached out and removed his paw from my chest, praying my heart would soon find its way from my throat back to my chest.

"I think I will like you," Kevelioc purred, licking my cheek with his thick, velvety tongue. "Now stand and we will begin."

In six days, I learned all Kevelioc promised to teach me, and though jumping was better left to the panther, climbing became effortless. Running through the vines and trees was refreshing, and it became a game. First I was the hunter and he the prey. Then we would reverse our rolls. I would become the prey and he the hunter.

It was not all a game, however. In the darkness of the night of the fifth day, I found myself tasting death in the face of a brown bear that blocked my path with his huge body, his giant paws swiping at my face.

The day had been extensively grueling, leaving my muscles weak and my senses dull. I was not prepared in body or mind to outwit or outrun this beast. I did, however, have the good judgment to stand quiet, confusing it long enough for me to grasp my sling and prepare to fight. Just as I was ready to send a stone into his heart, I could see something in the corner of my eye. In that instant the panther landed on the bear. His strong jaws and long canine teeth grabbed the nape of the bear's neck, killing him instantly.

"You have learned a good lesson," he said, moving close to me. "When you are as weary as you are at this moment, keep yourself hidden from potential danger."

"It was you who killed the two men who held me prisoner that day at the cottage," I said, stroking his back.

His dark eyes peered at me. "You have just discovered that?"

"Why did you not stay and walk with us?" I questioned.

"Why should I have stayed?" he answered. "My work was finished."

At the end of the sixth day, I had improved my skills enough that when playing the prey, I became weary, climbed high into a tree, and stretched myself on one of the heavy limbs. Then I wrapped myself in vines that hung from the branches, making it my bed. Some time later, I could see the panther below me, his nostrils flaring and his coat damp from exhaustion. I could hear his breath as his own weariness seemed to have overtaken him.

I was sure he had lost my scent for it was now wrapped in the vines. I remained still. Even my breath was silent. I felt rather proud of myself as I watched him from my hiding place. He looked around him, even glanced into the tree, but said nothing. He walked away only to return. Finally, he yawned, dropped to the ground, and seemed to sleep. I waited.

His eyes opened—he yawned once again, smacked his lips, and growled, "You can come down now, young lad. It is time to fill our bellies."

My heart was filled with disappointment by his words. I groaned and removed the vines from me. "How did you know?" I asked him when I was again on the ground.

"I did not know," he informed me, "but this is where I lost your scent, and I could not pick it up again. I saw nothing when I looked up into the tree for you had disguised yourself well. I only took a chance that if I could not find you on the ground, you had to be somewhere above me."

"That was not fair—you tricked me!"

He looked at me and smirked. "Trickery is part of the game, and you have learned something very valuable. Never let the words of your opponent defeat you. Make him prove them before you accept them as truth."

I sat beside him, feeling defeated in my foolishness.

He growled in sympathy and licked my arm. "This is the time of learning, Etcheon the Younger. This is the time to make mistakes, for these are the greatest lessons learned." He stood and nudged me to stand also. "Come now, I am very hungry, and if we do not soon find food, I will be forced to eat the prey before me."

Seeing the humor in his eyes, I laughed—spitting out my self-pity. A short time later, we had a rabbit cooking over the fire.

As the sun withdrew its light from the forest, however, Kevelioc's wisdom had become my wisdom. His skill and agility, mine as well. "You have passed the test, Etcheon the Brave," he purred. "You have learned all you need to know. It is time to return to Taraini's kingdom." He yawned. "We leave first thing in the morning." He placed his head upon his paws and fell asleep.

On the morning of the seventh day, a roar awakened me. "Was that necessary?" I groaned and lifted my aching body from the ground.

"Only for those who continue to sleep when it is time to travel." Kevelioc grinned, showing two very sharp fangs. He stood beside me, assessing me with his liquid eyes. "Are there any questions before we leave?"

"Yes. Is this truly the seventh day?"

He roared in amusement. "Of all you have experienced here, this is your question?"

"In all that I have experienced since I came to this kingdom, the experience of time has been the most unnerving."

He looked at me, and his eyes softened. "It is truly the seventh day, my friend."

"Thank you." A deep sigh of relief escaped me. Though I ached in every muscle and now carried cuts and bruises on the whole of my body, I was content.

As we began our journey home, Kevelioc walked close beside me, and I placed my hand upon his neck, in friendship.

"I think it best that we not tell the story of the bear," he said as the huge, gnarly Ancient of Trees came into sight. "It was for your understanding that I allowed the circumstances to play out before interfering. You need to know that I will protect you even with my own death, if necessary. You had to witness the strength so that you might have faith in the animal."

We said nothing more, but as we entered Taraini's kingdom, Kevelioc remained at my side, and my hand remained upon his neck.

"See the marks upon him? Some are deep enough to leave scars." Taraini sighed, leaning against the bark of the Ancient as she watched Etcheon and Kevelioc approach.

"They will be scars of bravery," the Ancient reminded her. "Be not saddened by them. They only prove he is who he must be."

7

Verch

WHEN KEVELIOC AND I RETURNED, we were greeted with more concern and less ceremony. I had taken care to clean the cuts and scratches, but they were still visible, as were the bruises, which I could do nothing about except allow them to grow darker and more obvious. The panther, nonetheless, looked just as he did the day we left. Perhaps there was one exception. I thought I noticed an air of satisfaction in his prance.

Taraini walked out to greet me, the look of compassion revealing itself beneath her smile. "I think a nice warm bath in water overflowing with healing herbs will be your celebration this day," she said, taking my arm as if to assist me.

"What you see are the rewards of his superior training," Kevelioc growled. "No more. No less."

"I would have been disappointed with anything less," said Barok. He flew around me proudly inspecting each discoloration and abrasion. "You are to be congratulated, Kevelioc."

The panther nodded with dignity, his pride visible in his eyes. "Etcheon was an eager student, and I am proud to have been his teacher."

"And now, I think we should let Etcheon bathe his cuts and bruises. Then we will ease his hunger," Taraini suggested. "When that is done, perhaps he will tell us of his adventure."

Once the herbs had soothed my body, and the table was cleared of all its food, I entertained with tales of my training. Kevelioc interrupted whenever he felt I had missed a point of necessary explanation. Neither of us spoke of the bear.

"It's time to take the third book from your pouch and read to us," Taraini said when all had been spoken of the adventure.

I eagerly pulled the book from my pouch and began to read.

"Ve mya tok ma sil stelo," loked el ber to os Elohm . . . ["I will make my own history," said the bear to his creator.]

"I will be the most fearsome of all the animals. I shall have the strength of three lions, the size of the giant, and the prowess of the tiger. Animals and humans alike will fear me, and I will rule over man and beast."

"Will you have no compassion?" asked the Creator.

"None for man, and little for beast," replied the bear. "But for my kind, I will show compassion."

The bear was indeed feared by all as he went about boasting of his superiority and causing the ground to quake with the magnificence of his roar.

One day he came upon a human boy. It was the first human he had seen. He licked his lips in anticipation. This will be a great day, indeed, he thought to himself. I shall taunt this man-child with my fearsome superiority, and then I will rip through him as if he were an insect.

When the child turned to look upon him, the bear was indeed fearsome, and the child began to tremble with fear. This pleased the bear and he began to dance about, bearing his ugly teeth, his roar causing the winds to stir against the ground, until even the ground itself trembled. His giant paws reached out and bumped the boy, his claws scratching the flesh.

When he was tired of the play, he clenched his jaws and reached out to rip at the body when suddenly he was attacked, and without warning, sharp teeth burrowed into his neck, taking away his life.

In the limpness of his death, he once again found himself in the presence of the Creator. In his confusion he asked, "Why, when I was the most powerful of all, could a simple animal, such as the one who took my life, have the advantage over me?"

"In all of your strength and prowess, you have not considered the wisdom of love," said the Creator. "Yet love is the greatest of all gifts one can give himself, for love is pure and knows no fear. In choosing to ignore its power, you bestowed upon yourself a weakness more potent than the strength of many lions. The panther protected the child out of love."

"But how could an animal love a human?" asked the bear.

"Because he came to know him," replied the Creator.

At the end of the story I allowed myself to look up. All eyes were upon me except for Kevelioc's. He was lying next to Taraini licking his paws, seemingly unconcerned with what I had just read.

"Love is unconquerable, is it not, Kevelioc?" she asked.

"Indeed," replied the panther. He raised his eyes to mine, and I could see his fondness for me.

That night Barok accompanied me to my room. "Kevelioc is very pleased with you," he commented as I climbed into my bed, "and he is not easily pleased."

"He is a great teacher," I replied. "Yet a question whirls around in my mind in need of an answer. When I read the stories, it is as if I'm hearing them for the first time. Yet all of you seem to already know them even before I open their cover?"

He fluttered about my bed as if contemplating an answer. "Methinks you ask too many questions for one who needs to sleep." Barok twittered softly and gathered the blankets around me with his talons. I suddenly felt warm beneath the blankets. "In reading the story, you now have a deeper understanding of Kevelioc's devotion, do you not?" I heard Barok's voice as if in my dream.

I felt my lips move as I murmured that I did. Then his voice slowly moved in the darkness. "Know that we all feel as Kevelioc feels. Now go to sleep. Tomorrow you will begin to understand that which disturbs you most."

When I awoke, the sun was casting shadows through the window, and Barok was nowhere in sight. Only silence greeted me. In the silence I heard the birds chirping and geese honking, their sounds echoing in the distance. I quickly dressed and hurried down the stairs. The rooms were mysteriously quiet and empty. The door to the garden stood open. Outside, instead of flowers and grass, I found dark, barren ground scattered with orphaned plants. Beyond young trees that cluttered the land, I could see a small meadow and a large lake. I called out to Taraini, my voice echoing in the quiet that surrounded me. There was no answer. My heart began to pound, and I felt as if I had been thrown into another strange and exotic dream.

As I walked to the edge of the meadow, I shuddered in the knowledge that I recognized the land. But where I walked was not as it was yesterday. It was in an earlier time when the trees were just beginning to create a forest.

Without warning, the earth began to tremble beneath me, and I knew that I must get back to the Ancient of Trees. I stumbled over the rocks and limbs as the ground quivered beneath me, its motion tossing me back and forth. I forced myself to focus on the door, open and waiting. At last, I was inside. I did not have to close the door, for it shut behind me as if a wind had blown it. The tree began to shudder with such violence that I was thrown against its wall.

"What is happening?" I shouted to the Ancient. But there was no answer, only the violent quaking of its body. Just as quickly as it began, the trembling ceased, and I was surrounded by darkness. I lifted myself from the floor, nursing new bruises while tolerating the renewed pain of the injuries sustained in the previous days. I could see stars beyond the window, their brightness defying the blackness of the sky. I hurried to the door. It opened at my touch, and I stumbled out into tall, unruly grass filled with wildflowers. Giant trees now surrounded me, the moonlight giving them an almost grotesque appearance. Beyond them, I could see a small meadow.

I walked to the meadow where the sky opened to me, allowing me to search for an identifiable formation. There I found what I was looking for. At least, in all this confusion, one cluster of stars remained true, and I found myself fascinated with the adventure. My heart pounded in the excitement as Barok's words came to me, and I understood. That which disturbed me most was now being made known to me.

I wanted to walk through the trees and the meadows—to comprehend this time in space. But the trembling began again, and I knew that I must return to the Ancient.

The next morning, Taraini watched me as I descended the stairs, the small carrier in my hand. "Your face is drawn and pale. Your eyes are lined with fatigue. Your hair falls about your face in disarray. And your body groans," she noted, sympathetically. "Yet your eyes are filled with questions."

"I feel just as I look, and my eyes tell the truth." I was about to sit down when Taraini took my arm.

"Let's go outside, beneath the Ancient, and I will explain." She nodded toward the door. When we were seated outside, she reached inside the carrier and removed something and handed it to me. "Inside is a round instrument called an astrolabe. Remove its cover."

I did as she asked, and when I held the instrument in my hand, I studied it closely. It was made of gold, its diameter about fifteen digits, its center raised slightly. Within its circle another circle was engraved. Straight lines crossing from one side to the other, both horizontal and vertical, were also part of its decoration. There were other markings that I could only conclude were markings of a language. Attached to the middle, a pointer moved freely around the circle.

"As you can see, this astrolabe bares a planisphere—a star map," Taraini explained pointing to the raised markings. The pointer in the middle is called the alidade. By sighting with the alidade and taking readings of its position on the graduated circle, angular distances can be determined such as longitude, latitude, and the time of day.

"Nonetheless, what you do not see is its only purpose." She took the astrolabe from me, turned it over, and pointed to a tiny clasp. "Hand me your crest," she said, holding out her hand.

I removed the crest from its mantle and handed it to her. Using it as a key, she inserted the tip of it into a small opening next to the clasp and turned it to the right. The back of the astrolabe opened. Inside I found a small dial, two lines—one vertical, one horizontal—and a circle, all with visible raised markings.

"This," she said, touching the horizontal line, "represents the timeline of earth as we know it. Moving the digit to the left of the center will take you to the past. How far is decided by the placement of the digit. Moving it to the right will take you to the future. The vertical line indicates the time of day, or night—the center being the middle hour. The circle is the rotation of the earth's axis." There was a pause as she looked at me intently, her eyes burrowing into my own. "Do you know what that means, Etcheon?"

"I can only imagine that the one who holds this in his hand has the ability to travel anywhere within earth's time," I replied, the discovery spinning in my head.

"Not only the earth's, but that of the universe, as well. But it also tells us that in its astonishing ability lies its danger."

I had not considered the consequences of its potential for evil. "Why is it always so?" I asked.

"Man has made it so," she answered. "But the astrolabe is safe while it is in your keeping." Using the crest she reset the clasp, once again concealing its secret, and placed both the crest and the astrolabe in my hand.

I closed my fingers over them, and my mind began to feel the power I held in my grasp. It was then that I understood the emotion of greed. It devoured me, its stench heavy in my nostrils, my stomach convulsing in the vapors. I reached out to Taraini, shouting for help, but my cries were silenced in my throat. She began to fade in the shadows that surrounded me. I could not move nor could I speak. I could only use my mind to fight the darkness that ripped through my head, its evil tentacles fighting to devour my soul. In all that I suffered, something within me began to reach and push the tentacles from me. I could feel them retreating, disappearing until they were gone. The shadows dissipated leaving me with little strength, and I fell to the floor, praying that greed would never tempt me again.

Taraini knelt beside me, her fingers wiping the beads of perspiration from my face. "Why did you not help me?" I said to her in a voice barely audible.

She wept, tears glistening in her eyes. "You did not need my help. You carry your own strength to devour that which is evil. If I had interfered, your strength to dispel it would have been weakened, and you would once again face the temptation of greed."

I nodded my understanding and made an attempt to stand up.

"Are you well enough to go on?" she asked soothingly, reaching out her hands to me.

"Yes," I said weakly, allowing her to help me to my feet. "Though my knees seem to have their own agenda."

"Then we will walk until they decide to listen to your command," she assured me. She smiled at me, unable to suppress a laugh—a laugh that brought life back to my being.

"Now that you have proven yourself worthy to carry the astrolabe—or the timepiece, as it will be called—place it, along with the crest, inside the mantle."

When the timepiece was safe inside the mantle, along with the crest—and the mantle was on the chain around my neck—she invited me to sit beneath the Ancient and rest.

I had gone back in time, at least five hundred years, then into the future, five hundred years—or more. I had done so at the whim of a giant tree, the age of the universe. It was the most extraordinary experience I thought I would ever encounter. I had visited the past. I had walked into the future.

Once again, questions began to fill my mind. "You told me that I received the gift of my ancestral clan. Is my mother not of the same clan as my father? Is my mother a time traveler? Did she travel through time to be with my father?"

Taraini looked at me and shook her head. "You are a man of many questions. Questions best answered by the Ancient, and I will leave it to him to do so."

"The Ancient traveled with me."

"Are you certain?" She looked at me, her brows furrowed.

"I am no longer certain of anything." I sighed, shaking my head. "The day Granna Fela died, my life began to change. Mr. Otherton's visit was the beginning of a strange transformation of events."

"And the questions continue to multiply, do they not?" she asked sympathetically. "I will answer those I can. Those I cannot I will leave to the Ancient."

"Then I will ask this. Mr. Otherton came from another time to bring me the papers, did he not, since he is the brother of Granna?"

Taraini nodded that he had.

"Granna Fela left a world she knew, and brought me through the portal, to another time, in order to save my life. Who is she if she is not my grandmother?"

"What Feladelphia gave up, she did so with no regrets. It was her gift to you. She is truly an ancestor to you." She paused, as if she was listening to another. Then, she nodded. "There are things better explained to you by the Ancient. This is one of them."

Suddenly Taraini cried out in pain. Her face drained of color and she fell limp against me. I wrapped my arms around her, holding her close, and feeling the erratic beating of her heart—not knowing what to do.

"Help me, Ancient," I shouted.

The Ancient's limbs began to sway about me, and I felt the trembling of the earth beneath me. I pulled Taraini's limp body closer to me. The words, *Evilious, Evilious, Explosious,* whirled through the air, and I felt my heart beat in rhythm with Taraini's. I covered her face with my own and closed my eyes against the nightmare—the words *evilious, evilious, explosious,* echoing over and over, in my head, until they faded away somewhere inside me.

I opened my eyes and looked into Taraini's face. Though her eyes were closed, tears fell from beneath her lashes. I gently brushed them from her cheeks, caressing her face with my fingers. Her lips moved slightly, calling my name.

"Shh," I comforted her. "I am here." Carefully, I lifted her in my arms and carried her inside the Ancient. There, I laid her on her bed, placed a coverlet over her, knelt beside her, and soothed her as she had soothed me only a short time before.

"Etcheon," she muttered, her eyes fluttering. "His power grows stronger. We have little time." She said no more, only closed her eyes.

I sensed a strange, eerie feeling in the space about me, and I shuddered and wrapped my arms around Taraini, trying to protect her from something I had no concept of. Barok's twittering entered my thoughts. "Do not leave her until the Ancient finishes."

The tree began to shake, just as it had when it transported me back and forward in time. I lay beside Taraini, holding onto her even tighter than before to keep us both from being thrown about the room. How long the shaking and trembling lasted, I cannot say, only that when it ended, Taraini awakened, her eyes wide with relief.

"The Ancient has taken us to a safer place," she said, her voice weak, yet a smile crossed her face. "You can let me go now."

"I will try," I replied, aware of the feelings in my heart. "Are you well?"

"I am, because you have saved me." She did not explain her comment nor what had caused her so much pain. Neither did she explain why the Ancient had taken us to another realm.

Her next words surprised me, nonetheless, when she said, "As you can see, we have little time to finish your training." She stood without my assistance, her full strength having returned to her, and beckoned me to follow. "The need to transport was necessary. You will see for yourself, that nothing within my realm has changed, only that which is beyond it."

She led me through the door and into the garden. It seemed completely undisturbed by what had just transpired. "Tomorrow," she continued, as if all that had happened had been expected and set aside, "you will talk with the owl. We affectionately call him Silence though his name is Verch. He is eager to speak with you."

I decided I must push the feeling of love, which came over me when I held Taraini in my arms, away from me. I forced myself to concentrate on what she was telling me and found myself eager to hear the owl speak. I waited as she called the owl to her. I watched him descend from his limb and settle on a rock beside her, only to turn and stare at me.

"I will leave the two of you alone now," she said, once she had introduced each of us to the other. With no other words, she turned and walked back through the Ancient's door.

I found myself uncomfortable with the owl, who continued to stare at me. In defense I decided to return his gaze. We sat for some time, our eyes locked, before he turned from me. I couldn't help but feel proud in my unspoken triumph.

"Do not think you are so clever, infant," he hooted harshly. "I turned simply because I grew tired of your face."

"Of course you did, elderly one." I laughed in defiance of his rudeness. "And now that we have that settled, what is it I am to learn from you?"

"Well done, infant," he replied. "Intimidation is a tool to reach into another's mind." His words bewildered me at first, and it wasn't until he turned and looked at me once again that I sensed a friendly air about him. "What I teach you will only add to the strength you carry within you."

Verch moved toward me, his feathered wings fluttering slightly. "It is the intelligence that controls the hand that yields the weapon. You may think the wizard, who stares down at you, has a power far greater than your own. As long as you think so, he will have. The magician's magic, tossed about you for his amusement, is only as potent as you allow it to be. But these things you have already been told."

He sat silently, gazing at me, as if determining my worth. "I have observed you this past year, infant," he said at last. "When you can do all that I shall teach you, your mind will be more powerful than that of any wizard. You will be able to see in a wizard's mind and know his thoughts, while closing him to yours."

The words of Verch were as hypnotic as his gaze. I was enthralled at the concept, impatient to begin.

The owl, instead, flew back to his limb and closed his eyes. For seven days he neither looked at me nor made any attempt to contact me. He slept. I not only began to call him Silence but also a few other names I will not repeat.

It was on the evening of the seventh day that Verch came into my room while I was asleep. "There is no time to sleep, infant, if you wish to become like a wizard." He hooted loudly in my ear, bringing me from a deep and peaceful sleep to a dazed awakened state. I lifted myself from my bed without complaint and waited.

"Hoo." He glanced at my clothes. "I see that you made yourself ready even before you slept, or do you sleep fully clothed every night?"

"It is only when I do not know who will be visiting me, and at what hour, that I remain dressed and miserably so," I retorted.

To that remark he hooted as if he was laughing. "I think you are ready to begin your instruction, infant. Follow me."

He exited through my window and settled himself on a limb. I did the same. Through the hours of darkness, we sat there, saying nothing, doing nothing. The only sounds that stirred the silence were those of the night. My eyelids grew heavy with boredom, but I dared not close them for fear I would fall asleep and perhaps fall from the limb.

When the sun appeared, Verch looked at me and hooted his instruction. "Go now, and sleep while you can. When nighttime comes, I will return."

Thus was my routine for how many nights I cannot say, for they all began to interlock. I simply know that time began to separate when I began to listen, not only to the sounds of the night, but to the sounds of the mind as well. It was as if the cells within the stem of my brain stirred and awakened from a long sleep. I could feel their presence. My eyes had vision in the darkness, and I became as the owl in my discernment.

When I had finally retained within myself a discipline, both mental and physical, Verch took me into the first level of meditation. Each night he would take me deeper and deeper until I no longer needed his help to maintain the deepest level. When he had accomplished what he had set out to do, he simply sat with me, waiting and watching. Then one night he asked what I had learned while sitting on the limb.

I looked at him with deep respect. "My first lesson was that of patience," I replied with a smile. "Was it not?"

He nodded that it was.

"The second lesson was of endurance and discipline. But perhaps the most important lesson was when I became aware of the capacity of the mind and its ability to perform."

"You have learned well."

I looked at this awe-inspiring creature beside me, besieged by his prowess. "I have been told by many that an owl is not wise, his eyes merely give the illusion," I said timidly, not wanting to offend, but only to explain. "Where the others have taught me the awareness of the mind, you have taken me even deeper in the ability to control it. You have taught me wisdom in its highest form. With that wisdom you have taught me shrewdness as well. Let me be your pupil for awhile yet."

"There is only one more thing I can tell you," Verch whispered to me, "and that is to listen to your essence, for it will be your teacher now. It knows of things that are right and of things that are wrong. If you allow it to communicate with you, it will bring all that you have learned into the circle of your awareness, placing them in their order. It will be your enlightenment against the darkness you will encounter." He said no more for a time, only watched me through large, round eyes. When he spoke again it was as if the breeze carried his message. "Listen."

I did as he asked and in the quiet of the spirit, I began to feel myself evolving. I became as the eagle, the Danes, the panther, and the owl. I could sense their strength in me.

"This will be your coat of armor and your great protection against all who come against you." He said nothing more, only closed his eyes to the sun as it spread its light upon his face.

I found I could not sleep. I called to Walkelin. When he came, I climbed on his back. "Run!" I shouted. Then I watched the ground blur beneath me, and I felt the freedom of the wind. When he finally came to a stop, we were beyond the mountains, inside a beautiful valley where slender trees surrounded a quiet pond.

"I think you need to breath in all that you now know, and you need to do it where no one can disturb you," he whickered.

"Not even Barok?" I laughed.

"Not today."

I sat beside the pond, my back against the soft bark of a small tree and closed my eyes. "I have changed," I said to my horse.

"I know," he replied.

"I feel a strangeness in me that I am becoming acquainted with, though I sense a fear of what I have become."

"And what have you become?"

"Perhaps that is where the fear lies." I sighed. "Have I become like a wizard or a sorcerer? Whatever it is, I sense a fear inside me."

"Why do you fear your strength?"

"It is a stranger to me, and I am a stranger to it," I said quietly. "There lies my fear. Am I nothing without it? Am I lost in whatever it is that I have become?"

"And to think that you are not yet finished." Walkelin nuzzled my neck. "But it can wait until tomorrow. Today you will rest."

I did as the horse suggested, closing my mind to all thoughts while he stood over me. Hours later, he awakened me. "Taraini waits for you." Walkelin said, laughing. "She mothers you in her concern that you might be hungry."

"This day without food has been good for me," I confessed. "My hunger reminds me that I am still human, and I am grateful to know that. Take me home, Walkelin."

Taraini watched as Etcheon came toward her. For the next three days, he would be tutored by Caspar-Arius. On the fourth and fifth day, he would council with the Ancient. On the sixth day they would make preparations for his quest. On the seventh, they would rest, and on the eighth day from this day, he would step beyond the tree. Already she missed him.

8

Caspar-Arius

"TONIGHT, MY FAMILY HAS AGREED THAT we should eat the treat of your village," Taraini said as I dismounted.

"I do not think anyone discussed the matter with me," Walkelin said, and snorted. "How does the treat of your village taste?"

I could see an enormous round almond cake sitting in the middle of the table. "Have you ever tasted the sweetness of cake?" I asked him, my mouth watering with the sight of it.

"And what is this sweetness of cake?"

I laughed at him. "It is the most delicious taste you could ever put into your mouth."

"Then I will try sweetness of cake." He shook his mane, snickering his approval.

To the side of the table stood the animals. Even Verch had ventured away from his limb and was perched upon the rock.

"Tell me," he inquired, pointing his wing at the almond cake, "when is this to be eaten? We are all anxious to try it."

"I'm afraid it is to be eaten last." I sighed, pretending sadness. "For it is the sweetness of the meal."

"The sweetness of the meal?" questioned the Danes.

"You told me it was the sweetness of cake," the horse insisted.

I explained that it was a delicacy full of sweet flavor, and Granna Fela would not allow me to eat it until all the vegetables, meats, and fruits were gone from my plate.

From a distance I heard two voices discussing the meal. "I would think that if we ate all our vegetables, meats, and fruits first, we would have no room for the sweetness of the cake," one voice exclaimed.

"Yet," replied the second, "if we eat the sweetness of the cake first, we would refuse ourselves the delicacy of its flavor to linger long after we have eaten it. Instead its flavor would be contaminated with those of the other foods."

"Still," countered the first, "will we enjoy the sweetness of the meal as much on a full stomach as on an empty?"

"Perhaps," pondered the second, "we would not fill ourselves so full of the meal if we were looking forward to the sweetness of the cake."

"But how are we to enjoy the meal itself, if we are thinking only of the sweetness of the cake?" argued the first.

I stood there, fully enjoying the discussion before me. I had never heard anything so frivolous yet so profound.

"I would like to introduce you to Caspar-Arius." Taraini chuckled as the oddest creature I had ever seen, appeared in front of me—a lamb with two heads.

My jaw must have dropped, for I felt Taraini's fingers beneath my chin, pressing it upward. I blinked my eyes more rapidly than was necessary, in my awkward attempt to think of something to say. I will say that the lamb seemed quiet amused at my reaction, and its gentleness drew me to it (or them), as it (or they) bleated delightfully.

Taraini placed her hand on the lamb's back. "Etcheon, meet Caspar-Arius; Caspar facing you on the left, Arius, facing your right. Now let us eat."

"I have never heard the almond cake debated so eloquently," I remarked, recovering from my shock and bowing to Caspar and then to Arius. They returned my compliment with a dip of their heads.

"I assume Caspar-Arius will be the next to instruct me," I said to Taraini, as she handed me a knife.

She nodded, then motioned for me to cut the cake. Ceremoniously, I cut and placed a slice of cake on each plate, setting one in front of each member of Taraini's family. Finally, I set the last piece in front of myself.

"Now," I announced, "this sweetness of cake is to be eaten slowly, savoring each bite." I broke a piece from my cake and placed it in my mouth.

Kevelioc snarled and licked at the cake with his tongue. Suddenly his mouth opened and the cake disappeared. With satisfaction, he slid his tongue across his mouth, then stretched his body, laid his head upon his paws, and with a soft purring sound, closed his eyes in contentment.

The Danes finished theirs with almost as much swiftness and enthusiasm as the panther, but the owl and the eagle took their time, savoring the sweetness. Walkelin nibbled at his as if it were a carrot while Caspar-Arius debated, with each bite, as to how an almond cake should be enjoyed.

I watched those who had become as close to me as a family, and sadness stirred within me.

"For three days you will sit with Caspar-Arius and learn to consider the consequences of each decision you make," Taraini said quietly, pulling me from my sorrow. "The debate of the cake was for your benefit. They were demonstrating that something as trivial as when to eat almond cake carries a consequence. There will be many times within a day, or perhaps an hour, that you will have to view both sides of a situation. It may be something as trivial as what to eat, or it may be a decision that must be made immediately in order to save your life or the life of another."

"How long before I must . . ." I found I couldn't finish my question. I did not want to know the answer for I did not want to go from this place. In all its peculiarity, it had become my home. Yet, even as the thought came to me, another stirred my conscious. *Your home is waiting to be rescued.*

"Methinks it is time for a story," Barok said, interrupting my thoughts with his eagle sounds. "Take it from your pouch, lad. We await your wisdom."

Forgetting my sadness, I pulled the fourth book from my pouch, opened its leather cover, and began to read.

> *"Vet el syld loged goen el vetae ta desvair uos sflek . . ."* [When the child looked into the water to find his reflection . . .]
>
> . . . he saw a face he did not know looking back at him. It startled him and he cried, "Who are you?"
>
> "I am you," the reflection answered. "Do you not recognize me?"
>
> The child leaned closer, his eyes narrowed, his lips tightened. His reflection returned his gaze, the eyes narrow, the lips tight. When he stepped back, the reflection became distorted in the water. When he stepped close, the reflection became clear once again.

In his bewilderment, the child asked, "Why do you not look like me if you are me?"

"Perhaps you do not see yourself as you truly are," his reflection suggested.

"What is it I do not see in me?" the child frowned as his reflection mimicked him.

"You do not see your courage."

The child was silent for a time and then asked another question. "Would my courage be seen in my face?"

"It would reflect in your eyes."

The child lay upon the grass to think. When he returned to his reflection, his mind was filled with more questions. "Tell me what I should see when I look upon my reflection that I might recognize my face," he begged.

"You will only see who you are," his reflection replied. "Who are you?"

"I am but a boy who has yet to learn courage."

"Your courage cannot be taught for it is either there or it is not," his reflection explained. "It is planted deep inside, waiting to be tested. Look into your eyes and see for yourself."

The child sought his courage and found it there, deep within him. Then he stared at his reflection once again, and he knew his eyes. "Tell me what else I must see to recognize my face," he said.

"You must see your goodness and your strength for they are in your countenance. You must know the power of your essence; it lies deep within your thoughts and reflects itself in your expression. Go and find these things then return and look into the water again."

The child did as the reflection asked. When he returned and looked into the clear water, he recognized himself at once and smiled. His reflection smiled with him. "I know you," the child said, and he was content.

"Now," advised the reflection, "you can go out into the world and be all that you are meant to be."

Taraini and her family kept their eyes upon me as I told the story. When it ended, she smiled, nodded her head, and reached for the book. I handed it to her and watched as she placed it in the pocket of her sheathing, just as she had the others.

"Tell me, Etcheon," she said when the book was safely put away, "what do you think of the story?"

"It seems," I answered, "that I have been a stranger to myself, not knowing how to acknowledge all that I have become. Perhaps I have been fearful of pride in what I am. Yet I see now it is not prideful to accept the gift that has been given, for in the gift lies the responsibility to use it wisely."

"You have recognized the story beyond the story and understand it well," Taraini assured me.

Walkelin snorted his approval, while Kevelioc circled me, his luminous eyes catching the moonlight and giving him the appearance of an enchanter. "Never doubt who you are," he roared with his teeth bared.

"I would give you the same advice," Barok whispered in my thoughts, while Verch sat quietly, knowing he had taught me well.

It was late when sleep came, and I awoke the next morning to an eagle's beak pulling at my hair. "Wake up, you sleeping lad," he chattered. "Your eyes cannot welcome the sun if you do not open them."

"Perhaps my eyes do not care," I said while suppressing a yawn.

"Will they care when they see the last piece of your sweet almond cake in the mouth of the panther?"

"There's a piece left?" I exclaimed, bolting from my bed.

"I do not know." The eagle laughed. "I was simply speculating. Now prepare yourself for the day. Caspar-Arius will meet you in the garden as soon as you have finished your morning meal. There you will once again become as a child in your learning."

I found no almond cake waiting, but Taraini set flat cakes and syrup before me. It was the first time I had tasted them since Granna Fela died. The almond cake was forgotten, and I ate with the hunger of the child Barok spoke of.

"Caspar-Arius waits for you," Taraini said when my plate was empty. "They will teach you well."

I walked to the garden where the two-headed lamb was discussing something between them.

"Now, Arius," I heard Caspar baa, "where shall we begin? There is so much we must teach him, and so little time."

"We can only start at the beginning and pray that he is quick to learn,"

Arius replied as she watched me come toward them. "And since he now stands before us, Caspar, let us begin."

A rock beneath me became my learning stool as I listened to the two approach the same subject from different points of view. My head became filled with their arguments and the swiftness of their words. It was a difficult day. They debated the weather, the colors of the forest, and weapons of war, among other things that have escaped my memory. But it was their debate of birth and death, at the end of the day, which caught my attention. In spite of the fatigue of my brain, I listened intently to their words.

"If, in our life, we are confined to this world of misery until we die," Caspar said, "perhaps it would be better not to have been born."

"Is there no joy on this earth, then?" Arius asked.

"Is there not more misery than joy?" Caspar asked back.

"Yet without misery, would we know joy?" Arius returned.

Caspar pondered only for a short time before she inquired, "Is it better then, to have been born—to have experienced both misery and joy in life, learning from each—than not to have been born at all, if one dies in misery?"

Arius wrapped her neck around Caspar's as if she knew she had won the debate. "If one dies in misery, having learned from both misery and joy, is it not his choice?"

"Baaa baaa," Caspar conceded. "You have left me with no reply, for which I am thankful."

The second day, now able to distinguish between the sounds made by Caspar and those made by Arius, I could concentrate on the intent of the argument with my eyes closed.

Caspar began with this question: "Would it not be better for a man to be silent if he cannot speak the truth in its entirety?"

"Oh, but think, Caspar," Arius said. "Would it not be better to have a fraction of the truth than none at all?"

"But what if a fraction of the truth bequeaths a message that can be construed and turned into a lie?" Caspar was thoughtful in her reply.

"What if speaking not at all brings the greatest danger?" Arius answered.

"Can a lie be less dangerous than silence?" Caspar turned to me and asked.

"No," I replied without hesitation.

"Explain." Their sounds were in unison.

"A lie steals from the truth. Silence protects it."

"Are you sure?"

I thought I was sure until they questioned me. "To analyze the truth within the words, the words are played against the truth," I said with uncertainty. "It is better to listen to what has not been said."

"You give an excellent argument." Caspar's baa was loud with enthusiasm. "And if you could trust no one even in their silence?"

"Then I would trust in my ability to read their minds through their eyes. There I would find the truth."

"Baa, the decision would lie in your own strength." Arius glanced at her twin and then at me. "Is that wise?"

Caspar did not wait for my reply. Instead, she argued, "Is not wisdom a greater tool than the sharpness of the arrow when one carries a powerful intuition and essence?"

Arius wrapped her neck around her twin's. "And the consequence of this decision would be?" she inquired of me.

I deliberated, yet found no answer. I could only reply that the consequence would not be known until the action was taken.

"Baa, baa, baaa." Arius's voice filled the air. Caspar joined her. They seemed pleased with my conclusion.

So went the second day and the third until, at the end, I joined in the arguments to the delight of Caspar-Arius.

"And see," Arius said proudly and pointed her nose at me when the third day had ended, "there is not a mark on him."

"Baa," retorted Caspar. "This gift has not yet seen battle."

"But in the using of the gift, he may not have to resort to the battle."

"Is it not the battle that will require his gift?" Caspar insisted.

"Only if he cannot outwit his enemy with his gift before the battle," Arius reminded Caspar.

"And if the battle is forced upon him?" Caspar stared into the eyes of Arius, both having remarkable fun.

"Then we will know if you were successful in your instruction," cried the eagle as he found his place upon my shoulder.

"Baa." Caspar-Arius joined their voices in confirmation. "It has been a profitable three days, Barok. Etcheon is ready."

"Then I will put him on my back and we will soar in celebration." Barok fanned his wings, leaving my shoulder and placing himself in front of me. I watched as he grew larger than I had ever seen him. "Climb on, lad," he said. "I shall take you for a ride you will not forget."

"You will fly with me?" I stuttered in disbelief.

"No, you will fly with me. Now waste no more time."

Without thought to the consequences, I did as Barok asked, and found myself lost in exhilaration as the earth began to shrink in size, and the clouds drew close. I forgot, for a moment, the tremendous responsibility that was mine, and the boy who was gone from me, returned once again. I shouted to the wind and laughed with the universe. There is no other explanation I can offer that would give the experience the honor it deserves; therefore, I will attempt none. I will only say that I was saddened to see the ground beneath my feet again and to see the boy I was once was overshadowed by the man I had become.

When we landed I put my head against his feathered neck and let a moment pass before dismounting. I thanked him, my eyes misted with tears.

The eagle cocked his head. "This is my gift to you, Etcheon the Younger." Then he flew away.

9

The Ancient

"ARISE, ETCHEON THE YOUNGER. Today you will confer with the Ancient of Trees." I raised my head and frowned rather fearfully.

"Do not be alarmed," Barok said. "There are things you must know that only the Ancient can reveal to you."

When dressed as the eagle directed, I stepped in front of the mirror. My hair was pulled back and knotted at the nape of my neck. The white shirt and chain, concealing the timepiece, hung from my neck. The vest, the soft comfortable boots reaching to the knees, the clataè, and the pouch hanging from its strap—all told the story of who I had become.

Barok dropped the sheath holding my father's dagger into my hand. "Belt it to you," he said.

When I finished, he flew around me, babbling something unintelligible to my ears. Finally he settled on the wardrobe and whistled. "Impressive. Methinks you are a clever man—a handsome man, indeed. There is only one more thing I must do."

I watched as he pulled a piece of transparent material from my pouch. "It is called Angel Fleece," he explained in a soft, reverent tone. "Taraini spins it from the sap of the Ancient."

When I touched it with my fingers, tiny flecks of light seemed to escape from its surface. They were like drops of morning dew, their fragrance as soft as their touch. "It is . . . amazing," I whispered.

"It is, indeed," he replied. "A piece protects your mother's scarf, as well. Now, we must tie a piece around your right arm, between the elbow and the shoulder." The eagle offered no more explanation, only assisted me in the task.

"Follow me, Etcheon," Barok kaa'd when the fleece was tied. He flapped his wings and led the way to the edge of the landing, away from the steps. "You will set your foot upon this step, and the next, and the next, until there are no more," he explained. "There you will find a door. It will take you where you need to go."

I looked at him and stared in disbelief. "I see no steps."

"Do not let your eyes deceive you," he advised. "Simply take the first step. It will lead you to the next and the next. Last time, the Ancient came to you. This time you must go to the Ancient."

I nodded that I understood, and with one last glance at Barok, I lifted my right leg as if to set my boot upon a step and the step appeared. Again, and again, I lifted my leg and steps appeared beneath my boot. With nothing but faith that each step would lead me to the Ancient, I continued to climb higher, until I stood in front of a small, unassuming door. It opened at my touch, and I found myself in a most amazing room. All around me tiny limbs had woven themselves into delicate trees, while vines and roses wound themselves along the walls, giving it the appearance of a terrace garden.

Twenty-one life-size statues of youth, wearing clothing much like my own, stood as if the garden had been created just for them. A quiver of arrows and a bow was strapped to their backs. In one hand they held a sling. On one shoulder draped a cestro. The sunlight touched the lifelike faces, while casting itself against the brilliance of their eyes, giving them the appearance as if they were looking directly at me, waiting for me to speak. I could not take my eyes from them, and I walked from statue to statue, captivated in the majesty of it all and feeling the desire to touch the delicate work that only the Ancient could have created.

When my fingers touched the right arm of one of the statues, glittering flakes of angel fleece fell against my hand, and I could see the outline of a narrow band of the fleece wrapped around the upper right arm of each statue, identical to the one the eagle had helped me tie around my own. *Was it symbolic?* I wondered, stepping away.

An archway appeared, leading me into another room. It was much like Taraini's sitting room, and it greeted me with a soft melody, so amazingly beautiful that it brought tears to my eyes. "Welcome, Etcheon the Younger," I heard a voice say.

I looked around to see who was speaking, but I could see no one. Yet a soft melody came from all around me and seemed to bring memories of another time. All that I knew and experienced from the time Granna held me in her arms as she walked into the Village of the Meadows until this very moment came to my mind, and I felt the pain and agony, the happiness, and the miracle of all who I had known and all that I had been taught.

The voice of the Ancient interrupted my thoughts. "I will answer your questions, now. Mayor Ratherberry kept his promise to tend to your cottage. Meadows will not fade from your memory, for it is there you learned perhaps your greatest lessons—those of goodness, gentleness, and kindness.

"I will tell you that Taraini is the daughter of a powerful wizard, and this is her home because it is her choice and that of her father. All that she has done for you, she has done out of the love she feels for you. The animals are her creation, so you would learn what she could not teach, and yet your learning is not complete. There is a part of you that slumbers still. It is you who will awaken that which slumbers. In all that you have learned within this kingdom, it is you who will be your greatest teacher."

The mood of the room began to change. It was as if the Ancient himself, was trembling. "There is one more thing you must know. Those who will seek your life, seek Taraini's as well. You must never speak her name beyond this realm or reveal your knowledge of her. Though her name must never cross your lips, it must stay protected in your heart. Do you understand?"

The Ancient's words frightened me. Not fear of him, but fear of my own folly, for I did understand. "Take her memory from me," I pleaded.

"I will not, for greater is the need that you carry her there. You will be happy that I did not take it from you." The Ancient's voice softened. "Let us talk of other things now."

"I am aware that time is not relevant in this realm. But I have come from a time that is, and I will go to a time that is," I reasoned. "Tell me who and what I am that I can travel through time."

A melody that stirred in his voice wrapped itself around me, taking me to a place where knowledge pierced my mind. By the evening of the second day, I knew the workings of the astrolabe, and its ability to act and react to my commands, even if they were to be revealed only in my thoughts. I knew the time-travel mechanism as I knew the beating of my own heart. It belonged to me and no one else.

I learned that all I was and had yet to become was a gift given to me by my mother—a gift that would be opened when I was ready to receive it. I could sense it slumbering inside of me, though I desired to let it sleep, for now.

"I have a special gift for you," the Ancient said when the day had ended. "Look behind you." I turned to see a bow and quiver of arrows leaning again the wall—the beauty and strength of which I had never seen.

"This weapon carries a responsibility, just as you do, Young Etcheon. It will be your protection as will the sling and the cestrosphendone. Two arrows, as you can see, are different from all the others—each in its own way. Keep them locked against the quiver. You will know when to use them."

I nodded that I understood. "May I ask yet another question?" I said, fearful of the answer, yet knowing I could not leave until I knew it.

"You may."

"Will I be able to return to Taraini's kingdom or see her again?"

"That is why you must keep her in your heart, for that will be your decision when the time comes."

His answer was all I could hope for, and I was content to keep her in my heart as he had said I must. "I will miss you, Ancient," I said sincerely, just as a soft breeze moved through the room.

"I will miss you also, Etcheon the Younger, son of King Etcheon and Queen Arcadia. I will know of your quest, although I know not which future you will create."

With those words, he bid me farewell and a leaf fell upon my face. I knew nothing more until I awoke the following morning in my own bed with Barok sitting upon my chest once again—the feathers of his wing caressing my cheek.

"I do not think I will miss you when I leave," I teased.

"I think you are right," he scoffed. "We have a day of rest ahead of us. Come, let us enjoy it together."

It was a day for resting, eating, remembering, and laughing. When I sat with Taraini, I felt as if I could not leave her side. Each time I stepped away, I felt cold and alone. It was as if I belonged here, not in some other time I knew nothing about.

I thought of the fifth book and found myself curious as to the story it would tell. When the sun began to set and Taraini had not asked that I read it, I removed it from the pouch and ran my fingers over the cover. There were many pages between the covers of this book. It was the largest of the five and would be a story long in the telling.

Before I could open the cover, however, she reached out and took it from me, caressing the cover as I had done. "It is not time, yet, to read it," she said softly.

I frowned at her, my eyes filling with disappointment. "When will it be time?"

"When it is time," was all she said.

I looked into her eyes, and I could see the sadness I felt in my heart. She laid the book on the grass between us.

I took her hands in mine. "What is it that brings such sadness to us?"

A single tear fell from her cheek onto the back of my hand. I felt its warmth and the love it carried. She had answered my question.

When it was time to leave her kingdom, she took my arm and walked with me to where I would step beyond the Ancient of Trees. She lifted my hand to her lips and gently kissed the palm. "It will be a remembrance of me," she said tenderly, wiping a tear from my cheek. "Now, it is time. Go quickly."

I looked away from her for only a second to see the path I would follow. When I looked back, she was gone. The eagle, the Danes, the horse, and the panther stood there in her place.

"Let us be on our way!" Barok screeched, moving closer to me.

"Where are you going?" I asked.

"You said you would not miss me, and I knew it was true for I will be with you to wake you every morning."

His words brought a frown to my face. "If you go with me," I reminded him, "you may never return."

"We know that," Kevelioc grumbled. "But we decided we have put too much into you to send you off by yourself."

"Do you realize that you may be sacrificing your lives?" I stammered.

"We may meet armies along our way," Walkelin neighed, "but they will face a legion."

I looked at them, and I honored them. I looked down at the timepiece in the palm of my hand, the hand that still felt the tenderness of a kiss, and the words touched my ears. "Always use the timepiece wisely, so that I will never be lost to you."

I pressed my thumb against a small dial, and together with the animals, I stepped beyond the tree. When it was too late, I remembered I had not put the fifth book into my pouch. I could do nothing now, but leave it behind, perhaps never knowing its story.

10

The Wizard's Plot

FOR SEVEN YEARS, ANCITEL HAD WAITED. His trickery had brought him favor in the eyes of this king, who in his own way was as treacherous as Ancitel.

Many years ago, Ancitel found his way to the underworld. Disguised as a lowly servant and keeper of the books of magic spells and potions, he hid his identity beneath the robes of the simplings: those who were born in the likeness of a human but having the aptitude to do only the menial tasks, and therefore, a disgrace to their kind. They were fed well enough and slept on mattresses of straw, but they were not allowed to remove the hood of their robe, for their faces were thought to be hideous.

While there, Ancitel studied magical books in the midnight hours, learning all he could about spells and potions. When he had what he needed, he cast the spell that annihilated the race of the underworld, leaving only the lowest of their kind alive to follow him. When he returned to his tower, he had what he desired: three of the most malicious books of potions and spells—and beasts to do his bidding.

The creatures were as hideous to the human eye as was the human to theirs. With the odor of the swamp clinging to their hides, they were willing to follow Ancitel's every command without question. In return he gave them a place to sleep and food for their bellies.

Of the three large magical crystals that adorned his wizard's table, none could show him the eagle that the soldiers claimed flew away with the boy. But they did warn him that the boy came back again that same day at the same place by the sea, just as he had disappeared. He was dropped into the arms of a woman who held a round gold astrolabe in her hand, and together they disappeared through a portal.

He studied the wizardly fables of the timepiece. In them he read of what the crystals had shown him concerning the woman. He sent his changelings back to their underworld to search for the one book that he had not found during his stay—the very one he now needed.

They searched until they found it buried deep inside an ancient chest, protected for centuries by a spell of its own making—a spell that had long ago dissipated into nothingness for lack of purpose. The evil had outwitted itself.

By midnight of the day that he sent his changelings to find the book, it lay helplessly in the hands of the wizard. He searched each page until he found the story—long forsaken, long forgotten—that told an enchanting tale. Though the tale was not complete, it told bits and pieces that allowed the wizard some knowledge, and he waited.

Ancitel had so cleverly planted his changelings, posing as insects, onto the coat of Otherton's horse. Then he sat back and let his large cyrstals reveal the cottage to him. Everything was going as planned until a drop of blood fell to the ground and chaos erupted. He watched, spellbound, as the changelings fell dead, and their bodies turned to ashes. All the power of his crystals could not show him who had taken their lives.

Anger raged while confusion flamed inside him. All the years he had spent in preparation had given him little in return. Now he would have to keep a watchful eye and wait with unmeasured patience until the day came when the young man would step back through the portal.

The day his crystals flared in color, showing him what he had been waiting for, he was as jubilant as he had been angry. He smiled. Though he could not see the face, there was no doubt as to who the young man was.

Ancitel warned the king to send his soldiers. After doing so, he sat back to ponder. With the potions and the magic he brought with him from the underworld, and the power he took from the minds of the wizards whose lives he had taken, he could have the boy, the timepiece, and perhaps a greater prize as well, if what the book—found in the chest—revealed was true. He would have all that and the worlds and kingdoms yet unseen. He would only have to be patient a few more days.

My nostrils picked up the scent of the sea. I listened to the waves as they slapped against the rocks, and I felt a strange awareness of where I stood. The sea was to the left of me, the woodlands to the right.

My heart began to pound. All that I had been taught could not prepare me for this moment. I almost felt in awe of what I had done in simply opening the timepiece and touching a small dial.

I watched the Danes take their place in front of me while Kevelioc stayed at my side. I could feel Walkelin's breath on the back of my neck and the pressure of Barok on my shoulder. I turned to the left. The animals followed.

I found it difficult to put everything in perspective. To me it had been over fifteen years. Yet the timepiece was set to return me to this place, at this moment in time, six days after Granna stepped through the portal with a boy of two years. The cry of the eagle brought me out of my thoughts, warning me that soldiers on horseback were moving fast in our direction.

I remembered a large crevice inside one of the rocks, away from the shore, that my mother said would hold many things. It seemed large to a child's eyes. Today, I prayed it was large enough to hold just one thing—me. "Follow me," I called out to Kevelioc. "There is a rock we must find. There I will hide."

"We will search while the Danes erase your footprints. It is our best hope," he growled.

With Kevelioc beside me, I moved swiftly and low to the ground. I knew finding the rock would not be easy, yet a familiar scent of a toy I had hidden in another time touched my nostrils. It was several cubits through the cluttered, displaced formations, and I knew where to lead the panther.

When we came to it, Kevelioc looked at me and then the entrance of the crevice. "It will have to do," he said and tucked and pushed until he had me invisible to the soldiers who were coming. There was barely room in which to expand my chest for air, but our actions had been none too soon. The men were so near I could hear their words as they talked among themselves.

"The old wizard said this was where we would find the boy," one of them said, his voice abrupt and commanding. "Search everywhere."

"We are searching for only one intruder?" I heard another voice ask as a foot appeared so close to my leg that I feared they would touch.

"Yes," the first replied. "Search every particle of this area, woodland, and shore."

Before I could consider the thought of only one being detected, the shrillness of Walkelin's neigh cut into the words of the men.

The soldiers marveled at the magnificent horse, thinking he was the intruder instead of a human.

" 'Tis a beauty, he is," another called out. "After him!"

Walkelin's whinny was loud and shrill and I was forgotten.

"They are climbing onto their horses," Barok called down to me. "It seems you are safe, for the time. The horse is a much greater prize." I could sense his enjoyment of the scene as it played out below him.

I pulled myself from the crevice, hid myself among the rocks, and watched, listening for any sound of the soldiers returning. My view was limited, however, because of the efforts of Kevelioc in keeping me from the eyes of the soldiers. But I could see enough.

Walkelin waited until the soldiers were very near, then he turned, leading them away from the ocean—allowing them to gain on him. Soon he was surrounded with a horse on each side of him, three ahead of him and three behind. He began to slow until all the horses were in a rhythmic trot. He slowed to a walk; the horses around him did the same. Then, he stopped, shook his head, and snorted.

"Have your tether ready," I heard their leader call out. They moved closer, their eyes upon him. He stood still, letting his head drop, then rise again. Suddenly, he raised his head high and stomped his hoofs, causing the horses in front of him to balk—giving him the room he needed. He ran, leaving the soldiers and horses behind. He led them far away from the sea. When he felt they would have no desire to return, he let his speed explode, leaving them in his dust.

"The horse has given them a run they will not soon forget," Kevelioc said beside me.

"Why did they think they were looking for only one?" I asked, brushing the sand from my clothes.

"It is simple," Barok said from behind me. "A wizard's crystal can find the opening of a portal. The temperature of your body radiates an atmospheric disturbance. The crystal found the portal and perceived only one because only one was perceivable." He said no more.

"What you are implying is that you do not exist in any given time, therefore he could not detect your presence?" I questioned.

"Excellent!" Barok squawked. "Now do what you came here to do."

"But how can you be here with me if you do not exist in time?"

He cocked his head, giving me a look of one who knew many secrets. "The science of our bodies is not the same as the science of those who live here or those who are travelers. The wizard has no knowledge of us." He glanced behind me. "Ah! Walkelin comes."

"I led them on a chase they will long remember." The horse snorted with humor. "But one I think they would prefer to forget."

The Danes joined us, panting. "The soldiers have returned to their king, who is called Yiltor," Gudrod said. "We followed them to the gates of the castle and listened to their chatter. Their egos have suffered. What happened this day will never leave their lips for they believe they were enticed by a phantom."

"And what will they tell this King Yiltor?" Barok asked.

"The eight of them have contrived a story to give him. They will say that the intruder was nothing more than a horse, too advanced in age to leave worthy prints. They will say that they blessed him with death and buried him before they returned."

"Will the wizard be fooled with such words?" I asked.

"It is my guess that the wizard knows who came through the portal and cares nothing for what the soldiers might say," Runolf replied.

"But their chatter was very helpful to our cause," Gudrod said. "They spoke of a place that sits high in the mountains, an hour's journey from the castle. This king travels there often and no one is allowed inside its rooms except he himself."

Barok nodded and turned to me. "Methinks if this king holds your mother and your father captive, it would be in a place such as this. I shall soon find out."

I studied the animals surrounding me. Taraini had truly given me a fine legion.

Suddenly, I sensed something or someone near. At the same time, Walkelin's ears shot up, Kevelioc's body became tense, and the Danes were immediately at my side. With a silent gesture, Barok lifted his wings and rose into the air as Kevelioc disappeared into the foliage. I removed the sling from my pouch and placed a stone in its leather.

It was then that a scream shattered the silence and a voice shouted, "Git frum dis p'rson, skully menace dat ye er, or dis p'rson will break da teef ye bare, wit a fist."

I could not help but feel the soul being harassed by Kevelioc was harmless and relaxed the sling. Without warning, what appeared to be a boy exploded through the vines of the trees and landed on his backside at my feet. He glared up at me and then stood, brushing the dirt and leaves from his clothes.

He did not seem to have the appearance of one who could injure a panther with his fist. He came to my chin in height; his likeness was that of a youth. His body was thin; his skin pale—almost iridescent. His hair seemed to suggest every color of a rainbow. His eyes were a deep blue; the pupils thin and narrow—like those of a cat in the daytime. He wore a covering made of cloth that bore the resemblance of angel fleece, its color the reflection of the sun. His leggings and boots were of materials I had not seen before.

He folded his arms across his chest, planted his feet on the ground, and looked me up and down carefully before asking, "Er ye Eteon?"

Though his pronunciation was strange, it was my name. "Why do you ask?" I asked cautiously, wondering why he would be searching for me or even know of my existence.

He stood there, silent, as if he was considering how he should answer my question. His eyes shifted to the animals, looking at one then at another until his eyes came back to me. "Tell dis p'rson, what do ye call yerself?"

"What do you call yourself?" I asked, staring at him as he was staring at me.

"Dis p'rson er Rafn," he said proudly.

"I am Etcheon," I replied.

"Coud ye nit say so?" he asked, showing his relief.

"Should I just tell my name to every boy who attempts to sneak up on me without requiring his first?"

"Dis p'rson er nit a sneker, as ye say, nit a boy. Dis p'rson er a Cara." I caught a note of defiance in his voice.

I reached out my hand to clasp his arm in friendship. "Rafn the Cara, I am Etcheon the Younger."

He hesitated only slightly and then reached out and extended his arm to me. In his clasp I felt his strength. It surprised me.

He caught my surprise. "Dis p'rson mayn't 'ave da mite of ye fur-legged fauna, but dis p'rson 'as a fist dat is strong. Der er dings to be said. Com."

I could see Kevelioc's eyes peering through the vines of the trees, while Barok was silent in his hiding. The Danes distanced themselves, in order to be alert to movement on either side of me. Walkelin fell back a few paces and then maintained a defensive distance.

"Yer fauna er of 'igh breed and a d'fendur to ye," he said as he led us back to the sea. "Is good fur ye er nit alone 'ere. Der er sum oo serch for ye to take ye. 'Tis good dis p'rson found ye ferst."

When we came again to the sea, Rafn turned to the east where there were rocks and waterfalls in abundance. We passed three small falls before he turned and beckoned for us to follow him. He slipped beneath a heavy spray of water where darkness awaited.

The shadows of a cave become visible the in mists, and I was amazed at the immense size of its cavity. Tiny bats fluttered about the ceiling high above us, their noise echoing against the rocks and crevices that surrounded us. And as warm as the sun had felt to me outside the cave, it had surrendered itself to the chill of the humid, thick air inside.

Rafn turned to me, his face now showing friendship. "Sit so yer eyes meet, and ye know words dis p'rson speaks er true."

The Danes barked and left us. "They will erase the signs of our presence," I explained to him.

"Dey er trustful of dis place?" he asked.

"They trust you," I answered.

11

The Cara

RAFN MOTIONED FOR ME TO SIT on one of the flat rocks near us. He sat on another, facing me. Pulling a cloth from his vest, he unfolded it and handed it to me.

I studied it closely, but it was written in a language I could not read. I looked up at the Cara, confusion written on my face. He simply smiled and nodded.

I studied the words a second time, and they began to form themselves in the language of my kin.

On the morn of the 8th day of the 8th month, in the 63rd year of the new kingdom, there will come through the portal near the seashore, one who will require the assistance of the Cara in his quest to fulfill the prophecy of the kings. The one who will come is called Etcheon the Younger. The Cara will conceal his presence from the crystals and protect him from those who seek him until they have seen him safely to the Hidden Kingdom of his Father, King Etcheon.

When I looked up at Rafn to ask what these writings meant, he was looking beyond me. He stood. I stood also, following his eyes to find another boy behind me. He was striking in his appearance. His dress was much like Rafn's, but he was taller and wore a thin coat of armor about his chest and a longbow and quiver on his back.

"Dis p'rson 'ill tak," the one with the armor said, his voice soft yet commanding. "Sit."

Knowing Kevelioc was in the shadows of the cave, watching closely, I did as the boy asked.

"Dis p'rson is called Kon." H reached out to greet me as I had done Rafn, and I took his arm in friendship. He sat across from me so our eyes would meet, and Rafn left us. "Da tong of da Cara er not of da tong ye speak," he apologized. "Do ye know da words spek'n to ye, as dis p'rson speks em?"

I nodded that I did.

"Den dis p'rson 'ill tak." He took the cloth from me and folded it carefully. Laying it beside him on the rock, he continued. "It is giv'n to da Cara to be 'ere fer ye. The Cara er to lead ye to da clan of yer fader." He paused and looked at me. "Der er sum oo know, as da Cara know, of yer cum'n—oo wood 'ave yer fer demselves."

"How do they know of me?" I asked.

" 'Tis wizard's magic dat took it frum da minds who knew. Ye 'ave com to change yer future. Dey wood nit 'ave ye do so."

"I have only come to find my father and mother and to free them," I responded.

He shook his head. " 'Tis true. Ye er to bring a new future."

"I can only hope that what I do changes the future for the better," I responded. "You said you were to escort me to the clan of my father. Where will you take me?"

"Fer b'yond dis cave." He picked up the linen and wrapped it in a leather cloth. "Now, Rafn cums wit ye food."

Rafn approached. He had a large leaf in his arms, filled with berries, fish, and flatbread. He set it between us and then took the linen and disappeared once again.

"Will you tell me about your people?" I asked as we ate.

He looked pleased that I would inquire and told me the most incredible story.

"Dis linen takes da Cara," he began, "fer many eoneaons." He glanced at the frown on my face. "An eoneaon is a t'ousand years as ye count time."

He took a bite of his flatbread then continued. "Da Cara er born to be p'rtectors of da universe—p'rtectors of its 'onor. Linen frum bark of ancient trees, not of dis world, were given to da ferst Cara fer p'rpose of 'ich ye see. All Cara 'olds a linen and knows da message as it cums to da linen." He stood and invited me to follow him. "'Ere ye 'ill 'ave safety frum dose oo seek after ye."

Rafn joined us, becoming our guide as we traveled perhaps two plethra before coming to another cavity. Without speaking, he turned to the left and continued for at least a stadion before stopping. "Dis place is deep 'idden," he said, pointing to a wall in front of us. Without further explanation he slipped through a crack in the wall and disappeared.

Startled, I looked at Kon, who motioned for me to do as Rafn had done. I did so and found myself surrounded by grassy meadows. In the far distance I could see the spirals of a castle.

"Da Cara take ye to yer clan, now." As he spoke, Kevelioc and the Danes joined us.

"Walkelin will follow from a distance," Kevelioc spoke into my thoughts. I nodded that I understood.

"Yer fauna er fait'ful to ye," Kon said with respect. "Dis p'rson trusts 'em."

Rafn took the lead, and we moved quickly and silently through the meadows and away from the castle. How far we traveled, I cannot be sure; then Barok's voice reached inside my head, warning us that the king's soldiers were just ahead of us.

Though Barok was communicating the directions we should go in my thoughts, the Cara needed no help. It was as if they knew, even before Barok did, the dangers ahead.

"Dose oo seek dis boy er close by," Rafn whispered. "Dis p'rson feels dem. Com anada way." He turned toward the mountain. Though no trail lay before us, he guided us to a small stream from which we could drink, and a place where we could rest for the night. There we ate fruit and bread from a bundle that fit on Rafn's back—a bundle that was made from the same cloth as the cloth of Taraini's sheath.

When I asked him about it, he smiled. "Dis p'rson 'as waited fer ye to ask. A c'rious soul dat ye er." He handed me the bundle. It was soft and light, yet strong. "It is made of linen nit in dis time—nit 'ere—nit in da time ye com frum."

I was about to tell him that I knew the substance of its fabric when my heart skipped in the thought that in revealing that knowledge I could have revealed her name. I handed the bundle back to him, commenting on the fine quality of its material. What I understood, also, was that although they knew of my coming, they knew nothing of Taraini's kingdom—that or they knew better than to speak of it.

"Tell me what you meant when you said you were created to be protectors of the universe and what you mean when you speak of a calling," I said, turning to Kon and changing to a subject that would require me to listen more than I would speak.

His eyes grew serious. "As ye er born fer da p'rpose of dis globe, Rafn and Kon er born fer da p'rpose of da universe. Ye dink yer calling is to rescue yer family. Nit. Yer calling is to save da 'onor of dis world." He paused and looked out into the night. "Da Cara er to see ye to 'im oo can give ye da knowledge ye need. In dis, Rafn and Kon 'ave p'rtected da 'onor of da universe. Is all da Cara 'ave done fer eoneaons and do fer eoneaons to come. Da Cara can nit interfere, only 'elp dem placed in der care, and p'rtect dem frum danja."

I looked from Kon to Rafn then back again. "How old are you?"

"Nit a babe, nit olden," Kon explained, unable to translate a more logical answer.

Rafn walked to Kevelioc, knelt in front of him, touched his nose, and spoke to him in a language I did not understand. Yet the panther responded to his touch and his voice, communicating with him through growls and purrs.

"Rafn 'as a love fer yer fauna." Kon smiled.

And it seemed that Kevelioc enjoyed his company as well.

We made no fire that night. Kon and Rafn simply placed me between them, and I was warm against the chill.

The next day, when the sun was at its peak, we were well into the mountains. We traveled fast, with no conversation—the silence marred only by the sound of our footsteps. Suddenly Kevelioc and the Danes turned right even before Rafn gave the signal.

Kon looked at me, a smile on his face. "Dey know da danja as da Cara know. Dem nit frum dis world, as Cara er nit." He seemed pleased when I did not disagree.

As the sun began to set, Barok flew low over the horizon. "The soldiers have set up a barrier to keep you from entering your kingdom. They are prepared for battle."

"As we er," Kon said when I told him what Barok had seen. "Dis p'rson must p'rtect ye til ye er safely taken to yer fader's village." He looked around him and led us into a knoll where we made camp for the night.

Just as the sun was beginning to rise, I felt a nudge. I opened my eyes to find Rafn beside me, his lips pressed in silence. I pulled the cestro from my pouch and watched Kon ready his bow. We waited.

Suddenly Kevelioc was behind us. "They have begun their search for you in the mountains. Ten come this way."

Kon signaled for us to be ready. There were four soldiers, one akaina away. Six close behind them. They seemed to know that something was behind the knoll.

"Their bows are ready," Barok cried, drawing the eyes of the soldiers upward.

"Wait until I have taken the one standing closest to the knoll," Kevelioc warned. "Then stand and make quick work of your weapons."

The Cara understood without my explanation, and we waited for the panther's signal. With the swiftness of his attack, the soldier had no time to react or consider his death. While the three were still trying to comprehend what had just happened to their comrade, our weapons hit their mark. The soldier to my left fell without a sound, a small hole between his eyes. Kon's victim lay dead with an arrow through his heart.

Thinking Rafn had no weapon, I turned to oppose the man, but he lay at the boy's feet, his neck broken. There was not time for Rafn to return to the safety of the rock before an arrow pierced his leg. Arrows soared in the fury of the solders, pinning us inside the knoll. As they let their arrows fly, they moved quickly toward us.

I readied the sling, now far more effective than the bow, and with little sound, a stone was flung without revealing its master. A cry was heard. As if it were a signal, Kon stood and let two arrows fly. The aim was direct and the victims fell. Yet, behind them, more came at us. The roar of Kevelioc brought them to a sudden halt, and they turned to see the fangs of a mighty panther.

"Send an arrow through his heart," a soldier cried out. But before an arrow could be released, the panther disappeared.

"Where did it go?" uttered another.

"Behind you," I whispered, as the panther's attack took the lives of three, while the talons of the eagle dug into the eyes of another. In the shock of what was happening, the four soldiers, still alive, lost their advantage to fear, and to the three behind the knoll. Before they could turn to defend themselves, they lay dead alongside their comrades.

"Your troubles are not over," Barok called to us. "Run. There are more coming."

Rafn grabbed my arm, his strength lifting me off my feet. "Com," he whispered.

We moved quickly through the narrow valley, the Danes staying close while the Cara led the way. Kevelioc and Barok stayed behind to confuse and frighten those who were in chase. Walkelin caused a fiery disturbance among the horses of the soldiers, sending them in all direction and causing chaos among the ranks.

Once we were beyond their range, and we could finally stop to rest, Kon placed something over Rafn's wound to heal it, then handed me fruit and bread from his bundle. While we ate, he pointed to the west, explaining the direction and the short distance we had yet to travel.

Rafn walked to Kevelioc. "Ye 'ave the gift of mind talk wit de fauna. Dis gift 'ill save ye many times, as it did dis day," he said, stroking the panther's fur. "Dis p'rson 'ill miss ye and yer friends." Then he turned to me. "Dis p'rson 'ill miss ye, Eteon. Yer calling, in danja, 'ill bring ye greatness." He nodded to Kon and, in that instant, disappeared.

I stood, stunned. "Where did he go?" I stammered.

"Da linen takes 'im to anada place," Kon said simply.

"But I did not say the things I wished to say to him."

"Rafn knows da caring of yer 'eart and da 'onor of yer being. Dis is more den ye can say. Now dis p'rson must see ye to da village of yer fader's clan. Quick!"

We traveled for another hour before Kon stopped near a grove of trees and directed my eyes to just ahead of us. "Der er da village of yer fader's clan. 'Ill be visible to yer eyes, but nit to yer fauna, nit any man but of yer clan. 'ere ye er safe frum da wiz'rd's eyes." He turned to the animals. "Dis p'rson must leave ye now." He turned back to face me, his eyes clear, his narrow pupils dark. "Dis p'rson 'ill miss ye, Eteon da Younger."

He handed me the bundle. "Dis 'ill stay wid ye. Is da wish of dis p'rson that ye, ner yer fauna, er be 'ungry." After he spoke these words, he disappeared just as Rafn had, and I could not help but feel sadness.

"I will miss them as well," Kevelioc said. "When I first came face to face with Rafn, and he spoke of doing me harm with his fist, I laughed. Now I have seen him take the life of a man in two movements of his body."

"I have as well," I agreed.

The animals stayed close to me, as I walked toward the walls of the city that seemed to blend into the hillside around it and the sky above it.

I studied the wall as I moved closer. When I reached out to touch it, it was as if I was touching the bark of a tree, yet it was not a tree, simply a reflection. Though I could not explain what I had discovered, the discovery itself stirred my memory. I called the Danes to me and placed my hand on Walkelin's neck. I closed my thoughts to everything but the words I whispered, "Avy Kyltom ve um el syld ov el rylm." [*Hidden Kingdom, I am a child of the Realm.*]

I could feel—rather than see—a gate appear. Beyond it was the city of the Purcatians. Walkelin and the Danes followed as I stepped forward and through the gate, leading them into the city of my people.

I walked along a path lined with flowers of every kind and color. It circled around gentle grass, white benches, large willowy trees, stone statues, and fountains of waterfalls. The path was of a soft tile, allowing my steps to be cushioned and quiet. The buildings before me were of glistening glass and dark timber. The city stood as if it was a painting from someone's vision, but the painting was missing the ingredient that gave it life—the people. I felt the sadness surround me.

Again I sensed someone. "Is someone there?" I called out in the silence, but no answer came back to me. I called out again. This time I thought I heard a voice. I turned to see a youth running toward me. His hair, the color of the sunrise, was long and loose. His shirt hung loose over leather trousers and his feet were bare. His age I could not guess. "Venillez, mya ye aidle vae? [*Please, will you help us?*]" he called out.

"Hval e ta ye dosa? [*What is it you need?*]" I asked when he stopped in front of me.

"They have taken our mothers and our fathers," he continued in the language of my father—the fury of anger evident in his young voice.

"Who has taken them?"

"The soldiers of Yiltor," he exclaimed. "We were not here, but in the ravine with our teacher, Klogan, when they came. They captured or killed everyone they could find. We were too far away for them to see, but we could hear the screams of our people and the shouting of the soldiers as they went about devastating our city. We were not prepared to battle in order to save them. Our slings and cestros were not used that day in our instruction and were left inside our homes. Klogan hid us, saying we must remain so in order to yet fight. We are the only ones left now. All of our kin are either dead or in Yiltor's prison."

The names *Yiltor* and *Klogan* were embedded in my memory the day I read of them inside the cave. I felt it remarkable that the Cara would guide me to the very place to which Klogan had written I would return. I looked at the boy with compassion. "What is your name?" I asked.

"Thorri," he replied.

"Thorri, can you take me to Klogan?"

"Yes, he has asked me to do so." The boy led me beyond the courtyard, to a small cottage where a man, much older than him, yet still young in years, lay on a bed. The right leg of his trousers, stiff with dried blood, had been torn open to expose a deep wound made by an arrow.

12

Klogan

"BRING ME SOME WATER," I SAID to Thorri. I knelt by the side of Klogan's bed. His brow was hot to my touch and beaded with perspiration. He was conscious but weak from loss of blood and the infection that had begun to eat at his leg.

Thorri nodded and left the room. When he returned, he carried a small jug of fresh water in one hand and a cup in the other. I forced water down Klogan's throat, then cleansed his wound. Just as Kon had placed fleece over Rafn's wound, I did the same to Klogan's. When I finished, he looked up at me and attempted a feeble smile.

"Thank you," he said, his raspy voice barely a whisper.

"You rest now," I said to him. "We will talk later."

Thorri was waiting outside the cottage, his face pale with worry. "It is my fault that he suffers now," he sobbed. "He saved my life, and in doing so, almost lost his own."

He blinked back the tears that appeared in his eyes. "I saw a soldier take my brother, and I ran from my hiding place to help him. But Klogan stepped in front of me and an arrow, intended for me, pierced his leg. He threw me to the ground, pulled the arrow from his leg, and covered me with his blood. I was to lie still and hold the arrow in a way that would look as if the soldier's aim had hit its mark. When the soldier approached, he saw the stillness of my body, the blood, and the arrow seeming to protrude from my chest. He came no closer."

Thorri swallowed. "It was difficult for me to lie still for he had my brother in his grasp, and my brother was screaming. Nevertheless, I did as Klogan asked." He looked at me, allowing the tears to fall freely.

"You did as you should have done," I assured him. "Now you must help me see to those you saved by pretending death."

"I do not . . ." His voice faltered, and he looked at me, his face posed in sudden understanding, and a smile appeared. "I thank you, sir, for your kind words. I had not considered the full consequence of my silence."

He looked in the direction at Klogan. "The soldiers took all the food and the animals. They took everything of value and destroyed what they could not take. There were no herbs or medication to help heal his wound."

I looked at the boy. "Have you had nothing to eat since that day?"

"For five days, we have eaten only the fruit left in the tops of the trees, along with bits and pieces left behind when the soldiers raided the kitchens. Klogan warned us not to leave the city, even to hunt."

I looked around me. Though the city had been pillaged, the streets were immaculate. "Why are there no signs of a battle?" I asked.

"Klogan helped us honor and prepare those who had been killed, for their journey home to the Heavens," he replied. "Then we repaired the city as best we could. He said these things would heal us."

"And did they?" I asked, trying to comprehend the immensity of this task.

Thorri looked at me, his eyes hard, his head held high. "No one can destroy our kingdom until we allow it. We will not allow it." His voice carried such conviction that I had to believe the healing had begun.

I returned to Klogan's bed, leaned down, and touched his forehead. To my relief his temperature was cooling. What he needed now was food. "There is a bundle on my horse's back," I said to Thorri. "Find it and bring it to me."

When the young man returned, he was carrying the bundle carefully in his arms. He watched as I removed fruits and breads from inside.

"Your bundle is made of such fine fabric," he noted. "I would think it would be too delicate for this purpose."

I smiled and handed him the bundle. "Take it out to the others and feed them, then keep it by your side."

He thanked me and hurried from the room. I turned to Klogan.

"I am Etcheon the Younger," I said to him. "Son of King Etcheon and Queen Arcadia."

"I know who you are." Tears streamed down his face and he reached up to embrace me. "I am relieved that you have finally come. I have watched for you, praying the words I had written would be fulfilled."

"I have read your words," I responded, "and the stories of those who came before you. I was saddened that there were no soldiers among you."

He handed his empty cup to me and wiped his lips. "Then you know the stories of those who wanted the weapons put away to protect the innocence of their children. Little did they know the price they were to pay because they refused to study the books of their ancestors."

Klogan winced with pain but refused to lie back down. "If you have read the books, you know all that happened until this day."

"I have read them all," I said.

Pain and fatigue were evident on Klogan's face. I wiped his brow and gave him more water to drink. "Lie down and sleep for now," I said to him. "I will see to the others."

"I must tell you one more thing before you go," he uttered, laying his head back onto the pillow. "Something that has not been written. Because your father was a wise king, he convinced me to teach the art of the sling and the cestro to those he would select. In all, there were twenty-one of the young chosen—their ages, fourteen through seventeen, perfect for learning. With the approval of their fathers, I began to tutor them. They are those who are with me now."

"These children know the cestro?"

A smile appeared on Klogan's face. "You still call them children—knowing their ages are so near to your own?" Then he nodded. "They know the art well enough," he said weakly.

I turned to see Thorri standing in the doorway. I studied him closely. It was difficult for me to believe that he was the age Klogan had implied or that he could use the cestro or the sling with any expertise. Yet I was reminded of the twenty-one statues in the rooms of the Ancient, and I wondered if the Ancient had carved them from a future he had seen.

Yiltor stood at his table looking over the map of the new world, a world that would soon be his. It was the perfect world for his kingdom—its borders vast, protected by both the sea and the mountains. But first he must rid it of those who stood in his way.

His wickedness burned in his eyes; his greed ignited his soul as his fingers touched the names of the lands he desired. To the northeast was the kingdom of Kvenland; to the northwest, Roskilde; below Roskilde was Trondheim. To the east, Cernonsix, the kingdom closest to his own, though not the kingdom he would conquer first.

It was the small kingdom of Etchon he claimed as his first triumph, and perhaps his greatest, for it was a hidden kingdom and the most difficult to conquer. No matter the size of the armies who wish to invade or the power of their weapons, they were helpless—for a hidden kingdom can only be conquered by one of its own. Perhaps *conquer* was not the right word for what brought destruction to the people of Etchon. Perhaps a better word would be *betrayal*.

He was not even sure of its existence, in the beginning. His only knowledge came from stories told many years in the past and handed down to the kingdoms of this day. The stories even hinted as to where it could be found if one were to venture into the rugged mountains to the east. Many had ventured over the years and found nothing, yet the story became legend. Though he knew legends came alive when truth is mixed with myth, he would take no chances.

He laughed when he thought of the shrewdness of his plan. He only had to find a wizard who claimed to have knowledge of hidden kingdoms. And though that in itself was perhaps more difficult than leading an invasion, it was an excellent strategy.

It took seven years in finding a wizard, but even the wizard Ancitel, with all his power and potions, could not simply find the Hidden Kingdom. However, Ancitel assured Yiltor there was indeed one. He called it the Kingdom of Etchon.

"There is no potion that will make it visible to us," the wizard explained to Yiltor. "We can only wait until my magic detects one of the Purcatians outside its perimeter. Then I will guide him to me and persuade him, through a simple brew, to betray his people."

It was another seven years in the waiting for one of them to walk beyond the protection of the wall and be influenced with wealth and station, to lead his army back to the invisible city.

It was a war that took fourteen years in obtaining the victory with only one battle that could not even be considered a battle. A battle is an encounter where both sides participate. The people of Etchon knew nothing of defense. They had become complacent in their hidden kingdom, thinking themselves safe and well.

Ancitel had advised the king to take the small son of King Etcheon and imprison him before he attempted the invasion. "It has been foretold among the wizards," Ancitel explained, "that the young prince alone would have the power to destroy any man who invaded the kingdom of his ancestors, for he carries the gift of his mother's blood inside him."

Yiltor had not bothered to ask what this gift was, thinking it was silliness added to the legend to make it more lively. Nonetheless, he had sent soldiers to the sea at the insistence of the wizard, who had discovered through his crystals that Queen Arcadia and her son ventured alone near the shore. Had the soldiers been swifter than the eagle that day, he would have had the boy.

Ancitel insisted that Etcheon had escaped into a theoretical future with the help of the bird. And now he came with the story that his crystals saw a portal of time open again—six days after the soldiers had taken the Kingdom of Etchon. Through this portal, the wizard claimed, the babe returned a young man.

Yiltor did have to admit that the wizard had value. King Etcheon was as pure as the wizard was evil, and Ancitel took great pleasure in his power over the Purcatian Clan. On the day the Kingdom of Etchon was captured, Ancitel flaunted his own greatness by presenting Yiltor with trophies of his supremacy: life-size prisms in which the king and queen were sealed—not dead but alive, able to hear his words. They were defenseless to take their eyes from Yiltor when he stood before them and told them of his plans. Yiltor had the prisms taken to his mountain fortress, where he displayed them as the first two trophies of his private collection. One day he would have six kings with whom he could discuss his glory. They would hear his words as he talked about his world that at one time had been theirs.

It was time to ride to his fortress and tell the king and queen the latest news. He called to his guards to prepare his horse and be ready to travel with him. All was made ready, and soon he stood before the prisms, a glass of wine in his hand.

"Although it has only been a week since we became so intimately acquainted, I feel as if we have known each other so much longer. It is because of this, I have come to bring you good news," he said with dignity. "Your son has returned, so the wizard claims. Nonetheless, I shall be ready for him when and if he should come in search of you—if even all that I have told you is true. One cannot be too careful."

When Yiltor finished with all he planned to say to them, he watched their frozen faces and thought he caught a glimpse of anger in the eyes of the king. Yet what disturbed him was the triumph he saw in the eyes of the queen. He shook the feeling from him and gloried in their silence.

A bird, the size of a sparrow, perched itself on the windowsill of the room in which Yiltor stood, listening to his words. He noted that the king was impressive in his appearance, standing well over three and a half cubits, his features notably handsome. His dark hair was long and neatly tied at the nape of his neck. He wore no covering for his head, no cape across his shoulders, no sword at his side. His clothes were simple. He certainly did not give the appearance of a wicked king.

When Yiltor finished his speech and left the room to return to his castle, Barok flew away. He had much to discuss with the panther.

Kevelioc watched the eagle as he came toward him. When Barok landed, Kevelioc told him that soldiers had been lurking about, but without a Purcatian to guide them, they could not find the wall.

"They have the cunning of a snake but lack its intellect," he scoffed. "I could hear them talking among themselves. One saying, 'The wall is this way.' Another saying, 'No, it is this way,' when all the time it was right in front of them. But tomorrow they will bring Petre back with them."

"But why are they here?" Barok asked. "Did they not take or destroy all things of value?"

Kevelioc growled, and his eyes grew angry. "It seems that Petre told Yiltor of metals in the mountains of the kingdom that can be melted down to make weapons." He turned from Barok, taking several steps toward the hidden walls. "It also seems," he snarled, "the wizard told him that the King's son has returned." He turned and fixed his eyes on the eagle. "Yiltor fears Etcheon because of the prophecy telling of the destruction of his own kingdom by the hand of the Purcatian Prince. It seems the soldiers are to search until they find him. When they have him in their grasp, they are to take him to the king."

"This king is cunning," the eagle said, telling Kevelioc all that he had seen and heard. "There is a darkness that surrounds him, and in it he finds his sanctuary."

I found Klogan awake and rested. His face had color and his eyes showed no pain. "You look better," I commented.

"It is because I am better," he replied. "Whatever this is that you wrapped around my leg has all but healed it. See for yourself." He removed the fleece and showed me a slight scar where there had once been a deep gash.

"I am told that it is called 'angel fleece,' " I said. "Perhaps that is what brings its healing power. It seems you are well enough to discuss the chil . . . those you have trained."

He looked at me, his face fighting to suppress a grin.

"I shall try to refrain from calling them children, though each counte-nance is as innocent as a child. Instead, I will call them Klogan's Warriors. We will make narrow bands of angel fleece to decorate the upper right arm of each warrior. This they will wear as an emblem of their bravery as well as a symbolic cloak of protection."

I was beginning to understand the power of the angel fleece. It was a gift to the warriors from the Ancient of Trees.

Barok's *ka-ka* invaded my thoughts. I stood to excuse myself.

"You are going to the eagle, are you not?" Klogan asked.

I looked at him for a moment before responding to his question. "Tell me how you know of the eagle?" I asked cautiously.

"I know that he took you away, and he was to bring you back." He smiled. "Come, I will walk with you to the wall." He stood without assistance and led me to the front of the city where a small grove of trees grew. "Walk through the trees," he said quietly. Then he turned and walked back to his cottage.

Barok met me just outside the wall. He told me of the wizard and his crystals—of the prisms that held my father and mother, and where the king kept them, hidden away from all eyes except his own.

"But they are alive?"

"They are alive."

"Thank you, Barok. That is what I needed to know." I sensed the panther behind me. "Tell me what you have found, Kevelioc," I said, turning to him.

When Kevelioc had finished telling all he had heard and seen, he added, "They are, nonetheless, unaware of Klogan and his warriors. But if the warriors were to step beyond the perimeter of the Hidden Kingdom, the crystals would warn the wizard."

"If we do nothing to prevent the soldiers from making their way to the mountains, it would mean they could simply take all the metals found there; make stronger, better weapons; and give themselves advantage over the lesser kingdoms by becoming a more fearsome army. If they think I am here, the soldiers will come prepared for battle."

"That is so," Kevelioc said, nodding.

"If these young warriors are trained as those of old," Barok said, "it would be possible for them to fight unseen, but it would also reveal that all the Purcatians had not been captured and imprisoned. Do you think it wise that we let the them defend their kingdom?"

I looked from panther to eagle. "Let them go to battle so they will be discovered," I said. "Then those who would know of their existence would also fear their strength."

"Methinks that is a good strategy," Barok acknowledged. "I will go to the palace of Yiltor and hear their strategy. Then when I return with the information, you will know how to prepare."

"And I will stand as sentinel outside the walls," Kevelioc growled.

"When it is possible, I will lead you to the place where your mother and father are held prisoners." Barok touched my shoulder with his wing and then lifted himself into the sky.

Kevelioc growled his disgust for Yiltor. With a gentle nudge against my leg, he disappeared into the shadows. I was left alone to return to the city with the knowledge I so desired, as well as the pain of knowing it.

Klogan was waiting for me when I returned. I hastily told him of my discovery and asked if his young warriors were ready for battle.

"I can tell you they are brave and well trained," he answered, "but to say they are ready for battle—I cannot—for they have never been in battle. I can only tell you what is in my heart, and my heart says they will fight without fear."

"Call them together."

When the young warriors stood before me, I could sense their strength. Their tender ages were hidden beneath hardened muscles—the innocence of youth beneath masks of bravery. I could not doubt Klogan's words.

"Tomorrow," I said to them, "an army will march to this city. They come in search of me and of the metals. We must decide what we will do."

Klogan stood and instructed his warriors to stand also. "If we do not fight, or if we fail in our attempt to defeat this king and those who follow him, not only will our people be as slaves, but also the people of the Kingdoms of Roskilde, Kvenland, Trondheim, and Cernonsix."

He paused and studied the faces of the twenty-one standing before him. "You have been trained to fight as your ancestors fought," he reminded them. "The records tell us that no one could defeat them. I tell you that no one can defeat you if you use those same strategies as I have taught you. There may be fifty soldiers or five hundred. There are twenty-one of you, but you have the advantage even over their hundreds. Do you wish to stay and defend the kingdom of your people?"

The young warriors stood silent, their eyes on Klogan. Thorri took a step forward. "We have discussed it among ourselves," he announced, "and decided that we will stand where you tell us, and we will fight as you have taught us." He stepped back into the line.

Klogan looked over his young army with pride. "Then, my young warriors, let us prepare for tomorrow."

I watched as he took them through the maneuvers. No target was too small for their cestros. Their quickness and their strength were well beyond their years.

Barok returned and watched from the limb of a tree. When the young warriors went to eat, he came closer and set himself on the small bench beside me. "The wizard has warned the king of your power," he said, "and Yiltor seems to have taken the warning to heart. He is sending sixty-three soldiers on the morrow at sunrise."

Barok was silent for a time as if in thought. When he spoke again it was of the young warriors. "So they have decided to fight?"

"They will not run away," I explained, "and Klogan stands with them."

"He has taught them well."

I could not dispute his words. They were young, blessed, and foreordained. They were the statues of the Ancient.

I said I would never again call them children, but they were still children in their innocence, even as they are about to battle for their lives, the lives of their families, and for the preservation of kingdoms. Therefore, in my heart I suppose I shall always think of them as such.

"I think it is time to introduce them to your legion," Barok suggested. "We will meet you in the courtyard where the young warriors gather."

I nodded and went in search of Klogan. When at last I found him, I told him all that Barok had said.

Klogan looked at me, his eyes narrowed. "If you have a legion, why have I not seen them?"

"Oh, but you have. You only need to know them," I replied.

He asked no more questions but left to gather his warriors.

When, at last, the five of us stood before the warriors of Klogan, I asked that they become acquainted with my legion and told them that together, we would defeat the enemy before us.

I motioned for Kevelioc to stand beside me. The young warriors gasped, their eyes wide, though not fearful.

"This is Kevelioc. He is of extraordinary strength and agility. His vision is intense. His instinct is powerful. He is silent and all but invisible to the enemy. His attack is quick—then he is gone. He is my protector, and now he is yours, as well."

Next I motioned to the Danes and they came to stand beside me. "The black one is called Ranulf, the brown, Gudrod. They are gifted in their scents. They will smell and hear those who come against us long before they can be upon us. Their speed and their ability to read the enemy will be one of our strengths. They will be your guides."

I gazed up at the eagle perched upon Walkelin's back. "Barok will be our eyes. He will direct our battle from the sky. Walkelin will be with me, for I will need his strengths as I battle."

The animals stood proudly, lowering their heads in respect for the warriors. The warriors asked that the animals walk among them so they could touch them. It was their way of saying that they would trust them with their lives.

I turned to Klogan. "Tell us your strategy."

He stood. "I will place seven of my warriors within the trees beyond the wall. There will be seven upon the wall itself. The remaining seven will be placed in these selected areas." He pointed them out to me.

"You have planned well," I said to him. "You will have the soldiers at a great disadvantage as you will be before them, above them, and behind them."

Klogan studied the animals at my side. "Who will you place with those inside the city?"

I put my hand on the panther's back. "Kevelioc will stand with those inside the city. The Danes will be with those outside the wall. The eagle will be with those above the wall."

The animals left us and took their posts as sentinels. A narrow band of angel fleece was wrapped around the upper right arm of each warrior. The explanation of its purpose was made known, and the warriors seemed pleased. It shimmered in its radiance for only a short time before becoming all but invisible to the eye.

Later, after Klogan and his warriors were asleep, I walked to the small hill behind the city. There I searched the sky and found that cluster of stars—tiny bright particles of the universe blinking as if transmitting a message that all things were as they should be. I felt emptiness in my heart for Taraini as those words came into my thoughts, and I was transformed, if only for a second, back to the Ancient of Trees and her smile.

The sound of Ranulf's voice cleared my head. "We are returning from the hills where we picked up the scent of two humans," he relayed to me. "They have been sent ahead to spy. We cannot harm them for they are to report back to their captain by morning. If they do not report, the captain will know something awaits them. We will leave the humans free to do what they were sent to do."

I hurried to tell Klogan of the Danes' discovery.

"The spies will see nothing that will assist them in the battle," Klogan assured me, "unless you decide to step outside the perimeter as bait." The humor in his eyes betrayed the intent of his words. Then his eyes became serious once again. "However, their caution tells me they fear your power."

"Do you fear for the lives of your warriors?" I asked.

"I'm concerned that they perform well," he admitted, "for that is what will save their lives."

We waited together for the sun to rise, ready to move as soon as Barok gave the signal—quiet in our preparation. Klogan girded his weapons of war about him. I did the same.

Just as we stepped outside, Barok flew over, telling us the soldiers were eight dolichos away and moving swiftly on horseback.

Seven young warriors slipped through the shelter of the walls. They carried with them oval shields and pouches filled with stones. Draped from their shoulders were the cestros and slings. They hid themselves among the trees, barely inside their perimeter. Seven more took their positions upon the high wall. Though I could not see the remaining seven, I knew they were in place.

In the silence that followed, one could hear the stream as it flowed along its banks, beneath the warbling of the birds. Soon Yiltor's army would be moving through the valley of the mountains, unaware that their enemy knew their every move.

13

The Battle

ANCITEL WORE HIS SILK ROBES THE color of crimson that contrasted the plain clothing of Yiltor. They stood together at the window of the king's chamber in the upper rooms of the castle.

"Don't worry, my king," he said, his voice smooth as the clothing he wore. "Etcheon the Younger cannot stand against sixty-three and survive."

Yiltor turned his eyes to the man who wore no wizard's hat, only thin crystals that were wrapped through his long black hair, which fell down his back. "Are you so sure?"

The wizard's mouth twisted and his eyes narrowed. "He stands alone, this boy."

Yiltor scowled at Ancitel. He did not trust him. He even feared him, at times. But he needed him. That knowledge alone disgusted Yiltor. "This boy somehow has the capability to transport in time, if what you say is true. I find myself curious as to how he does this."

A sly smile appeared on the wizard's face as he lifted his hand and turned it, allowing Yiltor to see the crystal that pressed against the palm as if it were the palm itself. "I do not underestimate him, or the power he obviously brings with him, but he is not a wizard. He holds no magic as I do. He cannot see what I see."

"And you have seen him though the palm of your hand?"

"When he approached the walls that are hidden from us, I did not see his face, for it was shaded by the brim of his clataè. But I know it was him, for the hat gave him away. I will say that you have sent enough soldiers to bring him back. Yet I would have sent no less, for if Petre is speaking the truth, the mountains within the walls of the kingdom will grant him many hiding places."

Yiltor wrapped his arms about his chest, his face revealing the thoughts that flogged his mind. "Much is at stake here, wizard. Let us pray that you are correct when you say he is alone."

"There is no prayer." Ancitel sneered, his face becoming dark and shadowed. "Only the power of the wizard's magic. This magic tells me there is no one with him. He is alone."

Klogan stood before me. In his hands he held several small, flat stones that glistened as they touched each other. He reached out and offered them to me. "They come from the caverns within our mountains," he explained, "and are the most accurate you will find."

I looked at him. "I am no more experienced in battle than your young warriors. Yet I feel as if I am well acquainted with its fury."

He nodded in understanding. "When the story of this battle is read, in years to come by those who will be our descendents, I pray it will tell of a victory won through courage and the knowledge of the sling and cestro. I pray it will tell how we defeated an army of well-trained soldiers in protection of our lives and the lives of our families. I pray it will tell of the son of King Etcheon and his legion."

He paused then and looked at me, slightly amused. "It will be like a legend with the telling of a man, a panther, an eagle, two Great Danes, and a horse, who came from the future to lead the pure of heart in battle."

I could not help but smile with him, for it truly would sound like a legend. "Let the story also tell of their teacher, Klogan, who gave them the knowledge of the cestro and the sling and taught them the art of defense."

Klogan's voice seemed distant as if he were talking to himself when he spoke next. "It will be a fearsome day—one that we shall never forget."

I agreed, puzzled with the bitter taste of fear that seemed to coat my tongue. I asked if he tasted it as well. He nodded that he did, telling me it was good to know the taste without yielding to its intoxication. "It will heighten our determination and make us mightier in battle."

"The soldiers are within one dolichos," Barok called to us from above the trees. He said no more but lifted himself back into the morning sky.

I looked at Klogan. "Barok tells me they are close."

He reached out, grasped my arm in a show of friendship, and bowed his head slightly. We parted, and I called to Walkelin.

"What is your strategy?" he inquired when he stood before me.

"Can you run faster than the wizard's magic?" I asked in return.

He shook his mane and snorted loudly. "My speed is far beyond the wizard's magic. As long as you are on my back, he cannot find you."

"Yiltor will surely place sentinels along the way for assurance that I be captured if I chance to escape those who come through the hidden walls. Barok will give us their positions, but you must be swift, and I must be accurate."

"Do not concern yourself with the swiftness of this horse," he whinnied. "You need only concern yourself with the one yielding the weapon."

"Then, for now, my friend, you will guard the mountains while I stand with the seven outside the walls. When Barok tells us it is time to ride, we will leave the perimeter of the kingdom and relieve the sentinels of their duty."

He threw his head up with nostrils flared. Turning from me, his hooves barely dusted the ground as he raced toward the mountains. He would be the only watchman of the mountain passes. Nonetheless, there was no need to have more. Yiltor's men had no way through them except to climb their cliffs.

I could not see the seven young warriors when I reached the trees, but I could sense their presence around me. I had just taken my place when Gudrod's words entered my thoughts. "Twenty-one soldiers have stopped and dismounted approximately four diauloi from the walls of the kingdom, while the others continue on. Those on horseback have changed their course slightly to the west. Runolf runs with them while hidden from them. Barok flies above them. It seems their strategy is in favor of approaching together from three sides."

I relayed the message to the one hidden in the tree beside me. The twittering music of birds told me the message had been received and relayed to all the warriors. Then the silence returned and we waited.

By the time the sun had filled the sky, Yiltor's army was in place—one division to the south, one to the west, and one to the north of the hidden walls. Six soldiers were left behind, two in each division, as watchmen. The only flaw in their strategy, it seemed, was their lack of knowledge as to the strength of their enemy.

Taraini's words, "*The greatest weapon you can possess is the weapon of knowledge*," would prove themselves this day.

The crystal in the wizard's palm glowed in pale hue as he watched Petre astride his horse, flaunting his arrogance. The Purcatian would lead those who were to approach from the west, when the signal was given. They would be the first to enter the invisible gates of the unseen walls.

An arrow appeared in the sky. The signal was given. From three sides, they began their march.

"Soon you will have your prince," he said to Yiltor, showing the king the palm of his hand. To himself he said, "And I shall have my timepiece."

I could sense the Danes coming closer—one from the south and one from the north. I could see Barok, high above those advancing from the west. The scent of the soldiers began to fill the air. Yet within their scent I became aware of something else. At first it puzzled me—then I knew. It was the scent of Petre. The scent of his greed and his arrogance was repugnant.

I could not see to the west because of the trees, but the young warriors began to twitter their bird-like sounds, relaying the message that soldiers and horses were approximately one diaulos away. Those approaching from the north and south became visible as I listened to the Danes communicate.

"They are now closing their ranks," Barok called from above, "and forming a half-circle. Their bows are drawn and ready. Prepare yourselves."

Once again the melodic warbling began, at my prompting, and the rustle of shields being raised was immediate. I slid my clataè low over my head, making sure the vest was tight around me, and we waited.

"The arrows are in the air!" Barok screeched from above us. His message was understood without interpretation, and we were ready.

The enemy was not foolish. Though their strategy was to keep their approach silent and unseen, their arrows were aimed for the trees, not the invisible walls beyond their ability to see. They would take no chances. The arrows fell where they were aimed. I listened to the soft clicking sound of the contact of arrow to shield, but I heard no cries of arrow to flesh.

An arrow struck the leather of my vest. Its force pressed heavily against my back, knocking me forward. Then it bounced and fell harmlessly to the ground. Even knowing about the strength of the vest, the test of its strength was amazing.

The arrows were silent, and the soldiers appeared below us. They dismounted and tied their horses to the trees where their arrows had found nothing. We waited for them to pass below us and into the clearing. There they stopped at the silent command of their leader, who held his arm in the air while conversing with Petre. As he lowered his arm, the soldiers formed three lines and waited.

Before us fifty-six fearless men stood facing a wall they could not see. They were well equipped with shields and swords, experienced in the art of war, and waiting for the command to enter the city. The sight was daunting. Would the young warriors begin to doubt their own valor because of it? I sensed nothing that would confirm or deny my concern until I heard the twittering of the morning bird—a command to ready the slings and cestros. The warriors slid silently down the trees and into the shadows.

Petre led the first row of men through the wall just as the morning birds conversed, and eight of those still waiting to follow, fell—simple stones stealing the life from their bodies—their deaths quick and silent.

Before the remaining soldiers could respond, sixteen more fell, the stones coming from behind them and above them. The five remaining soldiers raised their swords and their shields in defense, their eyes darting all around them. They could not see the enemy. They could not know that their shields would not protect them. Small stones found their mark and the five slid to the ground without as much as a sound or a glimpse of their foe.

The call of the morning birds filled the air, sending the message that the battle beyond the wall was finished. The seven warriors positioned atop its pillars could now focus their attention on those who had entered the city.

The soldiers followed Petre and found themselves in a quiet courtyard. Having no knowledge of what had just taken place outside the walls, they waited for the rest of the men to follow. When no more came, Petre quickly stepped to the outside of the gate only to find them lying on the ground, blood covering their faces and necks. Fear struck his eyes as he looked about him. He trembled in confusion and cowardliness.

He stepped back from the dead—pressing himself against the wall. He slowly lifted his eyes to the trees as if he knew what was hidden in the shadows and, for a time, remained motionless.

Suddenly he disappeared through the gate only to reappear seconds later, his eyes more frightened than before. I could only guess that what was visible to him here was the very scene he encountered when he ventured back through the gate. He began to slither along the wall much like a snake, in the hope of escaping—sure in the knowledge that one of his own blood would not kill him.

It had not been discussed as to what would be done with Petre. Perhaps it was better to let chance play into the outcome. I knew we could not let him get beyond the perimeter or the wizard would surely see him through the supposed magic. I was just about to call to the Danes when Kevelioc came through the gate, his eyes on Petre. His thoughts mingled with my own.

"What had to be done is finished. Now the traitor belongs to me," he said, silently closing in on the young man, whose age could be no more than my own.

It wasn't until Petre had reached the edge of the perimeter that a low growl turned him around to face Kevelioc. He froze, and his face filled with terror. Suddenly, he let out a scream and turned to run.

Instantly the panther had his teeth around Petre's neck. Dragging his limp body back through the wall, he laid him at the feet of Klogan and then stepped away.

Klogan thanked him, lifted the body into his arms, and disappeared.

Kevelioc looked at me and snorted. "He is not dead, only frightened into unconsciousness. I thought perhaps you might want him alive for your own purpose."

I nodded to him and turned my attention to the young warriors as they came from the shadows. I asked if they were well enough. They simply nodded, and with tears streaming down their faces, sat upon the ground in a closed circle, reaching out and taking each other's hands.

Thorri invited me to join them, but I explained that Walkelin and I had one more thing to do. He understood and turned back to his companions.

By the time Walkelin was beside me, Barok had given me the directions.

Walkelin nudged me in the back. "Climb on and let us finish this battle," he neighed, throwing his mane and stamping his hooves.

I did as he advised and, feeling the tenseness of his muscles, gripped his mane as he thundered to the south and the first two sentinels.

His speed was smooth. But as I tightened my grasp on the cestro, it came to me that I should not end their lives, but instead, send them back to Yiltor with fearsome stories of whirlwinds that knocked them from their feet, and wisps of dust that spoke to them with eerie voices. I relayed my thoughts to the horse.

"Let the thunder of hooves be part of their story." He neighed as he pounded the earth, letting the echo vibrate. "They hear us coming, but they cannot see us, and they are confused."

The two soldiers stood together only a short distance from us, their weapons drawn, their eyes searching.

Walkelin stirred the soil beneath him and let his speed control its movement as it spun and grew in intensity until it wrapped itself around them at the horse's command.

I spoke as a ghost through the dust, telling them their comrades were no longer alive and that they would be wise to carry that message to their king. "It is a warning of the power that now prevails inside the walls of the Hidden Kingdom," I assured them, my voice vaporous.

Then, as suddenly as it had appeared, the whirlwind was gone, leaving them hugging the ground and spitting dirt from their mouths.

Twice more we repeated this tactic before we returned to the safety of the Hidden Kingdom.

Ancitel wrapped his fingers around the palm of his hand. Once the soldiers entered the perimeter of the Hidden Kingdom, he had lost contact. His only option now was to wait. The wait, however, was much shorter than he had anticipated. The scream of the Purcatian shocked him, and he threw open his palm to a short glimpse of Petre before he disappeared from his view once again.

Next, the crystal in his palm revealed a fast moving whirlwind that suddenly materialized where the two sentinels stood at the south, moving speedily to the west, and finally to the north. It engulfed the men as it traveled, picking them up, then dropping them to the ground—leaving them powerless and fearful. Then, without warning, it disappeared.

"What is happening?" he screamed. He spat upon the crystal and rubbed it with the cloth of his robe. "Let me see inside the walls," he pleaded, his face flushed with anger. "Let me see inside the walls."

The crystal revealed only the sentinels unraveled in their chaos, riding swiftly to the south and the castle.

The king was instantly at his side. "What is it?" he asked harshly.

The wizard could do nothing but show him the palm of his hand and tell him what he had seen. "Have the six sent to you immediately upon their arrival," he said finally. "We must find out what happened."

Yiltor whipped his robe about him. "Tell me, wizard," he said furiously. "Where are the fifty-seven?"

"I cannot say for sure." Ancitel withered in the thought, wondering how the sentinels had been discovered.

"One mere boy, you said. Now I ask—did one mere boy do this? Is it possible that he could defeat sixty-three of my best soldiers all by himself?"

"One boy came through that portal," the wizard said sternly. "One who should never have left this realm in the beginning." He paused for a moment, letting his words remind the king of his warning. "If there are others with him, it is you that must take the blame, for it was you who said all the Purcatians are now in your prison."

Yiltor was taken aback at the wizard's accusation. Was it possible that his soldiers had not found all of them?

"Think for a moment," Ancitel continued. "Did Petre not tell us there were many hiding places in the mountains?"

Yiltor stood at the tower window and looked beyond the city walls, his eyes searching for signs of the six returning—his mind considering the things he had seen in the wizard's crystal. His face grew dark as he reminded himself of the missed opportunity to have this "mere boy" locked in the wizard's prison, just days ago. Ancitel had warned him, had he not? If he had sent his men as soon as the warning was given, this day would not have happened. "This is not good, wizard," he said finally.

"We must assume nothing until we hear what your men have to say," Ancitel answered.

When the soldiers stood before them, perspiration had mixed with dirt, leaving their hair caked, their faces streaked. Their eyes, red with grit, betrayed the fear that lingered in their thoughts.

Their stories were the same. First, they heard the thundering of hooves. Then, without warning, a whirlwind lifted them into the air before dropping them to the ground. They could see nothing through the blinding dust, but each heard the haunting voice.

Yiltor looked into the faces of his men. "And what, exactly, did this voice say?"

One of the soldiers stepped forward. "The message was the same to all of us. We were told that our comrades are no longer alive—that we would be wise to carry this message to our king, for it is a warning of the power that now prevails inside the walls of the Hidden Kingdom."

Yiltor listened, his face displaying remarkable calm contrasting the fury he felt within him. He dismissed the six, sending them to their quarters to bathe and rest.

He turned to Ancitel. "Go back to your books and potions of magic. Find how to rid ourselves of this son of King Etcheon."

Before the setting of the sun, the bodies of fifty-six soldiers lay side by side within the courtyard. Their helmets and armor were carefully placed above their heads, their weapons by their sides. Their faces, hands, and feet had been washed, their hair brushed. A soft cloth was placed over each body as a coverlet.

After this was done, the Danes, the horse, and the panther led fifty-seven horses into the meadows beside the mountains to graze. They then watched with me from the hillside as the young warriors went about their task with reverence and respect for those who had died this day. Barok soared silently above them.

"Explain what I see but do not understand," I said when Klogan sat beside me.

"These soldiers only followed the orders given them," he replied. "They are ignorant of the truth. Because they have been taught nothing but lies, their deaths are innocent, and we honor them for their bravery."

"It is a beautiful sight."

He smiled. "You are correct, my friend. These men deserve that much."

We sat in silence for a time until all was finished in the courtyard, and the young warriors sat among us. As the sun dropped beyond the horizon, the twenty-one began to sing, their voices filling the night with soft, melodic harmony. Their song was one of farewell to those whose spirits would return to heaven this night.

When they had finished, Klogan walked away from us and to the courtyard. He touched the cloth that had been placed over each body with fire, and the night became bright with the flame.

"They have been released from this earth now," Thorri explained. "The fire purifies the spirit so it can enter the greater kingdom." He motioned to the others, and they touched my shoulder as they passed, thanking me for standing with them against Yiltor.

Klogan returned to my side. "The story will read well, Etcheon the Younger."

"It will be a great legend among our people," I agreed, my body weary. The day had drained all the energy from me. I felt more tired this night than the day I returned from my training with Kevelioc. I could not help but smile when I thought of that day—the scratches and bruises I wore like medals.

"Your look is far away," Klogan said quietly, "as if you are remembering another time."

I fixed my eyes on him. "And I see in your face great relief, knowing that none of those who you care for died this day."

"You are very perceptive." Klogan sighed.

"Now that this day is over, tell me of Petre," I said.

He did not speak for a time, only gazed into the sky. "Petre was my closest friend," he said finally, his voice filled with sadness. "Until he wanted more than what this kingdom could offer him." He reached out and stroked Kevelioc. "Your panther's wisdom guided him when he chose to capture instead of to kill. Now Petre's fate can be decided by those of his blood."

"Where is he now?" I asked.

"In his home."

"Is he not guarded?"

"Not as you would think, but he will not leave his house." His face spread into a mischievous grin. "He hides there out of fear of Kevelioc. I told him that if he stepped outside his door, the panther would have him for a meal."

Kevelioc turned his head to me and groaned. "Tell him I only needed to smell the spoilage to know I did not wish a taste."

I was amused at Kevelioc's words. But I thought better than to pass them on to Klogan. Instead I congratulated him on his brilliance. "This day your young warriors have proven themselves worthy in battle. Tonight, they have proven themselves worthy of the blood that runs in their veins. Your strategy was as remarkable as their aim. But I need to ask a question I wish I did not have to ask."

"You want to know if they are ready for a more fearsome encounter," he interrupted, "because this is only the beginning. I will tell you this. I did not know how they would perform today, though I was not surprised, only pleased with their performance. They know what is ahead of them, but they are not afraid for they have you to lead them and me to stand beside them." He gestured toward the animals. "They have the Danes, the horse, the panther, and the eagle to stand with them. How can they be afraid?"

"We both stand beside them as we both lead them," I corrected him. "It is as it should be."

14

Yiltor

I AWOKE TO BAROK TWITTERING IN my ear. "I have just returned from the castle," he said in distaste. "Unlike you, the king spent a sleepless night. It seems the six you sent back to him had a very unusual tale to tell." He moved away from my ear and onto my chest—I believe to make eye contact and ensure he had my attention. "The whole kingdom has now heard it. Would you care to hear more?"

"Could it wait until I am awake?" I asked.

He pecked gently at my chest, causing just enough discomfort to bring my senses to a conscious state. I pushed him from me and groaned. "Thank you. I am awake, now."

"The people of Yiltor fear the unnatural power that controls the Hidden Kingdom." Barok perched himself upon the windowsill, his eyes narrowed. "But it is what I have to say, now, that is the most dangerous."

I could sense a change in his mood. "I sat in the window of a tower listening while the king and his wizard devised a plan. There are five hundred and thirty-seven Purcatians in his prison. His strategy is to use them as a ransom. You are the payment. Each day that he must wait for you to surrender to him, fifty of your people will die."

Having my people in his prison had given Yiltor the advantage, and I had not even considered this. "We may have saved the city, but have I lost the people?" I groaned, miserably.

Barok was silent for a moment then cleared his throat as one would before he revealed something profound. "You have mystified a wizard, exasperated a king, and frightened his citizens. Your legion is proud of you and stands ready for your next command. How do you propose we save your people?"

I looked at him. He would have nothing of my self-doubt. I took a deep breath, letting the air out slowly. "When does he intend to post this ransom?"

"Tomorrow he will send out a decree on which your crimes will be written as well as lies professing the Purcatians to be a threat to the lives of his citizens and their children. It will take five days for that which is written to be acknowledged throughout all the land. Therefore, he has allowed seven days before he begins his executions. The people will believe the words on the parchment because they know nothing except that which Yiltor tells them. They will cheer when the Purcatians are paraded before them in chains and executed."

I looked into the eagle's eyes. "Tell me, Barok," I said, "did I bring this about, unnecessarily?"

He neither hesitated nor did his eyes leave mine. "Know this, young Etcheon, you did not. Yiltor had already planned to rid himself of them. They are a nuisance to him as well as a burden. He looks upon them as if they were wild dogs and wishes to tend to them accordingly. At noon tomorrow, one hundred were to be sent to the executioner, their bodies dumped into the sea when the deed was done. This was to be repeated each day until all five-hundred and thirty-seven Purcatians lay buried in the deep."

I could hardly believe his words. "How do you know all of this?"

Barok cocked his head. "Unlike you, Yiltor is a man who likes the sound of his own voice, and who, in his arrogance, cares little what the bird sitting in his window hears. His captains think he is a gracious king to give you seven days in which to respond with your surrender before he begins to execute your people."

"Then we have seven days to free my father and my mother, conquer a kingdom, and rescue my people."

He nodded as a sigh escaped him. "There is much to consider, but know this also, young Etcheon, you have given us those seven days."

I nodded. "Call my legion to me. Together we will devise a strategy."

"I will do as you ask." He flew to the windowsill and called back to me. "Know this, young Etcheon, you are far more than you think. Do not fear that which you must do, for the sake of your kin or your legion, but do what you know you must do, for their sakes as well as your own." He disappeared beyond the window.

I hurriedly dressed and was about to open the door when a voice called to me. "Etcheon the Younger," I heard Thorri say. "Are you awake?"

"I am," I called back and opened the door to greet him.

In his arms he had the pouch that held our never-ending food supply. "May we have our morning meal with you?" He looked humble in his request.

In the courtyard beyond him, I could see twenty youth gathered around Klogan, laughing and talking, as if yesterday had never happened. It was refreshing to me, and I stepped out, inviting them to share the food from the pouch. Thorri opened it to Klogan and to me before he handed it to the warriors.

I sat beside the teacher. "It is interesting to me," I said quietly, "though they carry the pouch for me, they never open it until they have asked my approval."

He turned his face to me and smiled, but said nothing—only watched as each young warrior took a small amount of fruit and bread from the pouch and then handed it to the next. When everyone had food upon their plates, they bowed their heads in a quiet prayer of gratitude.

While they ate, their chatter was of pleasant things. It was as if they had no memory of the day and night before. I looked at Klogan. "Explain something to me," I said. "Have they forgotten?"

He studied the warriors for a moment and then placed his hand on my shoulder. "They have not forgotten, my friend. They will carry yesterday with them forever—not only the memory of the battle, but also the glory of preparing the soldiers for their return home." He took a bite of his bread, chewed it thoughtfully. "Now, may I ask a question of you?"

I nodded that he could.

"Yesterday, these children went into battle knowing the art of defense. Yet in the battle you gave them a greater knowledge—that of knowing their enemy's strategy. Which is the greater—knowing how to use a weapon with exactness or knowing the mind of your enemy?"

I pondered his question before answering. "Knowing the mind of your enemy gives you a great advantage. It could keep you from his path or give you the chance to foil his attack without having or needing a weapon."

He nodded his agreement.

"But what if in knowing his every move gives you the knowledge that he is about to end the lives of your family, and you cannot reach them in time to get them away. But you can intercept him before he reaches them?" I continued. "Your only alternative must be to end his life. But you need a weapon. Would you then wish for the bow, a cestro, or the sling—and the knowledge of their art?"

"Indeed, I would." His face brightened.

"Is it not better, then, to conceive that knowledge is not only knowing the mind of your enemy but knowing the art of defense as well?"

"You are implying that what I have taught my warriors is just as important as what you have taught them, are you not?" He grinned, pleasure evident in his eyes.

"I believe you already knew that, my friend," I chided him in humor. "You just wanted pleasant conversation."

What we discussed next was far from pleasant. "What do you plan for Petre?" I asked.

"We give him time to consider his crime. Then he must face those he has betrayed. He will be allowed to speak in his own defense. The warriors will listen. Then they will decide his fate."

"And you are not afraid that he will try to escape before this happens?"

"Oh, he will try. He now has had time to consider his choices. He is too arrogant to be humiliated in front of those he considers to be simple children. Even with the knowledge that Kevelioc lies in wait outside his door will not deter him for long. In his pride, he will consider himself capable of a well-plotted escape. If his attempt fails, he knows it would be less painful to die in the mouth of a panther than to stand before us."

"It seems you know him well."

"I know his mind because, not only was he my closest friend, but he is also my brother."

Klogan's voice was so quiet when he spoke the words, I thought I must have misunderstood. But as I looked at him I could see the deep sadness in his eyes, and I knew I had heard him correctly. There were no words that could sufficiently express my feelings for his torment.

"I am sorry," was all I could think to say.

"As am I, my friend." He sighed heavily. "It is my family who has brought this devastation to our kingdom and caused your family so much loss. I will give my life in your defense to prove my loyalty."

"You have nothing to prove," I assured him. "I know where you stand."

Yiltor held a parchment in his hand, holding it so only his eyes could see the words. "This decree will be sent to all the kingdoms in the land," he said, letting his fingers caress the words that were written. Then he turned his eyes to Ancitel and sat in his chair, leaning back and letting his boots rest on the desk in front of him. "It will take, I believe five days for the word to reach every man, woman, and child. Great whisperings and excitement will come from it, and many rumors will fly about as bees buzzing, causing much attention to be turned away from the boring, everyday life of the peasant and the wealthy alike." He handed the parchment to the wizard. Would you care to read what I have written?"

"Of course, Your Majesty. I would be most pleased." He took the parchment and began to read, silently.

"Read it aloud," Yiltor requested, "so that I might hear my words from another's mouth."

The wizard sighed and did as the King had commanded.

To the loyal citizens of my Kingdom,

It is in the highest regard for your safety and that of your children that I now go to the lengths of my responsibility. Nevertheless, it is after deep consideration that I write this decree to you, son of King Etcheon, to be read by all who live in this land.

Because you have brought death to fifty-six of my soldiers, without provocation, I issue this warning. If you do not surrender to me on the seventh day of this, the second month of the sixth year, fifty-six of your people, of whom I hold five hundred and thirty-seven, will be executed. Each day that you fail to appear before me, fifty-six more will die.

In your deliberation, let your conscience bear this thought: it is not I, King Yiltor, who must carry the burden for the death of your people. Instead, it is you, the son of their king.

I sign with my own hand.

Yiltor, King of the Land of Yiltor

Ancitel's menacing eyes were passionate. "You have done well, my King. You reach into the mind of this son of Etcheon and take away any advantage. He will have no choice but to surrender himself." The wizard thought for a moment then added, "It is wise to give him seven days. The citizens will think you more than generous."

In his mind, Ancitel had another thought. His changelings had failed to bring the boy to him, and he needed more time in which to find him. There was much at stake here, much more than there had been, before he learned what he now knew. These seven days would allow him time to work his sorcery in a way he had not done while bowing to this king he despised.

Yiltor pressed the royal stamp onto the parchment, beneath his name. "When all the kingdoms around us have a duplication of my decree, and because they fear my wrath, this Purcatian will not find safety anywhere."

Ancitel waited until the king had placed the decree on a table before he spoke again. "In the night, the crystal showed me vapors of bluish smoke rising above the hills where the Hidden Kingdom is thought to be." He opened his palm for Yiltor to see into the crystal.

"I see nothing but simple clouds, you fool."

"Look closer, my king."

His patience wearing thin, Yiltor grabbed Ancitel's hand and almost touched his nose to the crystal. In doing so, he breathed in the heavy scent of spices.

"Note the aroma emitted from the clouds."

Yiltor tossed the wizard's hand away from him. "What is this?" he growled, waving his own hand in the air.

"It is the burial ritual of the Purcatians. Oil, scented with sweet spices and highly flammable, is poured over the body. Cloth, made from silk, becomes its coverlet. A torch lights the flame and when it is over, all that remains are a few vaporous clouds of tinted smoke."

Yiltor stepped back. "Fifty-six bodies brought together and cremated within a few hours. Do you still believe he is alone?" His eyes flamed into Ancitel's. "Give me your answer, wizard."

Ancitel closed his palm, covering the crystal. "The answer is simple. You did not capture all the Purcatians."

"Ah! There you are." Kevelioc yawned as Klogan, Barok, and I approached. "Petre wishes not to stay. I was up with him most of the night, like a mother tending to her child."

"He attempted an escape?" I made no effort to hide the pleasure in my voice.

Kevelioc looked at me, bearing his huge fangs. "He is lucky he survived. But it was his preparation that stole my sleep. He thought himself so clever while I could only shake my head at his foolishness. This morning he carries the mark of a claw on his back." He closed one eye and laid his head against his paws. "Already, he is busy preparing for his next attempt."

"And there are those who would help," Gudrod announced from behind me. "While Runolf and I were patrolling the perimeter I took the mountain's edge. There I spotted three who look to be Purcatians in the ravine, preparing to climb the cliffs."

I told Klogan what the animals had said to me.

He chuckled at the panther's story but quickly sobered when I told him what the Danes had to report.

"I know the three. They are Petre's followers—Ingelric, Talvas, and Senfrie."

"Are they as arrogant and stupid as Petre?" snarled Kevelioc.

Klogan looked at me for translation but I offered none because Petre was his brother. Instead I asked him what he wished to do with them. He replied that the three were as arrogant and stupid as Petre, and we should treat them as the enemy.

"Did I not already mention that?" Kevelioc asked.

"I will take flight and see where they have progressed to," Barok said, "while you discuss the more apparent danger."

I agreed and proceeded to tell Klogan all that the eagle had revealed to me earlier. "It seems the real battle has not even begun."

"We both know that if you were to surrender yourself to him," Klogan assured me, "the Purcatians would still see death." He paused and crossed his arms, his eyes narrowed in thought. "When you first showed me your legion, I will admit that I doubted. I no longer doubt for I have seen them perform in battle in a way man cannot. You have with you the strength of many armies. My warriors and I will be proud to stand with you in whatever it is you must do."

"Do the smaller kingdoms around you stand with King Yiltor?" I inquired.

"They are all peaceful people, as were the people of Yiltor while his father was alive. There are claims that Yiltor plotted his father's death in his pursuit of power. He now controls a mighty army as well as the minds of the citizens. The smaller kingdoms fear him and, I believe, will do nothing to anger him. They are foolish in their thoughts that he will leave them alone, for his desire is to control them all."

Barok landed next to me. "The three have begun their climb," he reported. "Their voices echo against the rocks of the mountains as they talk. They are coming because they know Petre is alive. It seems the very laws he claimed were for the weak are those that now protect his life. They move quickly as if they know the trail, and they carry bows and quivers of arrows. Their plan is to enter the city at night, find where Petre is either hiding or being held prisoner, and rescue him. In their conceit, they hope to find the son of King Etcheon and seek their own ransom when they deliver him to Yiltor."

"Tell me of this law that protects Petre from death at the hands of his own people," I said after relaying Barok's words to Klogan.

"The law is written that no Purcatian will take the life of his own people. Nor will he take the life of any man unless his own is threatened."

"What is the punishment if one breaks this law?"

"The law is a simple instruction to teach respect for life and carries a punishment determined by the people. The law has not been broken for well over two hundred years." He stopped speaking, and I could see him pondering his words. "Nonetheless, Petre and his three followers have twisted its interpretation to fit their gluttony. In their minds—I will assume—they think they have taken no lives. They see no blood on their hands. What they cannot see is that their souls are soaked with it."

"What is your plan for the three who come?" I asked.

"See the narrow valley in the shadow of the mountain?" He pointed his finger. "The three will simply walk into a trap just before they step from its shadow, a short distance from the meadow where the horses are grazing." He looked to the panther. "I only ask that Kevelioc track them."

"I will watch over them," the panther said. "Humans can be quite entertaining in their stupidity. Perhaps they will present an agreeable pastime." He rose to his feet and nudged Klogan's back.

"I think he is ready." I smiled.

As they walked away, Klogan called back to me, telling me he would go to the classroom after he had spoken with Petre. There he would tell his students of the plan.

"We know what Yiltor is preparing," I said to the animals after Klogan left us. "Though I cannot help but wonder if the wizard has plans of his own."

"Your words have merit," Ranulf said. "As the soldiers traveled here, the captains spoke of their mistrust of the wizard. Though he pretends to be docile in front of the king, they feel he is much too clever—that his potions and his magic pose a threat and a danger to their people."

"And the king is not suspicious of him?" Walkelin inquired.

"I think," Barok interrupted, "they are much alike in their cleverness and their vanity. Therefore, their trust in each other is for the moment."

"Perhaps that very fact will serve us," I said. "Their cleverness as well as their vanity may well become their weaknesses."

"Well said," Gudrod agreed. "It is my thought that someone should follow the wizard for a time." He looked at Ranulf. "Is it not true that wizards hold kindly to dogs?"

I looked from Gudrod to Ranulf. "Are you proposing that the two of you become companions to Ancitel?"

"For a short time, and only as long as it takes to get the information useful to us," he assured me.

"Will he not become suspicious when you appear unannounced—his supposed magic unable to warn him of two Danes approaching his tower?"

"There is a myth that thrives within the land of the wizards," Ranulf explained. "It tells a story millenniums old, of a ship's captain who never set sail without his two dogs. One dark night they were swept into a hurricane, destroying the ship and all men aboard. Only the animals survived when mermaids took pity on them, giving them breath until they themselves could breathe beneath the sea. The mermaids promised them immortality if they would stay with them. The dogs agreed to do so only if every five years they could go ashore and be with man for a time."

"It is believed, if one believes in myths," Gudrod continued, "that whoever the dogs choose to befriend is granted one wish. It is also believed that no magic can detect them, just as no magic can detect the mermaids." He winked at Ranulf. "To give the myth more integrity, we will first take a dip in the sea so that when we stand before him, our coats are wet."

"You must promise to be wary of the wizard," I warned them. "And you must return in five days even if you have nothing."

"That is understood," the Danes replied. "We will leave now."

"Before you go, there is one more thing we must discuss," I added. "I must see my mother and father."

"I knew you would require that," Barok answered, perching himself upon Walkelin's back. "So I have a plan. Walkelin will carry you through the mountains, well apart from the path of the three. Once you are beyond the perimeter and near Yiltor's estate, Walkelin's speed will be beyond his magic."

"And once we are there?" Walkelin asked. "When my hooves are still—what will protect Etcheon then?"

"The Danes," Barok answered, tilting his head in their direction. "I will follow them. Once they have introduced themselves to Ancitel and have claimed his attention, I will return and guide you to the estate."

Before we could discuss the plan further, Kevelioc stood beside me. "It seems Petre thinks himself above a conversation with Klogan and refuses to speak." Kevelioc snarled. "He turned his back to avoid the eyes of his brother. The pride rises above the guilt. I smell it when I am near him, and I mock him with disgust." He turned to see Klogan coming toward us. "He wishes to speak to you," he said quietly before moving behind me.

I watched the teacher as he came closer. I sensed the anger inside him, yet his face reflected calm. "It is of no use—for the moment—to try and talk with Petre." Klogan sighed heavily, when he finally stood beside me. "I will try again tomorrow. For now, I will go to my students, and we will make plans for the four of our blood." He embraced me as a brother and left us.

"We must go, also," Ranulf barked softly.

"I do not wish to put your lives in danger, but something draws me to my father and mother. I cannot be of value to you—or to my people—until I sit before them and find what it is I must learn from them."

"Do not be troubled." Gudrod nudged me with his nose. "We know the wizard who does not know us. We have the advantage."

The Danes disappeared beyond the wall—Barok with them. When he returned some time later, he brought with him quite a story. "It was a trick beyond the wizard's magic," he called out, wrapping his talons around the limb of a tree just above me. "The wizard was filled with childish delight when the Danes presented themselves to him, for he knew of the myth. He welcomed them into his arms and methinks he has forgotten all about the Yiltor's ambition—at least for now." His eyes pierced mine. "We must go quickly to the estate, while the Danes have his full attention."

I climbed upon Walkelin's back. The earth beneath us became distorted and blurred—the grass changed to rocks to ledges and cliffs and to grass again, as we entered then left the mountains behind. We followed Barok to the place that only Yiltor visited.

As we came within its boundaries, the eagle's eyes became vigilant, leading me to a spot where I could dismount. "Follow me," he whispered in my ear, once we were inside Yiltor's private fortress. As fast as I could follow, he led me to a room where two glass prisms that entombed my father and mother radiated in the light of a small window, sending their prismatic colors throughout the room.

I had not prepared myself for what I would feel when I looked upon them. The emotion that swept through me took my breath and, for a time, I thought I would scream in anger or lose consciousness in the attempt to remain silent.

"Waste no time!" Barok flew about me. "Do what you must do."

I made myself gaze upon the lifeless yet living bodies, their skin having the appearance of porcelain. They were clothed in beautiful royal cloaks, the color of crimson. My mother's long golden hair fell around her beautiful face and over her shoulder. The ivory of her dress glistened as it caught the light reflected through the prism's transparency.

My father's appearance was a reflection of my own, his eyes open, yet unseeing.

All that I had learned from Verch came to me, and I knelt between the two prisms, my head leaning against the one that confined my mother, my hand pressing against the one that confined my father. I closed my eyes, letting my mind expand, and the essence flow within me. Slowly, I began to communicate my thoughts. "Mother! Father!" I reached out to them.

"Etcheon?" It was my mother's voice crying out in my head.

"It is," I answered.

My father's voice entered my thoughts. "How old are you, now, my son?"

"Eighteen."

I thought I heard a tearful gasp come from my mother. "You are a man," she whispered.

I looked from one to the other. Tears fell to my cheeks, unchecked. "Are you in pain?" I asked.

"Not a physical pain," my father's voice came to me. "But the confinement brings with it the agony of seeing only Yiltor's face and hearing only Yiltor's voice. That is his desire, and he gloats as he flaunts his power over us."

I could sense my mother's alarm as her next words pierced my thoughts. "We knew you would come, but do you not know that he is here this minute?"

It was then that Barok flew to my side. "Yiltor is outside." His sounds were hushed. "I am afraid I have failed you this time, young Etcheon."

"You have not failed me, Barok. It is me who insisted in coming." I touched the prism of my father. "Has he seen me yet?"

"He walked by, pausing only to say he would return for there was much he had to tell us. I think he wants us to concern ourselves, for a time, with what he might say."

I pressed my hands against the prisms and forced my thoughts into the thoughts of my father and mother, once again. "Tell me what it is I need to know so I can help you," I said.

The sound of the footsteps became louder, disrupting my thoughts. There was no time left. Within seconds, Yiltor would be coming through the door.

"In here," I heard Barok whisper. "Hurry!"

I turned and found him pulling at the lid of an old chest. The wood, black with age, had begun to rot, and I could only imagine the creatures that made their home inside its belly. But there was no choice. I did as he instructed, stuffing myself inside. Once the lid was closed, there was barely room for my chest to expand enough to breathe—reminding me of the crevice on the rock.

At the same time I heard Yiltor's voice, I found the eyes of a mouse staring into mine. He did not seem happy to be sharing his home and began to sniff about my face. I could only close my eyes and keep still, praying the rodent had no plans to take a bite. I heard the sound of a bottle being uncorked and liquid being poured into a glass.

"I'm sorry to have taken so long, but I had to select the right vintage—one that would compliment our discussion." Yiltor raised his glass in at toast, then tasted the red liquid. "I know you will want to know that your son has shown himself. Though I have not seen his face, I have seen his work. But he made a mistake in killing fifty-six of my finest soldiers." He paused for a moment, I suppose, to take another sip of whatever was in his glass. Then he continued, "Nonetheless, I do not think he did it alone. There is a possibility some of your people hid themselves during the battle in which we conquered your kingdom and are now aiding him."

I heard his footsteps again and, as I peeked through a small hole where the wood had rotted away, I saw him walking toward the chest. My heart began to beat wildly. I was certain I had been discovered, but when he stood directly in front, he turned, covering the hole with one leg while planting the other on top of the chest. The mouse's whiskers tickled my nose, and I fought to restrain a sneeze.

I could hear the scratching sound of parchment being unrolled. In the quiet of the room, his voice was thunderous, as he read his decree. I took a chance and moved my fingers to my nose and let out the stifled sneeze, as softly as was possible. Yiltor's voice suddenly became silent. I had made a mistake. I waited, listening. He removed his foot from the lid of the chest. I could hear the creaking of the lid as he began to lift it. Just then, the mouse darted through the hole, causing Yiltor to step back and remove his hand from the lid, allowing the lid to close again.

"Only a mouse." He chuckled nervously. "Now, back to the problem at hand. You must know that I cannot allow those of your kingdom to live." He sighed. "But we shall keep that truth from the prince."

I forced the hate that was surfacing away from me. It took all the owl had taught me—to keep my place, be still, and be patient—to listen without involvement of emotion.

I could hear Yiltor's footsteps—then silence—then his voice, again. "It seems I almost forgot to tell you that Ancitel is at his tower studying his books in order to prepare a most potent potion. He claims he will ensure us a victory, and that soon your son will be beside you once again." Then, without saying more, he left the room, and the mouse returned to his. I dared not move until Barok tapped on the lid of the chest. "He is gone," he called to me. "It is safe to come out."

It was with great relief that I lifted the lid and jumped out of the chest—happy to fill my lungs with air and be free of the intent of the creature inside the chest.

"We have learned much from a king who delights in hearing himself boast," Barok said. "But there is still much we have to know."

I turned towards the prisms. "Is he truly gone?" I asked, knowing I still did not have what I came for.

"Yes, he is gone, but have you sensed the Danes at all?"

"We have been rather busy," I reminded him.

"Then, be quick in what you need to do here, while I see to the Danes."

I touched the prisms, once again, and let three minds connect. "There is little time. Tell me what I need to know."

This time my father's words were as clear as if he were standing by my side. "There is one who can help you, my son. His name is Mythias. Go into the forest to the northwest of our kingdom. There you will find him. He will . . ."

Before he could tell me anymore, Barok, who had grown to a gigantic size, swooped down, picked me up with his talons, whisked me through the window, and carried me into the sky. He finally dropped me onto Walkelin's back once we were inside the Hidden Kingdom's perimeter.

"What happened?" I called out to Walkelin when I had my breath again.

"The Danes called to us with a warning. The wizard left them suddenly and returned to his tower, moving swiftly. We had no time left. Barok is flying there now to find if we were discovered."

Had I asked too much of my legion? Though I had to believe that if the wizard was now suspicious, he would not tell the king that he was chatting with two Great Danes, as a child would, while someone or something other than Yiltor himself was inside the room with the prisms.

When we approached the Hidden Kingdom, we watched as Kevelioc came toward us. He looked content, which could only mean the capture of the three, who were coming to rescue Petre, had gone well.

"I see you have returned safely," he said, observing me as he paced in front of me. "I think I would like to hear your story."

"I am afraid it is not yet finished," Barok replied, landing beside me. His eyes peered deeply into mine, as they did each time he had something to reveal to me. "Did you not wonder why you were taught rather strange and unusual lessons by such extraordinary teachers? Not only are we battling an army, we are battling a wizard, his magic crystals, and his books of potions brought from the underworld."

He broke his eye contact and stretched his wings. "In the wizard's conversation to himself, the Danes learned that he thinks Petre is dead. Ancitel has prepared a potion that will expose the Hidden Kingdom, its perimeters having been described by Petre. The power of the potion is in the form of a cloud that will settle over the city. Droplets of its poison will fall upon the invisible walls, exposing their existence, and at the same time, destroying anything alive within the city. The Danes tell me his plan is to send the cloud within a day."

The eagle inched closer. "Tell me, lad, how will we save the children?"

Knowing there was only one thing we could do, I answered. "We must get them to the safety of the cave by the sea." I turned to Walkelin. "How many can you carry on your back at one time?"

"As many as can stay on my back while I travel beyond the ability of the wizard's scope," he replied.

"Then we will tie three at a time to you. Now, take me to the Hidden Kingdom."

Klogan and the warriors were waiting for us when we returned. Thorri told the story of the three who would rescue Petre.

"We had thought that, because they were of our kind, they would not attempt to harm us," he began. "We carried no weapons, showing our trust in their integrity, but we soon found out that they were willing to kill us without conscience. They drew daggers from their belts after we had taken their bows and quivers and came toward us in an attempt to take our lives."

Raven took over. "I asked them if they thought drawing our blood would bring them riches. Senfrie explained that they cared nothing for our blood. He said we were naïve and foolish to continue with our beliefs, that the world was filled with gold, and a life that was beyond our comprehension. That was what they cared for."

Thorri walked to Kevelioc, who sat quietly beneath a tree and away from the conversation. "Before they could use their daggers," he continued, stroking the panther, "fearful and ferocious cries came from the shadows of the trees. The three froze where they stood, their eyes bulging and their mouths twisted in fright. All we had to do was to reach out and take their weapons."

When their story was over, Kevelioc let a roar escape through his open jaws, bringing cheers from the warriors. "Now, tell us your story," he growled.

I nodded to him and asked the warriors to listen carefully. The air about them became still, and they sat with me, their faces revealing that they somehow knew, as did Kevelioc, that this story would be the most fearsome of all.

15

Ancitel's Potion

"WALKELIN WILL TAKE THE HORSES into the back mountains where they can find streams and grass. There they will be safe from the poison of the potion. We will go to the safety of a cave, near the sea," I said when the story ended.

Klogan stood slowly and spoke with the gentleness of a father speaking to his children. "We will prepare to leave our city."

The warriors nodded their understanding and hurried away to collect their personal belongings. It was dark when we met again. The students of Klogan were quiet, allowing Thorri to speak for them.

"Tell us what we are to do," he said bravely.

"Three of you will climb on Walkelin's back," I explained. "I will place straps around you, to hold you to the horse, for his speed must be faster than the wizard's scope. When the first three are safely inside the cave, Walkelin will return for the next, and the next, until you all stand together again. Klogan and Thorri will go first and make sure no soldiers camp by the sea. I will be the last to leave the city."

"What of Petre, Senfrie, Ingelric, and Talvas?" Brettina asked as she stepped forward.

I looked at Klogan for the answer for I had neither seen nor talked to the four.

"I will have made a decision before—"

"Klogan, forgive me," Thorri interrupted, "but we believe that we should decide the fate of the four." He kept his eyes forward as if he dared not look at his teacher, for fear he would falter.

Klogan stiffened. He placed himself directly in front of Thorri and forced their eyes to meet. "Give me your argument."

"It is our mothers and fathers who are imprisoned," Thorri said, returning Klogan's gaze. "It is also our kingdom that is about to be destroyed."

A smile formed on Klogan's lips, and pride reflected in his eyes as he turned away from his warriors. He took a few steps to distance himself from them. "You wish to carry the responsibility of this judgment?" he asked, gazing into the night as if he was speaking to no one but the stars.

"We do," the warriors said in unison.

He turned back to them and waved his arm in gesture. "Then let it be so. Begin."

Three warriors, Albini, Raven, and Ferdin, stepped forward and stood beside Thorri and Brettina.

"We need to have Kevelioc brought before us," Albini said, handing a stick to Klogan.

He took the stick in his hand and asked, "Who will bring the panther forward?"

"He's guarding the four," Raven said, turning to me. "Etcheon the Younger, will you call him to us?"

I did as he asked, and Kevelioc came to my side.

"What do you want of me?" the panther said, skimming the many eyes staring at him.

"Have the four been filling your ears with strategies and plans?" I asked.

"Indeed," he said, scowling. "More than any panther—even one with my strength—would want to hear."

"Tell me what you have learned," I said, and explained why his words were needed.

He roared with humor. "What was it that Rafn called me—a skully menace?"

I suppressed a laugh of my own. "I believe those were his words."

"Those are the same words I shall use to describe the four, for the words are fitting."

He began to pace in front of the warriors and their teacher. "They take turns watching me, and while they watch, they talk. Their plan is to wait until I sleep or turn my back to them, then they will put a spear through me and make their escape. This escape will not be into the mountains or back to the

Kingdom of Yiltor, but they will stay and slaughter the warriors, one by one, until all are dead, then they will take the city for themselves and make a treaty with Yiltor for the minerals inside the mountains."

"Tell me, where did they get the spear they plan to put through you?"

"They used an old battered butcher's knife they found in the cottage to whittle it from the leg of a chair. They are now busy whittling away at the other three. By morning they will have their weapons ready."

He stopped pacing and looked at me, baring his teeth with a sneer. "They give no thought as to why these warriors have survived. They know nothing of the sling and the cestro that will stop them."

The warriors listened as I told them all the panther had said. When I finished, they thanked me and then walked away for private deliberation. Klogan stayed behind. I looked at him for an explanation.

"They will make a decision, then bring it to me, not for my approval so much as for the respect they hold for me."

"What is the purpose of the stick?" I asked, noticing it was still between his fingers.

"If I return the stick to them, as it is, it means I approve of their decision. If I break it in half and toss it to the ground, they know I disapprove and will not stand with them. The stick stands as proof. They will carry it with them until all is done, then it is placed where it can be seen from that time forward. Whether theirs is a victory or defeat, the stick will be a reminder."

He sighed and stared at the stick in his hand. "I have taught them many things. Now they will take what they have learned and use it for the survival of a kingdom. In their youth they have become very wise. I will not question their judgment."

From above us, we could hear the screeching sounds of an eagle. "The wizard has talked with the king," Barok called to me. "The potion will cover the kingdom just as the sun rises, tomorrow." Then he was gone again.

Klogan hurried to the circle of warriors to tell them what we had learned, then left them to their deliberation.

When the warriors stood before us again, Raven stepped forward. "We are twenty-one soldiers of the Kingdom of Etchon. We have been taught by the greatest of all teachers, and know the art of war as well as the art of virtue," he said proudly. "We are of the clan of Purcatious and know what we have decided is in defense and protection of our lives, and the lives of our mothers and fathers. It is in defense of our race, and our kingdom."

Ferdin stepped forward and repeated the evidence against the four. "Though it brings sadness to our hearts, the judgment against them is just," he said, when he finished. Then he stepped back.

Thorri stepped between them. "Klogan, we now stand as your army, and take upon ourselves the responsibility for the fate of the four who turned against their people. We will leave Petre, Senfrie, Ingelric, and Talvas as they are, preparing their attack, but without the knowledge of the poison that will enter the city in a cloud, for it comes at their invitation. Therefore, let them be the recipients of its deadly deed."

Klogan gazed into the faces of his students, searching for a feather of doubt as to the judgment. When he saw none, he stood and walked to Brettina. "Your judgment is fair." He handed her the stick.

Thorri turned to me and asked if I also approved.

I indicated that I did. I called Kevelioc to my side. "You will stay and guard the four until you see the cloud approaching. Then, my friend, you must leave the city and join us in the cave by the sea."

Kevelioc roared his understanding, leaving us to return to his duty while the twenty-one stood together, waiting for my words.

"Because the cloud comes soon," I explained hastily, "we must all be gone by sunrise. Walkelin will take Klogan and Thorri to the cave. When he returns, we will be ready." The two were tied to the horse's back. "Run," I cried out to Walkelin, and the three disappeared in the flurry of dust.

We stood on the hillside, watching for the whirlwind of sand to appear. The whirlwind would be Walkelin. I looked at the warriors around me and I thought of Granna Fela, who for fifteen of my growing seasons gave up everything for me. I asked myself if I could protect the children of my blood, as Granna had protected me.

Then, something occurred to me, and I began to comprehend the purpose of the twenty-one warrior statues that stood in the room of the Ancient, their faces framed with bravery. I was not the protector of the young warriors. They were mine. The Ancient had given them to me, just as Taraini had given me the animals. Just as Granna was given to me, by whom I did not know . . . not yet, at least.

The whirlwind suddenly appeared, and Walkelin was beside me. "All is well inside the cave," he assured me, while three warriors were strapped to his back. We stepped back and together we watched the horse disappear, once again.

Walkelin repeated this course through the night until just before sunrise. When, at last, I climbed on his back, I called to Kevelioc in my thoughts. "We must leave. Follow me."

"Do not linger," he warned. "I will be along, soon." Then his mind was closed to me. He wanted no debate.

For one last time, I looked around me, and I could feel the sadness of the city. It was as if it knew its life would soon be taken from it. "You will live again," I whispered. "That is my promise." I felt something stir inside me, and I opened my mouth. *"Protecious, Relivious."* The words seem to speak themselves, as if I was only the instrument through which they could escape. "Run, Walkelin!" I cried, leaving the four Purcatians to receive the reward of their deeds.

At sunrise a cloud filled with death drifted through the sky and settled on the city, moving to the north then to the east. When it no longer moved, it began to vanish until, at last, it was gone.

The emotion I sensed among the twenty-one and their teacher was one of revulsion as they silently gazed into the sky and watched the nightmare play out until there was nothing left of it. They knew they might never return to their home. They knew the bodies of Petre, Senfrie, Ingelric, and Talvas would remain unwashed and uncovered, inside the city, until they decayed into obscurity. They knew the battle to protect their race had become fierce.

When there was nothing left to see, the warriors turned from the entrance of the cave, gathered in a circle, and sat upon the sand. With their legs crossed in front of them and their hands entwined one with another, they began to sing. Their voices were soft at first, then slowly the song grew louder until their voices became thunderous, the gripping verses and mystical music filling the cave. Then suddenly the song ended, leaving behind the echo that whispered all that had been sung until even the echo itself was silent.

In that silence, tears stained the sand with their sadness. Not understanding, I turned to Klogan to see his eyes closed and tears falling from beneath his lashes. I waited.

When at last the warriors stood, they turned to us and said nothing, only touching our shoulders with their hands as they walked by. They went to the corners of the cave, where they rolled out their blankets, lay upon them, and fell asleep.

I turned to Klogan. "Explain this to me."

"The song they sang is symbolic of the oath they have taken in their hearts." His voice carried a touch of reverence as he spoke. "From this day, the twenty-one warriors will carry their cestros upon their shoulders, their bows in their hands. Their slings will be belted at their waists, their shields and quivers strapped to their backs. With these weapons, they have vowed to destroy the enemy as the enemy has destroyed their kingdom. They will not stop until all who would seek the life of the Purcatians are dead. Their prayer is that their hearts will still be pure when the battle is over."

"My prayer is that they will all still be alive," I whispered.

"There is no doubt in their minds that they will be," he replied, wiping the last of his tears from his face. "They have a great faith within them, taught to them as children. That is their courage. If one should die, it will be as it should be."

Before more could be said, Kevelioc limped into the cave—his eyes dull, his tongue protruding from between his teeth. I ran to him as he fell to the ground.

"Why did you stay when the cloud appeared?" I cried to him.

There was no response.

Without thinking, I pulled some angel fleece from my pouch and placed it on his nose and around his mouth. Klogan was quickly beside me, a bowl of water in his hands. Forcing the mouth of the panther open, he poured water against his tongue.

Walkelin stood over Kevelioc, warning me that the potion needed to be washed from his flesh. I shouted to the warriors to bring water from the sea. They didn't hesitate.

As the salty water was poured over the panther's coat, Klogan and I scrubbed away the poison, using the soft bark that cluttered the floor of the cave. When we had done all we could for him, we wrapped a blanket around him to give him warmth, as we dared not build a fire.

I stayed beside him to console him. In doing so, I placed my hand upon his neck and closed my eyes, letting my mind reach into his. His mind was foggy. Only bits and pieces came to me, but it was enough to know what had happened. The four had seen the cloud approaching and ran outside the cottage to watch. When it settled over the city, they seemed to understand its purpose. In fear, they began to run, using their spears against Kevelioc. They failed to hit their mark. Being no match for his strength or quickness, they became his prisoners. He did not leave the city until he knew the four were no longer alive.

What I had seen in the panther's mind gave me new understanding of the wizard's power. He may not see my legion through his scope, but his potions were powerful enough to take their lives. As soon as Barok and the Danes were safely inside the cave, I would insist they all return to Taraini's kingdom; I prayed that Kevelioc would live to do so.

I laid my head next to the panther's, letting my thoughts be his thoughts. Together we traveled back to woods where he was my teacher. "Just as you protected me—let me, now, protect you," I whispered. We slept, and in my dream I found myself standing beside the Ancient. I asked why Kevelioc could not stand against the potion.

"He has," I heard the Ancient's voice reply.

I breathed deeply, letting the weight of guilt dissolve from me. "I am so young, how can I do all that is expected of me?"

"Because you do not stand alone."

Suddenly the dream was gone, and the trembling of Kevelioc's body awakened me. I quickly wrapped his blanket tighter and placed my arms around him to give him warmth.

I watched as Thorri knelt beside the panther and gently laid his blanket over him. Then Brettina came and placed her blanket over Kevelioc. She laid beside him, wrapping her arms around his belly.

It seemed we all fell asleep, for when I awoke the hour was much later, the cave was quiet, and Kevelioc's body was still, except for the gentle rise and fall of his chest. I carefully removed the angel fleece from his face and stroked his neck. His eyes opened at my touch and he asked for water. I placed the bowl before him.

"I have had the most interesting dream," he said after he lapped enough water to fill a well. "It was a dream of a wizard's son."

With no other words, he closed his eyes and went peacefully back to sleep.

16

The Cave

"LOOK INTO THE CRYSTALS, MY FRIENDS," Ancitel said to the Danes. "There you will see the work of my potion. I am pleased, as you should be, of its success." His smile was as dark as the shadow of his soul.

He placed the crystals back on their velvet pillows and walked to the window where he stood, glancing at the ground beneath him. Then he turned back to the Danes, his robe weaving about him, his arrogance almost stifling. "I do not want the prince dead. I want him beside the king and the queen, inside his own prism. But before I place him there, I need the timepiece, and I am not a fool to think he would simply hand it to me. Nonetheless, I will take great pleasure in obtaining it. And when I have it safely hidden, those who serve me will hand the boy to Yiltor. Then, when all is in order, they will bring Yiltor to me."

He knelt beside the Danes and placed his hands on their necks. "Yiltor will soon send for me so that he may praise my magic. Before that hour, you must grant me my wish. I have been very patient, and I have proven my power to you, have I not?" He looked into the faces of the Danes and motioned for them to follow him to the books. "Come, I am waiting."

The Danes knew they had to pick a potion so the wizard would not become suspicious. Gudrod turned to Ranulf. "Go to the table and place your paw upon a potion. I will do the same."

When the ancient books were opened for them, Ranulf pushed aside several pages with his paw, before placing it on one requiring little effort in its preparation. He looked up at the wizard and barked.

Gudrod took another book, letting his nose sniff through several pages before pressing his paw against the ancient formula that filled more than two pages and barked.

Ancitel removed the Dane's paws and studied the formulas from both books. With his fingers, he followed the lines on the pages of each book. He began mumbling to himself, calculating, reasoning, and at first, doubting. Then, suddenly, he threw his hands into the air and turned to the Danes so swiftly that his long hair whisked about his face.

"You have granted my wish," he said, his eyes betraying their astonishment. "I am pleased with the potion that will bring the boy to me." A smile spread across his thin lips. "Now, you must stay until I have finished with its preparation, so you can see for yourselves."

The Danes wished to only be rid of Ancitel and the evil that flowed through his veins as if it were blood. For all that they wished, they knew they could not leave until they knew the power of the potion Ancitel would prepare to ensnare Etcheon.

As the sun began to set on our second day of confinement inside the cave, I sat near its entrance, waiting for Barok's return. Kevelioc's strength had restored itself, and Walkelin had taken him out for a run, leaving me alone to consider all that was now behind me and all that was still ahead of me. Yiltor's decree had given me until the seventh day. I had three days, after this day, before my people would begin to die.

"Methinks you are a tired soul," Barok said, landing beside me. "Your mind is so cluttered that I could not break through."

I gave him a weary smile. "I'm sorry, but it seems I have much to consider."

"I'm afraid I must give you more." He fluttered his wings then settled himself upon a rock, close to me. "Ancitel is brewing yet another potion. This time its magic is meant for you. He knows of the timepiece and wishes to have it hidden in his tower before Yiltor has you in his grasp. He thinks you will surrender yourself to save your people on the seventh day, as the king has written. That gives him little time to perfect his potion and snatch the—"

"Did the Wizard see the warriors as they brought water to Kevelioc?" I interrupted, not caring about some potion when all I could think about was the safety of the twenty-one I had hidden inside the cave.

"It was a terrible chance to take, but one that was necessary, of course," Barok concluded, "though the Danes made no mention of Ancitel's awareness of it. The wizard was most likely too busy with his own desires to catch the son of King Etcheon than to make himself aware of a few Purcatians running about near the sea."

It was then that I told him of the oath taken by the warriors. "Look at them," I said, my eyes directing his. "They have changed. As they eat their evening meal from a pouch that seems to give them never-ending nourishment, it also seems to provide them with a physical strength I've just begun to recognize. When I look into their faces, their innocence is no longer visible to me but buried beneath the burden they now carry. It saddens me to know that their childhood has been lost to them."

"If you were to look into a mirror," he uttered, "you would see the same in yourself." He lifted his wing and wrapped it around me. "Tell me, lad, what is your strategy?"

"I must find another place to hide the warriors, away from the wizard's scope. The cave confines their spirit. Where do I search? I must find a way to rescue over five hundred of my people from the prisons inside Yiltor's kingdom. How do I save them? I cannot allow myself to be wrapped in the wizard's potion—if what you said is true. Yet how do I avoid it when I do not know what to avoid?" I thought for a moment and suddenly the answer presented itself.

Barok looked into my eyes. "Methinks you have an idea floating inside your head."

"Why have I not seen it sooner? My answer lies in the forest of Mythias. Fly to it, Barok."

"It will be my pleasure." He lifted his wings and disappeared into the sky.

I called to Klogan, "Tell me what you know about the forest that lies to the northwest of the Hidden Kingdom."

He shook his head. "I know very little."

"Can you tell me how far it is from the city?"

"Perhaps two dolichos from the perimeter. Why do you ask?"

"I must travel there for reasons I will explain when I return."

"You risk discovery by Ancitel," he warned me.

"I will return safely," I assured him, and then climbed on Walkelin's back.

"Then I will not say farewell, for that word is best used for a long journey." He stepped away just as Kevelioc appeared.

"Will you ride with me upon the back of the horse," I asked, "or travel at your own pace?"

He growled and told me that he would allow his own legs to carry him and promised he would not be far behind. Then he let out a roar that told me he was completely recovered.

I laughed at him, and he showed his teeth to me. I waved to Klogan and then touched Walkelin's flanks.

"Barok has found the forest from the sky and waits for you," Walkelin said to me as the ground beneath us became a haze of color. "I will take you into its perimeter before I stop. We do not know if the forest is protected against the wizard."

It seemed rather a small forest from the distance. But as we came closer, it grew to be immense, and when I slid from Walkelin's back, I found myself inside one of the most unusual forest I had ever seen. Some trees grew fat and low, their willowy limbs winding in every direction. Their leaves, trimmed in gold, were all sizes and shapes and varied in the colors of greenish-blue and purple. Other trees grew tall and stately, their limbs filled with large leaves, blending their colors from deep green to yellow with a silver cast.

As I tried to walk between them, I stumbled over vines and limbs that had no rhyme or reason to their direction. Why Walkelin did not stumble, I could not imagine. "Are your eyes as quick as your hooves?" I asked.

He only laughed at me and gave me a sly wink. What it meant, I had no idea, but before I could ask, Barok appeared from the top of a tree.

"This forest is of enormous size," he said. "If one were to get lost inside its sphere, he might never find his way out." He perched himself on Walkelin's back. "From the air I could see no breaks in the trees. I had to come down into the limbs to find you. What we find from this point will be new to all of us."

We waited on the path until Kevelioc joined us, then together we entered the darkened shadows. Almost immediately, the thickness of the trees blocked the sun while, in the shadows, bones of human skeletons appeared all around us, their flesh having long ago nourished the ground.

I knelt down and examined a skeleton that lay close to my feet. It looked to be as long as one akaina. The bones were large in their frame and the skull was dense. I looked up at the animals. "I think we should let our instincts become our eyes, for now."

They agreed and we became silent, waiting and listening, letting our eyes adjust to the darkness. I could smell nothing but the scent of bark and spruce. I could sense nothing but the panther, the horse, and the eagle. Even the air around us was still.

Kevelioc was the first to move forward. We followed. I began to feel uneasy. My mouth was dry while my skin began to feel damp. The air became thick and suffocating.

Suddenly I felt something against my arm. When I reached out, there was nothing there, but I could sense the presence of something human. I could smell his scent, and so could the animals. We continued on with great caution.

Our progress became more and more difficult as Kevelioc led us deeper into the forest. Strange limbs seemed to purposely reach out, snagging my skin and hair, and tugging at my feet. The animals were no less burdened.

Kevelioc stopped. "There is a human just beyond the next tree. The rhythm of his heart tells me he knows we are coming."

"I come to see Mythias," I called out.

No one answered.

"I come to see Mythias," I called out again.

"Who be you who wants Mythias?" a voice called back at last.

"I am Etcheon the Younger."

"Who be Etcheon the Younger that I should show him Mythias?"

"I am the son of King Etcheon and Queen Arcadia," I said, stepping away from the animals and closer to the voice. "Mythias witnessed my birth and placed his name upon the document."

"You speak as an honest person, do you? If so, this document I should see."

I opened the pouch and, with the light of the crystal, found the document Mythias had written. His name signed with his own hand. "Will you step forward so I can see you?" I asked.

He laughed. "I step forward, I think not."

"Then I will not give you the document."

Loud grumbling noises came from behind the tree.

"I think he might be considering your proposal with distaste," Barok twittered, softly.

"Oh, I hear the tattling of an eagle, don't I?" The voice snickered. "Does that change my mind? I think not."

I sensed no menace in him, only stubbornness. I rustled the paper so he would know I had it in my hand. "I will trust you to take this to Mythias." I held out the paper and walked close to the tree. A hand hardly the size of a child's reached out and grabbed the document. The rustle of leaves told us whoever had the document was gone.

"Do you think you did the wise thing?" Walkelin asked.

"Methinks he had no other choice," Barok said. "Now we wait and see what happens."

"While we wait," Kevelioc growled, "perhaps I will search for sunlight and fresh air, away from the prying trees. You are welcome to come, or stay where you are."

"I think we will be happy to follow you," Barok said.

Before we could take our first step, however, the willowy limbs of the trees on either side of me began to wrap themselves around me, and I felt a chill creep up my spine. "Stop!" I shouted, trying to break away from them. But it was of no use.

The limbs were rapidly making their way up my legs, around my waist, and down my arms. I grasped the handle of my father's dagger and pulled it from my belt, blindly cutting away at the limbs to free my arms. But as I cut away, another would appear in its place, doubled in strength.

I cried out to the animals, only to see them tearing at limbs that blocked their way and prevented them from reaching me. It was like a nightmare—one from which I could not awaken.

The wizard and his potion came to my mind. Had he been so clever that he could work his magic this easily? Did he know of Mythias? Did he put the thoughts that I should find Mythias into my head to bring me here? Had I, so unwittingly, been imprisoned?

Then, as quickly as the limbs appeared around me, they were gone. The trees were moving away from me, or I away from them, I could not tell—nor could I see Kevelioc or Walkelin. Only Barok was with me, perched upon my shoulder, his size that of a small bird.

"Tell me what is happening," I whispered to him.

"Perhaps this is what we have come for," he replied.

It was as if we were floating, yet I could feel the ground beneath me as we approached trees, standing tall and majestic.

Beyond the trees I could see what appeared to be a gentle countryside, filled with rose bushes and fruit trees, and dotted with miniature cottages. The cottages were of all sizes and shapes and painted in the colors of a rainbow. Some were two stories high while others were three. The windows and doors were either round or square and, in some cases, both round and square. The tall chimney's billowed with smoke. It was an amazing sight. Though it is difficult to explain the feelings that passed through me as this small village appeared, I would have to admit that delight would come close to a definition.

Small, delicate forms were running in and out of the open doors of the cottages as if they were busily preparing for something.

I could not tell my legs to move or be still for they seemed to be following another's instructions, taking me closer and closer to the village, the forms beginning to take the appearance of men, women, and children—all in miniature.

When I found myself in the center of what I can only describe as an enchanting (and perhaps, enchanted) village, my legs took me to a small bench on which I had no choice but to sit. The air about me was filled with fragrances of lilacs and cherry blossoms. Had I been able to understand the situation I found myself in—I would have not questioned, but simply inhaled the calm that settled upon me.

Barok remained protectively perched upon my shoulder, and there was no attempt to remove him. "Methinks this is even more than what we were looking for," he said in my ear, "yet I sense no danger."

Neither had I, only mystical impressions passed through me, and I could not interpret their meaning.

Around us, tiny faces seemed to be smiling happily, reminding me of the little people in Granna Fela's stories. She had described them as chubby, unkempt, and mischievous. Though the miniatures before me were dainty and glittery clean, giving the appearance of fairies without wings, their eyes did dance with mischievousness.

Finally, one of them stepped forward. He stood only a cubit tall, and I would not venture a guess at his age. His face was thin and delicate, his large eyes the color of the forest. His silver hair fell to his shoulders and he wore a clataè much like my own. His clothes were simple (a long shirt belted over leggings), and he wore no boots, only soft sandals.

"Etcheon the Younger are you, then?" he said, and I recognized the voice to be the same voice as the one behind the tree.

When I nodded that I was, he turned from me and faced his audience. "The son of the king of the Hidden Kingdom, this boy claims he be. What say you?"

The miniatures rushed forward and began touching my clothes, pulling at my hair, and pressing their fingers into my face. A child's arm reached inside my pouch and pulled from it my mother's silk scarf. At the same time I could feel my father's golden dagger being removed from its sheath. I tried to tell them to put them back, but my voice was silent. My eyes seemed to be the only part of me that listened to my brain, allowing me to see the scarf and dagger disappear into one of the cottages. I was surprised they did not take the timepiece.

Once the scarf and dagger had been taken from me, the miniatures stepped back and gave me a quiet look, their faces no longer smiling but still pleasant in their appearance. The mischievousness was gone from their eyes—replaced by a gentle glow, yet I still could not speak or move.

"Perhaps I should look inside the cottage," Barok said and flew from my shoulder. There was no attempt to stop him. When he returned, he placed his beak close to my ear and whispered, "Methinks the cottage is an entrance to something much more elaborate than what we see here."

The miniatures seemed to have forgotten us in their preparations for what appeared to be a celebration. The men were setting long tables on the bricks of the village square while children decorated them with brightly colored cloths and vases of flowers. Women were scurrying in and out of opened doors, cluttering the tables with plates, glasses, spoons, and knives. It all looked elaborate and festive, but it made no sense.

Once in a while, a child would stop, touch my boot, look up at me, and smile—then hurry off again. It seemed I posed no threat to these tiny people. How could I when I could not even move or speak?

"Have they a power over me?" I asked the eagle through my mind.

"I think not," he answered. "I continue to sense no danger. For that matter, I sense quite the opposite."

I closed my eyes and remembered the lessons of the owl, allowing my mind to expand in meditation. I did not move nor did I open my eyes and, slowly from deep within me, I began to feel the melody of silence. Its harmony stirred my essence, and I became aware of everything around me. The trees, the village and . . . there was something else . . . something more powerful than the forest itself. I could not identify it. I could only let the melody rise in me, allowing the strength of the forest to be one with me.

Little by little, my legs awakened to my thoughts, and I knew to stand. The melody carried me inside a cottage, large enough for me to stand, though small enough for the ceiling to meet the top of my head. The miniature who had been a thorn in my side stood before me.

"Ready to meet Mythias, are you?" he questioned, a glitter reflected in his eyes as he looked at me, telling me he was enjoying the moment.

"That is my purpose for coming."

"Then Mythias is who you shall see." He bowed, slightly. "Through this doorway you will follow me. Alone you shall go from there." He motioned with his finger, turned, walked through the doorway, and simply disappeared.

Taking a deep breath, I stepped to the other side of the doorway to find him waiting. When I looked behind me, the room of the cottage was no longer visible. Instead, I saw the forest and a path leading into its darkness. I turned back to the miniature. In front of him, the path continued on.

"Slow you are to come through the doorway. Fearful of what your eyes might see, are you?"

I gazed at him. "There is no fear inside of me." I smiled, becoming quite comfortable with him. "Tell me your name so I will not have to think of you only as a miniature."

He laughed out loud, "A miniature you call me, then a miniature I will be, but a name is far better. The name Timberlin would sound good to your ears?"

"Yes, the name Timberlin sounds very good to my ears."

"Timberlin, I am." He glanced around him. "On this path I leave you. To Mythias you will go."

I looked behind me and ahead of me. "Which way do I go?" I asked.

"Which path you follow, you should know—if Mythias you know."

With those words he disappeared, and I stood there, alone, considering my next step and praying it would be the right one. Ahead of me were two paths, each going in a different direction. Only one of them would lead me to Mythias. Where the other one would lead me, I had no idea. Perhaps back to the unfriendly trees.

17

Mythias

THERE WAS NO EAGLE TO FLY above me or panther to guide me to Mythias. Nor did I have a horse to carry me swiftly there. But I had within me everything they had taught me. I was not alone.

I recognized the scent of the forest and knew the sounds of its creatures. My eyesight was intense, and I could see into the deep shadows of the trees and beneath their twisted limbs that covered the ground. I became still, listening to the conversation of the trees and searching out the one scent that did not belong.

I closed my eyes and inhaled, letting my instincts separate one from the other. Then a smile slowly made its way across my face. I turned away from those in front of me, stepping on a path that was not visible, the path that would lead me to Mythias.

The limbs that kept it well hidden seemed to be waiting in anticipation of my first step, so they could have my boots in their grasp. I watched them for a moment and let my mind recall the rhythm of the horse's hooves as he carried me into the forest. The rhythm beat within me, and my boots barely touched the ground as I ran over the top of the roots until, slowly, they began to retreat in their acceptance of defeat.

Marbled flat stone replaced the willowlike limbs. I could hear the sweet songs of the birds, and feel the sun's warmth against my face. The trees parted to reveal a meadow so beautiful and peaceful that it reminded me of Taraini's kingdom.

In the distance I could see smoke rising from the chimney of a lonely cottage. It resembled the beautiful cottages in the village, though it was immense in its size. The colors of its door and eves were brilliant red. A quiet garden spread out to the side of it. A wooden fence encircled it.

Standing near the doorway was a man with the height even beyond that of Mr. Otherton by at least a cubit. His back was to me, and I could see broad shoulders. His hair—the color of the clouds with shades of lavender and blue—fell almost to his waist. It was tied at the nape of his neck with a piece of leathered bark. When he turned to me, I saw an ageless, handsome face with a soft white beard, neatly trimmed beneath his chin, and gentle eyes that glistened with wisdom. He wore a simple shirt with trousers much like my own. Soft leather boots covered his feet.

"Mythias?" I asked, not daring to go any closer until I had been given permission to do so.

"I am." He smiled, waving his arm to invite me into his home where he offered me refreshments and a soft chair, both of which I was grateful to accept.

"You are your father's son in every way," he said, handing me the golden dagger. "Though I can sense the power of your mother's gift is strong within you." He handed me the scarf. "These are the proof that you are who you say you are."

"Would you not recognize me just by looking into my face?" I asked, curious as to why I had to be tested.

He looked at me and sighed deeply. "I knew you as a child, but the wizard Ancitel could have, by some magical miracle of his own, seen your face as you look now and would have liked very much to fool me with an imposter. I had to know that you were the true son of Etcheon. Only the true son could find the way to my home."

"But it was only that I could—" I began to explain, but he interrupted me.

"I know how you found me." Mythias smiled again. "Now I am sure you would like to see your friends."

"They are here?" I cried, astonished that he knew of them.

"Come, I will take you to them." He led me through his cottage to a door that opened to a beautiful garden of flowers and butterflies, soothing waterfalls and soft benches. There, lounging as if they had nothing better to do, I saw Barok, Kevelioc, and Walkelin. I laughed and ran to them, touching them—wanting to know for myself that they were real. When I was convinced, I turned to Mythias and studied his face. "Are you a wizard as Ancitel is?"

"I am a wizard, but not as Ancitel is," he corrected me. "My intentions and potions are for the good of man—not for his destruction or his enslavement."

I pondered his answer then I asked another question. "Why, then, did you not know it was me?"

He looked at me. "Know this, Young Etcheon. One wizard can fool another wizard. I have fooled him, and he has tried to fool me. This could have been his day to do so. It is a dangerous game that only he likes to play."

I nodded and we sat there quietly for a moment before I asked why he did not wear the robes of a wizard so that I could recognize him as such.

Humor glistened in his eyes, as he seemed to ponder my question. "Tell me, young Etcheon, how many wizards have you seen?"

I had to admit that I had seen none except in books where stories told of them.

"You will see my robes when it is necessary that I wear them, but I find them to be cumbersome and very uncomfortable."

I found myself laughing at him and with him at the same time, and I found myself feeling very much at home in the meadow of Mythias's forest. "You know why I'm here, do you not?" I inquired.

"I do," he replied.

"Can you free the Purcatians from Yiltor's prison?"

"Only you can free the Purcatians, my boy," he answered, his deep, brilliantly green eyes peering into mine. "It is your calling."

Frustration had become my closest companion and once again, I felt its temper. "For a year, I have been given answers that made very little sense to me or no sense at all. Once again, I have been given an answer I cannot understand."

"You will, young Etcheon," he said, gently. "You will."

"Yet Ancitel assists Yiltor," I argued.

He raised his eyebrows and tilted his head toward me. "Oh, but I can assist you. Ancitel's scope does not reach into my forest. I can hide your warriors until it is time for them to fight. I can create a battlefield where they can practice their skill. But most impressive, I can make you invisible to the wizard's crystals . . . among other things."

I paused only to take a quick breath concerning the last words he spoke. "You can make me invisible?"

He laughed. "Close your mouth, and listen to what I have to tell you."

Unaware that my mouth was open, I quickly closed it and waited for his explanation.

"First, the old goat thinks his scope reaches into my forest, but he is fooled. The bones you saw when you entered guard the forest from the magic he uses to find out all he desires to know. He knows nothing except of the bones that lie in wait for anyone or anything that might enter, uninvited.

"The soldiers he sent to explore and conquer were met at the edge of the forest by my army of skeletons, who stood against them and scorched them with the blood that still haunts the weapon that pierced their own bodies long ago. The weapon is of Ancitel's own making—it is made of steel, fired and primed in the underworld. Then he placed a spell upon it. Now that very spell works against him. He cannot enter the forest because of it, so he searches for a potion that will break the spell and turn the bones to dust. But the bones of those wizards are lives he took with those same weapons, who enjoy the game, and show him only what they desire for him to see, and it is not the dust of their bones. No one else dares to enter the forest, for they know the legend."

"Tell me the legend. My mind is filled with the mystery of it," I said.

"The bones are those of the wizards of many ages, who fought against Ancitel's evil, and lost. In their deaths, they found a power he knows nothing of. They chose to stay here in the forest of their ancestors, allowing their bones to be scattered around the perimeter to protect their descendents. Their bones live in our behalf."

"The tiny people in the village are wizards?" I asked in amazement.

He smiled at my surprise. "Would you believe that I was once that small?"

I blinked my eyes, unable to comprehend him less than a cubit in height. But I had to snicker in the attempt. "Tell me," I said. "Do they all possess your power?"

He shook his head. "They possess the power of their ages—that is all. Only a few will become like me, when their time comes. Though none of them aspire to become a full wizard, for it is not in their nature."

We sat on the bench and ate vegetables from his garden and drank juice from his grape vines, while Mythias told me how one becomes a full wizard and why only a few even desire its power.

"None of us know how we will accept that power when it is given to us," he explained. "It can bring joy in its goodness or it can turn one into the likes of Ancitel, who in his wickedness has decided his eternities. It is much simpler and safer, I might add, to remain innocent as a child, using the limited power only for good until your life concludes."

"When does their life conclude?" I asked, timidly.

"Let me think," he mused, squinting his face as if in deep thought. "The earliest conclusion of one's life, as I recall, is three hundred years."

I stared at him in disbelief.

He brushed the garden dirt from his trousers and winked. "Three hundred years is not that long in the eternities of time, young Etcheon. I am almost a hundred and seventy three, and I am yet a child in my learning."

He laughed at my expression and, once again, suggested I close my mouth. I did so, quickly. "Tell me more," I begged.

"I will tell only you that I was not happy when my clothes began to shrink. I, like those you saw in the village, was very content to be as they are. In truth, I miss those days." He paused as if he was brushing the thought aside just as he had brushed aside the dirt, and I thought I could see a spot of moisture in the corner of his eye.

He cleared his throat. "The story is ancient in its telling that one who carries the power also carries the responsibility for those who do not. It is their birthright."

He put his hand upon my shoulder and turned me to face him so our eyes would meet. "You are much like me, Etcheon, for you have been prepared from childhood for the responsibility you now carry. Your father, King Etcheon, has given you your birthright; your mother has given you her gift. You alone now have the power to save your people."

"Tell me of your bond with my father and mother," I said, feeling a stirring within when he mentioned them.

"I had heard the rumors that Yiltor was losing patience with his father for living so long, so it seems he invited a wizard to live in his tower to oversee those things that required a wizard's gift."

He stood and refilled my glass with sweet juice. "Did you know that wizards can sense each other's presence from great distances? They know if one or the other is good or evil. I sensed no goodness in Ancitel as I felt his presence. The forest protects my identity, nonetheless, and he is not totally aware that I am here, though he suspects and plays his silly games. When the King died, shortly after the wizard's appearance at the tower, I knew there were things I must attend to myself."

"The kingdom of the Purcatians?" I asked.

"It was my duty."

"Why was it not hidden from you as well as all other people?"

"Because I am a part of you or you are a part of me."

His words bewildered me. I had heard them before, only from Taraini. I felt as if he could see into my heart, for his look was one of sympathy. Yet how could he know what dwelt in my heart? How could he see the place where I carried her memory? I forced myself not to ask for an explanation. Not yet. Not until I could do so without letting her name linger unprotected within my mind.

He stood and changed the subject of our conversation, "Come," he said, "and I will show you the room where I work my sorcery."

Grateful that he gave me something else to think about, I followed him up the stairs, to a large wooden door. The word *sorcery* filled my mind with mystical thoughts, and I asked, "Is it real magic that you work?"

He lifted his hand and said two words—*Emocipus zaumos*—and the door opened, its brackets whining painfully with the weight. "Someday, I must fix that," he said, frowning. "They have been complaining rather loudly lately."

The door opened to the most amazing room I had ever seen. It was much larger than I would have imagined, and was filled with all kinds of unimaginable things that amazed me. The room was, indeed, filled with magic.

There were shelves lined with books filled with instruction to make magic potions. There were small bottles filled with colorful liquids, and large bottles filled with herbs and strange things I had never seen. There were stones and crystals of all sizes and shapes that were sitting on tables and benches. There were strange plants growing everywhere, some with large leaves and small flowers, and others with small leaves and large flowers. And in a corner sat a large cat, its fur white as snow.

Mythias walked to the cat, picked it up, and held it gently in his arms. "Sofrates," he said, "meet Etcheon the Younger." He motioned for me to come closer. "Etcheon the Younger, meet Sofrates."

I greeted the largest cat I had ever seen. His eyes were large, luminous, and almost frightening. Although his purr was soft, his claws looked very sharp, indeed. I would suppose this cat was very capable of taking care of himself, or anyone entering the room uninvited.

Mythias stood beside one of the large tables where a flat crystal, almost a cubit in size, lay atop a bulky book. "Here, I will tell my story," he said, taking the crystal in his hands. "This is my window to the world beyond my forest."

I listened carefully while he told how the power of a crystal depends on the goodness or the wickedness of the wizard's heart. "Ancitel has many large crystals to see the little things." Mythias chuckled. "While I have one that shows me all things. But if I should use it for gain or for evil purposes, its power will diminish, and I will be no better than he."

"Is the crystal powerful enough to see the hidden wall of my father's kingdom?" I asked, somewhat astonished, yet curious as to how this was done.

"Only at a certain time of the day," he admitted, "and only for a few seconds of that time. But it is all the time I need to know that which requires my attention. I know the king and queen as I know myself. I was with your mother and father the day your father wrote the letter you now carry in your pouch. It was a difficult thing they had to do, but it was necessary. I warned them of what I had seen in my crystal and insisted that Feladelphia take you away, for the good of your kingdom."

"Who was Granna Fela?" I asked.

Mythias puckered his face in thought. "I would call her an angel, for she is all of that. But, in truth, Feladelphia came from another sphere, at my request, to protect you in a way no one else could, for that part of your life that needed her tending. When her work was done, she returned, once again, to the sphere of her birth. But know that she is truly your ancestral grandmother with many years in the counting."

I noted that he said nothing of the timepiece she carried, or how it came to be in my possession. But, for now, he had told me enough. I did, in truth, belong to Granna.

The Danes watched as Ancitel pulled several glass bottles from his cupboards and consulted the pages where they had placed their paws. They could hear him mumbling words unknown to them as he poured liquid into a glass dish, the size of his hand. He would remove the corks very carefully, pouring one drop from one bottle, three from another, or ten from yet another, careful not to get too much or too little. He would lean over the brew and sniff the aroma much like a fine cook would do as he stirred. He slowly brought it to just the right temperature over the soft flame of a candle.

For hours he stirred and sniffed and spoke strange utterances, until beads of sweat appeared and his face became haggard. Finally, colorful vapors began to escape from the dish, floating freely in the air, filling the room with a strange fragrance—one that left the Danes light-headed.

"Bury your nose in the velvet," Ranulf instructed Gudrod.

Ancitel glanced at the Danes, and seeing their noses stuffed beneath their blankets, he explained. "The sweet fragrance overcomes you, I fear. But do not be concerned. Only the one this is meant for will be truly affected by its aroma." He lifted the wooden spoon so the Danes could see the slime that dripped from its scoop. It cast a greenish glow as it slithered back into the dish.

"It is almost ready." Ancitel sighed and pushed away the strands of hair that had fallen into his face, letting six beads of his perspiration drop into the dish. "The final ingredient to be added." He smiled as he continued to stir.

Abruptly, and without being commanded, the third crystal became alive with color. The wizard's eyes widened and he set the brew down, hurrying to the stone and staring into its intense glow.

"What do we have here?" he asked, his voice menacing as he ran his long fingers through the colors of the light. "Purcatians near the sea? How many are there? I see two . . . three . . ." His eyes continued to count though his voice became quiet.

Hearing his words, the Danes jumped from their velvet beds and began howling, their cries piercing Ancitel's ears.

He turned to them and covered his ears with his hands. "Quiet!" he shouted over the terrible, painful sound. Before he could say more, he remembered the brew and quickly turned to it. He carefully cradled the dish in his left hand and, with the smallest finger of his right, he swirled the brew gently and whispered his incantation, once again.

"Forgive my rudeness," he apologized when he finished. "You were trying to warn me of my negligence, and I mistook it for insolence. Had you not used your voices at that moment, the potion would have failed, and I would have failed, for there is not enough ingredients to begin again."

He felt the texture of the brew that remained on the tip of his finger. "The time is right to let it sit and cool. Tomorrow, I will stir its magic into a powerful potion—one that the son of King Etcheon cannot refuse."

He looked back into his crystal. "Now, I think I will call my little army of changelings together to rescue a small band of Purcatians from the dangers of the sea." The laugh that came from him was almost as piercing to the ears of the Danes as was their howling to his. As Ancitel summoned the creatures, the Danes looked at each other.

"We must warn them," Runolf said. "We must warn them of the creatures who are coming after them. They will not be prepared for what they will see and what they will have to fight against."

"Let me stay so that we will know what the potion does," Gudrod argued, looking up at the dish and stepped toward it. He could simply knock it from its place.

"Step away," Runolf scolded.

Gudrod did as he was told and lowered his head. "Have we no choice?" he said, sighing.

"We must leave things as they are in the wizard's tower," Runolf reminded him, "and we cannot leave one without the other, or we mock the legend, and the wizard will become suspicious."

"But what if I spit into the potion?" Gudrod asked. "Will it not weaken the power and give Etcheon some resistance?"

Runolf considered Gudrod's words. Then he stepped between the potion and the back of the wizard. It took only a moment for a touch of Gudrod's saliva to disappear into the bowl.

Six ugly creatures walked into the room a few moments later. Six more waited outside. "This is my army," Ancitel said, kneeling beside the two Danes. "They are changelings, and can take on the appearance of whatever I decide, in order to do my bidding. Because I released them from the underworld, they are loyal to me." He stood and stepped away from the Danes to his potion. "Stay, if you can, until I return." Then he walked from the room, the creatures following after him. The Danes heard the clicking of the door being locked.

"He thinks he can enchant us to keep us here, to do his bidding," growled Runolf. "But we will not be here when he returns. The warriors lives are in danger."

They turned away from the door, knowing it would not be their way out.

Allowing their senses to take over, they were led to Ancitel's sleeping room and beneath his bed. "There is air below the floor," Gudrod sniffed.

It was not easy for the two of them to crawl beneath the bed, for their bodies were large. Only the need to get away prodded them further. They pulled at the wooden flap until they lifted the corners high enough to slide it away from a dark, drafty hole.

Runolf reached into the blackness, letting his nose be his guide, and allowed his eyes to adjust. "There are steps leading down," he said.

Once they were both through the hole, they braced themselves on a small landing and worked the flap back into its place. Following the circle of stairs, they were soon outside the tower and free of the wizard.

By the time they had escaped the tower, the army of Ancitel was riding away.

18

The Woodland

AS THE WARNING OF THE DANES echoed through the trees of the forest, Walkelin's ears pricked up, and Kevelioc let out a roar that caused even the trees to shake.

"The Danes are coming, fast." He turned to me and growled. "Something dreadful has happened."

I looked at Mythias. "Tell me if you can look into your crystal and see what it is."

"I will need your crystal." He reached out his hand.

"The small crystal in my pouch?" I asked, disbelieving it would be of worth to a wizard. "It is only useful as a light."

"Hand it to me, quickly," he said impatiently. "I do not think we have time to discuss its value."

I did not question him again. When the crystal was in his hands, he pressed it forcefully between them until it glowed so brightly that its light reached through the sinews and the flesh of his hands and caused them to glow as brightly as the crystal itself. Then he put the crystal close to his face and slowly opened his hands. The force of the light filled his eyes until they began to glow as well. His voice began to echo in my head. "You must bring your warriors to me, Etcheon. Go now. There is not much time. The warriors do not carry your gift within them."

What gift? I wanted to shout. But I had no time to discuss it. I would leave it to be answered another time.

"I will go to the Danes," Barok cried. He spread his wings and ascended above the trees. "We will meet you at the cave."

"Perhaps you should carry me as well," Kevelioc growled, jumping onto the horse's back behind me. "There is no time for pride."

Walkelin snorted and his speed took the breath from our lungs.

My eyes were closed against the wind until Walkelin's voice came into my thoughts warning me that there were creatures, twelve of them, running toward the cave—their speed, that of a horse. I forced my eyes open to see them for myself. They were like those who came to the cottage long ago, and I shuddered at the sight of them. I blinked, and we were well beyond them. The waterfalls were before us, with the cave hidden behind it. Walkelin slowed his pace and then came to a halt at the opening.

Klogan ran toward me. "It is getting dark, and we had become concerned for you."

"We must get the warriors away from the cave!" I exclaimed. "Ancitel knows we are here and brings his creatures to find us. They are unlike anything you have ever seen."

Klogan did not doubt my word. He shouted to the warriors to prepare to leave immediately.

"There is another exit, deep within the cave," I said quickly. "Follow me. The Danes will erase our prints behind us." I could hear the sickening chants of the creatures. They were getting close. I motioned for the warriors to be silent, leading them into the depths of the cave.

"The opening is just ahead," I whispered to Klogan. "Take them deep inside the woodland."

"Where will you be?" He frowned.

"I will be behind you. Go, now. It will not be long before they discover you are not in the cave, and the woodland will draw them to you then."

When I returned to the other side of the cave, near the sea, the animals were waiting.

"There is more we must tell you, but it will wait until the twenty-one are safe," Runolf barked.

"Ancitel and his creatures are coming fast," I heard Barok speak in my mind. "They are near the cave."

I looked at Walkelin, Kevelioc, and the Danes. "Run with the warriors. Erase their prints and take them deep into the thicket while Barok and I create a diversion."

They did not hesitate.

I stood by the waterfall and watched Barok begin his descent. His screeching was a warning that the creatures had arrived.

"They stink as if they have come from the swamp," Barok complained, perching himself on my shoulder. "There are twelve, and Ancitel leads them."

"The cave is here," I heard a voice whisper, its sound echoing against the rocks. Twelve creatures quietly entered the cave, their wizard motioning for them to spread out while the flames of light that were their eyes, cast eerie shadows against the walls.

"Go down the tunnel to the left," I whispered to Barok, "and make just enough noise so they will think they have found the warriors. I will take the tunnel to the right and do the same. They will waste time searching before they find no one here."

"Methinks that is a clever plan." He flapped his wings and took flight.

Letting the warriors' footprints bring Ancitel's creatures farther into the cave, I made whispered sounds of chatter to draw them deeper. This I did, relying on the promise of the Cara to protect me.

They could not see me, nor could they see Barok. We were as ghosts to them, yet they could smell something human beyond their own stench. For several minutes, they crept along the dark tunnels and caverns, letting our noises guide them. They seemed confused—groping and reaching out with hairy claws while their eyes gave them light.

"Find them. We are wasting time," Ancitel shouted from beyond the cave.

"Smell them here, but my eyes see not a human," a creature near me shouted back. Then, with the swiftness of a snake, it turned to me. It sniffed, pounced, and grabbed. I had no escape, but to back myself into the solid rock behind me. He was so close that I could see the thick, yellow saliva drooling down his hairy face—the flame in his eyes looked directly at me, as if I was visible to him. He moved closer and his smell became almost intolerable. I quickly pulled Mr. Otherton's handkerchief from my pocket and pressed it over my nose.

The sound caught the creature's ears and it pressed its claw against the wall—where my head had been just before I dropped to the ground in an attempt to escape.

Suddenly a shout came from behind the creatures. "They have escaped to the woodland. Waste no more time here." It was Ancitel's voice. He obviously had seen the warriors through his crystal.

Yet the one who smelled my scent hesitated. I slithered against the other side of the wall as he took one more swipe—his claw slamming against the rock. Grunting in pain, he turned and hurried back to the entrance of the cave. Though the creature was gone, its scent remained, forcing me out of the cave and into fresh air.

"Methinks we have given the warriors time to get to the woodland, but another minute of that cave, and I would have choked to death. The creatures carry with them their own protection—that of their smell," I heard Barok say from behind me.

What he said was true. Their smell was their protection. They could have paralyzed me with its stench or rendered me unconscious.

"Walkelin comes for you," the eagle warned me. "Be ready."

The dust had no time to settle before I climbed upon the horse's back and gave him his lead. Ancitel and his creatures moved as if they were in slow motion as we passed them.

"Ancitel senses something but his crystal shows him nothing," Walkelin snorted. "You will have very little time before they are upon you."

Once I was inside the woodland, the chirping of birds led me to where the warriors waited. I stood by Klogan near the middle, while the warriors hid themselves in the trees. It was dark, but we could still see a little by the light of the moon.

Ancitel's voice carried through the thickets. He directed his creatures by using his crystal to guide them to the warrior's hiding places. The twitter of birds sent messages of attack, and the warriors were ready.

"My changelings have you surrounded," Ancitel's voice called out. "If you will surrender, no one will die. If you do not, well, perhaps some or all of you will die."

"I would suggest the same to you," Klogan replied. The woodland became silent again.

While we waited, I warned the warriors of the scent that would follow the changelings. Another scent, however, touched my nostrils and filtered into my mind. I tried to pull myself from it, for it blurred my thoughts. But my mind felt weak, and my body numb.

Barok was suddenly on my shoulder. "Pull your mind away!" he screeched into my ear, making sure I could do nothing else.

"Was that necessary, you silly bird?" I moaned, trying to shake the shrillness from inside my head.

"This silly bird will protect you—if you will listen." Barok gave my ear a hard peck and tossed my hair with his wing. "The Danes have not had time to tell you of the potion."

"It has been mentioned, but what is its power?"

"Better asked is what is its aroma?" the eagle corrected me. "I will tell you. Its aroma is sweet, soothing, deceiving, and dangerous. Let nothing enter your thoughts outside of your own and those I send you. Do not sniff the air. Force all but my squawking from your mind. Do you understand?" He did not wait for my answer but flew above the clearing and to the south, once again.

Not knowing what to watch for in my thoughts, I moved close to Klogan as if it would be a protection against whatever Barok had warned me of.

"I am afraid the warriors are enjoying this," Klogan whispered, and I detected a touch of pride in his words.

"I think you are enjoying this as much as they are," I whispered back.

"And you?"

I did not have time to answer. The chirping began again telling us the battle was about to begin. We could hear the rustling of movement all around us; suddenly, three changelings appeared at the edge of the clearing. Klogan stepped away from me, and I heard the hiss of his cestro as I sent an arrow from my own. The changeling, pierced with my arrow, did not fall as I expected, though the arrow was protruding from his heart, or where I supposed his heart to be. That was my mistake. It was not the last one I would make.

The huge, ugly creature pulled the arrow from his body, threw his head back, and let a strange shrill escape from his throat. Then he looked straight at me. "Yose to cum."

Before he could take a step toward me, I aimed another arrow and a stone at his eyes and his throat.

He grabbed at his throat, unable to cry out, his anger mixed with pain flaming in his one good eye. Still he came at me and grabbed me around my neck, leaving my body dangling beneath his enormous arm. I snatched my dagger and thrust it into his side. He swiped at the dagger and tightened his grip, giving me little air to breath. Even the arrows and stones the warriors aimed at him seemed to bounce off his thick coat of rough flesh and fur.

"Yose is not kill me. I's not be kilt." I heard him grunt. Still, the arrows and stones had injured him enough to make him stumble.

I did not have to guess what he meant. There were creatures lying dead about me. It had taken several stones and arrows to take them down, but this one was the curse of the wizard. The one sent to find me.

The strength of his hold began to send sensations of lifelessness through me. My eyes closed, my breathing ceased, and darkness clouded my mind. Then, as if something struck my mind with a force, I took a breath and shouted the words: *Filthy curse, be gone from me!* The creature began to tremble, and its arm fell limp from around my neck, dropping me to the ground. It fought to stand, stumbling forward and then sideways until it fell to the ground. I did not wait to see if it was dead. I needed to get back to Klogan.

I could see his sling and cestro swinging as if they were one, though they were in opposite hands. A wolf-like creature lay at his feet, one more was coming at him, teeth bared, inches away. Not knowing his skill, they did not live long enough to see it demonstrated, though the tooth of the second creature penetrated Klogan's shoulder before it fell against him, an arrow in his chest and stone in the middle of his forehead.

"They are not easy to kill," I stammered, my whole body aching and smelling of the creature.

"Neither are you, it seems!" He grimaced, holding his shoulder where blood covered his clothing. "I am relieved to see you, though you have smelled better."

"I could say the same of you," I said, and pulled the dead creature from him. "Let me look at it."

"It is nothing," he assured me. "Only a flesh wound. I will heal quickly now that the smelly, hairy . . ." His voice faded as he stared at the ugly thing that lay dead at his feet, watching it turn to ashes. He raised his eyes to meet mine. "Most hideous things I've ever seen!"

A loud command to retreat was heard from beyond the woodland. The rustling beyond the thicket told us the changelings had heeded the command. Now only the songs of morning birds reached our ears, telling of seven creatures whose bodies dissipated to ashes.

"They retreat only to regroup, count those still breathing, and conceive another tactic," Barok warned me as I tended to Klogan's wound. "The Danes stay at the edge of the woodland, hidden from their eyes, but not their voices."

We waited as the sun began to climb—the warriors in their hiding places, Klogan and I beside the rock, and Kevelioc close by. I was finding it difficult to keep my mind from the thoughts of the wizard and the potion. "Tell me how you learned the art of the cestro and sling," I requested of Klogan, hoping his story would distract me.

"I learned from my father, who learned from his father, who learned from his father, who learned from his father," he replied, offering no more to the story.

"Very interesting," I grumbled. "Is there no more to tell?"

"Why do you need to know when it is better that we keep our minds alerted to the enemy?" he asked as impatiently as I felt.

"For that very reason." I explained what Barok had screamed into my ear. "Until I know its power, I do not know what to do with my thoughts for fear they will open the way for Ancitel's potion to find me."

The chirping began again. "It seems I will not have to bore you with my story, for now at least," he said with relief. Klogan pulled himself up from the ground. "Someone is coming."

"The Danes," I said, their thoughts reaching into mine and warning me of a greater danger than I could have anticipated when I brought the warriors into the woodland.

"They are preparing to set fire to the thicket," Gudrod barked feverishly as the Danes came thundering through the brush. "The fire will burn from the north and the south. The cliffs to the east will offer you no escape, so they will wait for you as you flee to the west."

"Then we will not flee to the west," I said, and summoned Barok to fly over the woodland while Kevelioc and the Danes explored them, in hopes of finding a possible escape.

Klogan quickly gathered the warriors. All were alive, though some carried the gashes of the enemy's fangs and claws. Others had been pierced with the tips of swords. Blood was spilling and clotting against the wounds. "They are strong enough to run," he assured me. "Tell us what we are to do."

"We will go to the cliffs," I said. "Ancitel will be waiting for us to flee to the west. He will send none of the creatures to guard the cliffs. Barok will fly above in search of an escape through or around the cliffs. The animals search for a way to climb to their peak."

Within seconds, the smell of smoke was all around us. Our eyes watered and our lungs cried for fresh air as flames quickly consumed the dryness of the thicket. We could barely see the jagged edges of the mountains cliffs through the smoke. We fought to breathe as we stumbled through the underbrush.

In desperation, I opened my mind to connect with Barok and the others. It was the very thing he had warned me against, just before he flew away, but there was no choice. Rather there was a choice, and I had made it, knowing the consequence.

I could hear Barok in my mind as he communicated with the animals; I cried out to them to help us. I heard Kevelioc's roar and Barok's cry, and I watched as the warriors moved toward the cliff and the sounds of the animals.

Suddenly, my mind seemed to be dulled by the aroma that had taken my thoughts before. This time it was stronger, and I could feel myself slump to the ground, my mind muddled. Through the flames that seemed to dance around me, a man appeared. He was wearing a long, dark robe as black as the hair on his head.

"It seems I have found you, son of a king," he said, his voice echoing in my ears. "Now that I have your full attention, I will tell you what I need from you, and what you must do for me." His shadowed eyes searched for mine as he reached down to remove the mask from my face. "But first, I think I would like to see your face and look into your eyes."

I fought with everything inside me to defend myself, yet I could do nothing but lie there, numb. He laughed and spoke my name as if he knew me. Just as his fingers touched my mask, his eyes caught sight of the chain around my neck. I could feel his fingers touch it, wrapping his fingers around it.

"Perhaps I do not care to see your face when I can see the chain that possibly holds something very precious to both of us." His hand pulled at the chain until the mantle was in his sight.

Something deep within in me cried out, *Use your power, Etcheon. He must not touch the astrolabe.* Then I felt the awakening and a power much greater than I had ever experienced. The words *mononimus, treminous, presevious* roared from my lips, and the wicked laughing ceased—the fingers no longer clasping the chain.

There was nothing around me but space. It had no substance and still it held me. I feared it was the Wizard's potion taking me away. For a time, I continued in the trance. Slowly my eyes began to sting, yet they would not open. My nostrils were filled with the smell of smoke; my throat felt scorched. Something was pressing against my chest, but I could not lift my hand to knock it from me. I tried to speak but my voice was silent.

"There is no time to dawdle, lad. You must get up!" Barok screeched into my ear. "The warriors are in grave danger. The fire is upon them and they have no escape. You know what to do."

His words brought me to my senses, and for once, I was grateful to see him perched on my chest. I forced myself to stand and look beyond the cliff. I could see Klogan and his warriors pressed against the rocks, trying to escape the flames. The fire leaped up at the warriors, licking at their cloths and singeing their hair. Many had fallen victim to the smoke and flames.

The words of the Ancient came to me, telling me I would know when it was necessary to use the timepiece. Now was the time. But first I had to bring the warriors to me before I could use the timepiece to help our escape. There was no time to consider the options. "Take me to the bottom of the cliff," I called to Barok.

He understood and grabbed me with his talons. He soared to the rocks below, dropping me beside Klogan. The Danes and the panther gathered the warriors to me. "Hold on to each other so that we all are touching," I cried out to them, knowing we only had seconds before we would be engulfed in the flames.

I held the timepiece in my hand and let my thoughts speak out to it, just as the Ancient had taught me. I felt the strange sensation of waves passing through my body as a mist enveloped us, lifting us from the flames, as we held tight to each other. A meadow appeared beyond the mist and suddenly, we were inside the forest of Mythias—all of us—alive. Many were wounded, some close to death, but still breathing—smoke no longer filled their lungs; no fire licked their bodies.

"All is well," I heard Klogan say from behind me. "All is well."

I looked at him and saw the pain in his eyes from the wound in his shoulder. Yet he did not complain. "We must see to the warriors," he said, when I reached out to examine his wound.

As we did so, my eyes searched the faces of the youth I called warriors, and I could not control the emotions that swelled inside of me. As I knelt before Thorri, Mythias stood before me. "Timberlin and his wife, Miranda, have brought our people to see to the wounds." He stepped back, and I could see the tiny people of the village guiding the smallest horses I had ever seen, as they pulled tiny, bulging carts.

"You have done well." Mythias smiled and placed his hand on my shoulder. "Though I think Ancitel would disagree. Now let my people do their work."

"There are seven who would have died had you not acted when you did," the wizard confided later when we sat together, watching over the warriors. "Instead, they will mend well, as will the other five, whose wounds are minor. The rest only had scratches and mild burns. Tomorrow, they will all be ready to fight again."

"They should have all been dead," I said to him, "if not for the angel fleece they wear around their arms as a shield to protect them."

"That is part of it, but not all," was all he said. Barok landed on his shoulder.

"It is happening," I heard the eagle say in his ear. "It was most frightening to watch, yet thrilling to behold. I can explain it no better than that."

I looked from Barok to Mythias. "What is this secret you conspire to keep from me?" I was beginning to lose patience with both of them.

Mythias only shook his head. "There is no secret. It is all there for you. Do not be afraid of what you are," he scolded, though gently.

Mythias looked about him, observing Klogan's warriors. "They are truly an inspiration, are they not?" It was not so much a question as it was a statement to remind me of the strength of my kin. "Perhaps you should explain to them how they got here."

19

The Forest

"WHERE DID HE GO?" ANCITEL SHOUTED to the crystal. "I had the chain between my fingers when something whirled about him and forced my hand from it, and he suddenly disappeared. Find him!"

But the crystal lay dull and silent, telling him nothing. He closed his hand, clutching it so tightly that blood dotted his fingers. "Find the boy," he hissed, his voice angry yet desperate. Then he opened his hand to the blood-soaked stone and caressed it gently, uttering words only he understood. The stone became as red as the blood that covered it, and its light began to cast an eerie glow against its master's face and into his eyes. There he saw the forest that stood far from the sea.

For a moment he was puzzled. Did the boy have magical powers? He did not believe so. It was possible, nonetheless. The mist had come from somewhere. Could the timepiece have been used for transport?

Why had the boy chosen this forbidding forest of bones, a place of myths and untold mysteries, to hide in if, indeed, he was hiding there? But then what better place? The myth claims the forest is enchanted—filled with fairies, mythical trees, and scattered bones of those who attempted to enter. It tells of a wizard who claims the forest as his kingdom—the king of the fairies and the enchanter of the bones.

He had even attempted, a time or two, to find out for himself, if the story was true. But each time he rode near, he found himself disinterested, having no desire to step inside the ugly, unkempt jungle of hideous trees and jagged bones, and he would turn and ride away.

In a surge of curiosity, for whatever reason he could not explain, he had even tried a spell to see inside, without the trouble of the journey. Though his scope traveled deep, the view was the same—bits and pieces of skeletons everywhere, tangled with the trees. But in that adventure, and only for a second, he sensed a trace of wizardry.

With that came the desire to attempt another spell—one that would turn the bones to ashes and the trees to stubble. The spell could not filtrate, and his curiosity began to burn within him. What better place to hide than where no one else would dare to step, if the story were true and a wizard had the power to transport a boy from the burning woodland—and from the grasp of another wizard—to the forest.

Ancitel felt his body being drained of its strength. Using his blood to find the forest had not been wise, but necessary as well as fruitful. Something told him the boy was there. He would use more drops of blood to give his crystal the power it needed to bring the boy to him. It would be well worth the loss of a bit of his power to have the timepiece. With the timepiece, he would have all he needed. And he needed so much.

The cursed decree allowed only a few more days for him to find the son of King Etcheon. He had seen the power his potion had on the boy. The crystal that now carried his blood was becoming more and more potent. It soon would be able to place a spell over the forest or break the one that was said to protect it. With the crystal and potion together, he could reach into the forest and bring the boy to the tower and to relieve him of the timepiece.

The changelings gathered around Ancitel. The one who had failed to bring him Etcheon, stepped forward. "Empty cliffs. Empty woods."

Ancitel looked at the gangly, hideous, smelly beasts before him. With his wand, he cast a spell of a better fragrance about them. At least, if nothing else, they would smell better. There were seven missing, five remaining. He wondered if he would have to call more from the underworld—but not today. Today, he would have other things to think about.

"It is time we all became acquainted," Mythias exclaimed. "The tiny people who have mended your wounds are called the Quynaè. They have now prepared a feast for you. It will be the finest of all celebrations, for they will be welcoming the warriors and the animals, who the story foretold would come this day. Preparations began the very moment the unruly trees of this fanciful forest entwined their limbs about the arms and legs of Etcheon the Younger."

The warriors, having never seen the tiny people of the forest, were captivated by the Quynaè and their delicate beauty. Mythias, having placed Timberlin in charge, slipped away quietly, while the tiny man made the warriors laugh with mystical stories of the enchanted forest.

Brettina found herself drawn to one tiny female and thought she was the most beautiful and graceful of all the Quynaè.

The tiny person smiled up at her. "My name is Mirlanda, and pleased, I am, that you are here."

Brettina reached out and touched the hand of Mirlanda. "My name is Brettina, and I think this is a beautiful, peaceful place."

A pair of stunning dark eyes looked up at her. "Beautiful, it is. Peaceful, it is, most of the time." Then she laughed, and Brettina laughed with her. "If Brettina you be, something I have for you." Mirlanda took Brettina's hand and laid her cheek against it, letting the moisture of a tear fall onto a finger. "The knowledge of the forest, it be," Mirlanda whispered in her ear.

Bewildered, Brettina glanced down to see the teardrop forming itself into a blue pearl. She looked at Mirlanda, her mind filled with questions. A delicate finger pressed against her lips.

"To you, joy, not sadness, brings the pearl. When comes the time, your magic it will be," Mirlanda said. "Alone for you, it be. Hide it well, you must."

Brettina nodded and folded her fingers around the pearl, slipping it into her pocket. It would be their secret.

The aroma of cooked vegetables, fresh muffins, and sweet foods reached our nostrils as we followed Timbelin to the village. He claimed there would be singing, dancing, and eating until all the songs were sung and all the food was eaten. "Then," he announced, "Mythias will tell the story of how Etcheon saved the lives of the warriors."

We heard shouting coming from the village. "Coming they are, and beautiful they are."

We could see tiny people, dressed in their finest, stepping out of their houses to watch the legion of Etcheon the Younger. They waved at the eagle that flew above them and cheered.

"Come, meet the people of Mythias, you must," Timberlin said, his face bright with the excitement of the occasion.

There were no wings to carry the miniatures from place to place, yet they moved about as if there were. Their swiftness was remarkable as they greeted the warriors and the animals, showing no fear of either.

"The village, small it may seem, for big you are," Timberlin said, and laughed. "Our food your tummies will fill, no matter." He turned to those who were like him and spoke in a language we did not understand. Then he turned back to us. "Mythias comes. Sit, please. The soft grass your cushion, it be."

The miniatures waited until we were seated. Then they began to dance as they sang:

> Mythias the giant, our wizard he be.
> Though once a Quynaè, he was like we.
> His feet grow long, his hair grows white,
> He walks among us, a terrible sight.

Mythias's laughter was heard in the distance and the trees began to sway, a gentle melody whispering through their branches. The miniature people began to move to the melody with such elegance that it was spellbinding to us.

As they moved, they began to sing again. The song told of a Quynaè who, because of the goodness of his soul, was given at birth a gift more powerful than any other—the gift of a wizard's magic, wisdom, and understanding. He would stand taller than man—his duty far greater than a king's. He would be the guardian of the forest, the protector of his kind, and the sentinel for those who were Purcatians.

In sadness, he would accept this gift, for he would lose his beautiful appearance and become a giant in his size.

In gladness, he would accept this gift, for he would have power over any who would come against him or his kind.

In fearfulness, he would accept this gift, for he would be tempted to use it for his own gain.

In humbleness, he would accept this gift, for it was the most precious and sacred gift a Quynaè could be given.

As they sang, the wizard Mythias appeared, wrapped in a long flowing robe in the colors of the forest. His white hair was almost hidden beneath an elegant clataè that shaded and shadowed the depth of his eyes. He carried in his hand a gold walking stick. On the third finger of his right hand, he wore a large emerald ring that glistened in the sun. At his side walked a unicorn. Its mane was gold, its horn beautiful, and its coat so white that it cast a soft glow around the wizard, which gave him a magnificent appearance. He greeted his people with tenderness; then he walked to us.

"It has been foretold," he said in the silence of the music that flowed through the forest, "that the Quynaè would unite with the son of the Purcatian King. This son, so the legend claims, would bring with him, a legion—not of man, but of animals—from another time and another place. Together they would step through the portal, near the sea. The hour and the day set by a timepiece belonging to the prince."

He smiled, nodded his head slightly, and gave me a wink before he continued. "The legend only tells us one more thing, for what is yet to happen is yet to be written. That which is left for me to tell you is this . . ." He turned to me and touched my shoulder with his walking stick. "The legend claims that those who walk with him will not fear death nor shall death take them."

I looked up at him. He had given me an answer. His kind eyes met mine and in them I could see my legion surrounding the twenty-one. There were no more questions inside of me. His eyes told all.

He turned from me and continued his speech. "We welcome you to our forest. Here, you are our guests. Here, you will be safe from Ancitel and his crystals while you prepare to go to battle against those who imprison your people." He turned and waved his arm toward the tables, filled with food. "We have prepared a feast in celebration of this moment."

He tapped his walking stick against the ground, and everyone cheered. The celebration had begun. The beautiful unicorn stayed close to Mythias as the music of the trees filled the air and food was placed before us. The Quynaè sat among us, talking and laughing until our plates were empty and our stomachs were full. Then a bell chimed, and all was silent.

"Mythias, my son," Timberlin said so all could hear. "We have waited long enough to hear of this adventure. It is time for you to tell us how Etcheon rescued the warriors."

The people cheered as Mythias lifted his father onto a table so everyone could see him. "I think it is you who should tell the story," Mythias argued. "You know it as well as I do, for you sat with me as the story unfolded in the mirror of the crystals."

Timberlin seemed embarrassed at the attention and turned to whisper into Mythias's ear. Mythias nodded, and Timberlin cleared his throat, straightened his jacket, and put his hands into the pockets.

Everyone had gathered around him; all were filled with anticipation and shushed one another until everyone was silent. He sat at the edge of the table so he could see into all their faces. Then he began.

"I shall speak in the tongue of my kin, and though the warriors cannot know the sound of it, there'll be an understanding, and they'll be hearing the story as I tell it." He cleared his throat a second time. " 'Tis the lark of luck that brings the magic to my son. I'll not cry about it, nor will I brag. I'll only be telling the story.

" 'Tis a story of the swiftness of a horse, the eyes of an eagle, the agility of a panther, and the diligence of two Great Danes."

The audience cheered.

" 'Tis a story of a young prince and his legion, who guides his warriors away from a cloud of death, away from a cave of fear, into the woodland, dark with thickets, that is soon filled with flames. 'Tis a story of the wicked wizard, who plots with changelings from the underworld to do his bidding in battling the warriors, only to find the warriors much more skilled in their slings and their cestros than the beasts in their claws and their thunder."

Again, the audience cheered.

" 'Tis a story of the battle that was fearsome and fearful, for changelings do not die easily. They carry no heart nor blood to spear or spill."

He narrowed his eyes and looked deep into the faces of his audience. "First the prince had to save himself. The evil wizard appears through the fire and places a spell upon the prince. The prince lies on the flaming ground, unable to move—unable to speak. The wizard reaches out his hand to remove the protective mask from the face of the prince, only to see something else he wants more than to see the face of the prince. His fingers reach to touch just as something magical happens. The wizard's hand is pushed away, and a mist takes the Prince from him."

"What magic removed this Prince from the spell of the evil wizard?" the children all shouted. "Was it Mythias?"

Excelarr—the son of Timberlin—climbed onto the table and sat beside his father. "Hurry, Papè, tell us how the story ends," he begged. "Before I grow old with anticipation."

Timberlin looked at his offspring and sighed. "Then I'll conclude the story with this. It was not Mythias that saved the prince but the prince himself."

The eyes of the children opened wide. "The prince is as Mythias?"

"Could be true," mused Timberlin. "But know this—the eagle perches himself upon the shoulder of the prince. The panther moves to stand at his feet. The Danes take their place at his side, and the horse stands behind him. For a moment, it seems that time is silent. Nothing stirs, not even life."

He stood and motioned for the children to stand and look behind them. There they saw what Timberlin had described, just as he had described it.

"Now, see the twenty-one that stand with him? Are they not beautiful to behold? Honor the legion of animals that watch over them."

The villagers raised their voices in praise. In return the animals came forward and lowered their heads, while Barok lifted his wings and soared above the heads of the children. They screamed in delight.

The music of the trees began again, and Timberlin spoke, reverting back to the language of my father. "This battle, though we cannot fight," he said, "your sentinels, we be. Your sanctuary, we be. The forest, your home it be. Today and tomorrow and the morrow after, until is won the battle—until free, your people be."

I looked at the people of the Quynaè as they stood together in their square, their beautiful village in the background, and my heart was touched. "You have given us the gift of friendship," I said. "We honorably offer ours in return. You have given us a home until we can once again return to ours. For these gifts, we have nothing to offer in return except our deepest gratitude, and this promise. We will defeat King Yiltor and his wizard. We will restore the Kingdom of the Purcatians. Then we can repay your kindness by never revealing what is found in this forest to another. That will be our gift to you."

The Quynaè bowed, and we listened as they began to sing, the music of the forest surrounding them, once again.

It is a day for celebrating what
The legend foretold would bring
Twenty-one warriors, who walk
With the legion of a king.

When, at last, the only light was that of the moon and the stars, Mythias led us to his cottage where beds awaited us.

"Your legion sleeps in the garden and is quite comfortable," he said when we stood alone. "You too will sleep without dreams to disturb your rest, as will the others. Tomorrow, after our morning meal, we will talk of the future."

"I will not sleep until you tell me of my past," I said, desiring to understand it all.

"When there is more time, I will tell you a story of Etcheon, son of Arcadia." He smiled. "It will be a wondrous story. The Quynaè will delight in singing its praises. But for tonight, you will sleep."

As I lay in my bed, my thoughts turned from my desire to know my own story to the desire to know the story that would be woven in the following days. Would it tell of our victory, or would it tell of our defeat? But even as disturbing as this thought was, my eyelids became heavy, and I slept without dreams to disturb me, just as Mythias said I would.

The next morning, Timberlin appeared with a mischievous glint in his eye and announced that the trees were ready and hoped the warriors were, as well, for it was to be a great day for all of them. "Follow me, you will," he said to the warriors and smiled. "Take you to the forest, I will."

"You will stay with me this morning, Etcheon," Mythias said, as I was preparing to leave. "I have read the decree which was placed at the edge of the forest, tacked to one of the trees." He handed me the decree. I did not need to read it. I had already heard it from the mouth of the one who wrote it. Yet a question burned in my mind. "Why could I not have come back before my people were taken to the prisons of Yiltor?" I asked, tearing the decree into pieces in my frustration. "Why could I not have come back before my mother and father were placed in the prisms, so I could have warned them of Yiltor?"

Mythias placed his hand on my shoulder. "I think the time for you to return was set for a purpose you have yet to discover."

"Then tell me this," I continued. "Where did the timepiece come from?"

Mythias said nothing for a time, only peered at me as if he was searching my soul. When he spoke, at last, he did so, cautiously. "From the hands of Timberlin."

His answer shocked me and left me without words to reply.

"What you now know can never be spoken of again," he warned, turning to the door and motioning for me to follow.

He led me to a room of great dignity and integrity. It was something I had not expected to see inside the cottage of a wizard. Its walls were lined with books—its floor decorated with the furnishings of a king.

While I stood there, mystified by this magnificent room filled with a different kind of magic than what I had seen inside another, Mythias turned to me and simply said, "What is your plan, young Etcheon?"

"My plan has been turned around and around and upside down so many times, it has been lost to me," I admitted. "First, the wizard sends a cloud of poison to destroy all life within the walls of the city. Yiltor now knows where the walls stand. The past five days have been spent in defense. I have not had time to consider a new offense." I looked into Mythias's eyes. "You said you could make me invisible to Yiltor. Tell me how."

Mythias smiled and handed me a small flask. "Inside, you will find a sour-tasting liquid. Open it and place two drops on your tongue."

I took the flask from him, opened the lid, and let my nose sniff an odor that made my mouth pucker and my eyes water. "Ugh!" I cried. "What is it?"

"Something that will become very tasty to you before you have finished the last drop. Now do as I say."

Slowly I lifted the flask to my mouth, barely touching it to my tongue, and found it not as bad as the odor implied as two drops fell. I removed it, replaced the lid, and waited for something to happen. Nothing did. I put my hand out in front of me. It was still very visible, though a little weathered looking. I looked at Mythias.

"It is perfect," he said, nodding his head in approval of his work. "Look at yourself in the mirror."

When I did, I was shocked at what I saw. I was not invisible at all, but an old man with whiskers and a nose that all but filled my face. "I am old and ugly," I cried, turning to him in disgust. "What have you done to me?"

"I have made you invisible." He laughed. "Each time you put two drops on your tongue, you will become someone else in your appearance. Only you will know who you are. The one you are at this moment is my creation."

"It seems you have a vivid imagination. How long must I look like this?" I asked, praying it would not be for long.

"No longer than four hours. That is something you must remember when you take the potion. Always know the hour that you place it on your tongue."

"Tell me how to change myself back."

"You tire of your appearance so soon?" Mythias laughed again. "But first you must go out and walk among your animals. See if they recognize you."

I stared at him, thinking him a rather foolish wizard. Then a thought came to me, and I decided he was very wise, instead. "You say that I can make myself look like whomever I wish?"

"Indeed you can, and Ancitel will not find you in his crystals as long as you are invisible as Etcheon the Younger. Think of the possibilities." Mythias raised his eyebrows and waited.

"Perhaps a soldier in Yiltor's army or a guard who stands by his door," I speculated. "Even better, one who stands by the gates that hold my people prisoners."

"Or even Yiltor, himself," Mythias suggested.

A smile spread across my ugly face and a plan began to form in my mind. "I will see if the animals know me," I said, turning and walking from the room. The good and wise wizard followed.

"Good morning," I said to Barok as I met him in the garden.

"Good morning to you, lad," he replied as if he were unaware of my appearance.

At first I was stunned. "How do you know it is me?"

"Because he looks at you," Kevelioc scoffed. "Why would we not recognize you when we just saw you last night? Of course, this morning you are a more comical sight."

I looked back at Mythias who was seemingly impressed with himself. "Explain," I demanded. "You said no one would know it was me."

"And would you not want your legion to recognize you even when you are someone else?" he said with laughter.

"When I look in the mirror, I am an ugly old man to myself, yet the animals do not see the reflection I see?"

Again Mythias raised his eyebrows. "They see the reflection as you see it, and they see you behind it."

It was perfect when I thought it through. The animals needed to know me no matter who I was. "I think the plan is beginning to form." I grinned. "Now tell me how I become myself again."

"By putting one drop of the potion on your tongue, you will return to yourself."

I pulled the lid from the flask and carefully allowed one drop to fall on my tongue. Then I hurried back inside and to the mirror. Relieved, I found myself looking back at me. I turned to Mythias and, with deep respect, said, "I will never doubt you again."

20

Yiltor's Castle

"REMEMBER TO KEEP THE HOUR IN your head," Mythias warned. I climbed on Walkelin's back, my appearance that of a peasant. In the bag that hung from my side, I carried candles that I would sell in the market place.

"I will," I promised, looking up to see Barok circling above me. Kevelioc had gone ahead and would be close, yet outside the city walls. The Danes would stay in the forest today. Not knowing what I would find inside the gates of Yiltor's city, we would not take the chance that Ancitel might see them. Walkelin would remain outside the city walls, hidden in the shadows of the trees.

I touched the horse's flanks, and we left a whirlwind of dust and leaves as the forest became smaller and smaller to my view and Yiltor's castle became larger and more impressive.

I entered the city from the peasant's gate and was inspected by the guard. When he was satisfied that I was only a poor lad who was selling candles made by my grandmother, he allowed me to enter.

Once inside the city, a small bird perched itself upon my shoulder and guided me to the marketplace. I mingled among the other peasants and listened as they gossiped about the decree written by their king. Some of them thought it quite generous of him to give the Purcatian prince five days to surrender himself before he began to rid the kingdom of those held inside his prison. Others thought him rather cruel to have the Purcatians in his prison at all and wondered if the story of their capture had been false.

I only listened, pretending to be uninformed either way. While I listened,

I sold seven candles, giving me money to buy some food. I walked through the streets eating flat bread and apples, listening to Barok as he gave directions to the guards' hut.

"Many peasant boys sit near the wall and admire the guards," he informed me. "You will not be out of place."

I had been inside the gates for more than two hours when I sat beside another boy, pretending to admire the soldiers as he did. "Do you come every day to watch them?" I asked innocently.

He nodded that he did and then went on to narrate their movements throughout the day.

I listened quietly, learning what I needed to know. I bid the young boy good-bye and hurried on my way. Barok settled himself on my shoulder, once again, and dropped a letter into my hand.

"It was not easy," he kaa'd, proudly, "but I managed to obtain an invitation to the King's Court while a servant's head was turned the other way. The true recipient of this invitation is snoring from lack of sleep and does not know he has been invited. I think he will not awaken until tomorrow afternoon. If you were dressed as a wealthy merchant, you could attend the King's Court this evening."

"And what is a King's Court?" I asked, opening the letter and finding it to be an invitation to attend a lively discussion of business at the king's table. I looked at Barok. "Do you think it is possible?"

"It will be risky, but you do not have much time for dawdling."

"Then, let us study the merchants for a time, and I will make the change after," I said.

Barok guided me to the merchant's corner where pompous and prideful men paraded around in flowing satin robes. Their talk was mostly of business, but science, math, and astronomy found their way into their conversation as well. I could compete with them with my knowledge, I thought, but I would have to practice in order to become pompous.

"Take me to a place where I can make the change," I whispered to Barok.

He gave directions, and I found myself in a private garden that was shaded from windows or onlookers. I removed the flask from my pocket and brought it to my mouth, letting my mind envision a merchant. Then I placed two drops of my potion on my tongue and waited. The change was amazing to me. My hair was black as coal and my complexion dark. The robes and clothing were quite elegant, I thought, and easy to wear.

"Methinks you to be perhaps twenty years beyond your age," Barok surmised, "which means you will not be skipping about, yet will still be graceful in your stride. You are not handsome by any means, but prosperous looking. Stand straight with your nose lifted, and you will blend very well with those with whom you mingle."

I began to walk as I had seen the merchants walk, throwing my robe about me and keeping my nose up and my jeweled fingers in plain view for all to see my riches.

Barok corrected me many times before he gave his approval of the spectacle he saw before him. "You must play the part at all times while you are in the castle. There are those hired by the king to watch over the merchants. If you falter in your imitation, you will be caught and thrown into prison for masquerading as one of them, in an attempt to steal their purses."

I looked at him, concerned that I was not a merchant at heart.

"Be as Verch taught you," he advised. "Be watchful without watching, and listen without letting others know that you hear their words, if their words are whispered. Remain calm when you feel the volcano of fear inside. Your instincts and your essence will protect you if you remember this."

I took a deep breath and closed my eyes in meditation, preparing my mind to respond and my instincts to become alert. "I think I am ready, now," I said, after a short time. "That is if my face hides the volcano of fear you spoke of, for it truly desires to erupt inside of me."

Barok laughed. "Your eyes are steady and cold. You have learned well. Remember one more thing. Do not drink the juice that will be to the right of your plate. Drink only the water."

"Why is that?" I stared at him in bewilderment.

"The juice is not fresh but aged. In the aging, it becomes potent and carries a strong flavor. Once it enters your body, it affects the mind and loosens your tongue as well as your intellect. It softens the muscles and makes you stagger when you walk. It is also the favorite drink of the merchants, so you must find a way to let the juice disappear from your glass without letting it touch your lips. And you must pretend to be affected by the drink, as they will be."

I said nothing for a time, trying to imagine what he was telling me. I knew nothing of this world. I was truly innocent, as Mayor Ratherberry said. Could I pretend to be otherwise?

As if Barok was reading my thoughts (and I believe he was), he perched himself upon my shoulder and caressed my cheek with his wing. "Do not doubt yourself, lad," he said softly. "You are all that you have learned. It is your innocence that will protect you as well."

Before he could say more, we heard the merchants laughing and talking as they came near. The hour for the King's court had come. Barok fluttered about me, making sure I was well groomed. Then I stepped out onto the road and into the parade of seventeen merchants, who were making their way to the doors that would permit those who carried an invitation into the castle.

Once inside, I found myself in an enormous hall, elaborately decorated with silk curtains, elegant crystallized candles, and statues of animals of all kinds—each posed in the position of attack. I walked by them as if I had been inside this hall many times, though their grotesque appearance disturbed me.

Further into the hall, a long table set with fine linen clothes, silver plates, and goblets, extended from the back of the hall to the front. Eighteen elegant chairs made of fine wood lined both sides of the table. At the head of this table was a smaller table, turned in the opposite direction. Behind it were three chairs, much more elegant, and seemingly more comfortable than the eighteen.

I listened to the conversations and laughed with the other merchants as they laughed, agreed or disagreed with ideas of business, and discussed the weather and the constellations. All the while I flaunted my robes and jewels. As I did these things, I slowly moved closer and closer to the table where Yiltor would sit. My strategy was to sit close enough to him to see into his eyes. There I would perceive my enemy for what he was.

The hall was noisy with conversation until chimes began to ring. Their sound brought the room to silence. The merchants walked to the tables, and stood behind a chair of their choice. I did as they did, finding myself three chairs away from the table of the King.

All heads turned to the front of the hall, and I watched as King Yiltor entered the room. His appearance was impressive, his clothing elaborate. His red tunic bore the crest of his kingdom, stitched with gold thread. His leggings were black, his embossed robe gold and clustered with small emeralds. His crown glittered with fine gold, dusted with what I could only imagine to be tiny flecks of diamonds. His hair was loose and fell down over his shoulders. He was, indeed, a very handsome man, and though he smelled of lilac, the scent of his soul was foul.

I assumed the merchants would bow before him and was making ready to do so myself. I listened carefully for any movement around me, while my eyes remained steady on the king.

To my surprise, the bows were no more than a nodding of the head in acknowledgement of his entrance. He welcomed us as if we were his closest friends, instructing us to sit. Then he snapped his fingers, and food appeared from all around us.

The merchant to the right of me seemed to be studying my clothing as the servants of the king filled our plates with food, one goblet with water, and one with the aged juice Barok warned me of.

"I think we have never met," the merchant said, as the servant stepped away. "The weave of your robe seems to be that of the Kvenland Realm, yet it has elegance unlike the cloth of that kingdom." He reached out his hand and touched the silk cloth. "Indeed, I must say that the cloth is some of the finest I have ever seen. Tell me, which kingdom do you represent?"

Though I had not anticipated such a question, I had overheard him talking to another, while we waited to be seated, and I would use what I had heard to my advantage. I nodded to him and smiled. "It is a fine compliment you pay me, sir, for you too are dressed in very fine materials. I would say you are from the Kingdom of Trondheim."

He nodded, pleased with the compliment, and accepted, it seemed, that I was, indeed, from Kvenland. Without further comment as to my kingdom, he began to tell me of the new silk weavings he had seen in his travels.

As the evening proceeded, the merchants talked of business and wealth, and I learned that silver and gold coins carried more value in one kingdom than another, making business transactions somewhat difficult, at times. Light arguments arose, each merchant attempting to defend his kingdom's position.

I watched Yiltor as the merchants tittle-tattled back and forth about the predicament. The contentment on his face told me he was very pleased with the progress of this discussion. He allowed it to continue for some time before he stood and watched in amusement as the eyes of the merchants turned to him, their voices suddenly silent. The only sound was that of the chairs being disturbed as they stood also.

A pleasant smile appeared on his face as he lifted his goblet in the air, and when he spoke, his voice was sweet and thick—like honey. "I raise my goblet in salute to each merchant as if he was of my kingdom, where gold and silver carry more value than in any kingdom," he said with humility.

If his voice seemed humble, his eyes were not. I could see their cunning reflection, and I understood the purpose of this King's banquet. His scheme was to feed these men sweet food and the aged juice that left their minds weak. Then he would entice them with wealth, knowing their desire for it was beyond their loyalty to their own kingdoms. They had become his spies, as they talked freely of the vulnerabilities of their own kingdoms

I looked around me to see the faces of the men sitting at the tables. They raised their glasses in salute and then drank greedily. At his bidding, they sat once again. Oh, this king was a clever man.

"Do you not like the wine?" a servant asked when he reached to fill my goblet and found it full.

I still held my empty water goblet, which I had raised in the salute. I handed it to the servant. "I have finished the wine in this, however." I slurred my words, trying to make myself seem as the others around me. "You may refill it."

He nodded quickly and filled the goblet.

"I think the truth is, my friend," the merchant from Trondheim whispered into my ear, the smell of the aged juice heavy on his breath, "is that you do not like the wine." He handed me his goblet of water. "Give me your wine, and I will give you my water, so you may drink without worry, and I may drink what I enjoy most."

I laughed and handed him my glass in exchange for his. Then, he turned to the king and asked, "Sire, is it true, that you have over five hundred Purcatians in your prison?"

The room became silent. Yiltor looked at the man beside me, and I could see it was a question he had hoped would be asked. "It is, indeed," he replied as if it was a simple matter, hiding his excitement beneath shadowed eyes, eyes that were as easily read as his words on the parchment. This was the purpose of the evening.

"It is believed that they have not existed for many years," another voice called out. "Yet I have heard that they hide behind walls which are hidden themselves to make us believe this."

"What defines these people?" I asked, leaning forward so I could see into his face. "Do they appear different than you or me?"

The room grew quiet, once again. Yiltor turned to me, meeting my gaze, and I could see beyond the facade of a gentleman. I could see the beast. "Would you care to see them for yourself?" he asked happily.

I had not expected such an opportunity as this. "I think I would, if it pleases the king," I replied, a smile of my own meeting his.

"It pleases the king." Yiltor laughed. "And he will take all of you down to the dungeon of this castle, where you will see for yourself. Then you can tell those you bargain with, as you travel to all the kingdoms of this land, that King Yiltor does, indeed, have more than five hundred Purcatians in his prison, at least for a while yet. I wait upon a young prince to save them." He laughed again.

"And will you do as you have decreed?" another merchant asked.

Again, all eyes were on Yiltor, hungry for his answer.

"If King Etcheon's son does not present himself to me in three days time, it will mean that he desires that I do so. I shall not disappoint him." He looked at me once again. "But now, my friends, we go to the dungeon."

It had been his intention from the beginning to take these merchants to see the Purcatians. In obtaining his desire, nonetheless, he had also fulfilled mine.

He motioned for me to stay close to him. "I will show you what defines one that claims to be pure of heart."

I was careful to be observant as we followed him through a large, heavy door and down a hallway, and then turned to the left and down several steps. There we came to another door. He opened the door with a key that he removed from inside his robe and led us down several more steps before entering a hall. We turned to the right, the hallway becoming darker and narrower as we approached yet another door. At this door, he simply knocked. The sound of a key being placed in the lock echoed through the damp and chilly hallway. The door opened, allowing us to enter.

At last, we had come to the dungeon. It was dark, damp, and musty—carrying the odor of filth. I could hardly stand to breathe without covering my nose with the sleeve of my robe.

The guard, an ugly, stout, little man with little hair and even less teeth, lit torches for us to see the Purcatians clearly.

" 'Ere we er, sire," he grumbled, pointing his dirty finger.

I forgot the odor as I stared at the sight before me, barely able to control my anger or the convulsing of my stomach. *Do not let your emotions betray you*, I heard the owl's voice whisper in my head. I closed my eyes to the scene before me and brought my attention to Yiltor, who was saying something to the guard.

He turned to me and said, "Sir Merchant, come close." He did not seem to care to know my name. Neither did I care to give it to him. I simply did as he asked.

The guard opened a heavy barred door, disappeared inside, and brought out a flaming torch, which caused the room to have the brightness of day. It took all my strength to look at the women and children, huddled together. Nonetheless, I could see that even in their filthy clothes and unwashed faces, they were beautiful. Their golden hair, though tangled, shimmered in the flame of the torch. Their eyes revealed their intellect far more than their fear.

The merchants stood there, staring at them, dazzled by their beauty and amazed at the transparency of their skin and the glimmering lightness of their hair.

"I have never seen one before," I heard one merchant whisper to another. "They are just as beautiful as the stories claim."

"The stories also say that they considered themselves far above the common man," another said, his voice carrying a note of distaste. "Now look at them—filthy and smelly, just like a boar who wallows in the muck."

Many of the merchants laughed; however, many did not. I could sense their discomfort and pity for my people, but they dared not say anything that might anger the King. They simply remained silent while the others continued to discuss those behind the bars of the prison.

Yiltor's eyes were upon me, and I could see the conquering look in his face. "Do you see what defines them, now?" he boasted.

"They are a most beautiful people," I replied. "It interests me to know, however, and I pray I will not offend you, Sire, by asking why you have made them prisoners. For if the stories told of them are true, they are not a warlike people and pose no threat to any kingdom. They only desire to be left alone."

At first, Yiltor's eyes flickered with anger. Then he laughed, raising his voice so all could hear. "If you were younger, I would think you insolent and have you thrown into prison, but you are middle-aged, and homely, at that."

There were snickers from behind me.

"It seems you know your stories well. Therefore, your curiosity seems innocent enough, so I will tell you. The Purcatians sent four spies to my kingdom. They disguised their identity by painting their skin dark and dying their hair black. These men asked many questions of my people. They crept into my army tents and counted my soldiers. They studied the perimeters and the weak spots of my kingdom. But what they did not know was that I had my own spy—a wizard, who watched them as they went about doing their deeds. I had no choice but to do what has been done." He explained no further.

As I listened, I forced myself not to laugh, for his story, though a lie, had merit. A Purcatian was a spy in his city. My skin and my hair were darkened to disguise my identity, and I was asking many questions.

"Come now," he chuckled, "you have seen enough, and it is late. I must let you return to your inns and your beds, knowing that you have much to do tomorrow."

"But where are the men?" someone asked.

"Ah, yes." Yiltor frowned. "The men I have placed in another part of the prison. Would you care to tread deeper inside and down many steps with me?"

"I think not," a voice called from somewhere in the crowd. They had all seen enough and had enough of this dismal, smelly place.

"Thank you for allowing us to see those you have captured," I said when we returned to the hall. "I have read your decree, and I wonder if the lad . . . Etcheon, is it?" I glanced innocently at Yiltor. He nodded, and I continued. "I wonder if Etcheon will surrender quickly to save his people."

"Let us hope that he does," Yiltor replied, "but I am curious as to your concern."

Had I gone too far, I wondered. But a thought came to me from one of the books I read in the cave, giving me a response. "My grandfather told me a story, long ago," I began. "It was a story of his youth in which he happened to meet a boy whose skin was as fair as the morning dew and whose hair was the color of the sun. It was only a perchance meeting, and they did not even speak to each other, for the boy ran away. My grandfather had seen enough, nonetheless, to become curious. He began to study the writings telling of a race whose heart was so pure that it reflected itself in the color of the skin and hair."

I paused and let my eyes study his. "I was fascinated with his story, just as I was fascinated tonight, seeing them for myself." I lowered my eyes to the floor. "I must now ask your forgiveness for my boldness. My desire to see them was above my better judgment of respect."

Yiltor seemed satisfied with my explanation, and I bid him good night. As I left the castle, however, I sensed someone behind me, and I knew Yiltor had not trusted my words.

"Someone follows you," Kevelioc said to me, in my thoughts, "and you have little time left before you begin to change."

I felt relieved to hear the panther, for it told me he was somewhere nearby. Also, I had forgotten to keep the time in my head with all that I had seen. How much time I had remaining, I was not sure. But one thing I was sure of—I had to find a way out of the city without being followed. Also, I had to do so before I changed back into myself.

My merchant friend from Trondheim called to me. "Come walk with me. Your story intrigues me, and I would like to hear it again, and more, if there is more to tell."

"I only know what my grandfather told me," I said cautiously. "But he did say something I did not mention to the king." I proceeded to create a tale of the supposed grandfather, who followed the boy, to a place surrounded by streams and waterfalls, tall trees and bushes from which flowers of all kinds and colors blossomed.

"My grandfather said he watched as the boy disappeared beneath the waterfall," I continued. "Yet, when he followed, he found only a wall of solid rock. Every day for weeks, he would return to the waterfall and sit for hours, waiting to see if the boy would reappear. The boy did not. That was all my grandfather knew, but when I saw those in the dungeon, I knew his story was true, for his description of the boy was the description I saw tonight."

The merchant listened carefully to the story. "I, myself, wonder," he said, when I finished, "if the king's story is exaggerated. As I stood there, looking upon the beauty of the Purcatians, I felt nothing but pity for them, as did several of those around me. Perhaps it might be wise to caution the king of Trondheim."

I did not comment, for I did not know if he was truthful or if he was a spy for Yiltor. I thanked him for his company, and we parted once we were inside the inn. Though I had no room, I pretended that I did, and found myself alone, finally, in a dark hallway—a door to the outside at the end of it.

"The one who follows you stands not far behind you in the shadows," Kevelioc warned me. "There is also another who watches beyond the south door."

I found myself in a situation in which I had very little time to consider the options. I was beginning to feel the effects of the potion, and I knew I would shortly begin to change. I could run and allow them to give chase, meaning that I only pretended to be a merchant, and Yiltor would begin to suspect even more than he did at this moment, or I could pretend something else.

"Tell me where the one lies in wait for me," I asked the panther, in my mind.

"He stands in the bushes to the right, just beyond the door."

I walked through the door as if to clear my head. I pretended to be sick from the aged juice, forcing myself to gag and spit. Then I fell to the grass, began to snore loudly, and waited.

"Well done. Yet he who watches does not move," Kevelioc warned. "There is no time left."

I heard rustling among the bushes, then a growl whispered in the air. A gasp, much louder than the growl, came next, and I opened my eyes just in time to see a figure running toward the castle.

"Well done," I whispered to the panther. "Now we must leave—I have begun to change back."

"You have already changed," Barok said as I felt his huge talons on my shoulders, and my body being lifted into the air. "The two who pursued you are no longer a threat. I only hope that if someone should look upward, the moon will not give them the silhouette of a boy being carried off by an eagle. I will take you to Walkelin."

No one was looking when Barok silently carried me into the sky. No one, that is, except the wizard Ancitel.

21

Ᵽhe Prison

"TELL ME THIS, CRYSTAL," ANCITEL SAID, with as much calm as he could gather about him. "Why was this Purcatian not visible until now? Where did he come from? Did he drop from the sky just as he lifted himself back into its darkness?"

A thought came to him, and he began to stroke the crystal gently. "Show me, one more time. Only let the motion be very slow and deliberate I might have time to study it closely."

Once more he watched the boy come to life on the ground, but this time, he saw something that had not been visible to him before. There seemed to be someone else with him. No! Not with him. What was it he was seeing? The boy was evolving from one form to another, his mouth moving as if he was talking to someone. But there was no one there, only a shadow in the moonlight that came over him and lifted him upward and disappeared into thin air.

The crystal was revealing to Ancitel, something very disturbing—something that only a wizard could do. Had this boy wizard blood in him? He paused for a moment to allow that which he had just seen to penetrate his mind, and evolve, so that he could perhaps make some sense to it. He pressed his jeweled fingers together. His eyes became slits across his face, his mouth puckered as his mind worked through this possibility. Suddenly, his eyes opened and his fingers parted. It was a wizard's work, but the boy was not the wizard.

The tales of the forest were not tales, but truths. It was enchanted with a wizard's spell. Were the little people real, as well, he wondered? Were the bones proof that no one could enter it and live, except those who were invited in? These were questions he would not bother to answer. He had the only answer he needed. His crystal and the potion he had been given by the Danes—once enhanced—would bring about that which he desired.

Oh, this wizard was clever and powerful, Ancitel perceived, for he had not felt his presence—except for a flutter, now and then. There had been nothing more. Now he wondered if this wizard was the one he had been searching for, searching for more than a hundred years. He would be the last of his kind. The others, Ancitel had rid himself of, one by one, until only one remained—the most powerful of all—Mythias.

Could his fortune be so true to him that it would provide all his wishes in one bundle: Yiltor's kingdom, Mythias, and the timepiece? Ancitel threw his head back and let a sound resonate from deep inside him. It was not a sound that would touch the ears of a simple human. But it was a sound that would echo in the ears of a wizard, no matter how distant. No matter the spell that protected the wizard from him. And at that moment, he felt the energy of the wizard whose ears tingled and whose heart jumped as the echo vibrated through him. Mythias was, indeed, in the enchanted forest.

Ancitel turned to his book, his hands shaking with the excitement of his discovery. He opened the book he had opened before and turned to the page he had turned to before.

It was the potion that had been sent to the kingdom of the Purcatians to cleanse it of their existence. Only this time he would add one more ingredient that would make it even more potent. It had to be potent enough to break through the enchantment spell. One potent enough that even Mythias could not evaporate with a flip of his wand.

Oh, he had much to do, and so very little time to do it in. He looked at his clock and counted the hours left before the young Prince Etcheon would walk through the gates of Yiltor's castle and give himself up for the sake of his people. Even as he thought of the simplicity of the act, he knew the boy would not do this if he had the protection of Mythias.

What would the next hours bring, he wondered. What plan did the boy have up his sleeve? What should he be prepared for? "Questions, questions, questions," he shouted to the walls around him. "What will the answers be?"

Ancitel had not felt this much excitement since he had taken the lives of those who professed that good would always triumph over evil. Had he not proven them wrong? Oh, how he loved the answer . . . Yes!

Time was of the essence now. He would begin to prepare his potion. But before he sent the cloud to the forest, he knew he needed to lure the boy and the timepiece away from its perimeters. He gathered his crystal that glowed red with his blood and laid it beside the ingredient that would be added to the potion.

I did not sleep that night and morning came too quickly; the memory of the dungeon vivid in my memory. "What should I tell these warriors?" I asked Barok. "Should I tell them that their mothers and sisters are imprisoned in the most hideous circumstances?" I could feel the anger growing inside me even as I shared my knowledge with the eagle. "Should I tell them that their fathers and brothers are imprisoned in circumstances even beyond that?"

He put his face close to mine, the dark pupils of his eyes locking with mine. "Would you not want to know the truth, Etcheon? Have they not proven themselves to you? Have they not had experience enough to be prepared for what you must tell them? Make them wait no longer."

He was correct. I had to tell them. It was their right to know. I splashed water against my face, combed my hair, and walked out into the sunlight of Mythias's garden.

"Did your crystals reveal to you my quest?" I asked quietly.

"It did," Mythias whispered back, handing me a sweet juice and bread. "Your success was more than I anticipated, but what you saw in the prison must now be told to the warriors." He drew my attention to the faces of the twenty-one sitting beside their teacher. "Tell them immediately."

I set aside the juice and bread, stood before them, and began to tell my story. The warriors listened quietly, tears falling from their cheeks, as I left nothing unsaid.

"Were our mothers and our sisters unharmed, otherwise?" Brettina asked through her tears.

"There were no marks or bruises upon their faces or arms, only what I described, but they were still beautiful."

Thorri stepped forward. "Have you discovered enough that now we can prepare for battle against them? We have only until tomorrow."

"I know the way to the prison, and I know the streets of the city," I explained. "I know that not everyone in his kingdom believes that Yiltor is the generous king he perceives himself to be. I believe our battle will be with the soldiers only."

I held the map up so they could see its markings. "I have mapped out the city so that Klogan can prepare you for battle within its walls."

"The soldiers will outnumber them by the hundreds," I said to Klogan, after the warriors had disappeared into the forest to practice with their weapons. I handed him the map.

"It will not matter to them," he said gravely. "They will battle until they have won or until they no longer live. But I think they will live because they wear the protection of the angel fleece. They have prepared themselves to live, by taking their skills beyond that of any generation before them, and they stand with the prince."

I put my hand upon his shoulder. "Today, while you continue to teach them, my legion and I will prepare a strategy. Tomorrow, we will free our people from their prisons and my father and mother from theirs, as well."

He looked into my eyes. "The warriors carry the same look of bravery that I see in your eyes," he said gravely. "We will proudly follow you into battle." He bowed his head slightly, in respect, then turned and walked toward the forest.

I called my legion to me, asking Mythias to sit with us. "Listen to my strategy," I said. "Search for holes wherever you can find them, so that I may plug them. There can be no mistakes."

Mythias sat facing me while the animals stood beside me. "Let me first ask this question of you. Can your potions control my mind if I am strong enough within my mind to stop the magic?"

A thin smile etched in his face, and in his eyes I saw humor. "I wondered when you would get to the point of asking that question." He studied me for a short time before he continued. "I will tell you this. The mind is the most powerful of all magic, for it is the mind that creates the magic. But if a potion contains certain herbs that, when inhaled or sipped from a cup, causes illusions and weakens the mind—that is not magic. That, my dear boy, is the deed of an evil wizard."

"Tell me of the magic you used to change my appearance."

"It is a wizard's magic, one that I will not take time to explain to you, but I think you already know that only one with your gift can make it work, but know that it is only as powerful as you allow it to be. Had you not desired it in your mind, I could not have changed you."

"Tell me about the wizard's potions."

"Ancitel holds two books that carry very treacherous formulas. The Danes have informed me that the potion he has prepared for you is a mixed brew between two. That in itself causes the potion to become unstable. He tested it on you in the woods. We both know what it did to you.

"Timberlin removed some of its vapors from your nostrils and brought them to me. I found that the potion contains the poison of a certain herb flower that is so powerful, if inhaled deeply and continually, will do more than give a wizard control; it will destroy the mind. Think of his potion that poisoned your city. Was it not more powerful than you could imagine? The potion he has for you comes from these same books."

"But can you prepare an antidote?"

"Ancitel, I am sure, will put a special ingredient in the brew—drops of his own perspiration, which protect the potion from any other wizard's interference. If he has done so, I cannot neutralize its power."

I considered Mythias's words, before moving to my second question. "Tell me about the timepiece."

"Even if Ancitel had the timepiece, it would be of no value to him. Only you can direct it. Timberlin made it that way to protect you, as well as the timepiece, much like Ancitel protects his potion, I suppose. But once the wizard finds he cannot control it, he will use his potion's poison to force you to use it for his gain."

We started to discuss the strategy to free my people and my parents. As we discussed, Ancitel's potion seemed to creep back into the concerns of the animals. "Methinks your strategy has only one large hole," Barok squawked, finally. "You have forgotten yourself in all of this. Your strategy shields everyone but you."

"Barok is right," Mythias said. "You say you will lure Ancitel away from his crystals with the timepiece, so the warriors can enter the city, unseen by him. But you have not considered what will happen if Ancitel uses his entire potion against you—it could destroy your mind with its power—to get the timepiece. Do you not think that he will attempt to take from your memory all that is in it, even that which you are not to speak of while you are here? In the end, do you not think that he will take your life as well?"

I looked at him, stunned at his words. I could only wonder why it should surprise me that he would know what no other was supposed to know. I wanted to ask him, but I dared not speak her name. I knew, nonetheless, that which I held most precious to me, I had not considered.

"You would give your life for your kin," Kevelioc said. "But, in this battle, we must protect your life, for only you can save them."

The Danes remained silent, moving closer to my side. Walkelin nuzzled my neck, telling me he also preferred that I live. Ancitel's potion would play no part in our strategy. Instead, one of my animals would be with me at all times, and Mythias's potion would be my most useful weapon.

When Klogan and his warriors returned in the evening, I sat among them as they ate and listened to their chatter. It was not of war and battles, but of the star formations that had begun to appear above them, of mathematics, and of music. "These are intellects as much as they are warriors," I said to Klogan.

"They are intellectual warriors." He chuckled. "As is your legion. That is the best kind of warrior to be. This chatter is to let their minds rest from that which they must do, making them more effective when the time comes."

"Yet we are an army of twenty-eight against not only an army of hundreds," I reminded him, "but the desires of a most powerful wizard as well."

"Look at the teacher and his students," Barok said in my ear. "Look inside of yourself. Methinks your army is greater than any Yiltor could send against you, or the potions Ancitel could brew. Besides, if Yiltor is your prisoner, I doubt his soldiers—what will be left of them—will continue to fight his battle."

A smile crossed my face, and I was content to simply watch the warriors for a time, remembering the first day I sat with them, thinking they were children—and they were children well beyond childhood.

"If your tummies are full," I prattled as a mother would, when I saw their plates were empty, "I will tell you a story."

They moved close—sitting in front of me, their legs crossed, their faces filled with anticipation. Even Mythias sat down to listen. The Quynaè were already beside me. It seemed they loved a good story as much as the rest of us.

"My story begins a thousand years ago and tells of a people who were the first to learn the skill of the cestrosphendone . . ."

As the warriors listened to the story, they did not move, nor did their eyes leave my face, for the stories were their history, stories they had never heard because their ancestors refused to allow their children to read them. I watched their tender faces closely as they became acquainted with those who stood, a millennium ago, where they were standing now—near a battlefield. I could see their emotions rising in the tender melody that escaped the lips of the Quynaè, adding drama to the telling.

When I reached the part that told of a wise king who instructed a teacher to take twenty-one of his finest students and teach them the art of the cestrosphendone—preparing them for what he hoped they would never have to do—the warriors joined the Quynaè in their melody. Only now the melody became brighter until it reached a triumphant finale—a song of victory—when the story reached its end. There were cheers as well as tears shed when the story ended.

"I think you have a story to tell us now," I said, looking into Klogan's tired face. "What have you done with your day to make you look like an old man?"

His face brightened. "The trees provide us with the greatest of any defense we could imagine." Klogan laughed. "They sway when they should be still—fall when they should be standing tall. Their limbs slap at us without warning. We have learned to ever be watchful of them, to sense their every quiver." He paused and a grin spread across his face. "*Quiver* is a curious word to use in description, but I can think of no other." He stood. "Let us give you a short demonstration of our accuracy and quickness."

Kevelioc purred. The Danes sat on their haunches. Walkelin nudged me to full attention, and Barok buffed me with his wing. "Be alert," he said against my ear, saying nothing more. It seemed the animals already knew what I was about to find out for myself.

I watched as Klogan spoke into Thorri's ear. Thorri nodded and snapped the cord of his cestro, which hung at his side. Immediately, the warriors stood beside him, their cestro on their right shoulders—their slings in their left hands. A soft beat, sounding like that of a drum, surrounded us, and they raised their voices in the song of battle I heard them sing in the cave. As they sang, their slings moved with such quickness that unless one was watching for the movement, it would have been missed.

The song continued to grow louder as did the beat. The warriors removed the cestros from their shoulders and placed the arrows in the pockets. A swoosh was heard and arrows flew. Next, they took two steps. In that time, they had placed a stone in the pocket of the sling, and an arrow in the pocket of the cestro. They took one more step, and with the sling and cestro in motion, they demonstrated their ability to hit both of their targets at one time. Then their voices were quiet, the beat went silent, and they bowed. I had never seen anything so remarkable—so beautiful.

Music flowed once again, from the forest, and the Quynaè danced. At that moment, the unicorn stood among the warriors, as if a symbol of their goodness and strength.

For a time, I could not speak. My heart had taken my voice from me, leaving tears upon my cheek. I felt the excitement of their skill, and the burden as their leader. I could not lose one of them. Mythias's promise was my standard.

When my voice returned, I raised my hand to them. "You have given me the confidence of a king who has a thousand soldiers at his side, but you are greater than even five thousand. Though you wear the simple clothing of youth, your armor is the purity of your soul. Though your weapons seem simple, your skill is greater than any man's. We will stand together—Klogan and his warriors, Etcheon and his legion, the Quynaè and their wizard—and none shall stop us."

"You have spoken well," Mythias said quietly. The warriors waved their hands back and forth and thanked me for the things I had said. "Yet I sense there is a question that troubles your thoughts. I will answer it, so it will not linger. You carry the memory of the one who brought you to her kingdom in your heart. I carry the memory as well. Together we will protect it."

I thanked him, letting what he told me be enough for now. I looked into the sky, filled with the brightness of the moon, and searched for the one constellation that I now called my own. "Yes," I whispered as I found it's light, "all is as it should be."

As I slept I found myself in a dream. I was a child again, playing by the sea. A voice called out my name.

Ancitel, having returned from an audience with King Yiltor, now stood at the window of his tower. The king had gloated of his evening with the merchants, and his subtle comment on wealth that would bring many of them to his allegiance. He laughed at the conversation he had with one of the merchants, which led them to the dungeon so all could see the Purcatians. Except for his suspicion of that merchant, the night seemed to have gone just as Yiltor had planned. He had sent spies to watch the man, yet they brought back nothing, saying he had fallen into a drunken sleep on the grass outside the inn.

The king's purpose in calling Ancitel to his castle was not, however, to discuss the night before but to discuss the future. "Did the wizard have everything in order?" he had asked.

Indeed this wizard has, Ancitel thought to himself. He told Yiltor nothing of what the crystals had seen. The potion was waiting on his shelf, and he no longer needed Yiltor. He only needed the boy.

His laugh echoed in the emptiness of the room as he walked to the shelf and touched the small bottle that held his future, the reward that would take him anywhere he commanded—anywhere in the universe—and would give him power well beyond that which he already possessed. With his precious books, filled with brews of the underworld, and with time travel in the pocket of his robe, there would be no limitation to his wishes. The potion now called the boy to him.

22

The Wizard's Potion

THE MIST WAS THICK. I SHIVERED in the chill of its haze, wrapping my vest tightly around me. My eyes could not see beyond its darkness, but my ears could hear my mother's voice calling out to me, "Where are you, Etcheon?"

I heard my own voice cry, "I cannot see you. I am lost in the mist."

"Follow the sound of my voice, and I will guide you to me." Her voice was soft and gently moved me closer and closer to the sound of it. But, even in the dream, I knew something was not right. I was becoming aware of a scent that was familiar to me. It filled my nostrils, and I could not pull away from it. It entangled me in its vapors, wrapped itself around me, and pulled me ever closer to the sound of the voice that pretended to be my mother's.

The howling of the trees sent tremors through Mythias as they called out to him from the glowing crystals.

"What is it?" he mumbled, trying to shake the heavy sleep from his eyes—knowing something was terribly wrong, yet unable to bring his crystals into focus.

He pulled himself from his bed and stumbled to the table, his body barely responding to the demands of his brain. He could smell something in the air about him—something strange, yet familiar. Suddenly it came to him. It carried the same odor as the vapors Timberlin brought to him—the vapors from Etcheon's nostrils.

He forced himself awake, feeling his chest heave as his lungs screamed for air unpolluted by the vapors. He felt the weakness in his fingers as he reached out for the flask he kept at his bedside. It took his full concentration to pull it to him, remove the cork from its opening, then sip its magic. He needed only enough to make him resist the odor that swept through the cottage, so he could gather his wits about him. The trees were trying to warn him of something dangerous . . . something deadly.

His head cleared immediately as the liquid from the flask entered him. He grabbed the crystals that glowed in bright red. His eyes consumed the brightness of the first one. There he saw Etcheon walking through the forest as if he was asleep. The trees moved violently about, their voices shouting to him, but they could not reach out to touch him—to awaken him. Beyond them, not far in the distance, yet still outside the perimeter of the forest, the moonlight revealed to him something that caused his heart to pound violently against his chest.

Without a thought to his robe, he ran outside. A strange cloud formation he had once seen before was moving closer. Through its density, the moonlight shimmered in a nauseating green. It was Ancitel's cloud of death.

He ran back inside, grabbed his wand and, with an utterance he had not used in many years, swept the fumes from his cottage. Then he pulled an old dusty book from its place on a shelf. It was thin, the pages yellowed and wrinkled, revealing only a few instructions to one spell. But it was this spell that had been used to enchant the forest by another wizard long ago. He needed only three words. He opened the cover to the page where the words were written, and they glowed at his touch.

He could hear the voices of the trees calling to him from the crystal, warning him that the vaporous cloud was now above them. He threw open the door of his cottage and stepped outside. Lifting his arm, he pointed his wand directly at the center of the cloud, and shouted three words: *Expelchous, Demanous, Octorios.*

The vapors of the cloud began to roll into themselves, causing sparks to flame and consume the poison. The cloud grew smaller and smaller, until it finally disappeared.

Mythias lifted his wand once more and moved it slowly in a circle over his head, widening the circle with each rotation. "Protious, Chantotious, Octorios," he chanted until, at last, a effervescent glow spewed from the wand, sweeping through, over, and around the forest, spinning its magic until all inside the forest was free of Ancitel's potion. Then the spell of enchantment fell over it, once again.

"You have invaded my kingdom, Ancitel," he whispered under his breath as he sat, exhausted, beneath a tree within his garden. "You have taken Etcheon from my protection. Now it is my turn."

Barok landed on the limb of the tree. "You have cast a heavy spell, Mythias," he said. "One that will protect this forest for many years to come, but at what cost to yourself? You, like Etcheon, would give your life to protect your people. I bring your flask to you."

"Ancitel has taken Etcheon from us." Mythias sighed.

"That is something I already know," Barok uttered. "The vapors, which put us all into a sound sleep, cast its spell upon him and pulled him away." He dropped the flask into the wizard's hand. "Ancitel worked his magic while the Danes slept peacefully at the side of Etcheon's bed; while the warriors slept peacefully in their beds alongside him; and while I slept peacefully upon the post."

"The Quynaè also slept, along with their wizard." Mythias groaned. Cold anger began to stir within him—anger he could only feel against himself for allowing this to happen. "I have been too arrogant in thinking the first spell cast upon this forest would be all the protection Etcheon would need. I will not make another mistake."

I became aware of everything around me, though I continued to stumble through the forest, unable to stop, as if the dream still held me. The trees were reaching out to grab me, to hold me back, to protect me. But something was pushing them away from me, cutting away at their limbs, causing them pain, and I could not stop it any more than I could stop myself from moving closer to the edge of the forest.

Somehow, Ancitel had found me. The enchantment of the forest could not protect me as Mythias had promised. I was under the spell of the potion.

"Etcheon," I heard Ancitel say. "I need the timepiece. Once I have it, I will free your mother and father from their prisons. I will free all of your people."

In the back of my mind, a memory repeated the words I had heard, once before. *"Know your enemy and do not trust his words, for his mouth is filled with lies. Let your mind be your weapon as well as the mortal weapons that you carry. Let all that is within you, guide you."*

I tried to call out to Mythias, but my voice was stilled. I was about to call out to the animals in my mind when I felt Ancitel prying into my thoughts, tempting me to submit to his wishes, to believe his lies. I heard him laugh and realized he knew I had tried to connect with Mythias.

"I know the forest protects another wizard whose power is much like my own, but he cannot aid you now." He was silent for a time before he spoke again. "You are stronger than I had thought you to be, boy, but you are alone. Soon you will find that I am stronger."

Because my thoughts had been quiet concerning the animals, he did not know that, in truth, I was not alone. I had my legion inside of me. I was greater than he. I was more powerful than he could imagine me to be.

With little effort, I closed my thoughts to him as the owl had taught me, and considered my circumstances; analyzing what information I would need from him before I could device a plan. "Why do you not show yourself to me?" I asked innocently.

"Neither can you show yourself to me. But very soon I will take you from the haze, and then we shall see each other." While he was enjoying his power over me, he also unwittingly told me what I needed to know.

The air became thick with the scent of the potion once again. "I think you need more of that which brings you to me and opens your mind to that which I desire to know."

I willed myself to stop breathing though my lungs craved air. With my head swooning for the lack of it, I pulled Mr. Otherton's handkerchief from my pouch and quickly folded it at an angle. Knowing Ancitel could not yet see my face, I quickly wrapped it over my nose, tying it behind my head. I could wait no longer, I had to breathe now or lose consciousness. "Allow only the scent of fresh air to filter through your threads," I whispered.

The cloth seemed to press itself against my nose, allowing only fresh air to enter, and my head began to clear.

I pulled the mask down from inside the clataè, letting it drop over my face just as the haze around me suddenly disappeared. Nothing around me seemed familiar except for the morning sun, rising to my left, telling me I was facing south—toward the sea and the tower of the wizard.

"Why the mask?" I heard Ancitel mutter. "Why always the mask?" His words told me he could now see me, but not the handkerchief.

Barok flew about the room, eyeing one crystal, then another until he ran out of patience. "Is there nothing there?" he squawked finally.

Mythias shook his head. "Ancitel was clever to add his perspiration to the potion. It shields Etcheon from me, though I know how he found him."

He put all the crystals back in their velvet cradles except one. This one he set in front of him so Klogan could see, pointing his finger to something inside. "Do you see the drops of blood?"

Kevelioc ceased pacing and moved closer to Mythias. "What does it mean?" he growled, glaring at the stains.

"If a wizard uses his own blood to stir his magic, each drop takes with it a portion of his strength, a portion that is never returned to him. The blood you see is Ancitel's. It flowed over the crystal, giving it the power to see well beyond its own capabilities. He took a great risk, for the longer the crystal takes to do as the wizard asks, the greater the loss of the wizard's blood. Nonetheless, it seems to have taken no more than twenty-eight drops before the crystal was able to break through the shield that guards the forest—to find Etcheon. Once that shield was broken, he could send his potion through. Once the potion was inside the forest, it would put everyone under a spell of sleep, but it would pull Etcheon to him."

Klogan looked sharply at Mythias. "Does this mean he knows of the Quynaè, the warriors, and you as well?"

"He knows only of Etcheon and of me, by now," Mythias answered. "No one but another wizard could have disrupted the cloud of poison he sent to destroy the forest."

"What of the warriors?" Kevelioc growled. "Are they able to go to battle?"

"I have removed the potion and its power from the forest. No one will feel the affects of it influence."

"Then let us rouse them," Klogan suggested. "The sun is beginning to rise, and we must change our strategy back to that which we chose not to use. We will be ready to leave as soon as Timberlin is ready to transport us to the walls of the city. We will attack while Ancitel is preoccupied."

When Klogan stood before his warriors he told them of the cloud, and Ancitel's potion that had taken Etcheon from them. "The strategy has now changed," he explained. "It will be as Etcheon first planned."

Thorri stepped forward. "Etcheon will be there when he is needed," he said confidently. "We will prepare to leave."

Klogan started to follow, then hesitated, and turned back to Mythias, noting the change in the wizard's appearance. The spells had taken much of his strength. He would need Etcheon. "What of the young prince?" he asked, knowing the wizard would understand the meaning of his question.

Mythias shook his head. "Only he can help himself now. His power is fully awake in him even as he is being pulled into Ancitel's spell. He will know what to do; we need not worry for his safety."

Klogan nodded that he understood and went to command his warriors. When the time came for them to leave, Mythias stood before them. His eyes were lined with fatigue, yet they sparkled with life as he wished the warriors well. His movements were slow but deliberate, as he presented them with shields made from the bark of the trees that lived in the enchanted forest. "These have the protection of those made of steel, but can be rolled and hidden beneath your clothing when they are not needed," he explained as he demonstrated their agility.

Klogan thanked him, unable to dismiss the weariness in Mythias's eyes. "Are you well enough?"

"Do not worry about me," Mythias assured him. "My strength will return in time. It is Etcheon that takes my thoughts. Yet I dare not fret too much for fear he will scold me when he returns." He smiled and Klogan could not help but smile in agreement.

Together, they watched Timberlin come toward them. Like his son, he was a handsome man—today, looking even younger. His hair was hidden beneath a clataè that sat low over his eyes, shielding the excitement that glistened in them. His tunic, the color of the forest, fit him well and gave him the appearance of one in command. On his belt hung what appeared to be a gold watch.

"It is time," they heard him say to the warriors, and Klogan nodded to Thorri.

The young warrior climbed upon Walkelin's back. The sound of the horse's hooves echoed as horse and rider disappeared.

"I think we will take the easy way," Timberlin said to Mythias, giving him a mischievous wink, as he motioned the warriors to gather around him. Then he opened the watch, touched a small dial, and they too disappeared.

"Show me the timepiece, Etcheon," Ancitel demanded, as if he was talking to a child.

I wondered if he could simply take the timepiece once it was visible to him, or was it possible that he could not take it from me at all? Would I have to give it to him in order for him to possess it?

"Why do you wish to see a timepiece?" I slurred as if the potion had hold of me. "Do you not have one of your own?"

"Do not pretend that you are innocent, boy," he hissed, and I could see his face. His eyes were filled with fire. His long black hair danced about his pale face as he glared into his crystal, feeling very much the conqueror. Did he know that I could see him, I wondered? With that thought another question came to my mind, and I asked myself, *How it was possible that I can see him?*

"Remove the mask," he commanded.

The mask? Had the wizard unwittingly answered my question? Was it the mask that gave me the power to see him? Was that what Tararini meant when she said, "There will be times when its protection will be your power"?

I could feel Caspar-Arius inside of me now, and my mind debated with itself. Why does he not simply wave his wand and remove it himself? Is it because he knows there is something about the mask that restrains him? Does he fear it or does he simply wish to play games? Yet, if it is a game he plays, does he not waste time that is quickly fleeting from him?

I concluded that he did not have the power to remove the mask. Perhaps he even feared it. "I cannot," I said without emotion. "It is enchanted."

He roared with laughter. "And you expect me to believe that?"

I waited until his laughter ceased. "Believe what you will."

There was silence, and I could see his face above the flare of his robes as he turned to the crystal again, the fire in his eyes rekindled. "You have overcome the potion," was all he said. Suddenly a heavy mist swept over me, the scent of the potion attempting to penetrate the threads of the handkerchief. It could not, and the mist disappeared.

Ancitel seemed stunned. "Perhaps you are a wizard," he growled, his face twisted in anger. I thought I could see a touch of fear there. "You have overcome the most powerful potion I could brew for you." He forced his voice to appear menacing, though dread seemed to steal through. "I should wonder if you are the wizard of the forest who placed a curse upon my cloud." There was a pause, and I could see the thoughtful look upon his face as he wrapped strands of black hair around his jeweled finger. "No, I think not, for you were under my power at the time. There is yet another."

A menacing smile appeared, and his fingers came to his chin, tapping it as if the rhythm gave him deeper deliberation. "I think I shall let you see me as I see you. Then we can talk as if we were equals. But you must remove the mask to be fair to me."

I wondered if I should tell him that I could see him already. No, I would keep it a secret, for now. "I cannot remove the mask. It is enchanted, just as I said."

His wand appeared. "Shall I remove it for you?"

"If you can." I knew as well as he did that if he could have removed it with a twitch of his wand, he would have done it already. I could sense a weakness in him as I looked into his eyes, and I became bolder.

He walked away from the crystal, and I lost sight of him for a short time. When he returned, his eyes were dark and sinister as was his smile. "You shall see what I can do."

Suddenly I found myself in a dark labyrinth. As the night vision of the owl came to me, I could see thickets all around me, large prickly thorns protruding from their creeping limbs and slithering stems. Large rocks, spidery trees, and a black shadowy hollow loomed where the thicket ended. I pulled my sling and my cestro from my pouch, knowing that within a short time I would need them.

"I see you have come prepared," he mocked. "But first, let me show you something." With a twitch of his wand, two prisms appeared deep inside the hollow. "Are they not beautiful?" He paused and looked into the crystal, a dramatic pout etched in his face. "Oh, I do wish you would remove that silly mask. I see no reason for it, except that it hides your eyes from me, and I cannot tell if you consider my masterpiece to be as inventive and captivating as I do."

He pulled his face away and sighed. "But then that is the purpose of the mask, is it not? You fear if I see into your eyes, I will know you for what you are. Oh, well, we will discuss that another time. Let us continue with what is at hand. I think you know what is inside the prisms, so I will tell you what you do not know. I have created a game for you. The thickets will come alive, opening and closing many paths for you. I wonder: will you make it through the maze and find the one that will lead you to the hollow, and through it to your mother and father who lie inside their prisms? The sport of the game will be for you to reach the prisms before I destroy them."

The face of the wizard disappeared, and the air became silent and still. The labyrinth, and whatever lie in wait, was as still as the air. Minutes passed and nothing moved. Neither did I. I sensed the wizard had left me to think about the game before he offered me an alternative. I was not disappointed when he spoke again, for his words were as I knew they would be.

"Or I can offer you another choice." His voice was cunning and whispered when he spoke. "You could simply use the timepiece to take you to your father and mother, without ever having to play the game. There, I will free those you love in exchange for the timepiece. You will be with your people, and I will have faded away through a portal."

There was silence while he waited for my reply. I did not reply, only readied my weapons.

I heard him sigh, and his face reappeared. "I see you have decided. Then let us make this game even more . . . should I say exciting? Or would *deadly* be a better word?" His lips curled around the word as he spoke it. Then a thoughtful frown crossed his face and his jeweled fingers caressed his chin. His eyelids shadowed the scheme that glistened in his eyes. Yet, even before he could tell me, I knew what he had planned. I felt a chill run down my spine, and the taste of fear touched my tongue.

Inside the castle, Yiltor paced back and forth in front of the window that gave him a view of the road beyond the gates of the city. Each time he passed it, he paused, glancing quickly at the road, hoping to see the boy. Each time, there was only an empty road.

He would be patient, he decided. After all, he had the advantage. Yet he could not help feeling just a little vulnerable. After all, it was he who was pacing the floor.

The sun was almost at its highest peak. The first of the Purcatians to be executed stood beside the steps to the castle, for all his citizens to see. Their hands were bound, their appearance filthy. Yet, he had to admit, in all they had endured, they were still an enchanting race. He would be glad to be rid of them.

Once again, he peered out the window as he passed it, and still no sign of Etcheon the Younger. He was growing tired of the game. He crossed the room and threw himself upon some pillows on the floor, his face posed in a spoiled, childish pout. He would not allow this simple boy to give him grief. Was he not the King? And where was Ancitel? Should he not be here with his crystal that would show them where the Purcatian was hiding?

If the boy was not standing beneath the steps of his castle soon, he would simply stand at his window, and raise his arm as the signal. Then, he would let it drop and listen to the cries as the women and children felt the pain of death.

"Horse approaching," called one of the guards from atop the wall of the city.

A conquering smile slowly spread across Yiltor's face. He casually arose from his pillows and walked to the window. Pretending disinterest, he glanced out just long enough to see a lone rider coming through the gate on a majestic horse. He was somewhat enchanted by the horse, yet satisfied to see the boy approach.

Would Klogan and his warriors soon be at the gate of Yiltor's city, I wondered? Would they execute our first plan of attack? Not knowing the answer, my strategy had to be as if they were ready to do just that. Though I feared what lie ahead of me, I knew that it would take the wizard's attention away from his duty to the king and, in that thought alone, I felt as if I had already won the game.

"Tell me, Ancitel," I called out to him, forcing him to keep his eyes on one crystal only. "Does the king wonder why you are in your tower instead of at the castle with your crystals in your hands, waiting for me to surrender?"

"I wonder why you ask?" He scowled. Then he turned away, giving me the opportunity to reach into my pouch and retrieve Mythias's potion. I hid the miniature bottle inside my vest.

I heard him laugh, but when he turned back to the crystal, there was no humor in his face. At first I thought he had somehow seen me do what I had done; instead, he had seen a rider on the back of a majestic horse, moving toward Yiltor's castle.

"Who rides in your place?" he demanded to know.

Once again Ancitel had told me what I needed to know. "Perhaps it is Etcheon himself," I replied.

The wizard smiled, leaning close to the crystal, once again. "No, I think not. It is a Purcatian, but it is not Etcheon. Etcheon stands before me. His mask does not cover his presence, only his face." He paused and studied me for a time, his eyes revealing his desire to be finished with me. He was losing patience.

The cold shadows of the thicket closed in around me. I could hear the snarling echoes from the blackness of the hollow. I had to wonder if they were real or some kind a magic trick to confuse and frighten me. The scent that touched my nostrils, nonetheless, was real. It was faint, at first, then it became more pungent. At least one creature, other than myself, was real and inside this maze.

I could hear Kevelioc inside my head, and I became as a panther, pressing myself to the level of the ground, and allowed the earth to send its signals through my hands. My ears were sensitive to sounds, my eyes seeing all that moved and sensed all that did not. In an instant, I became aware that the danger was not ahead of me, but behind me. "There is a changeling, an akaina tall, behind you," I heard Kevelioc's growl, whispering in my ear. I crouched and turned swiftly, slipping the sling and the cestro into my pouch and taking the dagger from its sheath. I could see the movement of the vines and briers, exactly where I knew the changeling to be.

It did not want my life, but only take me to its master. Whether it be in an conscious state or near death, I knew it would not matter. It entertained the wizard, and he needed me only to be alive enough to willingly hand the timepiece to him. Stones or arrows would not stop this creature from its quest. But slitting its throat deep and wide with my dagger would leave little life within it.

Ancitel had, apparently, cast a pleasant aroma spell over the creature because its scent was hardly the disgusting stench of the last time I encountered the likes of it. But the animal scent was still there, and it was becoming stronger. Then I saw it, in the corner of my eye, coming towards me. It appeared as a wolf, only much larger; thick yellow saliva dripped from long, sharp fangs. Its eyes were large, fearsome, and liquid.

It approached as any agile, four-legged creature would approach its prey. I watched it as it watched me, ready to spring.

I willed myself to become still, following its eyes with my own. As I did so, I found that I could read its eyes and hear its thoughts. It was playing with me, like a cat plays with a mouse before it strikes. It circled around me, teasing me and snatching at me with its claws. I circled with it.

Its eyes narrowed and its muscles rippled. A low growl escaped its throat, and it pounced. I sprung to the left, receiving only a gash in my leg as its huge claw reached out for me.

"Excellent move," I heard Ancitel cry out with glee. "I am pleased you are making a sporting game of it."

Again the creature began to circle me, and I listened to its thoughts. It had not expected so much quickness from me and was considering its next move. Twice more it struck and received a gash in its side from my dagger, and I received more wounds from its claws.

"It is time to end this," Ancitel's voice rang out, and the scent of the potion entered my nostrils, and my senses dulled. I could no longer focus on the creature, nor his thoughts. It was all I could do to make my hand grip the dagger. "Take the potion from the air I breathe," I whispered to the handkerchief, barely able to form the words with my mouth. But even as my mind began to clear, the creature was upon me, his claws tearing at my flesh, his teeth bearing down upon me, the fangs already cutting my arms and legs. The pain was more than I thought I could bear, and I felt my life slipping from me.

"That is enough," Ancitel called to the creature. "I want him alive enough to hand me the timepiece. Bring him to me."

The creature lifted its paws from me and backed away, the thrill of victory glowing in it eyes.

It reached down to drag my body to the tower, and though the pain in my body was excruciating, I willed myself to stand—to lift my dagger and throw myself onto the unexpected beast. With one arm, I grabbed its head and pulled it back. With my other arm, I plunged the dagger deep into its neck, slicing its throat.

The creature howled and clawed at me furiously, trying to get me off its back. A wisp of air escaped from its lungs, then it lay dead beneath me. I rolled from it and fell to the ground, barely able to breathe, myself. My strength was spent. I just lay there with blood dripping from my wounds, deep and shallow, and waited to hear the voice of the wizard.

"Well, young prince, you surprise me," he said at last, the humor gone from his voice. "And as you have defeated your foe, I will allow you to get to the hollow without more interference."

I did not acknowledge him. I simply pulled myself up to a standing position as best I could and, with great difficulty, shut my mind against the sound of his voice, and forced myself into a deep meditative state to get rid the pain. If what Verch claimed was true, I could control the bleeding that was beginning to soak my torn and riddled clothing.

". . . and while the sand is falling, you stand there . . ." I heard the wizard's voice cackle. Then he was gratefully silent, his eyes glaring at me through his crystal. "What is this I have before me? One with the power to . . ." Once again, he stopped speaking, and his face disappeared, only to reappear a few moments later. "I think I see a wizard in my grasp. I had not expected this." His eyebrows raised and his eyes laughed at me. "Is it possible that you were sent through the portal to the home of the Ancient?"

How would he know of the Ancient? I thought to myself, surprised at his words.

His voice disrupted my thoughts, and I prayed that he had not invaded them. "I will hold you back no longer." The labyrinth disappeared before me and all I could see was the hollow, the prisms glowing inside. And all I felt was the pain of numbness, knowing I had let this evil wizard outwit me in the end.

Or was it the end, I began to wonder? Did he want to imprison me because he feared what he now suspected? Had he begun to sense my power?

A sudden surge of pain rippled down the left side of my face. I touched the wound with my fingers. It was not deep, but ran from just beneath my eye to the tip of my chin. A drop of my blood fell upon the blade of my dagger, mingling with the hair of the beast that was on the edge of the blade. When they became one, flames ignited, and lapped at the hair until there was none left. When the proof of the beast was gone from the blade, the body of the beast disappeared as well.

"As I thought. The blood of this boy runs so pure that it devours the blood of a beast with its flame, and I wonder . . ."

I was tired of hearing Ancitel's voice. Tired of his mocking sneers. Tired of his face in the crystal. Still I could not stop myself from walking toward the hollow.

"Is the hollow where you really want to go?" I heard the voice of Caspar-Arius whisper. I touched my face and found no wound. Could it be that the beast was only a test, to find the proof of wizard's blood? Had I allowed myself to be a pawn in Ancitel's magical game? Was he simply waiting until I got to the hollow before showing me his real power, or did he now believe me to be a wizard, also—afraid of my power?

He called it a hollow. Perhaps it was exactly that—empty, without life. If I entered, would I ever emerge? Or would my life be swept into nothing-ness—everything inside of me void of life? It would be simple to get the timepiece from me then. I would have no strength to fight him. Whatever he asked for, I would give to him, freely. When he had the timepiece in his hand, would he then leave me forever trapped inside the lifelessness of the hollow, or was the hollow itself, and all around me, simply an illusion?

I tried to get into his thoughts, but it was useless. I was weak from loss of blood, and barely able to keep my thoughts locked against him.

It was then that I decided I would not go into the hollow. But to make him think I believed him, I continued toward it while pulling the small bottle from my vest. Holding it tightly in my hand, I forced the lid from it. But before I could place two drops of the potion on my tongue, the shadows of the hollow reached out and grabbed me, pulling me into its darkness.

"I could not take a chance that you would change your mind," I heard the wizard cackle, his voice surrounding me, filling my mind with his words. "The hollow takes you from my sight, but not my power. There I shall leave you for a time and allow the darkness to take from you all that makes you live, except for the beating of your heart. Then I shall come to you, and we will talk of the timepiece."

His words became silent as the darkness began to invade my mind, and the cold vapors of nothingness pierced my body, drawing me deep into its belly. It was as if I was suspended in an airless tomb—no gravity to pull or push me. Time did not exist, and I felt soothed—without responsibility. How long the hollow held me, I did not know nor did I care. I closed my eyes and let nothing exist.

"It is time to give me the timepiece," I heard the wizard say, and my mind welcomed his words, though my soul did not—nor did my heart. Inside of me, a battle raged between the conscious and unconscious, between the spirit and the mortal. Yet, in all the conflict, I found myself reaching for the timepiece, unable to stop myself. I could see his hand reaching out to take it when, from somewhere within me, I heard the screeching of the owl. "There is no hollow. It exists merely in your mind."

"Verch," I cried out, but the nothingness silenced the words as they left my lips. Yet the words had come from my soul and not even the nothingness could silence my soul. I gazed at the timepiece in the palm of my hand, the wizard's fingers reaching to wrap themselves around it, and I knew I had to force my mind awake—my body to come alive. When at last I could feel the pounding of my heart and my brain begin to function, I willed my hand to close itself around the timepiece just as Ancitel's fingers touched its mantle.

"You fool!" he shouted. "Give me the timepiece, or I will see that you remain in this nothingness until you become nothing yourself. I will leave your father and mother imprisoned within the crystals, neither alive or dead, forever. You will know that your kin died because you failed to free them. The game will be finished; these are the only memories I will leave with you. You will have nothing else, and I will have the timepiece in the end."

I closed my ears to his words and forced my brain to believe the hollow did not exist. Suddenly, I began to feel the agony of awakening from a nightmare. The depth and darkness of the hollow began to fade away. I could see the sea in the distance, the forest behind me, and the wizard's tower with a figure in a window. His face was aflame with anger and frustration. His wand was in his hand, ready to weave a spell, and his voice pierced my ears with the ranting of the incantation.

I had no time to think, only to react. The small bottle was still in my hand. I quickly touched it to my tongue, picturing a sparrow in my mind.

I began to tremble violently, something that had not occurred before in a transformation. Ancitel's spell had begun to work, and I had to take the image of the sparrow deeper into my conscious.

I began to whisper the words *sparious, ignamious, pocaious,* over and over until the whisperings became loud in my ears—until the trembling became even more violent and, suddenly, I flew as a sparrow into the sky and onto the windowsill of Ancitel's tower.

Not seeing me, as his eyes were focused on the wand, Ancitel believed his spell had thrown me back into his pretended hollow. He threw his head back and laughed a most wicked laugh. Lifting his robe, he twirled it as he danced. His long black hair, entangled in small crystals, fell about his face and gave him the look of one who had lost his sanity.

When his dance ended, he became somber and his eyes filled with bitterness. "You are a foolish boy to love," he hissed, acid biting into his words as he spoke. "For love becomes an enemy when it makes you think with your heart." He glanced up at me, but seeing a sparrow on the windowsill, paid no more attention. He continued on with his words for a boy, who was no longer his prisoner. "I suppose, in a way, I envy you." He sighed. "At least you had something to love."

Suddenly, he stopped speaking and turned to the crystals, staring deeply into the one ablaze with light. Forgetting the memories that love had once touched him, he began to stroke the crystal as if it were a kitten and to speak to it as if it had life. "The Purcatian who pretends to be the boy has entered the city, it seems. But what else do you show me?"

His eyes narrowed. "There are more, and though they are Purcatians, they appear more like peasants, scattering themselves about." He backed away from the crystal, puckering his face in a thoughtful frown. "What do they hide beneath their peasant frocks?" He tapped his fingers against his chin, letting the rhythm ignite a sinister thought. "Perhaps I should tell King Yiltor that an army of peasant children, who wear their battle robes hidden beneath their rags, wait to fight against his army."

He removed his robe and replaced it with one more fitting when bowing before a king. "I will return, Etcheon, who floats about in the darkness of my hollow. And when I do, I think you will be pleased to give me the timepiece." Then he walked from the room.

I had outwitted the wizard—at least for now. Without another thought to my narrow escape, I fluttered my sparrow wings and set my course for the kingdom of Yiltor.

23

Etcheon's Strategy

THE BEAUTIFUL GARDENS, TALL slender trees, and magnificently carved statues surrounding the outer walls of Yiltor's kingdom told all who passed by that it was a kingdom of wealth. Soldiers standing guard atop the wall, wearing the finest tooled armor, reminded all who thought to do battle that the kingdom was well protected.

Klogan knew that today this show of wealth would be an advantage to his warriors, giving them hiding places and clear targets.

When the attention of all who stood guard was upon the horse and rider, the cry of the morning bird was heard, and those who guarded the side gate of the city fell silently to the ground. Ten warriors entered the city, dressed as peasants—their hair bound in wraps, their weapons hid among ragged clothing. Ten remained outside its walls.

Once inside, Klogan directed them to mingle among the people. "But stay close together," he instructed. "When I give the signal, you will return to this spot."

The warriors nodded that they understood, but they had not prepared themselves for what they saw as they moved along the crowded street.

The eyes of the people were focused upon women and children, standing in chains, on the steps of the castle—their faces and hair darkened with the soot and grim of a dungeon, their clothing torn and filthy.

Brettina grabbed Raven's arm, her face wet with tears. "I cannot pull my eyes away from them," she whispered.

"The sight of this will only cause us to fight with greater purpose," he responded, pointing to her tears. "Best wipe them away."

The warriors did not have long to wait before the chirping of a bird brought them back to the gate they had entered. Their eyes revealed to Klogan that they had seen what he wished them to see. He quickly gave them their instructions and sent them to their hiding places just as the guard at the tower gave the order to open the gates.

Thorri lowered the mask of the clataè over his face. "Go forward," he commanded Walkelin. "Make your steps slow and deliberate. Let yourself prance about and your nostrils flare. We shall entertain the king and his soldiers, who watch us from the walls of the city while the warriors find their hiding places."

His heart began to pound with excitement as he drew closer to the gates. The air about him was still. The voices of the soldiers, who stood at their posts upon the wall, were silent. Yet he could feel the coldness of their eyes upon him. He was aware of the eagle, soaring above the city. It was the signal that all was in place. Even then, he did not quicken his pace. Wherever Etcheon was, he would need time. Thorri was sure of that. He would give him as much time as he could.

As he drew closer to the gate, the blaring of a trumpet warned of his arrival, and the gates opened before him.

The streets were filled with peasants and wealthy alike, waiting to see Etcheon the Younger, the boy who had killed fifty-seven of the king's soldiers. When they saw the size of his horse, they stepped back. When they saw the mask that shielded his face, they called out for him to remove it, for they wanted to see his face.

He did not acknowledge those around him but simply continued on until he was directly in front of the prisoners. A guard stepped forward and raised his hand.

"Stop where you are," he bellowed, "and remain on your horse until the king, himself, commands you to dismount."

Thorri nodded slightly and touched Walkelin's neck. The horse snorted and raised his front hooves just enough to send the guard stumbling backward.

When the guard had his feet once again beneath him, he pulled his sword, aiming its point directly at Walkelin. "Keep your horse still, or I'll run my sword through his heart," he growled in his anger. But the deed had been done, and the people seemed to have enjoyed the exhibition.

The sun began to bring with it the shadows of the afternoon. The sword that guarded the horse and his rider changed hands three times while the horse and rider remained as a statue—silent and still.

No one knew of the soldiers who lay dead outside the walls of the city, for all eyes were on the boy wearing a mask and riding a magnificent horse.

"Barok!" I cried out in my mind as I flew over the city.

"Etcheon?" I heard his eagle cry shrill and eager. "Where are you, lad?"

"I am the sparrow above Yiltor's castle."

Soon Barok was swooping over me. Clutching me in his talons, he flew away from the castle.

"Where are we going?" I called to him.

He did not answer but continued in his flight until we were near the enchanted forest. There he dropped me gently on the ground, beneath a tree. "I cannot see Etcheon in you, bird, so I ask that you turn yourself back," he said. "I need to know you are indeed who you say you are, before we talk."

When I was myself again, I could see relief mixed with fury in the large pupils of his eyes. "You are covered in blood. It seems, from the wounds covering your body, that it is your own blood. Your clothes are in threads. Your face is as pale as the clouds above us. Tell me what happened."

"First, I must know where the prisms are that hold my parents."

"They are on display on the steps of Yiltor's castle, for all to see in celebration of this day."

The relief I felt made me light-headed, and I slid to the ground against the trunk of the tree that held me.

"Are you well enough?" Barok asked, fluttering about me like a mother hen.

"There is something I must tell you before I answer that one." I brushed the tears away with the back of my hands. "Ancitel knows of the Ancient. Does he know because, somehow, I unwittingly let him reach into my memory?"

"He did not get his information from you," Barok assured me, wrapping a wing around my shoulder. "He was introduced to the Ancient as a small child. The Ancient was to be his teacher. But Ancitel mocked him, making light of that which was good. He was a selfish boy, who was told he was a wizard long before he should have known. His father was a selfish wizard, so was his mother, but they were not evil as their son. It was his black heart that the Ancient could see, and he found no goodness in him. When his father discovered the truth, he decided to cast a spell upon Ancitel that would turn him into a statue. That way, he would always have his son near, but he could not become an embarrassment to him. Only when Ancitel found out, he disappeared and was never heard of again. But his name was not Ancitel when he was young. It was Telican. You can see he simply rearranged the letters.With the help of those just like him, he traveled to the underworld to study the dark arts. His soul became as dark as his heart."

"Why was I not told this?"

"I only found out myself," Barok admitted, "when Mythias searched the crystals for his name." He peered into my face, and I could see the concern on his. "You must rest, lad. We will wrap those wounds with angel fleece so they can heal quickly. There is much to do."

"You must take a message to Klogan for me," I insisted. "Ancitel's crystal was not fooled by the costumes of peasants. It revealed the warriors to the wizard. Now he is on his way to warn Yiltor."

The eagle moved to a limb, low on the tree. "Yiltor has commanded that the son of King Etcheon remain on his mount and stand as sentinel next to the prisms of the king and queen until he sends for him. For over an hour, Thorri has sat silently on Walkelin's back at the steps of the castle, as he was told to do. Of course, he hopes to be left there until you arrive. He has great faith in you, lad, as do all the warriors. But we must make you well before you try to save others."

Before more could be said, I heard Mythias calling my name. "I see you have outwitted the old wizard," he said as he came near, wearing a smile upon his face and a look of apprehension in his eyes at the sight of me. "You have won the battle, but you bear many scars. I will take you to my cottage and wrap you in angel fleece. There is not much time."

"Can you not simply touch me with your wand and heal the wounds?" I asked, impatient to be on my way."

"I suppose so, though it will be more painful."

"Then do so, and I will try not to cry out in pain," I insisted, knowing more pain than he could inflict.

"Then I shall fly to the castle to warn Klogan," Barok said, and left us.

"And as I heal you," Mythias insisted, removing his wand from his sleeve, "I want to hear how Ancitel whimpered as a child when he could not imprison you."

"He thinks he has me in his hollowed prison still," I gloated, wincing in pain as the wand touched a small wound. I told him the things I had told Barok and what Barok had told me about Ancitel. The second touch of the wand brought greater pain than I thought it would, but a deep wound began to close itself until only a scar remained.

"I am afraid you will carry that scar for the rest of your days," Mythias apologized. "The wand can only do so much."

As he continued to inflict his healing pain, Mythias talked. "Thorri sits on Walkelin's back while Yiltor sits inside his room. He sends more and more Purcatians to join those on the steps of his castle for his own amusement. But what he does not know is that Timberlin has hidden himself among them and carries with him his timepiece. When the time comes, he will bring all who stands on the steps to the forest."

"Your forest and your people have been more than kind to us. Your father watches over my people. You, great wizard, have watched over me as if you were my father. You have been my mentor and my friend. How do I thank you when there is no way I can repay you?"

"Oh, but there is a way," Mythias said, placing his hand against my forehead. "Do not be afraid of who you are."

I stood, the pain gone from me—the wounds healed. "I am no longer afraid of what I am. Ancitel saw to that." I grinned and put on clean clothing.

"I think I believe you. Now tell me your next move."

I explained to him the only plan that seemed to come to me.

"It is a good plan," he said. "I can see Barok returning now. Take him and go quickly. I will make things ready for you. Then I will deal with Ancitel. He has stirred my anger to depths I did not know I had, and my soul is darkened because of it. Until I avenge myself, it will remain so; therefore, I must either defeat him or I will become like him." With those words, he was gone.

Knowing Mythias's heart, I no longer concerned myself with the thoughts of Ancitel. I placed two drops of the potion on my tongue and became a large rat.

"Ugh!" Barok said when he arrived. "Methinks you are an ugly thing, but I will carry you anyway." With that he snatched me in his talons and lifted me into the air. Soon the castle became visible beneath us, and I could see Thorri astride Walkelin. Beside him, the prisms glittered in a circle of light, giving them a most incredible appearance.

People were crowding the street. Some were walking by Thorri, the prisms, and the captives to get a closer look, while others stood by, waiting for Yiltor to appear. All about them, soldiers stood at attention.

Barok landed behind the castle, leaving me on the ground to find my way inside. To my surprise, I found that a rat's access into the royal court was effortless. I only prayed that I would not meet any real rats in my travels.

As I scurried past the kitchen, I could see the king's servants eating their midday meal. Six rats waited patiently near the door of the kitchen for the tidbits that would be theirs when the meal was over. They paid no attention to me. I simply scampered through the hallways and down the stairs finding that I could slip through holes much smaller than my size, with a little effort.

When I came to the door that would be opened by the guard, I removed the bottle, which had shrunk in size as well, from the fur that covered me. I was anxious to return to human form.

I placed two drops of potion on my tongue while, in my mind, I envisioned Yiltor. When I felt his appearance, I could not help but think that in becoming him I had become only a larger rat.

I tapped on the door as Yiltor had done that night I dined with him, and the door opened. The same ugly little guard peered up at me.

"I wish to have all the Purcatian men brought to me," I said, using the same voice Yiltor had used.

He eyed me with curiosity for a time, and I wondered if I had failed in becoming the king in every respect. "Er ye wantin' all hunert of em, an er ye wantin' 'em to be washed up?" he asked finally in a raspy little voice.

"Just bring them to me," I said with as much impatience as I thought Yiltor would show.

"Which room do I take 'em?" he asked again.

"With a hundred unkempt men, which room would you advise?"

"Aye." He nodded. "I'll unlock it and open the windows."

To my relief, he led the way to a room—dingy and damp—where three dusty windows, high above us, allowed just enough light to see its putrid state. A rope hung from each window. These he used to open them and then left me to consider an escape while he went deeper into the dungeon.

I called to Barok in my thoughts, and he appeared through one of the windows.

"I do not know how much time we have before Yiltor appears on the steps of his castle," he warned me. "The citizens have begun to grow restless, but Thorri has not moved from the softness of Walkelin's back."

"Then I pray the guard brings the men quickly." I sighed, looking at the windows high above me. "I fear our escape will take some time. Tell me what lies beyond these walls."

"Only briary and bristle," he said. "Beyond a narrow path that works its way around them, there is a small woodland to hide the men and a stream where they can bathe. Mythias instructed Mirlanda and the Quynaè to prepare food and clothing, which are being carried by the Danes and Kevelioc. They will be waiting for the men when they get to the woodland." He hesitated. "I must say that I have seen miracles worked this day in all that the Quynaè have done for us."

"Then let us pray that the miracles continue," I said softly, "and all goes as we have planned." He agreed, and we waited for the guard to bring his prisoners. It seemed we had waited a long time already, and I began to wonder if the guard had seen through my disguise and that soon Yiltor would be walking through that door. I was about to reconsider my situation when I heard chains scratching against the solid floors.

"Fly out into the hall of the prison," I whispered to Barok, "and find the key that will release the chains."

I could hear the guard shouting, "Git on, smelly varmits. Yer stench is makin' me tummy swoon."

A small bird disappeared through the doorway as the men were ushered into the room. I was not prepared for what I saw. Their hair was filled with webs and nits. Their bodies were darkened with filth and left unprotected from the cold, for their clothing had been taken from them except for a loincloth. They squinted in the shadowed light of the room and shielded their eyes with chained hands. Their ankles were swollen from the shackles that bound them together.

I could hardly bear to look at them without my heart aching. I wanted to kill the ugly little man, who continued to belittle my people by striking them with his club and calling them foul names. But I had to pretend to enjoy and encourage his offensiveness, knowing it would mean nothing when the day was done.

When all the men were inside the room, and Barok was back inside the room, a key in his beak, I commanded the guard to leave us. He nodded and held his nose as he passed the prisoners, glad to shut the door against them.

There they stood, one hundred men, the tightness of their chains, and the chillness of the air causing them to huddle together. They stared at me with eyes that showed nothing but the dullness of their senses.

"Who is your leader?" I asked, trying to ignore their dreadful appearance.

They did not respond.

I removed the bottle and placed one drop of potion on my tongue. Their eyes widened as they watched the transformation, and I asked again who led them, as they had no king.

I heard the sound of chains softly clanging against each other as an older man, standing close by, raised his hand. "I do. I am Nepron," he whispered, his voice raspy from lack of water. "But who are you who can change from Yiltor to a man wearing the clothing of our kin?"

"I am Etcheon the Younger," I said, speaking as softly as he had, not knowing if the little guard was listening behind the door.

As my words were whispered from one to another, tears began to fall from their faces, and I watched as their eyes became alive. Yet they remained cautious.

"Etcheon the Younger was taken away only a short time ago, not years," Nepron responded. "How can you be that babe?"

"I was taken away to another time," I explained.

"Then what we have been told is true." He bowed and commanded the others to do the same.

Barok flew to me and dropped the key into my hand. "Do not bow to me, only listen to what I say." I showed him the key, then raised it for all to see and put my finger to my lips.

They nodded that they understood.

"I know your bodies are weak from all that has been placed upon you," I said to Nepron as I unlocked his chains, "but I will ask that you think of your families and let that be your strength to do what I will ask of you."

Although his sores caused by the chains were raw and bleeding, he raised his head and broadened his shoulders; his steady eyes hid the pain. "You need only tell us what we are to do, and it will be done."

Impressed with his courage, I continued. "Climb up the ropes and escape through the windows. Once you are outside, the eagle will lead you into the woodland. There will be a stream where you can bathe. There will be clean clothing for you to wear and food for you to eat. When everyone is together, I will tell you what you must do next."

Nepron took the key from me and continued to unlock the chains, while all that I had told him was whispered from one to another until all knew what they must do.

As quickly as the chains were removed, the men were climbing the ropes, each man assisting the other, until all that was left as a reminder of their presence were the bloody chains. I felt the emotion of deep anger as I looked about me, and I wanted to shout my vengeance.

"They are all safe in the woodland," Barok's voice broke through the silence. "Put away your thoughts, lad."

I looked up at him. He tilted his head, and I nodded to him. I reached my hand out to open the door. A chill ran down my spine when I saw my own hand before me. I had not yet turned myself back into Yiltor. Quickly, I placed two drops of the potion on my tongue. Feeling the transformation come over me, I remembered the words Mythias spoke to me the day he handed the small bottle to me. *It cannot change you unless you desire . . .* Unless I desire. Could only a wizard's desire bring power to the potion? I opened the door, closing it behind me. "I shall leave them where they are, for now," I said to the guard. "Lock the door."

"Aye," he uttered, taking the key from his pocket. When that was done, he asked if he should check on the prisoners from time to time. I assured him that they were not going anywhere with chains binding them so close together. He grinned a nearly toothless grin, grunted his approval, and unlocked the door to the hallway so that I might leave.

As soon as I heard the click of the lock, I hurried to the door to which I had no key. There I stopped, turned myself back into a rat, and hurried through the halls and corridors.

I was almost to the door that would take me outside the castle when I saw a rat, almost twice my size, glaring at me from less than a cubit away. Its long tail curled high above its back and its beady eyes seemed to have no need to blink. Its mouth opened to reveal a full set of sharp teeth, then relaxed into what seemed to be a grin, though I could not tell if it was smiling or preparing to take a bite out of me. It moved slowly toward me, leaving me unsure of what to do. I could only watch it closely and paid attention to the shiftiness of its eyes as they darted back and forth from me to something in the shadows, to the right of me. I turned my head slightly to see what caught its eye, praying it was not yet another rat. To my relief, I saw several large bread crumbs and a small piece of cheese. The huge rat was only challenging me for the food.

I looked back at the rat, lowered my head, and stepped away cowardly, letting it pass. As soon as it was occupied with its prize, I darted through the doorway and out to the courtyard.

When I was myself once again, I hurried to the woodland and the men of my kin. The huge rat could have his cheese, and if I ever had to become a rat again, I would envision a much larger one.

When I reached the stream, I could hardly believe my eyes. Before me stood a hundred men I did not recognize. Their hair was flaxen and free of nits. Their bodies were clean, their clothing soft and comfortable. Barok informed me that Mirlanda had sent a bag of special herbs with which they washed their bodies and their hair.

"The herbs refreshed their bodies and killed the nits in their hair, bringing back the beauty of its color," he said, his *ka-ka* echoing through the air. Barok flapped his wings and perched himself upon my shoulder. "What of these men before you?" he asked. "I see that they are polite, gracious, refined, and educated, like the warriors. But they are not warriors. They do not know the sling or the cestro. Nonetheless, they do know how to carry the bow."

Nepron walked to me and reached his hand out in friendship. "We must thank you," he said. "Not only for the herbs which swept the filth from us, but for the clothing and the food as well. In the prison, the food offered us was boiled carcasses of rats. At first, we refused it, but hunger overcame us, and we forced ourselves to at least tolerate it to stay alive."

He paused and motioned to the men behind him. "I am speaking for all when I ask you to tell us your strategy, for we will do whatever you require. But first, may we inquire about our families. Are they still confined within the walls of the prison?"

I told them of Timberlin's plan, and they were content to hear my strategy. "Come with me," I said, leading them through an unguarded gate where one hundred horses waited and where bows, quivers of arrows, and a hundred arm shields lay on the grass. As I told them what they were to do, I could see the courage come alive in their faces.

"Methinks they appear as an army of spiritual beings!" Barok whispered in my ear when the Purcatians sat upon their mounts. "The Quynaè possess a wonderful magic, do you not agree?"

I nodded as I gazed at them. Their fair skin and golden hair glistened in the sunlight. Their white tunics were clasped at the waist with gold braids. Their leggings and boots, made of gold-crusted leather, caught the brightness of the sun, creating an illusion of divine light. These things gave them the appearance of spiritual beings. The quivers and bows on their backs, and the shields strapped to their arms, gave them the appearance of an army that would confuse Yiltor's soldiers long enough to do what needed to be done.

Mythias smiled as he gazed into his crystal. He was pleased with the army it showed him. Etcheon would not need him any longer, and it was time for him to set out for Ancitel's tower. He gathered his potions together and placed them carefully in his pouch next to his crystal. Then, he slipped his wand into the snugness of his inner sleeve.

The unicorn stood silently by his side as he prepared, knowing his plan before the wizard would tell her.

"It is a dangerous thing I am doing, I know," he admitted when she shook her head at him. "But there is no other way. I should have done it long ago, when he first came. I only hope I have not waited too long."

She said nothing, for she knew the wizard was right.

Mythias stroked her mane. "I will leave you to tend my forest and to protect the Quynaè until I return."

The unicorn nuzzled his neck. Then she watched him as he disappeared beyond the perimeter of the forest.

"I think it is time to visit the boy," Yiltor said and yawned. He had enjoyed these hours relaxing on his pillows, thinking of things he could say to the son of King Etcheon before the executions began.

"Have the rest of the women and children brought to the steps," he called to one of his servants.

"It shall be done, Sire," said a voice from the shadows of the room.

Yiltor heard the echo of footsteps before it was quiet again. He looked at himself in the mirror, admiring the reflection that smiled back at him. The royal sword was belted about his waist. The royal robes were wrapped about his shoulders, and the crown, in all its glory, adorned his head. Two guards waited to open the door for him as another called out to the people that the king was approaching.

He decided it was a beautiful day for an execution of this grandeur as he stepped out to greet those who called him king and those who despised his presence. He smiled at himself wondering which was the most exciting—to have power over those who are your servants or to have power over those who hate you.

All the Purcatian women and children now stood upon the steps, their backs to him. Those who were his servants bowed graciously to him. It was as grand as he had planned.

He raised his hand to greet his people. They rose and waited for him to speak. "I think it is time for us to become acquainted with the son of King Etcheon," he said with eloquence. "But first, I must ask him to remove the mask that shields his face." He looked directly at Thorri, "Do so now, Etcheon the Younger. Let my people see the face of the boy who murdered their fathers and sons."

Walkelin's nostrils flared and his eyes were aflame as he raised his powerful head. Yiltor hesitated and a touch of fear flickered in his eyes. He was not prepared for the magnificence of the animal that carried the prince. Then he brushed his concern away for now. He would let nothing disrupt his pleasure at this moment. He looked directly at the boy, but Thorri did not move nor did he speak.

My eyes searched for Klogan in the crowd, finding him not far from me. I warbled a soft cry and his head turned. When he spotted me, he moved slowly in my direction.

"I am glad to see you," he whispered. "Are you well?"

"I am," I whispered back. "Are the warriors in place?"

"They are."

I told him of all that had happened, of the one hundred men, and of the new strategy. "Can you send the message to the warriors?" I asked.

He nodded, turned, and disappeared.

"I will ask once more," Yiltor said and sighed, taking a step closer to the horse and rider. "Remove the mask, Etcheon, son of King Etcheon II."

Still Thorri did not move or speak.

"Do as you are told!" a guard shouted, stepping close to the warrior, his spear raised.

"Perhaps he is not the son of the king; therefore, he is not who you are speaking to," I said from my hiding place.

Yiltor looked about him in surprise before his face turned to anger, while another guard immediately came forward, shouting, "Who dares speak to the king in this manner?"

"Riders are coming from the east, Sire. At least a hundred!" a guard shouted from atop the wall, drawing Yiltor's attention away from the rider he thought to be me.

"What banner do they carry?" he bellowed.

"It is difficult to see," a soldier called back to him. "The sun blocks a good view."

"Have twenty soldiers guard these Purcatians," Yiltor hissed to the man behind him. "Have ten more guard the horse and rider."

"They have come close enough for us to see them clearly," a guard from the tower shouted, "yet too far away for our weapons to do them any harm. Their appearance is like nothing we have ever seen before."

A guard stepped away from his lookout and cried. "Their armor is as bright as the sun. It blinds our eyes to look at it."

"They wear no helmets or breastplates," another said, his voice hushed, yet all could hear, "only an arm shield. It is their clothing that blinds us. Their hair shines in the sun as if it were on fire."

"They carry bows," another called out, "yet they do not lift them in preparation for battle."

"Then they are fools," Yiltor said, sneering. "Make ready your weapons."

"But, Sire," another guard cried. "They look as if they are spiritual beings.

If that is so, it will be useless to raise our weapons against them, for they cannot die."

"If you believe that, then you are a fool," Yiltor fired back at him. "Do as I have ordered." Cursing under his breath, he moved quickly up the steps and to the tower. "Show me what you see," he growled when he stood beside the soldier.

The soldier pointed his finger. The king shielded his eyes as the soldiers had done. What he saw sent a chill through him. "Find Ancitel and bring him to me," he growled. "Waste no time."

"Yes, Sire." The soldier turned and disappeared down the steps.

The king turned to his captain, who stood beside him, waiting for his orders. "Make ready three hundred men. We shall send them out to greet this small army who seems to gather the sun about them."

The captain nodded and hurried away.

Those who had come to observe the execution of the enemy scattered quickly, having lost interest in the Purcatians—their own lives now their concern. All that remained in front of the castle were the prisoners and the soldiers who guarded them.

When the three hundred soldiers were mounted and ready, the captain commanded the gates to be opened. The bolt was lifted, and the chirping of birds filled the air. As the soldiers moved through the gate, the guards who surrounded the Purcatians fell to the ground without as much as a single cry.

I ran toward the Purcatians and looked for Timberlin. He was hiding not far from the women and children. "There is no better time," I whispered to him.

Timberlin gave me a broad wink as he touched his finger to the dial of the small gold astrolabe in his hand. When the women and children did not disappear, and Timberlin still stood beside me, he looked at me and frowned. "Ancitel is close by and has cast a spell."

At first I did not understand, then I heard the wizard's voice coming from behind us. "There are young Purcatian soldiers in the city," he shouted so all could hear his voice. "Their flaxen hair is hidden beneath the peasant's cap—their weapons beneath the peasant's clothing." He pointed to the soldiers lying dead on the steps of the castle. "See the victims of their weapons."

Fury stirred Yiltor back to his senses. "Search for them!" he screamed from atop the tower to the soldiers below who stood about, waiting to be told what to do. "And when you have found them, bring them to me."

While all attention was on Yiltor, I hurried to Walkelin. "Take Thorri beyond the city wall where he can change into the clothes of one of the dead soldiers." Then I looked up at Thorri. "Return and do not leave the prisms."

He nodded that he understood, and the two of them disappeared just as I heard the warbling of a morning bird.

Outside the city, the captain of the three hundred called out to the mysterious army. "Drop your bows and step away from your horses."

There was neither a reply nor an attempt to do as the captain commanded. Again, he warned them. "If you do not drop your bows and step away from your horses, this army of three hundred will fall upon you and leave no one alive."

Again there was no reply, but the bows of the Purcatians were armed, and at the command of Nepron, arrows flew through the air.

"Raise your arm shields," the captain shouted. But there was no clanging of arrows against metal nor cries of soldiers falling to the ground. Instead, the arrows fell harmlessly short of them. The soldiers lowered their shields to see only the dust of a hundred horses in retreat.

The captain turned to his army, knowing now that they would believe his words. "These are simple men who have thought to fool us with their trickery." He turned back and called out to Yiltor. "We will find them, Sire." Slapping his horse with his reins, he led his soldiers away from the castle.

Yiltor let his attention return to Ancitel, the Purcatians, and the guards who lay dead at their feet. He closed his eyes, rubbed them with his fingers, then opened them again. "Have I found myself in a nightmare?" He flung his robes behind him in his hurry to get down the steps of the watchtower. "Where is the rider? The one that pretends to make me the fool."

Then, as if he had forgotten his anger, his face softened and he walked to the prisms, taking his time. When he reached them, he ran his fingers over the crystal and spoke softly to the king who lay inside. "It seems the boy has run away and left you—the very ones he came here to save, so it is said."

"Sire," a soldier called to him from beyond the steps of the castle, "what would you have us do?"

"Bring these prisms to my private chambers," he said. "Surround them with guards. Then have the prison guard bring me ten of the Purcatian men, still held in the dungeon.

"Sire," another soldier shouted, "there are no soldiers guarding any of the gates outside the city wall."

"Place more guards at the gates!" Yiltor bellowed. Then he glared at the man who had failed to warn him. "Tell me, wizard," he said, his eyes dark with anger "did your crystals not warn you of this?"

"Did I not warn you that if you brought all those you held in your prison to the steps of the castle, it would be a difficult task for my crystals to warn me of any intruders?" Ancitel asked, his eyebrows raised in innocence. "Yet in spite of all of this," he waved his long-fingered hands over the Purcatians, "the crystals were able to find twenty-one who were pretending to be peasants."

Yiltor looked about him, his eyes devious. "And where are the twenty-one you speak of?"

"They keep themselves separate from those you see. But I must tell you there is another wizard about. I can sense his meddling. Before you are the women and children he had hoped to take from you. He cannot take them as long as I am here, for I bound them with the swish of my wand."

"Sire," a soldier called to him, "I have twenty men to guard the prisoners."

Yiltor paused in thought before replying. "With your twenty men, take the prisoners back to the dungeon, but do not leave them until you are commanded otherwise."

The soldier retreated and soon the women and children were being forced back through the doors that led to filth and darkness.

"Look through your crystals and find me the twenty-one you speak of," Yiltor demanded. Turning his back on Ancitel, he walked back through the doors of his castle.

Timberlin stood with me in my hiding place while we listened to the command. "You must not worry for them," he whispered. "Watch over them, I will. What you must do, you will." Then he slipped away from me and back among those being led to the prison.

Once the king was in his room, he pulled the robes from his shoulders, wrenched the sword from his side, and threw his crown at his servant. "Take them away and then bring the Purcatian men to me."

He fell upon his pillows and ranted like a spoiled child, pulling at his hair and tangling it in his fingers. "Is there another wizard as Ancitel claims? Is it his army that wears the armor that draws the sun?" he whispered to himself. "Or is it only a trick—a serpent's game?" He stood and walked to his mirror. "I will not be fooled by this trickery . . ."

"Sire," his servant interrupted him. "The prison guard wishes to see you."

Yiltor frowned. "See him in."

The servant left the room only to return with the unpleasant little elf of a man.

"Speak," Yiltor said, waving his arm as a gesture.

"Somthin's amiss, Sire." The little man's words were breathless.

Yiltor gave him hardly a glance. "Say what you have come to say."

"Did ye not com to my prison this mornin' and say fer me to bring the men to yeh?"

Yiltor turned slowly, his face losing its color. "I did not."

"Then a person lookin' jes like yeh did," the little man insisted. "I was to bring the men of the Purcatians to the waitin' room. I did as he commanded, fer I was lookin' at yer face. When he left, he tol' me to leave them where they were till he returned." He paused. "I did as he commanded, fer I was lookin' at yer face."

Yiltor put up his hand to silence the guard. "Where are the Purcatians?"

The guard stepped backwards, trembling with fear and knowing what he had to say would make the king furious. "Th-th-they are gone, Sire."

The look on the king's face turned to disbelief—its color changing from ghostly white to crimson red—his eyes ablaze. "They are gone?" he asked, the words spewing from his mouth.

"Aye, Sire," the man replied, barely able to control his fear. "Whoever it was, wore yer face, yer hair . . . yer whole being."

Yiltor turned his face away from the ugliness of the man, to consider what had come from his toothless mouth. "He wore my clothing, you say?"

"He did, Sire. He knocked same as yer's. His talk was same as yer's."

Yiltor began to rub his temples with his fingers in an attempt to relieve the throbbing pain in his head. "Leave me," he said, groaning.

The guard did not hesitate but turned and disappeared through the doorway, relieved to be out of the king's sight.

Yiltor walked to his window and stared out beyond the wall, searching for signs of his army. There were none. He muttered to himself as he turned away, his mind dulled in the knowledge that a boy could outwit him. Certainly this mere boy could not be the wizard Ancitel spoke of, yet he seemed to have a power beyond that of a mortal. "If this son of a Purcatian king has powers, why could he not take the two prisms I hold as ransom?" he asked openly, his fingers caressing the lock of hair that fell across his cheek.

"Sire," he heard a soldier call from the room just beyond the one in which he stood. "Where shall we place them?"

He glanced through the doorway to see the prisms being carried on wooden carts. He strolled to them and touched them with his hands, as if he wanted to make sure they were not simply an illusion. He arched his right brow and a thin, sinister smile spread across his face. They were, indeed, genuine, as were the two imprisoned inside the crystallized glass. Without glancing up at the one who had asked the question, he waved his fingers. "In the middle of the room where I can see them." He turned away, and then turned back again and touched a corner of the prism that held the king. "Surround them with guards. Let there be no opening where one could reach them with even a touch of a finger, as I am doing now." He removed his finger and left the room.

He returned to his window. The one hundred soldiers were not spiritual beings as his men had supposed. They were one hundred Purcatians, taken from his prison by trickery. But they had not inflicted the wounds that ended the lives of his soldiers. The boy was somewhere close. "Where are you, Ancitel?" he shouted.

"Here, Sire," the wizard replied, walking to the window from the shadows of the room. "What would you have me tell you?"

Yiltor turned and looked into the face of Ancitel. "I think you already know, wizard, but I wonder if you know something else you have not told me." He motioned for the two guards at the door to stand behind the wizard. "Tell me, where is the boy and his timepiece?"

Ancitel frowned deeply, his eyes steady, and his thoughts on the spell that held Etcheon prisoner inside his tower and on the timepiece that would soon be his if he did not allow himself to be tricked by this king. "I have heard of a timepiece," he said slowly, as if he had not heard the accusation. "It has been discussed among the wizards for hundreds of years, but no one can describe its appearance, for no wizard has ever seen it, if it even exists." He paused, allowing the intention of his words to linger, while he attempted to read Yiltor's eyes. But the king's eyes were veiled. His face was shadowed.

Ancitel sighed deeply and continued. "As for the boy, my crystals tell me he is among the twenty-one who pretended to be peasants." Even as he spoke, his hand that held the crystal felt a tingling. He opened it and the brightness filled his eyes. "Sire," he said softly. "At least one Purcatian is somewhere within the rooms of your castle. My crystal will show us where."

The light disappeared from the crystal before it could show the wizard more. Suddenly, it came alive again. This time its light was so brilliant that it burned as a flame against his skin. He gasped in the pain, dropping it to the floor. With eagerness, he knelt over it and brought his face close, without touching it. His eyes glowed in the color of its brilliance for only a second, then the light was gone and the crystal was dark again. "Someone pretends to be me inside my tower," he gasped in disbelief. Without any further explanation, he grabbed the crystal and ran from the room.

A soldier standing at the foot of the prisms stood still, hardly daring to breathe as Ancitel passed by him. He could see the wizard's hand that held the crystal change slightly in color, but the wizard was in too much pain and had more dangerous thoughts in mind to notice.

24

The Trap

THREE MOVED SILENTLY, SEARCHING AND LISTENING in the shadows of the darkness as a horse approached. They waited until a soldier emerged from the thicket and waved to the rider. When the soldier and rider disappeared back into the thicket, the three followed and listened.

"How did you know where to find us?" a voice asked.

"I knew to find you here, Captain," the rider replied, hastily, "because the army you pursue is of the Purcatian clan. There is no explanation of how they escaped nor where they found the armor you saw when they stood outside the gate. But there was no question as to where they would lead you, giving them the advantage. But I bring you news that you are to bring back these Purcatians, dead or alive."

Another voice was heard. "These mountains are no different than our own, Captain. The terrain is perhaps a little more difficult, but I have seen worse."

Another voice broke in, breathless, as if the man behind it had been running. "We think we have found their location, Captain. If so, only rocks and recesses protect them."

"Then at dawn we will let three hundred arrows fly," the captain replied with confidence. "We will raise them high so when they fall, their points will drop down upon them like raindrops. Then, we will move in."

The three who listened retreated—returning to their leader and telling him all they had heard.

Nepron called all the men around him, and then knelt upon the ground and drew a circle in the loose dirt. He made an X with his finger. "This is where Yiltor's soldiers hide," he explained, his eyes connecting with the others. He looked up at one of the three who had listened, near the thicket. "Zephra," he said, "you will take thirty men and go into the city. We have entered and found it free of the poison the wizard sent."

He turned to another of the three. "Johel, you will take fourteen of those men and hide yourselves upon the wall."

He drew a circle outside the circle and said to the third, "Anton, you and I will take the others and we will form a barricade around these soldiers of Yiltor. There are trees and brush enough to hide us, and they will be our protection when their arrows drop like raindrops, away from us. We will take no more lives than is necessary, but we will take them all, if we must."

He stood and brushed the dirt from his hands. "They will be surrounded, but not helpless. They have weapons we do not possess. They outnumber us, three to one. As soon as you see the arrows fly, aim your arrows no higher than their heads, for we will also be a moving target as well. When our arrows reach them, they will know they are surrounded and will make adjustments in their strategy, while we continue to make the changes needed to cause them confusion. Only the men upon the wall will remain where they are." He paused and looked into the faces of the men before him. They were satisfied. As soon as the darkness fell, they were all in their places.

Just as the rays of the sun appeared, Yiltor's army was ready, their arrows pointed high in the sky.

"Release them!" shouted the captain.

Three hundred arrows filled the air, the swooshing sound capturing the silence. But when they landed, there were no cries of pain.

Suddenly arrows came at them from all directions. They had not anticipated such a move, and many cries of pain were heard. When it was silent again, thirty-six of Yiltor's soldiers lay dead or wounded.

"We do not wish to kill more of your men, captain," Nepron called out, his voice echoing through the air. "Please surrender yourselves. Be our prisoners until we have regained all that is ours, then we will return you to your city."

"You must think me a foolish man to agree to such an arrangement when my army outnumbers yours by so great a number?" shouted the captain in return. "I would, instead, suggest that you show yourselves so that we can do battle, fairly."

"And you would think me a foolish man to do so?" came the laughing reply.

"Then we shall battle until one of us has fallen." With that the captain ordered his men to position themselves in a large circle and aim their bows twice more, then pull their swords and pursue their enemy. He had seen no swords belted to the Purcatians, only the bow. A bow was no match for the sword when looking into the eyes of the enemy.

Arrows sliced the sky, coming at them from above and to the right. Seventeen more soldiers fell to the ground.

"We ask you, once more, to silence your bows," Nepron called out, "and we will silence ours."

"I have never experienced such a battle," the captain muttered to himself, in frustration. He counted the wounded and the dead, knowing his army still outnumbered the enemy by remarkable odds. "Within the hour, I will give my answer. Until then let us both silence our weapons," he responded.

"So it shall be," came the reply.

The captain's face wrinkled into deep lines as he attempted to confine the Purcatian's voice, but it seemed to come from all around him. He thought of the information given him by the youth, Petre, who said the men of the Purcatians were intellectuals, weak and spineless, knowing nothing of battle strategies. The boy was a fool, just as he had been, to believe such a tale. They may not be trained in battle. Nonetheless, they had the knowledge needed for battle.

What was thought to be a simple task would prove, instead, to be quite the opposite. This small army may even have his men surrounded, giving them the advantage in spite of their limited weaponry. This would prove to be a most difficult day and keep them from returning to Yiltor's kingdom for several hours.

Then it dawned on him. This *was* the strategy of the Purcatians, and he had been deceived to think otherwise. He had unwittingly led his men into a trap.

Outside the city wall of Yiltor's kingdom, the bodies of all the dead soldiers now lay side by side, their helmets placed above their heads, their swords at their sides. The trees hid them from the eyes of those upon the wall. When the task was done, the warriors climbed high into the massive trees and waited.

I hid myself near the steps of the castle—the prisms gone now, and the streets deserted. I called out to Barok in my thoughts. "Tell me all you know," I said to him, as soon he rested his talons upon my shoulder.

"Kevelioc tells me that your kinsmen are showing surprisingly effective aptitude toward defensive strategy. Their leader, Nepron, a knowledgeable historian, seems to have learned enough to become a leader and a man of great influence among the hundred. You need not worry about them. Nepron has a voice of logic that intrigues the captain of the king's soldiers, and though there have been deaths and wounds among the king's men, the voice of logic now brings an agreement of retreat on both sides, for the time being."

The eagle fluttered his wings and squawked something I could only assume to be laughter. "What do you find so humorous?" I demanded.

"To think of a battle fought with words instead of swords, until agreement of harmony is obtained, is something I would like to see written, so all can know of its possibility." He lifted his wings and perched himself on the limb of a small tree that hid me from the eyes of the soldiers.

"Can Ancitel see inside the Hidden Kingdom?"

"The Danes tell me a drop of a dog's saliva, that somehow fell into the potion as it was ripening, changed the composition of the poison and now prevents him from seeing into the city."

I could not help but feel pleased with the Danes.

"It also pleases me to tell you that Mythias is now inside Ancitel's tower. Now, tell me, what is your strategy?"

"The strategy seems to change as the hours pass."

Suddenly Barok tilted his head, and I heard his voice in my head. "A soldier approaches from a hiding place. Prepare yourself."

"Did I hear you mumbling to a bird, stupid peasant," a craggy voice from behind me said.

I wrapped my hand around the handle of my father's dagger and waited.

"Turn around and let me see your face," he said, snorting, "or your insolence just might put a blade through your heart."

I could hear the sound of his knife being lifted from its sheath just before he grabbed my peasant's cap and pulled it from my head. I heard the intake of his breath as my hair fell loose.

"Just as I suspected," he hissed, and grabbed me around the neck from behind, pulling my head against his chest. He placed his knife against my throat, and his mouth against my ear. "Perhaps I will first cut out your gullet, then remove your heart and present it to the . . ." His voice suddenly faded and his look was one of confusion. Then his eyes became lifeless and the knife fell from his hand. As he slumped to the ground, I quickly turned to see Klogan become visible behind him, his sling in his hand—his body pressed against the wall so he would remain hidden.

He glanced around, then turned his attention back to me and whispered. "We will take him to lie with his comrades."

When the soldier lay beside his dead comrades, a warbling cry came from high in one of the trees, and Raven was soon beside us. "A short time after the wizard entered the castle, many soldiers also entered," he warned. "Many more are searching for us through the city."

Klogan raised his hands to his lips and the cawing of a hawk warned all of the warriors to leave the city and meet under the protection of the trees. Only Thorri would remain.

"Find Mythias," I said to Barok. "Tell him what has happened. Ask him if he has found a way to control Ancitel. If not, we will retreat until he has. While I wait for you to return, I will go inside the castle and listen to the king discuss his strategy with his soldiers."

The eagle eyed me through his dark pupils. "And what, or who, will you become in order to get through the door of the castle—a soldier? Or a rat, perhaps?"

"Perhaps both," I replied. He cocked his head, gave me a questionable look, and then lifted himself into the sky. As soon as he disappeared, I called Walkelin to me. "Go to the Hidden Kingdom and talk with Kevelioc. Then call the Danes to you from where the soldiers make plans to do battle against our people. When you have all you need, return."

It was then that we heard a soldier give the command to search through the trees and shrubbery outside the wall for the enemy. "The warriors know what to do," Klogan assured me. "When we meet here again, we will have all the information we need for a new strategy." He placed his hand on my shoulder. "You are a strong leader, Etcheon the Younger. We will retreat and do nothing until all is known, and a new strategy is before us."

There was a pause in his voice, and a tremor came into his voice. "Will you do one more thing . . . for me?" he asked.

I looked at him and, for the first time, I saw fear lining his face. "Anything," I promised. "What is it you need?"

"My wife and baby daughter should be among the women and children." He choked back the tears as he spoke. "I could not see them among those who stood upon the steps before they were taken back to the prison. I must know if they are still alive."

Why Klogan had not told me that he had a wife and a child, I did not know. But I did know, at that moment, he thought he was asking for more than he should, and it was difficult for him to do so.

"I will find them and tell them you are well, and soon they will be with you again."

"Her name is Angli," he said, softly.

How could I not admire his strength? I stepped back from him and removed the bottle from inside my vest. There was little left, I noticed, and I hoped I would only need to use it one more time. I let two drops touch my tongue and I became the detestable rat I had hoped to be rid off. But, for now, it was my dearest friend.

Mythias, pretending to be a stranger, inquired about the huge tower as he walked along the road that led to it. The people he met were not unfriendly but cautious in their telling of the wizard who lived there. He learned that an old mute woman, who lived in a small cottage next to the tower, was the only other person allowed inside.

"It is a strange thing, though," one man said, as he talked of her. "I have known her all my life, and she could speak fine enough before the wizard came. It has made us all very wary of him."

It pleased Mythias to leave a bag of gold on the woman's doorstep with a note telling her she would never have to enter the tower again. He watched her closely as she opened the door, gathered the bag to her, and read the note. Then he placed two drops of potion on his tongue and became the old woman.

Making sure his steps were slow and careful, he hurried at an old woman's swiftness, knowing Ancitel was watching his approach from a window high above him. When he reached the door, it opened. He stepped inside and found himself in a room that reminded him of a witch's cellar. Dust, webs, huge pots filled with herbs, and other odds and ends used in the making of brew cluttered the room. There was scarcely space for the stairs that twisted up through the center of the tower to the room where Ancitel lived.

The door above him opened. Ancitel appeared, his robe flaring about him as he hurried down the stairs. He was muttering to himself about the affairs of the castle becoming wearisome. He did not acknowledge the old woman, only tossed a list of duties at her as he passed.

When Mythias could no longer hear Ancitel's footstep, he placed two drops of the potion on his tongue and became the wizard he had come to destroy. Once inside the room, he had only to glance about him to know where to find what he needed. He hurried to the crystals and carefully studied them.

Calling to the crystals in the voice of the wizard, Mythias told them to show him everything they had seen at the castle—one more time. The crystals showed him the warriors, dressed as peasants, and the army of three hundred, encircled by the Purcatians. He now understood Ancitel's abrupt exit.

With a wave of his wand and a few well-spoken words, all the bottles and jars filled with herbs and potions fell from the cupboard and tables, shattering as they hit the floor. Next, he touched the wand to the largest crystal. "Show me your master," he whispered. The crystal responded, and Ancitel became visible to him from inside the king's private chamber.

"I sense a Purcatian inside the castle, not far from this room," he heard Ancitel say.

"Disordious, demoris. Destroy the crystals!" Mythias cried out, and slapped his wand against the crystals, shattering them one by one, each one draining more of his power as it shattered.

When the last crystal fell to the floor in pieces, Mythias fell also, his strength depleted. Barely aware of his thoughts, Mythias knew one thing clearly. Shattering the crystals would bring Ancitel back to the tower and save one of the warrior's life, at least for now.

He knew he must find a place to hide. He forced his shaking hand inside the pocket of his robe and tried to wrap his fingers around the small bottle, but the fingers lay limp as if they were paralyzed. He closed his eyes and made his mind focus, trying again to grasp the bottle. With greater effort than he had thought possible, his fingers finally answered to his command, and he brought the bottle to his lips. Just as Ancitel entered the room, he became the old woman again, lying on the floor.

Ignoring the woman on the floor, Ancitel ran from his cupboard of broken bottles and ruined potions to the shattered crystals. He screamed and shouted, his robe whipping about him and his hair flying about his face. Mythias thought he had never seen a finer tantrum.

Suddenly Ancitel became quiet and Mythias could feel him coming closer to him. "Old woman," he said, gently. "Awaken and stand before me."

Mythias did not move.

"Old woman?" Ancitel touched the body with his wand, causing currents of pain to surge through Mythias. "Awake and stand before me."

Mythias screamed out in pain, but whatever magic Ancitel used to cause such pain seemed to bring strength to Mythias, as well. He stood as the old woman and looked into Ancitel's face, and he knew this wizard, from another time, another place.

"You are not who you pretend to be, old woman," Ancitel whispered, and touched his wand to her again. The pain felt good to Mythias, for it awakened his powers, and he smiled to himself. Perhaps he should let the wizard continue with the game, for a while yet.

"Tell me, who is it that tries to destroy my magic before I become impatient and let the wand burn you alive?" Ancitel raged, his wand iridescent in it glow.

"Wizard," Mythias said at last. "Do you delight in harassing old women with your wand?"

Ancitel stopped sharply and stepped away as a smile appeared on the old woman's face. He knew who had destroyed his crystals—one wizard who once had more power than he possessed. "You!" he hissed. "I thought you were dead. For more than a hundred years, you have been dead to me."

Mythias raised the miniature bottle to his mouth and let a drop of the potion fall onto his tongue. "Isn't that remarkable, for I thought you to be dead, as well."

Ancitel watched the transformation with astonishment. "But I enticed you into the pit of acid and poison myself. I stood there and watched as it ate away your flesh and destroyed your bones. You could not have survived."

"That, of course, is true," Mythias admitted. "Nonetheless, I did not care for its flavor. One taste of its fury, and I decided to take myself elsewhere."

Seeing no wand in Mythias's hand, Ancitel held his tightly, ready to use it. Yet he could not help but feel caution sweep through his body as he replied. "Tell me, where did you take yourself, as you so curiously put it?"

"You think I would give away my secrets?"

Ancitel laughed, remembering that Mythias had once been his friend—remembering that which ended the friendship. "Did you hope to finish me by destroying my crystals?"

Mythias looked into the darkness of Ancitel's eyes and felt sorrow. "Only the evil that you represent. There was a time when your friendship was as gold to me."

Sensing Mythias's sorrow, Ancitel turned from him, abruptly. "Do not feel sadness for me, wizard," he mocked. "I am content with who I am."

"And who are you?"

Ancitel turned back to Mythias—his eyebrows arched, his eyes flaunting his arrogance. "I have yet to discover who I am, for I am yet in my infancy." He closed the distance between them. "Let us instead answer the question as to why you have come, and why you attempt to destroy me."

"I am afraid I came at your bidding," Mythias said simply, arranging his robe about him.

Ancitel frowned, taken aback at Mythias's words. "Explain," he said.

"I think it is you who should explain," Mythias corrected him.

"You have not changed, Mythias, and I find myself growing tired of this game of words." Ancitel lifted his wand and eyed Mythias carefully. "It must have taken much of your strength to destroy my crystals, and though you pretend, I think you are in a weakened state. I think you are simply using your words to keep me from returning to the castle." He paused, and his eyes narrowed. "You are trying to save the Purcatians, I think, but know that you cannot."

"They do not need my help any longer," Mythias said, a triumphant smile spreading across his face.

Ancitel pondered Mythias's words. "You think by doing all this," he gestured to the broken glass and the clutter all about the room, "and bringing me back to the tower, you have done a great deed?" Ancitel laughed, and it echoed around him. "You know nothing, Mythias."

"If you say so," Mythias answered, crossing his arms and putting his hands inside the ample sleeves of his robe. He turned and walked to the window—wrapping his right hand around the wand hidden in his left sleeve.

"Yet, if I know nothing, then why should I linger?" He removed a small crystal from the pocket inside his right sleeve and held it tightly in his left hand.

Ancitel watched him, cautiously. "Perhaps you have come in search of the Purcatian prince?"

"I suppose you have him hidden somewhere?"

"In a place where no one will ever find him, and where he will stay forever," Ancitel replied, his voice suddenly soft. "Unless, in a moment of weakness, I release him. Though, if I should release him, he will not be the same prince that came to save his kin. He will be as the babe, who was sent away to another time, all gooey and sopped."

Ancitel paused to pick up a handful of shattered crystal, watching it as it fell through his fingers. Then his eyes turned as cold and menacing as his voice. "But I shall not think that far ahead. I cannot release him until he has given me something very precious to both of us." He wrapped his long fingers around his black hair and removed one of the crystals that adorned it. "You have not destroyed all the crystals that carry my magic," he said to Mythias. "What would you like to see?"

"Show Etcheon to me so that I can believe this tale you weave," Mythias demanded.

"You ask to see the boy, and I will show him to you, but first I must prepare you." He raised the hand that held the crystal, touching it with his wand. The crystal evaporated into a mist. He raised his hand to his mouth and blew the mist into Mythias's face—spreading its hypnotic scent through his nostrils and into his eyes.

The face of Ancitel become twisted and distorted. The sound of his laughter penetrated through the mist, as twisted and distorted as his face.

Mythias could hear the words as if they were delivered from far away. "It will be a painless trip. Soon your mind will be senseless, and finally, it will know nothing at all, and you will be with the Prince of the Purcatians."

The words awoke Mythias's anger. He gripped his wand tightly and pulled it from his sleeve. With all that was in him, he shouted, "Proceio!" His wand began to quiver, and blue flames flowed from its tip, devouring the mist until it was no longer visible. "I think not," Mythias said, taking a deep breath to clear his head.

Ancitel stepped back in fear, surprised by the power of the magic used to break his spell. Nonetheless, his mind worked rapidly, and he pretended to only be entertained by what he had seen. "Did you see the prince?" he asked innocently.

"I did not, and neither will you, for Etcheon has escaped your spell as well."

Ancitel's breath became shallow and his eyes narrowed as he fought to contain his anger. "And you know this as a fact, I presume?"

"I do. I also know that you wish to have the timepiece, so I will tell you this: The timepiece will work for only Etcheon. If you held it in your hands, it would be nothing but an astrolabe."

"What kind of a fool do you think I am?" Ancitel asked, tossing his arms about him. "It is knowledge well-known among all wizards that the time-piece will honor whoever may have it in their possession."

Mythias drew the crystal from his sleeve and looking into it as if it were revealing something valuable. He knew Ancitel could not keep himself from it. Suddenly Ancitel's fingers tore it from Mythias's hand. "What is it you see, wizard?" he asked, looking into the crystal.

Mythias touched the crystal with his wand. "The spell you placed upon Etcheon, and into that same spell you will now go." He waved his wand, and Ancitel began to fade from him.

"What have you done to me?" he screamed as he began to sink into the spell.

"It is what you have done to yourself," Mythias answered, and listened to Ancitel's voice fading into nothingness, while his wand fell to the floor next to the crystal. Mythias picked them up and set the crystal back in his pocket. He did not break the wand, but laid it on the floor, among the shattered glass. Waving his wand above it, he cast a spell about the room, and everything that belonged to Ancitel, disappeared, leaving the room clean. When it was all done, Mythias ran down the stairs and out of the tower into the sunshine, feeling ever so good to have it done.

As he walked by the old woman's cottage, he quietly touched the wand to her gate and spoke a few words unknown to anyone who might be listening. Then, with a smile of contentment on his face, Mythias walked on. When the woman awoke in the morning, she talked to all who came by her cottage.

25

The Rat's Advantage

AS A RAT, I COULD MOVE swiftly and without notice through the halls and up the stairs of the castle. When I reached the floor where I supposed I would find Yiltor's rooms, I found my eyes level with the boots of soldiers instead, having to make a quick retreat to protect myself from them. But in retreating I heard their conversation.

"If the wizard claims Purcatians are in the castle," one of them said hastily, as they hurried down the hallway, "why did he not stay and find them with his assumed magic crystal?"

"It seems he suddenly vanished just as he was about to begin the task," another voice answered.

I left them to their work, praying Ancitel's sudden disappearance was the work of another wizard far greater than he.

Two soldiers, who looked as if they carried rank, came up the stairs and turned to the left. I followed, and they led me to the room I needed to find. I scarcely could believe my good fortune when I saw the prisms, Thorri, and the king all in one chamber.

"The wizard has disappeared!" Yiltor shouted to the two soldiers, as they entered. "Send men to his tower and bring him back to me." He sunk back into his pillows, uttering something ugly under his breath.

I hurried to the prisms, and to Thorri, wondering how I could get his attention. I scampered over his boots. He glanced down, but did nothing more. I nibbled at his boots, drawing the attention of the soldier beside him.

"Seems you have found a friend," he whispered, "that, or you have smelly toes." He gave Thorri a friendly grin, before turning his attention back to the guarding of the prisms.

Thorri looked down again, and I could only sit on my backside and put my front paws together, as if I was pleading to him. He frowned and was just about to kick me, when Yiltor's voice boomed from behind him.

"Take only the children to the steps of the castle. The executions shall begin with them." I could see him pacing back and forth, his body ridged and his eyes ablaze.

"But, Sire," an elderly man warned him. "Do you not think that a display of that extreme will turn your own people away from you?"

"Not if they believe that it is their children's lives or those of the Purcatians," Yiltor replied, his face twisted. "Write the words I tell you, then have soldiers ride through the city, reading the decree to all the people."

The elderly man shook his head but seated himself at a small table and began to write:

To all who are citizens of this realm, hear the words of your king.

By means of witchery, the men who call themselves Purcatians have escaped our prison and are now an army against us. With help from the dark powers, their prince and those who stand with him have invaded our kingdom. They hide among our people clothed as simple peasants and use their weaponry to kill our soldiers, leaving our children unprotected. It is my decree that unless all those who disguise themselves surrender, the children of their kin will be brought to the gates of the castle where they will be executed at sunrise, in order that our children may be saved.

A smile appeared on the face of the elderly man as he set aside the writing pen. "You are a clever king," he said, holding the paper for Yiltor to see.

Yiltor merely glanced at the decree before ordering ten replicas made and ten soldiers made ready to carry the word to the people.

I could sense the anger rising in Thorri, but he remained still. Taking the advantage of the commotion of preparation, I twittered as a bird, bringing his eyes back to the rat that sat at his feet. Noting that the attention of the soldiers was on the king, he knelt down close to me with a look of confusion on his face.

"Say nothing, only listen," I whispered. "Do not worry about the children—they will be safe."

Thorri's eyes widened in disbelief, but he lifted me with his fingers and placed me in the palm of his hand, putting his ear close to my mouth.

"I believe the king will not stray far from the prisms, giving you the opportunity of hearing his strategy as well as watching over my mother and father. Are you safe enough?"

He nodded that he was.

The soldier beside him nudged Thorri. "Best leave the rat be," he advised, "the king comes this way."

I jumped down. Thorri stood and tilted his head in thanks to the soldier who had warned him.

I hid myself in a corner, as the soldiers stepped away from the prisms. I watched as Yiltor caressed the prisms, looking into my father's face.

"Well, King Etcheon," he said, his voice as silk. "Your son has succeeded in freeing your men from their dungeon—making them appear as glowing soldiers. He wants to confuse those who serve me." He paused and sighed deeply. "How he did this, I will admit I do not know." He lifted his hand from the prisms and turned away, dramatically tossing his robe about him. "Though it was a clever trick, I will show him that he has gained nothing by it."

Just then there was a knock, and a servant opened the door to the two soldiers who had been sent to the tower. They walked into the room and bowed slightly. "The wizard is not in his quarters, Sire," the first announced.

"There is nothing in the tower, Sire," the second one continued. "It is as bare as if it had never been occupied."

Yiltor closed his eyes and took a long breath. "Do we not still hold the most precious of the Purcatians, their king?"

The men around him nodded their heads in agreement.

He walked to the window and looked out beyond the borders of his kingdom. He had been wickedly deceived. But it would not keep him from his quest. "Then we shall continue as we have discussed." Even as he talked with such confidence, I could sense the apprehension inside of him. It was time to go to the dungeon.

Just as I was about to pass through the kitchen, a broom appeared in front of my face, and the kitchen maid shouted, "Skeet out, you grimy rodent!"

I felt the sting of the broom as it struck me, and I scurried for safety behind the cupboards. I did not have time for this, yet I had no other choice but to wait in the shadows until the maid went back to her chores. While I waited, I listened.

"'Tis my hope they ner'r find him," I heard the voice of an old woman say. I poked my head around the corner of the cupboard to see the back of an old woman and the face of a girl, no older than the warriors.

"Shhh!" the girl scolded. "Ner'r know what ears might listen."

"Ah, my ears caught a bit of blabber, they did," the old woman said, saying nothing more until the girl begged her to go on. "Quite a story I heard when the soldiers came near the door, their mouths working as much as their eyes." She softened her voice, and I had to move closer to hear. "They breathed a tale of children given to weaponry not known to us. Tiny arrows and bitty rocks, they carry, that kill as easy as swords or bows."

"Tis only a tale," the girl scoffed. "Though t'would be nice, if true."

The old woman chuckled. "Twenty soldiers who guarded the Purcatians, so the blabber goes, now carry bitty rocks and tiny arrows in their throats and foreheads, while no breath flows from their lungs."

"If the blabber be right, as you claim," the girl said, slowly, "perhaps there'll be another tale to learn from the ugly little guard when I take his nightly meal."

The old woman reached for a bucket. "Go now, and take a dab of water to the poor women and children who must abide his presence."

The girl hurried out to fill the bucket with fresh water from the well. When she returned, the old woman set a plate in her empty hand and slipped a key into her apron pocket. "Hurry now. Be kind and smile at him, then he'll be blabberin' as did the soldiers."

I scampered down the darkened halls and stairs ahead of her, and then wiggled my way beneath the doors until I was inside the damp and filthy hole of a dungeon. I looked about me. The guard was sound asleep upon his stool. Beyond him the iron gates of the prison stood open and empty.

I heard the knock upon the door. "Guard, 'tis the kitchen maid with the evening meal."

The guard opened his eyes, and smacked his lips at the thought of food and company. He slid the key into the lock, opened the door, and stepped back so the girl could enter.

"Good evening, Graylon," she said, a pleasant smile on her face. "I've brought you some fresh bread, meat, and sweet yams for your meal." She set the plate before him, glancing at the empty prison. "I brought water for the prisoners, I did, but where can they be?"

"Yiltor commanded they be hidden deep, so Purcatians who pretend they be soldiers cannot find them," he said, grunting as he tore the loaf of bread apart, and filled his mouth.

"May I take them this bucket of water for drinking?" the young girl asked, pretending to be humble and also smiling sweetly, as the old woman suggested.

He shook his head and motioned for her to put the bucket down beside him. "It'll stay here 'til I chew me meal."

"Will you promise to take it to them?" she asked, touching his unwashed arm.

He glanced up at her, his eyes softening. "Twill get to 'em." Then his brows drew close together in a frown, and he gave her a long look. "Do ye feel sorry for em?"

"Only that they are women and children." She returned his frown with one of her own. "As you should feel sorry. What if it was your mum?"

"Girl, I've got no mum. Women and children are of no concern." He stuffed his mouth with yams and bread and chewed on them as he studied her more closely. " 'Tis a promise I give ye, because of yer soft heart, the water'll go to em."

While she waited for him to finish, so she could take his plate back to the kitchen, he told her of all that happened through the day. She listened and took his plate when it was empty. She returned to the kitchen with a juicy tale to share with the old woman.

When the girl was gone, the guard picked up the bucket and slowly descended the narrow, slippery stairs that led to the place where the women and children were kept. I followed.

Well into the damp darkness of the dungeon, silence filled my ears. I could see nothing but the light of his lantern, and the ghostly shadows it cast as he continued to descend. Finally, he stopped and unlocked a heavy wooden door. Raising his lantern as high as he could above his head, he held the bucket of water in front of him. "The kitchen maid felt sorry for the lot of ye. Drink as ye wish," he said, dropping the bucket in front of the bars. Taking the light of his lantern away from the bucket, he turned, locked the door, and hurried away.

When the light was no longer visible to them, I could hear Timberlin's voice, and the dungeon became bright with light. I dared not waste the potion, so I called to him with my voice. Tiny as it sounded, he squinted his eyes, searching. "Hear your voice I can," he said, his voice guarded. "But see you, I cannot."

I scampered close to him, stopping just a few steps from him. "Look at the rat in front of you."

He did as I asked, looking rather startled. "Etcheon?" he cried, kneeling beside me.

"It is me," I assured him, "and now you must listen to what I have to tell you. Ancitel has returned to his tower for reasons known only to him, or perhaps Mythias ordered him there, I do not know. Will your timepiece tell you when the curse is no longer holding you?"

"Know, I will, when press the lever I do." He removed the timepiece from his vest pocket and opened it. Touching the lever, he gave me a sorrowful look. "Too far below the ground, the astrolabe shows." He slipped through the iron bars. "A key, we must have, or unlock the bars, we cannot."

"I will have to go back to where the guard stands watch," I said. I dug beneath the dried or rotted remains of roaches and rats, just to get through the small opening beneath the wooden door. As I squeezed my way through, however, I felt something hard move beneath my paw. I struggled to push the rot and dirt away to find something bent and rusted. "Timberlin," I called. "I think I have found a key."

I grabbed it with my paws and attempted to pull it from its hiding place. It was too heavy and slipped back into its hole. Once again, I attempted to free it, using my teeth as well. But I could not break it away.

Timberlin reached his arm under the door and found the hole, but his arm would go no further than to allow his fingers to touch the tip of it. Using my paws and all the strength a rat could have, I strained to push the key into his hand.

"Have it I do . . . not," he grunted, his arm completely vanishing beneath the door. He clutched the object in his fingers, pulling with all his strength, until it finally gave loose, and he had it in his hand. "Have it I do," he said and grinned. His arm was covered with the remains of whatever died beneath the door. Happily, he brushed it from him and hurried back to the iron doors.

"Angli," he called out, handing it to a woman whose beauty could not be denied even beneath the grime and straw that clung to her hair, her face, and her clothing. "With this, unlock the door, if it will."

A young child clung to her dress as Angli carefully eased it into the lock. The noise it made as she twisted the key echoed so loudly throughout the chamber that we feared the guard would hear it, and he did.

I squeezed under to the door and watched for him, while the sound of his footsteps came closer and closer to the door. He leaned his ear against the door but did not attempt to put the key in the lock. When he was satisfied that the sound had not come from this dungeon, he shrugged his shoulders and returned the way he had come.

I followed him until I watched him lay his lantern on the chair and fluff the straw beside it. When his bed of straw was as he wished it to be, he laid himself down and was soon snoring loud enough that I doubted he would hear anying more.

When I returned to Timberlin, however, the voices of soldiers echoed through the hallway. "We are too late to take them to the forest," I explained quickly to Timberlin. "The king has ordered the children executed. Wherever the soldiers take them, go with them and see to their safety."

Timberlin nodded. "Fear, you must not," he said. Then he turned to the women and children, explaining what was about to happen. He warned Angli to lock the door while reassuring them that the children would be safe in the forest before one of them could be harmed.

The soldiers brought light back into the dungeon with their lanterns. They unlocked the prison door, grabbing thirty children from their mothers. We could only watch as they forced them through the door and up the steps. They did not notice the miniature person or the rat that followed them.

I had to know Yiltor's plan for the children. Why would he take them now, instead of waiting until the sun had begun to rise? As I hurried through the hallways and up the steps to his chamber, I was greeted only by the silence once again.

I squeezed beneath the door of the king's rooms. All was quiet. It was late at night. Fresh soldiers stood guard, while those who had guarded throughout the day slept. I looked for Thorri, finding him against the wall beside the door, his eyes closed, his breath even. He was asleep.

I put my whiskers close to his ear, tickling them in hopes that he would awaken without arousing those around him.

"I only pretend to be asleep," he whispered softly. "I have been waiting, hoping you would return. The king has decided to take the children to the soldier's quarters. There they will be guarded by two hundred of his men, dressed in full armor, who will surround them, three deep. He no longer trusts the protection of the dungeon now that the Purcatians escaped its depths."

"Timberlin is with them. They will be in the forest before morning," I assured him. "Now I must get to Klogan. Do nothing to arouse suspicion. Only guard the prisms."

Thorri nodded, and I was again squeezing my body beneath the door, scurrying down the stairs as a rat would. Soon I was outside the walls of the city, deciding that being a rat had its advantages. I pulled the potion bottle from within the fur of my rat's coat, opened it, and let a drop fall to my tongue. It was a relief to be myself again.

I chirped quietly and listened for a return reply. There was none, but Klogan was beside me in an instant. Before he could even ask, I told him I had seen Angli and his daughter. "They are well, and your wife is a beautiful, brave woman."

"Thank you for bringing me this wonderful news!" He cried, unashamed of his tears.

"Nonetheless, I have not told you everything yet."

His eyes met mine and I did not need to tell him more. "My daughter?"

"She stands with the other children who are to be executed before the sun rises," I replied. "But she will be afraid only for a short time. Timberlin is with them. As soon as they stand outside the castle, they will be taken from this city to the forest and the Quynaè."

"I am grateful to you," he said, bowing slightly in respect.

"And the warriors?" I asked.

"The warriors are safe. The soldiers barely glanced up into the trees as they searched for some reason. Whatever it is, I am grateful. They also did not venture among the leaves where no one walks. Had they done so they would have found their dead."

A smile fell across my face. "I think I am grateful you are on my side in this battle."

It was then that Kevelioc and the Danes joined us. From the Danes we learned that Yiltor's captain and Nepron have come to an agreement. When the sun rises, they will meet and talk. "I believe Nepron has intrigued the captain with stories of the ancient warriors who could battle against armies ten times greater in number and defeat them, leaving those who still lived, retreating in haste."

"It seems the captain and many of his men do not agree with the king's desires, and hope to find a solution that will pacify the situation they find themselves in," Kevelioc growled. "Your people have chosen Nepron as their captain and plan their strategy as generals would."

It was decided that we could leave the three hundred to Nepron and his army of intellects.

26

The Sacrifice

THE SUN HAD BEGUN TO RISE. The children were huddled together in soldier's quarters surrounded by soldiers, just as Thorri said they would be, though I could not see any signs of Timberlin. Barok's twittering reached into my thoughts, and I looked to the sky to see him approaching.

"I have just come from the tower," he said proudly, landing on a rock beside me. "Mythias thought you might need this. There are only three drops left inside, so he cautions you to use them wisely. Now what of your news?"

I told him of that which had transpired and was yet to take place. "The children will soon be taken to the safety of the forest now that Ancitel is no longer a threat."

My pouch suddenly felt warm against my side. Confused, I opened it and found the crystal glowing. The voice of Mythias whispered my name from its core. I held it in my hand and stared at the miniature face of the wizard.

"Ah, there you are," he said. His face, weary and lined with fatigue, sparkled with humor. "Close your mouth and listen."

I was unaware that my mouth was open and did as he requested.

"Ancitel is wrapped in the web of his own doing, for now," he warned. "If he can escape, I do not know. I have destroyed all that he would need to do so, except his wand. You need to remember that, for if I had broken it, its evil would have flung itself upon me, and I do not have the strength at this time, to fight it or destroy it. I have given much of my power, and it will take time for it to restore itself. Know this also, I am sure he is much too clever to not have a secret or two up the bellowing sleeves of his preposterously elegant robe."

I wanted to laugh at Mythias's description of Ancitel's robes. But the somber thought of Ancitel becoming a nuisance again darkened my mood.

"I must ask you," Mythias said, "have you not outwitted a most powerful wizard? Did you not use your own power against him and escape? He now knows that you are not a mere boy. He knows that you are a wizard, Etcheon—one of the most powerful ever to be born. Use it against him. That is how you shall change the future."

As if something had taken the air from him, Mythias stared at me through sunken eyes. "Do what you must do and do it now . . . destroy Yiltor . . ." His voice became frail as if it was difficult for him to speak. "Destroy the wizard who . . . who has freed himself, . . . demonstrating his power by attempting to pry into my mind. . . . to find you . . ."

His voice was now so weak that I could not hear what he was trying to tell me. I could only see his face become as a piece of stone. I called out to him, but the brightness of the crystal slowly dimmed and then lay dark in my hand. I stood there and stared at it, hoping it would come alive again when noise and confusion erupted from inside the city.

"Where did they go?" a soldier shouted.

"They disappeared before our eyes," another cried out.

Klogan and I looked at each other. With all that was still ahead of us, we could tuck a small victory beneath our peasant hats. All of the children were now safe in the forest with Mirlanda, and the Quynaè were tending to them.

With this small victory, however, greater dangers lie ahead for those still inside the prison. Yiltor would no longer waste time in waiting for the prince to appear. He would begin the execution of the women even before the sun began to set. We positioned ourselves just inside the gate and listened.

"The king demands silence!" shouted the guard who stood beside him on the balcony of the castle. Stepping away he bowed slightly, and Yiltor stepped forward.

"Explain," he called down to the soldier in charge.

"Sire, we surrounded the children, three men thick. Our eyes were straight upon them when they suddenly disappeared before us."

"Bring the women," Ancitel said calmly, stepping from the shadows into the light. He was arrayed in his finest robe, and his long black hair shimmered with the tiny crystals entwined therein. His hands twisted in the air. "They will not disappear."

Yiltor glared down at the wizard for a moment before speaking "Where you have been all this time?"

"I have been doing the king's bidding by eliminating the wizard Mythias, who thought he could rid himself of me."

"And who is this wizard that he should want to rid himself of you?"

"Once a dear friend, but now an enemy—one who desires to protect the Purcatians. Those who have disappeared from your kingdom are now safe inside his."

Yiltor shook his head, his hand gripping the iron rail that surrounded the balcony. "You have destroyed him?"

"I have not but have left him alive." Ancitel paused and looked around him, then focused his eyes on the king once again. "Not alive, as you and I are alive, but alive as the king and queen of the Hidden Kingdom. He is my trophy, and I shall display him on my mantle, a statue made of gold and stone." The wizard snickered with the thought.

I knew, now, why Mythias's face appeared as it did. I had no time to waste. I had to find him before Ancitel had control of his spirit. For once that was done, he could control the forest and the kingdoms.

The distant cries of a hawk—the signal telling Klogan that the warriors were near and waiting for his command—came from behind us.

Klogan turned to me and waited.

"Our strategy will be as I presented it, in the beginning," I said. My eyes drilled into his, warning him not to argue.

"I will not argue, for I know what must be done." Klogan reached out his hand in friendship. "When this battle is over, we shall have much to talk about."

"It will make a wonderful story that will be written down and told to the children of our future." I climbed upon Walkelin's back, my mask covering my face, my clataè pulled low over my forehead. My vest was tied securely around me. The bow and quiver of arrows given to me by the Ancient were strapped to my back, while the sling and cestro lay hidden in the pouch that hung from my side.

"You are truly a warrior-prince," Klogan said. "When you return, Yiltor will not doubt who it is that rides a giant horse so bravely into their city."

"I will enter Ancitel's mind and tell him I have gone to save Mythias. He will follow me, though the spell he will cast to prevent Timberlin from taking the women will surely remain. You know what you must do to save them. I go to save Mythias and rid us of Ancitel."

He bowed to me and then stepped back to let me pass.

"It is time to go," I whispered to Walkelin. The muscles in his body quivered with excitement, and everything around us began to move in slow motion as he set his hooves to the ground. Only one sound seemed to follow us—the vaporous voice of the wizard warning me that he would find me where Mythias lay, dead outside his forest.

"To the forest," I called to Walkelin in my thoughts. "We must get to Mythias." I had hardly finished with my instructions when the forest lay before us.

"Beware Young Etcheon, and stay on my back," Walkelin snorted. "All is not as it seems."

I did as he requested, holding tight to his mane as we stepped into the perimeter of Mythias's forest. We were greeted with silence. Not even the rustle of trees reached our ears. Then a breeze touched me, ever so softly, and it whispered in my ear. "You must find him before Ancitel inhales the last breath he will take. That breath will give him Mythias's life, and all that he possesses, even the forest itself—and all who live there. The forest will die; you and your kin will die."

I could feel the pain of the trees and hear their groans in the breeze as it passed by me. Walkelin snorted and shuddered beneath me.

The wisdom of the Ancient came to me. In all that had happened—with all who had been a part of everything that encircled my life—I was the only one who could decide which future would be mine and the future of my people. Why was I not afraid?

"Because you are not alone," the voices of my legion whispered from within me.

In the darkness of the night, the moonlight gave life to the skeletons. Through a mist that clouded my eyes, I saw the essence of their souls. "I will bring Mythias to you," I said, bowing slightly in respect, for they were to be respected as great wizards.

Once inside Yiltor's chambers, the king turned to Ancitel, his face ugly, his fingers wrapped around his sword as if he intended to use it. "Tell me, wizard, why is everything disappearing before me if this wizard is under your spell?"

"This is not the work of a wizard," Ancitel muttered quietly, as the king's face came close to his own, "but that of a wizard's father."

Yiltor paused only for a moment as if his mind was questioning the words of the wizard. Then he threw his arms into the air. "What are you babbling about?" he demanded.

Ancitel did not reply. Instead, he walked out onto the balcony, pulling a lock of his hair over his shoulder so that his hand could hold the crystal that bound the lock. Touching the center of the crystal with his finger, he brought it to life so his eyes could see within it. He requested that it show him the one who had taken the children. But even as he searched, he knew he would not find Timberlin. The little pixie was too clever to allow himself to be seen inside a wizard's crystal. His efforts were not a total loss, nonetheless, for his crystal revealed the presence of Purcatians.

"Show them to me," he whispered. "Show them to me, now!"

The crystal became bright in his hand and his eyes caught the glow, seeing them just as he had before. Their weapons were hidden beneath peasant clothing, their flaxen hair beneath ragged caps. They were inside the walls of the kingdom, some close to the castle—others not far away. What he saw next made him very curious as to the strategy of these children soldiers. For now, he would tell the king only of the one, who stood at the prisms.

He slipped the crystal back into his pocket and let his eyes wander to those who guarded the prisms as he stepped back into the room. "It is said that he who fathers a wizard has but one power himself," he reflected. "The power to protect the people of his blood, whether by magic or by his own wit."

The king studied him for a moment. "You are telling me these children are no longer here because the father of a wizard made them disappear?"

"What I am saying, Sire, is this: though Mythias is no longer a threat to us, for as I have taken his life, his father has taken the children. That is his power, his only power."

Thorri listened from his place at the foot of the prisms, as Ancitel talked of his trickery in capturing Mythias and of the forest where he supposed the children to be. Suddenly, the voice was silent. Then whispering rippled through the air, and he could feel a chill run down his back. "Bring him to me," he heard Yiltor say.

The guard standing next to Thorri stepped away as a soldier grasped the young warrior's arm, forcing him forward and into the room where the king stood waiting.

Ancitel tilted his head slightly, letting his eyes examine the young man dressed in the soldier's uniform. "Remove his helmet," he ordered.

Rough hands pulled the helmet from Thorri's head, taking strands of dark hair with it. He did not wince or cry out. Instead, he stood tall—his eyes steady, waiting for whatever was to come.

"Now, I wonder how you managed this," Ancitel continued, running his fingers through Thorri's hair until its true color revealed itself. "Are there more of you wearing soldiers' uniforms, I wonder?"

Thorri remained silent, neither looking at the king or the wizard, only keeping his eyes forward until Yiltor stepped into his view. "I need to know how many of you avoided the capture when your city was invaded by my soldiers."

Thorri stared directly at the king, saying nothing.

Finally, Yiltor stepped away. "Make him talk," he instructed Ancitel calmly.

"As you desire, Sire."

Thorri felt pain in his mind as the wizard's fingers touched his forehead. Spasms gripped his muscles, and he fell to the floor, his thoughts combining with those of the wizard—Ancitel asking the questions, Thorri providing the answers.

A sly grin appeared in the corner of the wizard's mouth. He decided to say little of what he had learned from the boy. What stirred him was the thought that if these children were able to take Yiltor's kingdom, the better for him, for he would take the kingdom for himself when they were finished. It would all be so simple.

"He is the only one inside the city," the wizard lied. He looked down into Thorri's face, noting the youth had not cried out though his face was twisted in pain. "His purpose is to keep watch over the prisms. There are twenty more just like him. They are not close, but they are armed with weapons, so we must assume they will come, as he has. Your captains have never seen the art of their strategies, nor their weapons—both more sophisticated than your own. But they are children, like this boy you see before you. When you take his life, the word will reach those who are like him." He looked down at the young warrior and sighed. "Then all who are children, such as he, will flee."

"Let it be so," Yiltor said, and flipped his robe with his hand as he turned away from Thorri, knowing it's edges would catch the young warrior's face and cause him more discomfort. He sat in his chair, taking time to decide what the punishment would be, then called a guard and explained to him what was to happen. "Let the sound of the trumpet signal his death," he said sadly.

"It will be done, Sire." The guard bowed and left the room.

Yiltor snapped his fingers and two more soldiers stepped forward, standing on either side of Thorri. "Take him now," he commanded, as if he were simply discussing the weather.

They reached down and lifted Thorri from the floor, dragging his limp body from the room.

The king and his wizard stood on the balcony—the wizard knowing he had regained the king's favor, the king thinking it would all be over soon and the land he so desired would be his. The two of them listened as a trumpet sounded and the guard announced that a Purcatian had been found hiding inside the castle, his purpose—to kill the king. Therefore, he had decided his own fate. He was to die by the very sword he planned to use against King Yiltor.

Klogan and his warriors could only watch as the execution was carried out. Thorri was forced to stand with his hands tied behind his back while his flaxen hair was shaved from his head. As the locks fell to the castle steps, they were ceremoniously swept into a bucket and passed to the king.

Yiltor raised the bucket high above his head. "See how easy it is to shave his head . . . to be rid of his golden locks . . . to take away the proof of his blood. But let us take the blood itself, and we shall see for ourselves how pure it is."

He let the bucket fall from his hand. The sound of it hitting the stones of the steps brought with it the cry of death as a sword was plunged into Thorri's heart, his blood spilling onto the golden locks that had scattered against the steps, turning them red.

Yiltor could not help but feel disappointed by the boy's lack of fear, even in death. It seemed to take away from the taste of victory, though the death brought him satisfaction.

Brettina, who loved Thorri, stood helplessly by, unable to do anything but watch him fall, his face calm, his eyes clear. The ache that clutched at her heart took her breath, giving no sound to the cries that escaped her lips. She wanted to shut her mind to the scene before her, but her eyes were set on Thorri's face.

Before Thorri took his last breath, a song of the sparrow stirred the air, and the warriors stood quietly, holding their positions. There they would wait until the women were brought from the dungeon. Timberlin would rescue them before they would begin their battle. They would honor this warrior, who gave his life for them.

"See, he did not disappear," Yiltor said to all who watched, his arms folded firmly across his chest.

"While you tend to the women, leave Prince Etcheon to me," Ancitel said calmly. "Before this day is over, he will be imprisoned just as the king and queen are. Then you can spend the rest of your days reminding him of his misguided arrogance, his foolish pride, and his ultimate defeat."

"Go, then," whispered Yiltor. "I will wait until you return before the women shall be executed. I wish him to see the execution himself. But you must return him to me before the sun sets."

"Oh, indeed, I will, Sire." The wizard disappeared.

From his hiding place behind a pillar, Klogan heard the words exchanged between king and wizard. He turned to move back into the crowd when, without warning, he felt the tip of a sword prick his back.

"Get from the castle steps," a voice scolded, "before the king decides to have you executed, as well."

Klogan lowered his head and moved away. It was then, out of the corner of his eye, that he could see the women of the Purcatians being driven, like cattle, to the stage of their death. At the bottom of the steps twenty soldiers waited, their bows armed. He prayed he would see the face of his wife one more time before Timberlin took her to the forest or the executioners took her life.

His eyes were drawn to Thorri's mother as she bent over her son. He listened to her cries as she gathered him to her, then removed her shawl and laid it over his face. He watched as a guard took her arm with noted gentleness, helping her to stand.

27

The Wizard's Revenge

"MYTHIAS," I CALLED OUT IN MY thoughts. But I could not reach him. Yet, I did not believe he was dead as Ancitel said. I would know if he were dead, just as I knew that he was still alive.

Finally, I brought Walkelin to a halt and sat quietly upon his back, clearing my mind of all thought. I waited. *Do not look for Mythias as the wizard, but the consequence of a wizard's sting.*

I slid from Walkelin's back. "We need only watch for Ancitel to come, and he will lead us to Mythias," I said to Walkelin. He neighed in agreement. We both could sense a disturbance around us. Ancitel was not far away.

"Will the potion do to you what it does for me?" I asked, pulling the bottle Mythias had given me from my pouch.

"He will not see me, though you can, if that is what you mean."

"What you are saying is that you can become truly invisible while I have to become a rat?"

"Have you ever thought to simply be invisible?" Walkelin asked.

I gave him a stern look, knowing I had not. "That will be my request now," I replied. I removed the lid of Mythias's bottle and dropped the last two drops of the potion on his tongue. The empty bottle disappeared from my hand.

I then took my bottle from the pouch and used the last two drops of the potion on my tongue. This bottle disappeared, as well. If we were truly invisible we would have to remain so until the potion's power had evaporated from within our bodies.

I put my arms and hands in front of me, and they were visible to me. "Can you see me?" I questioned Walkelin.

"As well as you can see me," he replied. "But I believe we are invisible to any other."

I climbed upon his back. "I pray that we are, for I can see Ancitel in the distance. He is coming our way."

When he passed by us, he suddenly paused and turned, his eyes searching behind him. A frown appeared upon his face as he looked to the right of us, then to the left. Finally he looked straight at us, or I should say, straight through us, for we were truly invisible to him. He would have seen us the moment he turned if we had not been. He continued on, seemingly more cautious.

It was then that I noticed the long staff he carried in his hand—Mythias's staff. Curiously, he did not touch it to the ground, but carried it as if it were a prize he had won and did not want it soiled. He seemed in no hurry, his steps were slow and careful. He would pause from time to time to listen and search the terrain behind him.

An hour passed. Still he continued his pace. "Could it be that he knows of us and plays a game?" Walkelin said in my thoughts.

Before I could reply, a strange and haunting song escaped Ancitel's lips.

> In ancient times, while at its birth,
> Earth's death was yet recorded.
> The past looks to claim its own,
> While the future lingers, then is gone,
> Long before the present can await its coming.
>
> Oh, 'tis a strange tale that the ancients sing,
> Of a man who comes from the future to bring,
> The travel stone made in the ancient of days,
> To understand what it is the future portrays,
> When it is stolen by an ageless wizard's cunning.
>
> 'Tis the tale of travel from future to past,
> To claim the magic and the wizard's mask,
> From the one who holds its secret and buries it deep,
> Beneath the earth, while another's eyes are closed in sleep.
> From such a tale as this, can there be no turning?

Though the words were twisted into riddles, I understood their meaning. The future would be of my making, if I were to kill him, or his to do with as he wished, if he were to take my life.

He was either aware that I was somewhere close enough to hear his song, or his song was for Mythias's ears. I could not be sure. Either Mythias had buried the mask, and the magic, deep within the forest where a wizard, such as Ancitel, could not enter unless he had taken all that Mythias had, or the mask was the one I wore, and he would claim it as he claimed the timepiece.

As the song ended, the wizard stopped abruptly, a plethron from the perimeter of the forest. In a voice that defiled the air, he called out to the forest, raising the staff above his head. "I have that which belongs to your master. Inside his staff, he sleeps. I have taken all the secrets he holds within him. Now, I shall inhale his last breath, taking from him the secret that will make me your master instead."

He tapped the staff against the ground. The rays of the sun seemed to catch its movements as it slowly molded itself into a stone statue—tall and majestic. The clothing belonged to Mythias. The arms were outstretched as if posed in battle. The face was etched with fierceness, the eyes—angry. The long, white hair fell down the back and was wrapped with a cord, while the beard was trimmed and short.

The shock of it caused me to gasp for air. The sound reached Ancitel's ears, and he turned quickly in the shadows. I could see the deep furrows of his brow while his eyes were but black slits etched in his face.

He removed one of the many crystals braided in his hair and rubbed it gently with his fingers. "Show me the young prince," he said, his voice soft, yet I could hear it as if I were speaking the words.

The crystal's glow reflected in the wizard's eyes. Then it vanished and Ancitel raised his head, his eyes searching once again. I knew that he had seen a ghostly horse and rider somewhere near, but the crystal could give him nothing more.

Placing his crystal in his pocket, he called out to me. "I am pleased that you are here, Etcheon the Younger. Whatever potion you have used to make yourself invisible cannot last for long. I shall wait until you are, once again, yourself. We have much to discuss."

In his eagerness to find me, he revealed how he had escaped from the prison of the hollow and what he was now capable of. The crystals braided in his hair were not only for the appearance of his vanity, but his weapons against his destruction. I counted eleven of them, all carefully placed in his hair, so it would be difficult for anyone to take them from him. Nonetheless, he had made it possible for me to get to the one in his pocket. It should be an easy snatch with hands that were invisible.

"It has been over three hours since we took the potion," Walkelin reminded me. "Whatever we do, we must do quickly."

I knew what I must do. I removed the timepiece from my pouch, opened its cover, and set it to take us to the hour Mythias spoke into my thoughts, telling me of Ancitel. "Come," I said. "We will learn how the wizard turned Mythias to stone."

"I cannot go with you," he neighed in my thoughts. "But the early shadows of the evening brings with it the last hour of the spell. You must hurry before you become visible again."

I understood. I quietly walked to Ancitel and reached out to his pocket, thankful that his robe was loose about him. I reached my hand into it and found the crystal. To wrap my fingers around it proved difficult, for he jerked his body around, and I felt the chill that ran through him. His eyes narrowed, piercing the air in front of me as if he could see me. No longer caring if he felt movement inside his pocket, I grabbed the crystal and quickly moved away.

"For what reason have you touched me?" he cried. He had felt the loss of a crystal without knowing—thinking it was my touch that made him shudder.

The good wizard had been right when he suggested that Ancitel might have something up his sleeve, only it was not up his sleeve but braided into his hair. He was more clever than Mythias had thought him to be, and now Mythias was his prisoner. Why had Mythias not considered the crystals? Or did he not have knowledge of them?

"Ah!" a voice rang out behind me as I ran to the statue, the potion having evaporated inside me. "I knew it would not be long before you would appear before me."

I turned to Ancitel when I reached the statue, holding the timepiece in my hand. I could see in his eyes the flames of greed flickering brightly. I could feel his voice inside my head, telling me to give the timepiece to him. I looked at him and closed out his voice.

The flames in his eyes were extinguished by his disappointment. "So wizardly prince, I think you have been tutored by the best." He paused and took a deep breath, rubbing his chin with his jeweled finger. Then he pulled at his locks of hair, twisting his fingers around them until he held two more crystals in his hand. He pressed his hand around them, forcing them to cut into his flesh. Blood began to drip from between his fingers, and his eyes closed. "Bring the timepiece to me," he whispered.

Suddenly, my hand began to burn, sending pain through my fingers, and I let go of the timepiece. Instead of dropping to my feet, it sailed through the air, Ancitel's fingers guiding it to him.

"You will not have it," I growled and leapt after it, my teeth bared, my eyes fixed on the timepiece. Just as it touched the fingertips that reached out to grasp it, I clutched it to me and ran back to the statue.

He stepped back, surprised at my speed and agility, yet he did not fail to see his blood smear across the gold of the timepiece. I pressed one hand against the statue and was just about to press the small pin on the timepiece, when his words stopped me.

"You cannot keep it from me, now," he said, sneering. "My blood has touched it, seeping into its belly, staining its glass, and tainting its gold. Into whatever time you take it, I will be there, for it carries my blood."

I reached down to wipe away the red stains, but they were no longer visible. *Let your own blood burn it from the timepiece,* I thought to myself, remembering the blood of the beast on my dagger. Quickly, I removed the dagger and pricked my finger, letting my blood fall on to the timepiece. White flames ignited, licking at the wizard's blood until it was no longer there. "You have been a good teacher," I mocked.

Ancitel's eyes became like ice. He realized his folly in revealing to me the secret of my blood.

I kept my gaze steady upon him. "Your magic means nothing to me."

"Then I shall bargain with you for the timepiece, once again." He walked to the statue. "But first I will tell you a secret. Mythias's people and the Purcatians are one people."

He must have sensed my surprise, for he smiled, removed his robe, and placed it over the frozen arm of the statue before he said more. "You did not know?" His eyes all but twinkled as he savored his words.

I sighed deeply, pretending to be bored with him. "And what I do not know, you will surely tell me."

"Yes, perhaps I should." He blew dust from the statue, his voice humming the song he had sung not long before. "And perhaps I will, for it will profit me as much as it will destroy you." Then he told me how the Purcatians came into being.

"You have told me nothing that would profit you or destroy me, as you said," I replied.

"Oh, but I am not yet finished." His tongue slid along his upper teeth in anticipation. His eyebrows arched, and his face revealed the thrill of his secret. Then I knew that he had somehow forced from Mythias the knowledge that would give him power over me. He spoke the name I dreaded to hear—"Tarainisafari"—letting it fall from his lips as if it were plated with gold.

In my shock, I felt the pain of the crystals as their brightness tried to force its way into my mind. It took all that I had been taught by the owl to deny it entrance. I suddenly felt the strain of fatigue, wanting nothing more than to sleep . . . to sleep forever.

"Press the pin, now," a voice screamed inside of me.

"I believe it is time to bargain," I heard the wizard's voice as my finger pressed hard against the pin that would return us to the hour I had set.

I could see Mythias walking by the edge of the sea, near the forest. He seemed to be relying on his cane to keep him from falling to the ground in fatigue. His face was ashen, his hair straggly and falling about his face as if he were a beggar without a comb. My heart felt pain as I watched him.

Then, I saw Ancitel waiting near the forest, his crystals glowing in his hair, giving him strength well beyond that of the good wizard, who had given much of his power to destroy all that was in the tower. I watched as Ancitel began to walk toward Mythias, and I could hear his words.

"Did you think I could be sent to a prison of my own making and not escape? Why have you not prepared yourself for a true battle against me? Is there no strength left in you? Are there no potions in your robe?" He cackled. "You become as an old rotten wand, forgotten and unused."

"And did you think that I would not prepare myself to meet you again?" Mythias replied, his voice tired and strained. "What seems to be may not be at all."

"You battle with words, old man. That is all you have left."

"Perhaps. Yet one can be deceived in his arrogance, do you not agree?"

The scene before me, and the words Mythias spoke to me in my thoughts, did not draw a parallel. This scene was more fearful—more revealing.

Ancitel removed a crystal from his hair. "This is my protection against you," he said when the two wizards were close enough to touch, their eyes locked. "Magic that appears only to be simple hair dressings, worn for vanity's sake."

Without warning, Ancitel forced his hand against Mythias's forehead. I heard a cry of pain escape Mythias as his eyes glowed with the brightness of the crystal that forced his memories and his thoughts to surface.

When the wizard moved his hand, I sensed the anger in Mythias. He raised himself to his full height, his strength burning in him. He reached out his hands to seize Ancitel. In that instant, Ancitel took a wand from inside the sleeve of his robe, pointed it at Mythias, shouted three words, and Mythias became stone.

I stood there, stunned. Why had Mythias not known what was coming? Had his senses been dulled with the loss of his strength? He had given everything for the sake of . . . of what? Was there something I had missed—something yet to learn? Was there something that he could not teach me without leaving me alone?

Ancitel's voice interrupted my thoughts. "You will forever remain a statue until one comes to free you."

I listened, my mind absorbing Ancitel's every word . . . every movement of his hands . . . the expression on his face, as he flaunted his victory. Then he paused and looked carefully into the stone face. "What? You ask how one could free you? Is that your question? I will tell you, for there is no one to hear."

Yet there was one who would hear. One who listened as the wizard told of the spell that would turn a man to stone and the spell that would release him.

"What is that you ask?" He raised his eyebrows as he leaned his ear close to the statue, in the pretense of listening, his dramatics almost comical. "How shall I take your last breath if you are a statue?" He backed away and sighed deeply, throwing his hands into the air. "Questions, questions, questions. You are simply full of them. But I will tell you, for only the two of us will know, and only one of us will still be alive to remember."

I listened as he told the stone statue all I needed to know. I watched as he put the crystal he had pressed against Mythias's forehead to his own. The crystal came alive once again, and all that had been taken from Mythias now belonged to an evil wizard. And he became ecstatic with all that flowed into him.

"I have all I need, or will ever need, from you." His voice was cruel as he spoke. "My crystal tears away the tenderness that surrounds the heart and steals all that is hidden there. You could not keep her locked away from me any more than you could lock me away in a prison of my own making."

He folded his arms across his chest and began to pace in front of the statue, his fingers caressing his chin. "Yet a thought comes to me," he said slowly, letting his fingers circle in the air. "You have always been a man of secrets and uncanny shrewdness. Could there be something I have not considered? Surely you knew what would happen when I found you again, knowing you had become weak . . . having given too much of your power." Ancitel paused and looked closely at Mythias's statue. "Yet, in all your cunning, what you once took from me shall be mine again, while you stand, forever, a statue of stone."

Again, I had not been prepared for all that he had said. He spoke of Taraini as if he knew her . . . as if he loved her. His words stunned me, and I had to force my mind to shut them out of my head. It was time to reset the timepiece and press the pin. I knew what Mythias's strategy had been when he called out to me in my thoughts. He was ever bit as shrewd and cunning as Ancitel claimed him to be.

I felt the trembling, and I stood, holding the timepiece in one hand and pressing the other against the statue of Mythias.

"I believe it is time to bargain," I heard Ancitel's voice say, again, his eyes fixed on the timepiece, his lips smacking with the desire to hold it.

"And what are we bargaining for?" I asked, innocently.

"Did you not hear me say her name?" He looked at me with pretended annoyance. "Very well, I will say it again. We will bargain for Taraini, the daughter of Mythias, of course." This time he said her name with elaborated eloquence. Did he truly love her, I wondered, or was his desire to possess her as he did the creatures and the books of the underworld?

When I did not reply but instead gave him a look of confusion, he laughed at me. "You think you can fool me into believing that you do not know of whom I speak, or perhaps it surprises you that I even know her."

I only knew the Ancient had warned me never to mention her name, but to carry it with me. What would happen if I allowed her name to cross my lips, I did not know, but Ancitel did, it seemed. No matter, I would pretend innocence. "If Mythias has a daughter, why did I not meet her in the garden of his cottage?"

He ignored my question, and I sensed the impatience in him. "You only have to say her name to remember." What was it that I would remember?

Think only of what you must do now, Barok's voice said inside me.

"If she is Mythias's daughter, she is not mine to bargain with. Only he can do such a thing." I goaded him, hoping he would tire of this game and strike out at me so I could do what I had to do.

"Say her name!" his voice echoed in my head.

"Why should I say her name when you already know it?" I shouted, pulling my eyes from his.

He turned from me, muttering something to himself. When he turned back, he walked toward the statue, pretending to concentrate his thoughts on the cord that held Mythias hair. "The gold piece you hold in your hand can take you anywhere you want to go, in this universe or another. And with it you hold the unknown possibilities of existence. With it in my possession, I could cause an eruption of time, transporting into another world, into another time. These things I learned from Mythias as I reached in and took from his memory all that I desired."

He paused and looked at me, as if for the first time. "Mythias was the one who sent you away, knowing I was aware of your power and other things I will not bother to discuss with you at the moment. But this I will say. I was the one who wished your father's kingdom destroyed. Yiltor was only the pawn. Mythias and I battled for the timepiece, just as you and I do now, using words as weapons. He is a very clever wizard, sending the timepiece with you, not telling you that you were of wizard blood, to protect your innocence."

It was true. I was a wizard. I also knew why my innocence had become my strength. The memories of another time began to flow back to me. I pushed them away. This moment was where I had to be.

"I sense there is something inside you that hides from me, refusing to explain itself to me. Something that makes you more than Mythias . . ."

"What is it you want from me, Ancitel?" I asked.

"Have you not been listening to me all this time?" he complained, the scent of his anger like acid to my nostrils. Yet the scent of his fear of me was stronger.

I could feel the greatness of all that had been taught to me by the animals. I welcomed the wisdom that flowed within me as I fought against his evil. He could not break the barrier that held him from me.

He whipped his robe at me. "Say her name, you fool!"

The crystals that hung from Ancitel's hair began to blaze as his wand appeared from inside his robe. Pointing it directly at me and speaking an enchantment, the wand released what appeared to be a bolt of lightening. Its force struck me in the chest, taking the breath from me—my flesh feeling as if it had been set aflame.

"All you need do is to speak her name, and she will come to you," his voice whispered into my mind. "Then I shall take her from you, and all that Mythias has shall then be mine."

I reached into my pouch and grasped the crystal I had taken from his pocket, saying nothing.

He touched his wand to my mouth. "Call to her."

Her name began to rise in my throat, and I could not stop it.

"His magic is only as powerful as you allow it to be," I heard Kevelioc growl. "Speak the words that will free you."

"Help me," I cried out in my thoughts.

"Let the crystal help you."

"Take the spell from me," I said as I pulled the crystal from my pouch, and the pain disappeared. My mind was free.

Ancitel's eyes were wild as he saw the crystal in my hand. "That belongs to me," he whispered harshly. "It is of no use to you."

"Yet it has taken away the pain of your spell," I said.

Ancitel's laugh became a cry of anguish as his beast burst into flames. He glared at me, his eyes fixed upon the crystal I held in my hand.

"You were right when you said that Mythias was cunning and shrewd. You walked right into his elaborate trap. You have lived too long, Ancitel, and have brought enough evil to this world." I took my father's dagger and forced the point into the center of the crystal I held in my hand. Ancitel began to scream as cracks etched their way along the surface.

I forced the dagger deeper until the cracks caused the crystal to break apart. As it began to shatter in my hand, I shouted the word, "Entropio." I watched the wizard's eyes begin to bulge from their sockets. His mouth fell open and his tongue protruded above his bottom lip. The poison of a potion of his own making filled his body with its acid. What was left of him slowly turned to stone—his face having lost all of its flesh. Only the wand and the crystals that hung from thin fibers of stone remained untouched.

When the wand fell to the ground, I picked it up and placed it in the outstretched hand of Mythias's statue, just as Ancitel had explained it should be done. He did not know that his glorious recitation of his spell was his undoing. "Anocio, inquil, recrudesce," I said, repeating the words exactly as the evil wizard had said them.

Slowly, the statue began to lose its stone-like appearance until the good wizard Mythias stood before me. He shook himself from head to toe and stretched his arms and legs, laughing as he did so.

"And what is it that you find so humorous?" I asked.

"Oh, young Etcheon, was it not a clever plan?" he replied joyously. "And you did not fail me. My gratitude is as enormous as is my relief to be human again."

He reached his staff into the air, then brought it forcefully to the ground while saying the words. "Flamonious leticna."

The crystals that hung from the statue's head disappeared. "They belong to those whose bones lie in the forest. Now that they have been returned to them, their lives will be returned to them as well. Ancitel did not recognize those he murdered without their flesh. He only saw skeleton bones, not knowing it was his doing."

I simply watched as Mythias joyfully went about his task, seemly totally oblivious to the fact of all that could have happened. "Why did you allow Ancitel to cast a spell upon you that could have imprisoned you forever?" I asked when he was finished. "Why did you not tell me of this amazingly frightful plan?"

"It had to be," was his only explanation.

"What if circumstances had been different, and I did not even know to come?"

"Because I knew I would only have to speak to you in your thoughts, and you would know to come." He smiled.

"Yet, in saving you, have I not also sealed my father's and mother's fate?"

Mythias's brows shot up. "You believe this?"

"What am I suppose to believe?"

He looked at me with sympathy just as Mr. Otherton had done. "You have not only destroyed an evil wizard, you have saved a good one. More importantly, you have saved a king and queen. His spells cannot exist if he does not."

I looked at him in surprise, relief flooding me. It seemed all so simple, looking back. It was the only way I could save my mother, my father, my people, Mythias, and be rid of Ancitel.

"You are beginning to see the size of the picture." Mythias's voice was gentle, yet stern. "And still there is much to do until it is finished. Listen to my words, Etcheon, son of a wise king . . . son of a wizard queen. There was no chance in what has been done. We have—"

"Why did I not know I was a wizard in the beginning?" I interrupted him.

"Because first, the books had to be written where you would learn to be a good wizard. Where you would learn how to use your powers that are so great within you—only for good. Where you would learn that you are still an infant in your learning."

"That is why Ancitel wanted the books?"

"If he had the books, he could devour them, then destroy them, as if they had not been written. In so doing, he would destroy you. That is why the unicorns protected them. We could take no chances."

He smiled gently and put his arm on my shoulder and placed his wand in my hand. "Feel its power, Etcheon. See it glow at your touch. No one else can make it do so. Yours is a power greater than mine, greater than Ancitel's. He knew this. Had we not sent you back when we did, he would have used the dark powers to steal you, teach you, and make you like him. Then he would have taken from you that part that was greater. After which, you would become a handsome statue in his garden of stone. Yiltor was simply the pawn. Your kingdom, part of the game."

"So he told me," I said. "But I am not through with my questions. The enchantments that I heard spoken—pulling me from danger or the wishes that I felt deep within me that were granted were of my own doing from the beginning." It was not a question. I suppose I just needed to hear the answer spoken from his mouth.

"It was, as you already know," he said, taking the wand from me and putting it back where he had taken it from.

"When this is all over, I want you to tell me all that you know about me. Then, I want you to tell me about your daughter and how it is possible for her to be your daughter," I said.

He shook his head back at me. "When this is all over, I will not need to tell you anything at all. You will already know."

"And the animals?" I eyed him, suspiciously. "Are they part of me as well?"

He only nodded his head. "Now, we must go to the castle of Yiltor. You will free your father and mother, take back that which belongs to you, and if you have any more questions, which I doubt, I will be more than happy to give you the answers."

28

All Are Not the Enemy

THE HOUR GREW LATE AND ANCITEL had not returned. Yiltor's patience had worn thin and it was time to rid himself of these Purcatians that had given him so much agony. He called for the guards to ready themselves.

Klogan had waited for Etcheon to return with as much patience. Nonetheless, they would follow the plan.

"For the women, do not fear," Timberlin whispered from somewhere above him.

He cautiously lifted his eyes and there, hidden in the leaves of the tree beside him, sat the tiny man—a wink of his eye and the smile on his face revealed he knew something Klogan did not.

Klogan tilted his head in acknowledgement and together they watched Yiltor raise his hand, the signal for the soldiers to ready their bows. When his hand dropped, the cry of a hawk rang through the air as the soldiers let their arrows fly. Before the arrows could touch the flesh of the women, and just as Klogan caught a glimpse of his wife, the women disappeared—as did the body of Thorri. The arrows of the soldiers dropped harmlessly to the ground—as did the soldiers—much smaller weapons finding their mark.

Yiltor stood motionless, his mind unable to accept what his eyes had seen. Soldiers in full armor scurried to surround him, pushing him back through the doors of the castle. The townspeople, showing the excitement of an execution, paused only for a moment to consider what they had seen and scurried far away from the castle steps. A warbling was heard. Then all was quiet.

From inside the king's rooms of the castle, Yiltor paced back and forth, mumbling to himself. Ancitel had lied about the Purcatian soldiers. How many were inside the gates of his kingdom? Yiltor called for one hundred guards to surround the castle, five hundred more to guard the city. One hundred more stood upon the walls where large bows, strung with ten arrows, waited to be fired at whatever enemy might appear. One hundred soldiers also began to search every building, be it house, barn, or business, for the Purcatians. Not one corner of the city was to be left concealed. Soon eight hundred soldiers stood as protectors of Yiltor's kingdom while twenty-four surrounded the prisms.

When all was set in place, Yiltor called to his scholars—those who studied the supernatural powers of the ancients. "Bring together all your knowledge," he commanded them, "and come with me. We must rid ourselves of this evil wizard who has it in his mind, and perhaps in his power, to take away my kingdom as well as that of the Purcatians."

Four men, their hair and beards gray with age, followed Yiltor to a room far above the living quarters of the castle. It was a library, of sorts, filled with books that, for many years, had not been opened.

"Here you will find that which you do not know. Study these books. Add to that which you do know. Then we will learn how to destroy the wizard."

The men sat around a dusty table, opening books that smelled of age and covered with the webs of dead spiders. Yiltor paced up and down the room, as he always did when his mind was a muddle, waiting, watching as the scholarly men searched the pages filled with ancient words, seeking the answer to the King's question: "How does a mortal man destroy a powerful wizard?"

Finally, Yiltor left the old men to their musty books and returned to his chambers, and to the prisms where twenty-four soldiers surrounded them. Twelve stood, the prisms pressed against their backs. Twelve stood three steps away. All had their swords drawn and ready.

In the doorway, the overseer of his army waited to be heard, his eyes etched with fatigue, his face lined with troubled thoughts.

"Sire," he said, giving a slight bow. "May I speak with you?"

Yiltor motioned him closer. "Speak."

"We have lost one hundred and twenty-six men, at counting. The wounds are all very much alike. It seems that the weapons were aimed to cause instant death, so there would be no suffering."

Yiltor's brows furrowed, but he did not attempt to interrupt.

"The twenty, if not more, are somewhere inside the city, not beyond it, as the wizard claimed. They cannot escape nor can they do real battle against us. We are too many. Though the night draws near, the soldiers will not sleep but will continue their watch. If yet a few more soldiers die, we will have the enemy."

Yiltor took a deep breath and rubbed his chin, letting all that the overseer reported settle in his mind. He stepped to the window where the moon now cast shadows on the quiet streets below. The only sounds that touched his ears were the echoes of the soldiers' boots upon the cobblestones. "Tell me," he said soberly. "How are they dressed?"

"Sire?"

"These Purcatian soldiers. What do they wear?"

"We are not sure. While some have said they are dressed as peasants, others claim they have stolen the armor of our own soldiers."

"I believe those who hide among us are not the fools we think them to be." Yiltor stood on the balcony his eyes searching. "An army of twenty can hide themselves much more cleverly than an army of fifty or a hundred?" He let a deep sigh escape as he turned back to the overseer. "We have never battled against children, if they are, indeed, children as was the one we discovered and executed. We have never battled against an unseen army whose weapons are unknown to us. We have never been in battle where we have yet to raise a weapon and already more than one hundred of our own lie dead. We have never battled against an army who are dressed as we are, unable to distinguish them from our own. Tell me, overseer, how do we rid ourselves of them when we do not know what we are looking for? When we do not have the wizard to point them out to us?"

The overseer's eyes flashed with spite. "And where is your wizard, now?" he asked, having felt nothing for Ancitel except jealousy and distrust. "Do you think he cares for your victory? Nay, he cares only for his own comfort, his own gain—and for the timepiece that draws him to the prince."

Yiltor felt the alarm surge within him. "What do you know about this timepiece?" he demanded, glaring at the man before him.

"Only that it is real, or so the stories of the past reveal it to be." He studied the king for a moment. "Have you never heard the stories of the timepiece, Sire?"

"Only that they are stories, nothing more."

"Then how do you explain the young prince, who, as a babe, is swept away in the talons of an eagle and after six days, returns as a man?"

"What proof do we have that he is that child?"

The overseer paused for a moment, to reflect. "We have none. It is, as you say, a story. Nonetheless, your wizard believes it and has for the years that he has been here. I believe he knows something we do not know. That is why I believe the stories."

Yiltor could not disagree with the overseer's argument, and was about to say so when he heard the commotion beyond his chambers.

"We must see the king," the voice of one of his scholars called out.

The four old men swept into the room as if they had forgotten the ailments of their ages. Their beards were touched with webs, and their faces powdered in gray. Dust from the books that had been opened and from the chairs that had been sat upon clung to their robes. A thin, narrow book was clasped in the hand of the one who led them. Its cover was of snakeskin.

"We have found a way," a scholar, who carried the book, said with more excitement than he had intended.

The unsightly appearance of the astute old men brought a touch of humor to Yiltor while their words brought hope for revenge. "Explain," he said.

The scholar opened the book to a certain page and handed it to Yiltore. "In this book they write that they rid themselves of a wizard who desired their kingdom," he explained. "You will notice that it is much the same story as we are dealing with today. Also, you will notice that they have proudly put their pen to the page to tell how it was done."

All stood silently as Yiltor read. "Most amazing," he uttered to himself as his eyes followed his finger down the page. "What is this thing called an alicom?"

"'Tis the horn of a unicorn," the scholar replied. "And known to be magical."

Yiltor looked up at the scholar. "You will tell me, of course, how we are to find this alicom—this horn of a unicorn—when a unicorn has not been seen in hundreds of years?"

The scholar smiled and stepped away while another stepped forward. In his hands lay a beautifully spiraled, though whimsical looking object— an alicom. "It was not an easy task, but it has been found," the scholar replied.

The king stepped back from the alicom, almost fearful of it, as if to touch it would bring him death. He turned from the man who held it in his hands, hiding the strange sense of fear that bristled inside him. "Take it from me and do what needs to be done."

The warbling of a sparrow told the warriors to remain where they were, for the night. They made themselves as comfortable as possible, on the thick limbs of the massive trees, whose leaves shielded them from the view of the soldiers.

Klogan kept watch over his warriors from atop the stone wall, dressed in a soldier's uniform. A helmet protected his face while the blackness of the night darkened his skin. Here he would stay, walking among the soldiers and listening to their conversations, until the sun began to rise. He did not sleep or speak. He only listened. When he slipped from the wall, at the light of day, he knew what he needed to know. Not all the soldiers of Yiltor wished to fight a battle that was not within their understanding of bravery or loyalty. But they would defend themselves and their city.

He slipped beneath the trees where his warriors slept when he felt a tug at his sleeve. Alarmed, he placed his hand over his dagger and turned his head slightly. From the corner of his eye he could see the face of a child looking up at him. Not knowing if this might be a trick, he did not relax the hold on his dagger, but turned slowly to see into the innocent eyes of a boy. On his head he wore a peasant's cap. His clothes were worn, yet clean, and the look on his face was one of great adventure and bravery.

The boy put his finger to his lips and motioned for Klogan to follow, disappearing through a gap in the wall, hidden by heavy vines.

"Shh," warned the boy when their faces met again. "The soldiers are close. Come."

Klogan followed, and soon they were back inside the wall and in a small courtyard filled with fruit trees and vegetable vines.

"This is my house," the boy said, pointing to the small, dainty cottage—its back door open as if someone was waiting for them to enter. "Do not worry," he whispered. "My brother waits to talk to you."

Klogan's eyes examined the room as he entered, his senses keen. A woman, standing just beyond the door, smiled at him, inviting him to sit on a stool beside the table. "We honor you in our home," she said softly, setting a plate of bread and cheese and a goblet of water in front of him.

He thanked her, accepting the food and drink. He had not eaten for several hours and was truly hungry. The woman stepped away and nodded to a young man who stood at the door. Klogan could see that he was a soldier. His muscular build and his stance gave him away.

Klogan instantly grabbed his dagger and stood to face the man, but the boy cried out, "Listen to what my brother has to say, please!" There was only a slight pause in the child's voice. "Come brother, tell him what you know."

The young soldier stepped into the room and took a long look at Klogan. "Please remove the helmet so I can see the color of your hair."

Klogan studied the young man standing boldly in front of him. His skin was tan, his eyes intelligent, his hair almost black. In spite of his armored uniform, he had a look of refinement, as if he should be a student, not a soldier. "First, you tell me what it is you have to say?"

The soldier stepped back, pulling the boy and the woman behind him. "You can see I have no weapon. Yet I must know if you are a Purcatian before I say what I have to say to those who have come to save their kin."

Klogan sighed deeply, slowly set the dagger on the table, and removed his helmet. "As you can see, I am a Purcatian," he replied with caution. "But how do you know me?"

The soldier pulled the small boy out from behind him. "You can thank Lloch for that. He has been blessed with a curious mind. He sees things others miss, and as you have witnessed, he is fearless. Our mother has raised him well." He gently took his mother's arm and led her to a seat. "Please sit and we will sit, also."

Klogan looked from one face to the other of the three who stood before him, and only after they had seated themselves, did he do so.

"My name is Raini," the soldier said when they were all seated. "I am a soldier in the King's Army and stand as a guard at the prisms that so cruelly confine your king and queen. I must tell you that I do not agree with what King Yiltor is doing, nor do many of the soldiers. I must also tell you that I stood beside the young man of your clan, not knowing who he was, and felt of his goodness and friendship." He paused, smiling unknowingly. "Even a rat became his friend."

Klogan could not help but smile with him, being a friend of the rat himself.

"I did not know he was of your clan," Raini continued. "But when they drug him from the castle and executed him, I knew I could no longer stand by quietly, doing nothing but my duty when my duty was not one of integrity."

"His name was Thorri," Klogan said sadly. "He was one of the bravest of my warriors."

"You are their leader, then?"

"I am."

The young man nodded. "The king keeps the prisms close to him now, guarded by twenty-four soldiers. Last evening, while I stood with them, I listened carefully to all that was said. When I told this story to my mother, Lloch said that he would bring you to me and I could tell you, so more Purcatians would not die." He proceeded to tell Klogan all that he knew about unicorns and alicoms, ending with the words of the scholars. "Can you tell us how this is done?" he asked.

"When the point of the horn is pierced and one blows into it, it emits a silent sound so soothing to a wizard that it subtly puts him into a dream sleep. In his dream, he follows the path of the sound until it brings him to the one who controls the horn. And who, from that day, controls him, for he never awakens from the dream. His breath slowly dies within him until, at last, he is drained of life. In death his soul is lost and his body becomes a heap of ashes."

"Why the horn of a unicorn?" Lloch asked, his eyes filled with the excitement of the mystery. "And why only wizards?"

Klogan explained. "The unicorn represents purity and goodness. The horn has powers of magic unknown to wizard or man. All that is evil lusts after the life of the unicorn to steal the alicom for its magic. Yet nothing evil can touch a live unicorn and not be stricken. And though they may live, and the unicorn die, they suffer the pain of their evil deed through eternity."

"Do those who are evil know of the consequences when they go after the unicorn?" Lloch asked.

"They believe their power is beyond that of the unicorn."

"But it is not," the boy said with conviction.

"It is not," agreed Klogan.

A contented smile spread across Lloch's face, and he moved closer, afraid of missing a single word of this remarkable story.

"But if, by chance, a unicorn simply dies and is found by evil men, its horn can be removed and used for evil purposes," Klogan continued. "Nonetheless, know this. The unicorn is a sentinel of a good wizard, and watches over him, yet does neither control or command him, though, at times, suggests."

"My mother does the same." The boy giggled.

The shadow of a smile etched Klogan's face, as he continued. "If the horn taken is sounded, it reaches the ears of the unicorns first. They call out to their master, warning him if the purpose of the horn is good or evil. If it is good, they do nothing more, for the sound only brings the soothing sounds without entrapping them in the dream. But if it is evil, they hurry to the side of the wizard, and there they stay until the horn is silenced."

Lloch released the air that been trapped in his lungs from the intrigue. "I wonder if the horn in the castle is good or evil?"

Klogan wondered that as well, knowing if it was evil, Mythias and Etcheon would be brought to the castle. He would have to leave that concern to the unicorn that watched over Mythias.

"How can we assist you in your battle against the king, when the wizard is no longer a threat to him?" Raini asked.

"There are many who will come to your aid, who live inside the walls of this city," Raini's mother said. "Soldiers are now checking every house for those of your kin. Some are noisy and boisterous, claiming they have already found five—teenage boys and girls—not even the age of Raini. They hold them in the king's chambers. Others are quiet, seeming almost ashamed to be a part of this."

"I don't even know your name," Klogan apologized. "Yet you have been so kind."

The woman smiled. "Amber is my name. We are the family of Captain Anusara, one of the king's most trusted soldiers." The smile left her face, replaced by a look of simple pride. "My husband is a great soldier, though not always in agreement with the king. He was sent with three hundred soldiers to follow the hundred who appeared as angel warriors outside the gates of our city. They have yet to return, and I am concerned for him as well as I am concerned for your people."

"I can promise you that your husband is safe, if he does not do all that the king demands, at this time," Klogan assured her. "The hundred are intellects. The one who leads them will most likely discuss war and its ultimate ruination with your captain and his men—either captivating them or boring them into a deep sleep, rather than to actually engage in battle."

Amber laughed. "I think I will believe you after all that has happened. So strange have been the events."

285

Again, Raini asked how those who were with him could assist when the time came.

"There will be a way, if you truly wish to help."

For several minutes they talked and when Klogan was ready to leave, a strategy had been arranged between them. "Perhaps when this is all over, I can introduce you to my warriors and their prince. They will all thank you for what you have done. And now, I must go."

"I will take you back to the tree where I found you," Lloch said.

"I would be very grateful if you would," Klogan replied, though he already knew the way.

When he returned to the wall, he walked as a soldier would to the great trees, pretending to search the area. He put his fingers to his mouth and sent a signal that brought Raven to him almost immediately. "How many are in the trees?" he asked abruptly.

"Eleven," Raven replied, eyeing him closely.

"And the others?"

"Near the castle, shielded by the shrubbery and flowers."

More than an hour passed and Klogan still did not hear the warbling of the sparrow from five of his warriors. Suddenly, Raini stood beside him.

"I have found many who feel that an injustice has been done to your people. There were three inside the king's court itself: One who stood at the prisms, as I did. One who is a servant of the king. The third—an elderly scholar, who was with those who found the book of instructions and the horn."

"Have they begun to blow the horn?"

"It has begun." Raini's harsh laugh rang unexpectedly through the air. "Even as the king waits for the wizard to be returned to him, he rants like a spoiled child who has not been given his way." His expression became serious once again. "Are those you lead, safe?"

"Because of your warning, fourteen are safe. The soldiers were correct, who claimed five were being held prisoners in the King's chambers."

"There are many, inside these walls, who will stand by your side," Raini reminded him.

29

Etcheon's Victory

THE BREEZE WAS GENTLE AND soothing. My eyes closed slowly and a path entered my dreams. I had not felt so warm . . . so calm . . . so peaceful. Suddenly, Barok's cries drilled through my mind. And though I tried to push it away, it only increased in intensity. I could not shut him out.

"Go away," I shouted to him.

"I will not, and you will wake up!" he squawked back at me.

I could feel the pain of his beak pecking on my ear. I could feel Walkelin's nose against my back, my clothing clenched between his teeth as he dragged my body away from the path and toward the forest. Once inside, he let me go, and I stumbled, falling hard against the ground, and the melody was lost. My eyes opened. "What . . . ?"

"There is no time to discuss *what*—just stand and look."

Something about Barok's tone warned me to do as he commanded. When I stood, I thought I saw Mythias coming toward me, a unicorn at his side.

"Her name is Ufradis," I heard him say, stroking the unicorn's mane. "Come. Let her cure you of your illness."

I looked at him as if he had gone mad. "I have no illness, though you look somewhat like an illusion to me."

He laughed. "Your sense of humor is returning. That is good. Now do as I ask, and I will explain."

The unicorn came to me, and I laid my head against her neck while Mythias told me the strangest story of a spell that was placed upon the unicorn horn.

"More than a thousand years ago," he began, "members of a great wizard's council thought it wise to use that which is pure to fight against that which is evil in such a way that evil's sorcery would have no defense. They went in search of that, which evil could not touch—the unicorn. In the purity it represented and still represents, a horn belonging to one who had died was given to the wizards. They were told what they must do to give the horn the power they desired it to have. But they were warned of the consequences if it was ever used for anything other than what they requested it to do."

He paused to inspect my eyes and my tongue. "You are well enough, now. Let us sit beneath a tree while I continue to tell the story. "

I was happy to do as he asked. Though I seemed well enough, my limbs seemed quite limp.

When we were settled, he continued. "Though it may have seemed wise at the time, as the years passed, the spell became corrupted and was turned against the great wizards by those the spell was meant for. Now, when the horn sounds, all wizards are placed under its spell. But as always, when wisdom is corrupted, greater wisdom is born, and in that process we have learned that the unicorn has become our protector against the horn of its breed."

"Your story is a strange one," I said, shaking my head. "Why is it that the forces of good and evil battle in all life?"

"I suppose that is how it is meant to be. Yet, in all my years, good has always triumphed and will do so as long as we protect those who have the power above that which is evil."

He paused and looked around him. "When the horn is silent, we will know that the statue of Ancitel stands before the king." He laughed. "Would that not be a scene to behold? Though I think he will be disappointed another wizard is not there also, for surely Ancitel has told him of one who hides in the forest. We will take no chances in thinking he does or does not know of our wizardry. Sadusarias will be here soon. If the horn sounds again, he and Ufradies will be our protection against the illness."

"How can the statue of Ancitel . . . ?"

He did not wait for me to finish asking my question. "Whether he be stone or warm flesh, dead or alive—unless, of course, he is in ashes—the sound of the horn will draw him to the castle."

I looked at him, and I could see the humor in his eyes, as he could see the humor in mine. We were both imagining Yiltor's face when he found Ancitel in his chambers. "He may even think the horn caused Ancitel's frightful condition," I said, "and he will feel glory in his victory over the wizard."

"On the morrow, when the sun begins to rise, we will rest in celebration. But for today . . ." He pulled his wizard's robe about him and placed his wizard's hat upon his head. "Is this how you think a wizard should appear before a king?"

"Only one as handsome as you," I said. "Now, I will prepare myself and we will go to battle."

"Sire," one of the soldiers called to King Yiltor. "Your scholar calls to you. There stands inside your chamber the ugliest statue we have ever seen. Come, see for yourself."

Yiltor followed and stood before the stone statue of Ancitel, finding it difficult to make out the face of the wizard, it was so hideous. But the clothing was the clothing of the wizard, and confirmed their suspicions.

"Is it the horn that has done this to him?" Yiltor asked the scholar, who had read the instructions and blew the horn until this statue stood before him.

"It does not say in what condition the wizard will appear," the scholar answered. "So I cannot give you an answer."

Yiltor took his time walking around the statue, his arms folded across his chest, his fingers resting on his chin. "He is surely dead, is he not?"

"He cannot be alive, sire. But, if you doubt, we can crush the statue and heat what is left until all is turned to ashes."

"Do it, immediately," Yiltor said, his whole body perspiring in the need to be rid of this statue and what it had represented. Without looking back, he left the room and shut the door behind him.

"King Yiltor, the prism that holds the Purcatian queen bears a crack along its middle," a guard called out to him as he entered the room.

Yiltor pushed the guards aside and touched the crack, following it with his finger. "Bring some sealing wax and pour it over the fracture," he called to his servant. He turned away from the prisms, calling for the guards to bring the five who sat in chains and follow him to lower rooms of the castle.

"There will be no display of execution for the five. I want them dead before we parade them. Do you understand? I want them dead when Etcheon comes to save them!"

Before he could say more, a shout rang out from the tower. "A lone rider comes."

"Get those five to the lower room and do as I requested—now!" He turned from the soldiers and walked to the balcony.

He listened to the bustling noise of the soldiers' voices. Then silence erupted as the gates slowly opened, revealing the bay horse and rider for all to see. The rider was magnificent in his white tunic, unusually tooled vest, and brown leather trousers. His boots, reaching nearly to his knees, were peculiar, yet finely sewn. The clataè on his head gave him an air of mystery as its brim fell low over his brow, shadowing the mask that shielded his face.

A fine quiver of arrows was strapped to his back. In his hand, he carried an amazingly beautiful bow, larger than most. The string glistened as if it was made from silver. Yiltor had no doubt that this was the prince. On the hill beyond the wall of the castle, he saw what appeared to be a unicorn. He shut his eyes and opened them again. The unicorn was gone.

The eyes of the soldiers looked up at me as I passed. I thought I saw looks of apology in many of them, while others showed the eagerness for battle. But all stepped back, as if they feared the horse I rode.

Walkelin stopped at the steps of the castle, and I waited for Yiltor to appear. I saw movement inside the partially opened castle doors, and a servant stepped out of the shadows. In his hands, he held a parchment. From it, he read: "Son of King Etcheon, kneel before King Yiltor and submit yourself to him. Acknowledge him as your king, giving him all that you own which is all the land of your father, King Etcheon."

The king stepped forward, wearing his royal robes, and I could read his thoughts. I had all but humiliated him. Now he wanted revenge. He wanted all to see me kneeling before him, begging him to preserve the lives of my kin. He did not know how the Purcatians disappeared before him, yet he assumed that I thought they were still inside his prison, and he would use this against me.

He looked at me and sighed. "I am afraid I have some sad news for you. The one who pretended to be you died upon these steps." He walked to where a pool of blood lay dry against the stone of the steps. "Here lies the proof." He turned back to me and sighed again. "As you had to miss it, I shall tell you the story."

When he finished, he stopped and gazed down at me. "It was you, I believe, who placed him there." He came closer. "You could not save him any more than you could save five more of your children soldiers who have just been executed in the lower rooms of the castle."

I remained on Walkelin's back, numbed at what he had said. The mask now shielded my emotions more than it shielded my identity. "Tell me, King Yiltor," I said, my voice cold. "How did it feel to execute a young Purcatian warrior? Did it make you feel more like a king?"

Yiltor's face turned pale, yet his voice remained calm. "I will dismiss your insults. You have no army to battle against my soldiers. You have only children, who fight for you."

"How many of your army lie dead from the wounds delivered by these children? A hundred? Two hundred, perhaps," I contended, "while three hundred more are held prisoners by those you considered nothing as well."

Yiltor was silent for a time. He had heard nothing from his captain about capturing the hundred, but that did not mean he had not. Why, then, should he believe this boy before him? A look of triumph arched his face, and he ignored the words of Etcheon. "How large is your army, now that six lie dead? Less than twenty, I suppose, if Ancitel has given me the correct numbers."

"If my small army, as you suppose, can kill two hundred of your trained soldiers, how many can fourteen or fifteen warriors kill before you begin to understand you cannot win?"

The king shook his head, his face filled with satisfaction. "You say I cannot win? What shall I do, then, to prove that it is you who cannot win?" He paused to rub his chin as if in deep thought. Then his hand came away from his face and fluttered in the air. "Perhaps a simple display will give you a demonstration of my intention." He raised his hand as a signal for the guards to bring the dead bodies of the warriors. "Would you care to see the five whose lives were snatched from them with a simple movement of my hand?"

I reached into Yiltor's thoughts, and I could see that he thought the five were truly dead. Yet I also sensed the beating of their hearts. Not all who were commanded by this wicked king were loyal.

It was time. I lifted my hand and removed the mask, giving the warriors the signal to be ready for battle. "You see the face of the one whose identity you wished to steal. What more you ask of me, I will not give."

Yiltor placed his hands on his hips as his eyes met mine, and I could see the envy and the hatred he held for me. "You are the image of your father, and there is no doubt as to your identity." He raised his arm. "Now that I know it is truly you, I will show you that you are no threat to me." I was conscious of the movement as he prepared to drop his hand—the signal to execute me.

In that instant, the shadow of a large eagle swooped down and lifted me from my horse while fourteen warriors stood, their cestros in one hand, their slings in the other. The soldiers were not prepared for what they saw. Twenty of the soldiers, who guarded the king, fell upon the steps. Then the fifteen warriors disappeared.

Fear expressed itself quite well on the face of Yiltor. He backed away, his eyes darting all about him, his voice screaming for the soldiers to attack.

More soldiers surrounded their king, pressing against him, pushing him back into the safety of his castle.

Captains were shouting for the citizens to return to their home and lock themselves in until the enemy was found and eliminated. If they did not leave, they would be considered the enemy and treated as such. The citizens acknowledged the command and fled. Nineteen lingered, though, out of the sight of the soldiers. In the shadows, they waited.

"We do not wish to kill more of you," Klogan called out. "Nonetheless, we are prepared to do so. The choice is yours."

Yiltor was so enraged, he could neither speak nor move, nor could the guards around him. The nightmare of what was happening held them captive. Their swords were still, their arrows silent.

"Find them and kill them all," the king shouted to his captains. He glanced into the sky, his eyes glazed with madness. Then he wrapped himself in his robe of cowardliness, turned, and made a speedy retreat, disappearing inside the castle, behind the thick protective walls.

From my view astride the eagle's back, I could see more than three hundred soldiers inside the city walls, while two hundred more, outside the city, guarded any escape. I could hear the sounds of swords being drawn and the strings of bows stretched. And I could see a single unicorn standing on the hill, watching me as if he was watching over me, and I knew he was.

"Constellations of the universe, those of my ancestors, let this world step out of rhythm, that I might control time." The words roared from deep within me, pushing themselves out and up into the firmament. The ground below me began to tremble. Soldiers, with swords raised to strike both the horse and the rider, suddenly moved as if their bodies were sleeping. Their cries and shouts were almost unintelligible in the slow escape from open mouths.

Out of the corner of my eye, I could see the unhurried flight of an arrow aimed to pierce Walkelin's neck. Barok flew down and I simply reached out with my hand and seized it, wondering if all around us had been caught in the warp, or if we alone had been pulled into it. It did not matter. Whatever force had allowed me to control time, I would be truly grateful to it. Many of the warriors would have seen death before this day was over.

"This is an interesting strategy," Barok said, as we watched the soldiers from the sky. "They are like silly statues."

I agreed. The movement of their pose in battle was so slow it was almost hypnotic.

I heard the whistling sound of the warbler, and I saw a soldier, his hand reaching out to clasp Klogan's in friendship, but his movement was caught in the warp. With a puzzled look, Klogan dropped his hand and backed away, turning his head from side to side and seeing what he could not comprehend. The five who were to be executed were no less puzzled. They hurried to him, their weapons ready.

"Take me to Klogan," I said to Barok.

"As you wish," he twittered, seemingly enjoying himself.

Klogan welcomed me. "What is happening?" he stuttered.

"I believe we are experiencing a wrinkle in time," I answered, still trying to fully comprehend what had happened myself.

Klogan's eyes narrowed as he studied me. "This is remarkable, and of your making, I suppose."

"If that's what you believe, then it is so."

"It is what I know," he answered, turning to the young solder caught in the time warp. "Let me tell you of him. His name is Raini. There are many here who do not agree with their king and have aided this young soldier—and who will aid you, as well."

Kadren, one of the five who had been held prisoner inside the king's chambers, rushed to my side. "There is something else you must know. The prisms that confine your father and mother have a crack that extends the length."

It was as Mythias had promised. Ancitel's spells died with his own death. I gazed up at the balcony that would take me into Yiltor's chambers.

"We will gather the weapons," I said to the warriors. "But keep your own weapons ready. We do not know how long this spell will linger. Let us be quick."

They nodded their understanding and hurried away.

As a soldier's weapon fell, his eyes, wide with bewilderment, would follow its descent. Then his eyes would rise to stare at his empty hand. So slow was the process, it was as a comedy of errors . . . a ballet of fools. But we did not laugh as we went about taking the weapons from the hands of the soldiers. This was a deadly play, yet to see an ending. Before the task was complete, however, the time warp began to dissipate.

"Get to the top of the steps with your weapons ready," Klogan called out to his warriors. "Throw the swords and bows behind you."

Barok gathered me in his talons and lifted me to the balcony of the castle that led into the chambers where the prisms waited for me. "I will be close by," he said, "if you need me."

I thanked him and slipped inside the room where shadows wrapped themselves in darkness, leaving the light struggling to survive in the flames of candles that surrounded the crystalloid prison of my father and mother. Iridescent light glistened at the edge of the crevices that forced themselves deep into the prisms—almost deep enough to free the bodies that lie beneath them. I could hear the sounds of the crystal dividing itself, again and again. Soon it would shatter.

It was then that I saw him, his face and hands visible in the candle's flame. He was standing over the prisms, his voice soft, whispering words I could not hear. I moved closer.

". . . as there are many things I would like to discuss with you, if we only had time," I heard him say. "But, alas, there is no time left. Your son has come with his army of children to take my kingdom, and perhaps his thoughts are of you as well. Yet I am afraid his efforts to find you will only bring him sadness, for as my kingdom dies, so will you."

I could see him holding something in his hand. As the light touched its metal, the dagger became visible. He ran his fingers along the edge of the blade, continuing to speak. "Soon the crystals will shatter and then I will shatter your hearts with the blade." His eyes seemed sad in the soft glow that touched his face. I wondered if he had never felt love, and I almost pitied him.

The shattering of the crystal brought an almost joyous sigh to his lips. "It is time."

I raised my bow—the string drawn—the arrow aimed and ready. Just as he was about to plunge the dagger, I called out his name.

He turned and looked at me, his face showing no surprise, only his madness.

I let the arrow fly. It pierced his chest, plunging itself into his heart, and I whispered, "A gift from the Ancient."

Yiltor gasped and staggered backwards. "It seems you have fulfilled the prophecy," he stammered in pain, as the blood flowed freely from his wound. Then death took him, and he fell to the foor, his cold eyes staring up at me in their lifelessness.

His servant, standing nearby, bowed to me. "There are no soldiers in the castle who wish to do battle against you," he assured me. "Nor do I wish you ill will." He turned and fled from the room.

I ran to the prisms, which had completely shattered. Taking my mother in my arms, I lifted her from the bed of glass and laid her on the king's pillows, then returned for my father, who had begun to stir. His eyes cleared and he looked up at me, then to the empty space beside him.

"She is waking, just as you are," I said to him, helping him to stand and feeling the weakness of his body against me.

He embraced me, then stepped back from me. "You have come, as was promised. Now go and help those who need you."

I nodded to him and hurried to the balcony where Barok waited. "As you can see below," he said, "more have come to join this army, though many no longer have a weapon, through no fault of their own." He tilted his head toward me and gave a sly wink. "All still seem a bit confused, though their wits have begun to return to them. They prepare to march against the warriors."

He turned my attention to the arches and pillars of the castle where the warriors stood, visible to the enemy, their cestros in one hand, their slings in the other. Raini stood with them, his bow strung, his sword at his side. They stood in two rows, ten in front and ten behind—waiting. In front of them, the panther paced, his teeth bared, his eyes flashing their eagerness for battle.

"Look to the castle wall where the soldiers stand, unable to string the many arrows in their long bows. Do you wonder why?" He paused and looked into my eyes, his own filled with humor. "I will tell you. One cannot string a bow if his hands are tied together with cords. The friends of Raini have seized the wall. The battle will only be against the soldiers on the ground."

I could see young soldiers standing upon the wall, their swords in their hands. A servant of the king and two elderly men dressed in scholarly robes also stood as sentinels. Behind them, angry soldiers sat, bound in cords, their mouths stuffed with cloth.

"The evil ways of a wicked king cannot change the souls of those who are good, and there are many who are good among these people," Barok advised me. "The battle for true freedom cannot be won without them."

"What of the soldiers beyond the wall? Why have they not come through the gate?"

Barok fluttered his wings and cocked his head at me. "I shall let Mythias tell you."

Before I could reply, I heard Klogan call out to the soldiers. "If you will stand back and let this battle end without another death, we will step away, and let it be so."

The one who led the soldiers shouted, "Are we not more than a hundred who stand against children who think they can kill us all with their small weapons?"

"Take the body of Yiltor in your talons and fly with him so all can see that he is dead," I commanded Barok. "Lay him at the feet of the warriors, then we will know how many wish to continue this battle."

"Excellent strategy, young Etcheon." Lifting Yiltor's body from the floor, Barok flew from the castle.

"See," I shouted from the balcony, "your king is dead. Do you still wish to battle?"

The silence that penetrated through the soldiers was stifling as Barok flew low so there could be no doubt as to the identity of the man he carried. The blood-soaked tunic added proof of his death. Slowly, the sound of swords falling against the cobbled street broke the silence.

Barok circled, then landed on the steps of the castle, laying the body of Yiltor in front of the warriors and covering Thorri's blood with the blood of the king.

The gates opened and Mythias came toward us, astride his unicorn.

Behind him rode Nepron and the captain of the three hundred, side by side. And behind them, their armies followed.

"I bring good news," Mythias called out to me. "The soldiers outside the city wall have decided to stand with us. And, as you can see," he turned and motioned to Nepron and the captain, "so has the king's captain, and those under his command."

Raini ran to his father and embraced him. "The battle is over," he said.

The captain of the three hundred turned to face the people. "This was not a war against a fearsome enemy," he shouted, so all could hear. "But a war of a madman, desiring more than what he had. It is time to end this madness with the death of its architect. Who stands with me?"

One by one, all who stood before him dropped their shields and swords and removed the helmets from their heads. The sound of the discarded weaponry stilled into silence.

"Then let us take care of the wounded and those who have died for a cause unworthy of their loyalty," Klogan called to them when they were silent again.

There was common agreement. As one, they gathered the wounded and the dead.

The bodies of close to two hundred were laid side by side, in four rows. Their helmets and their armor were placed above their heads, their swords at their sides. The warriors washed their faces and their hands, then combed their hair, while Lloch and many of the peasant children gathered the soft, thin material that would lay over each body as a coverlet.

When all was done, the warriors stood near them and began to sing the song that would introduce their spirits into the heavens. The moon appeared. When all was ready, the warriors lit the material, one by one, until all were aflame.

Klogan stood by my side and we watched. "There will be a wondrous story to be told and written about this day," he said solemnly, as if he was almost sad it was over. "You are truly your mother's child."

I studied him, my brows furrowed, thinking of his last words. "Have you known all along?"

He placed his arm upon my shoulder. "I have studied all that has been written. Do you think I would not know? Do you think I would have let your strategy become mine had I not known? I with my warriors, wearing the protection of your angel fleece, could battle the king's soldiers, but only you could battle the wizard. Only you could destroy him."

"But what of Thorri?" I asked, fighting the hurt that tore at my heart.

"The story has not ended yet. Thorri's life or death is with the Quynaè."

I started to ask him if going back in time would bring Thorri back to us, but he interrupted me, turning to the warriors. "It was Etcheon, the son of Arcadia, who is the daughter of Jokell, who is the son of Sverdin, who is the brother of Timberlin, who brought the time warp to us."

The warriors raised their arms and waved their hands in silent honor to the wizardly prince.

Klogan turned back to me and put his hand on my shoulder. "You come from a ancestry of pure wizardry. There is no fracture in the line of descent. Your mother carries the blood of your ancestor Jokell, who also could control time. That gift has been granted you because of your worthiness.

"*Can a person control time?*" *I had asked Taraini.*

"*If he is strong enough within his mind,*" *she had replied.*

"*If there is greater power, is it possible for a person to restrain time for more than himself?*"

"*It is.*"

The words came back to me, her voice soft in the strains of my heart,

"I knew you had yet to discover what you were capable of," I heard Klogan say, "and the time was not then to discuss it. Now is the time, Etcheon, son of a wizard mother." His eyes looked beyond me. "Go to them."

I turned to look where his eyes directed me. There I saw my father and my mother step through the door of the castle.

I could no longer hold my emotions inside. The tears fell unattended. I hurried to them, wrapping them both in my arms. I felt the warmth of their flesh. They were truly alive. Their eyes held mine, and I could see their love for me. "It is over," I said.

"No," my mother said, softly. "It has only just begun—the future you have given us."

30

Time In Its Dimension

QUEEN ARCADIA SLIPPED INTO HER son's room, to sit beside him and watch him as he slept. She could sense the power within him. It thundered to be unleashed, to awaken and increase. Mythias had been correct when he held him that day, telling her of it and advising her to put him in Feladelphia's care, for his protection and for his preparation. But letting him go had taken from her all that a mother gives to her child. Tonight, she would do something she had not done in many years. She removed a wand from her cupboard, spoke three silent words, and touched Etcheon gently on his forehead.

Placing his sea scope beside him and a soft leather-covered book in his arms, she said softly, "I love you, my child."

The little boy opened his eyes and looked up at her, then down at the book in his arms. He slid from his bed and climbed upon her lap. "Read to me, Mommy," he said, handing her the fifth book.

Etcheon's eyes glittered with excitement, as his mother held him in her arms and opened the book to a most amazing story. "This is a story of a young boy's voyage when he leaves behind his princely childhood to become what he was destined to be—the protector of his people," she explained as she took her son's hand and placed it on the first page, knowing the words she read would bring back the memories to him. "Tell me what you feel when you touch the pages."

"It is a story filled with danger . . . and magic . . . and wizardry." The boy giggled, running his hand gently across the first page.

"Then listen to all it has to tell you." The queen smiled. Yet her smile seemed rather sad to him, and he reached up to pat her cheek with his little hand. She felt the tenderness of his touch and the charm of his curiosity as his fingers tapped gently against her lips, eager for her to begin. She forced the tears away from her eyes, letting them linger in her heart as she began to read.

The story told of a young prince who was taken away to another land, in another time, by a woman of high standards and intellect. There, she watched over him and taught him of the quiet things in life, and educated him in intellectual learning. She taught him integrity and wisdom, purity and truth. She taught him to be kind and made him a gentleman. All this she did to prepare him for that which he was to become.

Etcheon listened as his mother read, and his memory came alive with the words written on the pages. "Her name is Granna Fela," he whispered to his mother.

"Yes, it is," his mother replied, resisting the tears that begged to surface. Then she continued in the telling of the story.

"When all that she could teach him had been taught, she released him to one of his own kind. One who lived within a magical realm, under the protection of the Ancient of Trees, far from those who would harm him, and take from him that power that lay deep within him—yet to be awakened. Here, he was tutored by those who would prepare him for that which he was to become—to awaken that which would make him the most powerful wizard ever to have lived."

The little boy's memory began to stir again within him and he leaned closer, touching the words on the page his mother was reading.

"When his training was complete, and it was time for him to step beyond the Ancient of Trees, those who taught him gave him the gift of themselves to carry within him. But he is not told that these are wizardly gifts."

Tears began to form in the little boy's eyes. "Where are the animals?" he asked.

"They are safe." His mother comforted him and he seemed a little older when she looked into his face. She wished she could wait for another day to tell him the rest of the story. But she knew she must continue.

She read of the good wizard Mythias, of twenty-one young warriors, and a man named Klogan, who walked and fought at the side of this prince—this son of a wizard. She read of the battles fought and won to save their kin and their kingdom against the wicked king, who sought for the prince's identity—and the evil wizard, who desired to take the breath of his enchanted life from him.

The little boy laughed when she told how the evil wizard was turned to stone and all that happened because of it.

He listened quietly when she read of the wounds that left their scars but did not take the lives of the warriors. For their lives were protected by the wizard's son and a simple band of angel fleece. Then tears fell from his eyes as she read about the one who could not be protected—the warrior Thorri, who died a hero's death and was given the greatest honor that could be bestowed.

As she read of Thorri, music of the forest rose from the pages of the book, filling the room with its magic. The songs circled about the room, their words appearing as tiny butterflies, fluttering about, bringing joy to the young prince. And he grew a little older.

"It is a wondrous story, is it not?" He smiled at his mother.

"A wondrous story with no ending, for it is a story that has only begun for the young prince," the king said, taking the book and lifting Etcheon onto his lap and planting a kiss on the little boy's cheek. Then he leaned over and kissed his wife as well, whispering into her ear, "I am glad you have used your magic to bring back a memory."

For hours, they played and laughed, the king and his son. Then the queen whispered into her husband's ear. "It is time to say goodnight."

The king sang a lullaby and rocked his son to sleep.

"The Ancient tells me that Etcheon has given us a beautiful future," Arcadia said, caressing the little boy's hair. The king laid him on his bed and covered him with the blanket.

She sighed deeply, letting her eyes linger on Etcheon's sweet face, and the words of the Ancient came to her, telling her that because of his goodness and his great wizardly power, the timepiece would take him again and again, a step beyond into futures of things that are past or into the beginnings of futures yet to come.

Mythias entered the room to watch the child sleep. He remembered the day he had warned the queen that her child was the one they had been waiting for. He placed the astrolabe in the little boy's hand. Etcheon stirred, clutching it to him, as if he already knew its secret.

"Tomorrow, when he awakens," he reminded the queen and king, "he will be a man again, and he will remember everything. We will have to let him return to that realm in which he finds the most happiness. Taraini waits for him."

Arcadia knew Mythias was right, as did the king, and they knew they would have to let him go. But tonight, he was theirs again—a child again, if only for a short time.

Just as Mythias had said, the boy awoke a man, and the man remembered who he was and all that he had experienced. He felt the power within him and was glad for it, wanting to awaken all that he was and all that he could be—knowing he was the Purcatian Prince, a wizard, and a gentleman.

He spent the morning with his mother and father. There was much for him yet to learn from them.

As they talked, Queen Arcadia told him of her own childhood, of her father's, and of her grandfather's. "Your grandfather could sense your gift while you were yet in the womb," she explained, "and taught you many things even before you were born. He would place his hands on my belly and reach into your mind, transferring the spells and powers. I could feel the movement of your little body as your mind became alive with the knowledge and magic that existed in his."

"Why have I not met him today?" the prince asked, thinking it strange he had not made himself known to him.

"He is with you," the king explained. "He is the constellation that watched over you and continues to do so. He is the one who gave you the power to control time. It is his gift to you."

"I know him, then" the prince replied, "for I saw him in the constellation. I called out to him when I needed direction, and he became my friend. It sounds rather foolish to say it aloud, but nonetheless, it is true."

The queen smiled at her son, admiring him, loving him with all her heart. The king felt the pride of a father who had become acquainted with the man his son had become.

The rest of the day, Etcheon enjoyed the people of his father's kingdom, rejoicing with the warriors, listening to the stories that would be told to the children of the children who played throughout the city.

In great ceremony, Thorri's name was engraved on the shield of each warrior, and his story became one of great sacrifice, yet of a great honor that was to be his reward.

Etcheon walked with Klogan and held the stick that would be placed, with honor to the warriors, in the city square for all to see, so the sacrifice would not be forgotten.

Then, as the sun began to set, he felt a tender caress on the palm of his hand. He touched it and the memory of a kiss placed there by a beautiful woman stirred inside him. He smiled, kissed his mother and embraced his father, waved to all his kin, and removed the astrolabe from his vest. Taking the crest, he unlocked the timepiece, set the dial, and pressed the pin as his mother closed the cover of the fifth book.

He could hear the music as the light flickered through the trees. He stepped into the light. "Hello, Taraini," he whispered.

"Hello, Etcheon," she replied, as she ran into his arms. "I have missed you so."

He held her, feeling of her love, not wanting to let her go. "I have missed you even more," he whispered back.

The eyes of the two children were bright with the mysteries of the story, as they sat on the large stump in front of the Ancient of Trees, the Danes on either side of them. Barok rested on my shoulder, while Kevelioc relaxed on his paws near the tree. Verch pretended to be asleep on the limb above the children, though I doubted that he was. Walkelin grazed with the unicorn near the garden, while Caspar-Arius was content to debate the future of that yet to come.

"Why did Thorri have to die when he was protected by the angel fleece, father?" Silvermist asked.

"His bravery lifted him above this earth," I explained. "He no longer needed to prove himself."

"But what of his love for Brettina? And what of her love for him? Did that not matter?"

"Remember the blue pearl Mirlanda gave to Brettina, telling her it was her magic?" I reminded her.

"Yes, but where was its magic?"

"When Thorri's body was placed in the village square so all could honor him, Mirlanda whispered in Brettina's ear. Brettina smiled, took the pearl from her pocket, and knelt beside Thorri. She laid the pearl next to his heart and kissed his lips. As their lips touched, a light began to glow around them, becoming brighter and brighter. Then, as suddenly as it had appeared, it disappeared, taking Thorri and Brettina with it."

"Where did it take them? Tell us, Father," young Thorri cried, "before I grow old with anticipation."

"Remember the constellation that guided me?"

"Your grandfather." Silvermist smiled. "They live in the constellation."

"Yes." I returned her smile. "They live among the stars, a place of great honor for both of them."

"It is a happy ending," Thorri admitted.

"There is no ending, Thorri," his sister scolded him. "Is that not right, Father?"

I nodded that she was correct, but before I could say more, she interrupted. "But tell us, how can the Hidden Kingdom be hidden when those of Yiltor's kingdom know where it is?"

"And who is the new king of that kingdom, now that Yiltor is dead?" Thorri added, the look of concern in his face matching that of his sister's.

"'Twas an easy spell, as your grandfather Mythias would say, and he did say that very thing as he cast it." I smiled, remembering the touch of his wand to the steps of the castle, and suddenly we were standing beyond the city, watching the people going about their business while their king, King Anusara, reigned with benevolence and wisdom. At his side stood Queen Amber, and their two princely sons, Raini and Lloch.

"I thought there would be no better king than one who had been a wise captain of the army," Mythias explained, removing his robe and his wizard's hat. He gave me a broad smile and a delightful wink. "The events of the past days have been taken from their memories, and no one in the Kingdom of Anusara has ever heard of such a thing as a Hidden Kingdom."

"Grandfather is truly a powerful wizard, is he not?" Silvermist looked up at her mother.

"But not as powerful as father," Thorri reminded her adamantly, his eyes revealing a touch of childish pride.

Taraini ruffled her son's hair and smiled at me before answering her daughter's question. "He is, indeed," she replied, her voice touched with emotion. "One day, when you have learned all the animals can teach you, you will become like him, yet even more powerful because of your father. Then, you will know your destiny. Another book will be written as another story will grow and become as a legend, because of you."

"Why is it that the animals must teach us first?" Thorri's question was fair and intelligent.

"From your mother, you are being taught the kindness of the heart and the tenderness of the soul. When you know that well enough, you will learn the agility, the dignity, and nature of the panther and the Danes. They will teach you to smell and see beyond the surface of the man or animal, to know if you are faced with good or evil. This will give you the advantage and the quickness to strike, if what you face is evil, or to stand back, if it is good.

"The lamb and the owl will give you the wisdom and discernment that will guide you as you use the gift inside you, for good. The eagle and the horse will teach you loyalty and the strength of bravery. But the most power-ful lesson they will teach is that you are your greatest teacher, and you must carry the responsibility for that which you teach yourself."

"Then, will you and mother teach us the magic and sorcery?" Thorri's voice fizzled with excitement as he looked into his father's eyes.

"The magic and sorcery are already within you." I could not help but smile as I brushed my son's forehead with a kiss. "We will only awaken it—when it is time." I lifted him into my arms as Taraini reached out for Silvermist's hand. "For tonight, nonetheless, it is time for you to sleep."

"It was a wondrous story, was it not?" the little girl asked as the covers were being tucked around her and a kiss touched her cheek.

"Oh, it was . . . and it is still . . . and will be for hundreds of years to come," her mother whispered in her ear as the little girl's eyes closed in sleep.

"I think it is time for all of us to sleep," Kevelioc said, yawning. "I have lived it, yet I could not pull myself away from the story."

"Only because it is a story that will never lose its splendor in the telling," Barok said, sighing.

While the children slept, the Ancient watched over them, its limbs having weaved beds of comfort where gentle dreams floated about them. The unicorn stood close by. His coat of brilliant white and his mane of gold cast a calm glow of protected love about them. Their mother and father kissed their children's sleeping faces, and then walked out into the night where a constel-lation shone brightly above them.

"Sometimes I think about the handsome boy who came that night, long ago, and I miss him in my heart," Taraini whispered to Etcheon.

"Sometimes I think of the beautiful young woman who greeted me that night, and I think I loved her the moment I saw her," Etcheon said, taking her in his arms.

"That is because you loved her, already." She smiled, looking up into his eyes. "It is a most remarkable experience to travel in time. But, tonight, I am grateful that time is not relevant, and all is well in the kingdom of my father and of yours."

"I think of all that has happened and the wonderment of it all," Etcheon replied, caressing Taraini's lips with his own.

"And I think of all that is yet to come and the wonderment of it all," Taraini answered, letting her lips embrace those of her husband's.

"All is as it should be," Barok said softly in the night.

"And they all lived happily ever after," said the panther.

The horse neighed, the Danes barked, the lamb baa'd, and the owl hooted in agreement, while the Ancient smiled in the contentment of the evening, knowing Etcheon had become what he was meant to be—known for goodness. But it also knew that evil returns with a vengeance. When that time came, the children of this great wizard would be ready to fight beside their father.

In all this, it also knew on this night, when all were asleep, Etcheon would climb the hidden stairs to the room where the statues of the twenty-one waited to greet him, and where he would sit among them, as if in a vision, where they could talk of the future yet to come.

The statues were a gift the Ancient had carved with more care than first intended—a gift given with more love than anticipated. Perhaps, there were still universal emotions to be taught, and perhaps the all-knowing Ancient itself had something yet to learn.

Appendix

Name Pronunciation Guide

Ancitel – an-seh-tell
Anusara – an-u-zar-uh
Barok – bur-oak
Brettina – brit-teen-uh
Cara – care-uh
Caspar-Arius – cas-par air-ee-us
Jokell – joh-kell
Kevelioc – kev-lee-ock
Klogan – kloh-gan
Kon – kawn
Lloch – lock
Mirlanda – mur-land-uh

Mythias – muh-thy-us
Nepron – neh-praun
Quynae – kwi-nay
Rafn – raf-en
Raini – rain-ee
Ranulf – ran-olf
Tarainisafari – te-rain-ih-sa-fa-ree
Thorri – thor-ee
Timberlin – tim-ber-lin
Verch – ver-ch
Walkelin – wok-eh-lan
Yiltor – yeel-tor

Explanation of Measurements

1 foot = 1 orgyia
10 feet = 1 akaina
100 feet = 1 plethron
600 feet or 6 plethra = 1 stadion
2 statia = 1 diaulos (1200 feet)
6 diauloi = 1 dolichos (7200 feet)
1 cubit = about 18 inches
1 eaneaon = 1000 years

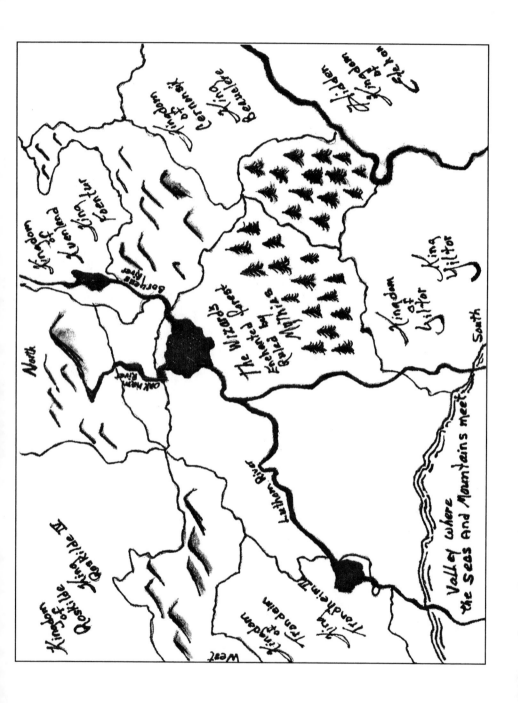

About the Author

Prince Etcheon and the Secret of the Ancient is JoAnn's fifth book and first fantasy. She found it to be an unbelievably exciting experience to simply take the imagination to a realm without borders.

Her first book, *Miracles for Michael*, was a story of simple miracles that changed a little boy's life and touched the lives of all who reached out to take his hand.

Journey of the Promise, Pages From the Past, and its sequel, *The Silent Patriots*, take the reader into the world of mystery.

JoAnn continues to divide her time between writing, painting, singing with the Southern Utah Heritage Choir, searching out her ancestors, and serving in the St. George Temple with her husband, Brent. They are the parents of four sons and grandparents to fifteen grandchildren.